SOUTHLAND NOIR

Cover image courtesy of Shutterstock.

This book is a work of fiction. Any resemblance to actual events or persons, living or dead, is entirely coincidental.

"Southland Noir by Douglas Clark. ISBN 978-1-63868-134-2 (softcover); 978-1-63868-135-9 (hardcover); 978-1-63868-136-6 (electronic).

BY DOUGLAS CLARK

BELFAST
TAKE FIVE
SHELL GAME
EVERMORE
CRITICAL MASS
FAULT LINES
PROVOKE THE DEVIL
THE IRISH SPY
ENDGAME
HUNTING ODESSA
THE AMERICAN SPY
HAVANA
MOSCOW WINTER
SOUTHLAND NOIR

To Josie for evermore.

SOUTHLAND NOIR

A NOVEL

DOUGLAS CLARK

CHAPTER 1

County Cork, Ireland | 1920

For the past year, armed rebellion progressively escalated in the latest attempt to free Ireland from British rule. After centuries of oppressive domination as a colony of the British Empire this latest rebellion held real possibilities. A combination of British missteps resulted in most of the Irish population openly voting for independence in the 1918 election. The backing of a large segment of the Irish population therefore made possible an armed insurgency. Where past rebellions failed, the Irish Republican Brotherhood founded in the middle of the nineteenth century now provided the necessary organizational structure for engaging in armed rebellion. With widespread popular support the IRB could rely on material support and intelligence to militarily confront the British in guerrilla warfare. Widespread passive resistance by the general population turned all of Ireland into a zone of British military occupation.

The political journey of Egan Walsh was like so many willing to give over their lives in the cause of Irish freedom. His family had an activist history in the Irish Republican movement. His paternal grandfather participated in the Fenian Rising of 1867. In the failed Easter Rising of 1916, Egan's father provided secret material support for the rebellion and his is older brother Cormac lost his life fighting for the Irish Republican Brotherhood.

Having recently graduated from University College in Cork, Egan joined the staff of the *Cork Examiner* newspaper. While he supported the aims of rebellion, he argued with his brother and father that armed rebellion was premature. The Irish population would not revolt against British rule. Thousands of Irishmen were serving in the British Army in France. The IRB did not have the manpower or weapons sufficient for insurrection.

Egan's views proved correct. Cormac died of wounds sustained in the unsuccessful 1916 rebellion. While the rebellion did not enjoy popular support in Ireland, the subsequent executions of the ringleaders by British military tribunal infuriated the Irish. Then in 1918 with British military losses in WWI mounting, London attempted to enforce conscription in Ireland. This final insult resulted in wholesale rejection of the prevailing majority Irish Parliamentary Party in the 1918 general election. The new republican Sinn Féin Party openly advocating independence overwhelmingly swept the election.

Immersed into reporting for the republican-leaning *Cork Examiner*, Egan Walsh turned to more active resistance by joining the Irish Republican Army constituted mostly from members of the former Irish Republican Brotherhood and other dissident organizations. The IRA was now the official army of the Irish Republic as declared by the outlawed revolutionary Irish parliament, Dáil Éireann in 1919. As the war progressed into 1920, those active in the IRA could no longer hold regular jobs because of widespread arrest by British security forces. The beleaguered Royal Irish Constabulary soon ceased to function as a viable policing organization of the British with the general population shunning all contact with RIC constables.

British Army units poured into Ireland to provide military security resources. Westminster passed the Restoration of Order in Ireland Act in 1920 to maintain the fiction that London still maintained civil control of Ireland. The British then augmented the RIC with thousands of unemployed former WWI British Army veterans. Thousands from the ranks signed on for the good pay. Informally known as the Black & Tans for their inconsistently mixed uniforms, they operated largely independent from the Army as a mobile policing force. Providing for an elite strike force, the British additionally established the Auxiliary Division of the RIC comprised exclusively of former British Army officers. Ostensibly as part of the RIC, the militarized Black & Tans and Auxiliaries engaged in a reign of terror. Unarmed Irish citizenry suffered terrible acts of brutality intended to break support for the IRA. Along with the burning of houses, creameries, and other means of livelihood, these former British Army veterans indiscriminately resorted to murder and torture. The Act further provided for British Army court martial jurisdiction for trying IRA combatants with authority for imposing death sentences.

The IRA resorted to counterterrorism as the only response given their inferiority in numbers and weapons. The Anglo-Irish War began to look like another brutal British colonial war in 1920. Yet this war was different. The Irish invoked worldwide sympathy. America with its large ethnic Irish population sided with Irish independence. Much of the funding for the Republican cause came from American private donations. The Irish cause looked very much like the situation of the American colonies 150 years earlier. In the United Kingdom, public sentiment resented the unpopular military crisis in Ireland while Britain suffered economically from five years of WWI.

Yet for everyone actively engaged against British security forces, the larger political issues became reduced to the immediate dangers and hardships of engaging in a desperate guerrilla war. One in which capture might end in death at the end of a hangman's rope, or *shot while trying to escape*, or *died of wounds*, a euphemism for torture. Such a life on the run bound each IRA fighter to his comrades. It equally bent and twisted everything normal in each participant's life. Egan Walsh's experience was no exception.

By autumn of 1920, Egan Walsh commanded the Clonakilty Company of the 2nd Battalion of the IRA 3rd Cork Brigade. The brigade was better known as the West Cork Brigade for its area of operation. County Cork and Dublin represented the highest concentration of armed confrontation with the British throughout the war. Unlike other armies, each IRA unit elected its commanders. Walsh was a natural leader.

3

September and October saw continual back and forth killings between both sides. IRA headquarters set out a plan to create mobile strike forces to inflict casualties on the Black & Tans and Auxiliaries. The strategy was born out of the necessity to demonstrate the military viability of the IRA while optimizing the effectiveness of the IRA's limited weapons and ammunition. Within the West Cork Brigade, WWI veteran Tom Barry organized an active service unit, commonly called a flying column, of IRA selected from across the brigade. These experienced and disciplined fighters would move through the countryside mostly on foot to execute attacks against vulnerable British forces. They specifically directed those attacks against crown forces engaging in brutal activities outside the realm of accepted warfare conduct. Since inflicting terror on the supporting civilian Irish population characterized the Black & Tans and Auxiliaries, the only counter measures available to the IRA were to inflict equivalent brutality on the enemy.

———

By November, Egan Walsh's duties in the IRA expanded from commanding a company to becoming brigade intelligence officer. In that capacity, he conceived a plan to ambush the hated Essex Regiment based in Bandon in the heart of the IRA West Cork Brigade territory. Of all the regular British Army forces stationed in Ireland, the Essex were the most brutal, rivaling the excesses practiced by the RIC Auxiliaries. Trained in counterinsurgency tactics, they even had a unit specializing in torture. Much of the Essex brutality was due to their intelligence officer, Major Arthur Percival.

Walsh's plan to ambush the Essex impressed Tom Barry. Every morning two or three lorries traveled from Bandon to Cork City and returned each evening. It was to be the first ambush of Barry's newly formed flying column. On the morning of 22 October, thirty-two IRA occupied positions outside the village of Tooreen. Walsh commanded the section tasked with attacking the second lorry.

4

The engagement proved a resounding IRA success. Suffering no casualties, the IRA killed five, wounded four, and captured six British soldiers of the hated Essex Regiment. Equally important, they seized fourteen rifles and 1,400 rounds of ammunition along with several Mills bombs and revolvers.

In reprisal, members of the Essex Regiment went on a violent rampage against Brandon. Of those participating, some included soldiers released unharmed by the IRA earlier that day.

Unfortunately, British reprisals took a more targeted form. This attack costing the lives of British Army regulars required a decisive response. The Essex intelligence was first rate. They targeted suspected IRA sympathizers and families of known IRA members. Among those were Dr. Dillion Walsh and his nurse wife Agnes. Fixtures in Clonakilty. Their son was known to be IRA. Dr. Walsh therefore became suspected of providing medical treatment to injured IRA.

Wanting to deflect such a direct reprisal as the work of the RIC instead of the Army, Essex Major Percival alerted the RIC Auxiliary Division Southern headquarters in Macroom, 25 miles north of Clonakilty.

By telephone to the commanding officer, Percival said, "The bloody *Shinners* murdered five good British troops yesterday. Survivors of the attack identified Egan Walsh as a leader in the ambush near Tooreen. Walsh's father is a local doctor and known to provide medical services to wounded IRA.

"Regulations restrict Army operations to only those directly involving enemy combatants. This is more within your policing portfolio. The Colonel would appreciate you including Dr. Walsh among those targeted for removal for active support of rebels. Clonakilty is an IRA hotbed. Best to eliminate the services of the doctor and his wife and torch their home which serves as an IRA medical facility."

Within days, two lorries carrying fourteen RIC Auxiliaries swept into Clonakilty. Targeting Dr. Walsh provided a perfect reason for inflicting their unique brand of barbarity. This from former British officers that never indulged in such acts during conventional combat of WWI. This essentially colonial war brought out an all too familiar pattern of British cruelty against subjugated colonials defying the might of the British Empire.

It was early afternoon under an overcast autumn day. The Walsh house was a large stone home with a slate roof built seventy-five years earlier. Located on the northern outskirts of Clonakilty, it was surrounded by a typical stone wall separating the property from grazing pasture of a neighboring sheep farmer. No mistaking the residence marked with a prominent sign at the road.

The entry to Dr. Walsh's surgery was through a separate side door in a single-story wing of the two-story building. Ten Auxiliaries took up positions to cover any threat. Both lorries carried mounted Lewis machine guns with each taking up a position to cover both directions of the road passing by the Walsh house. Four Auxiliaries entered the surgery armed with revolvers.

Dr. Walsh was attending to a local farmer having injured his forearm when the Auxiliaries made a noisy entrance.

The Auxiliary in charge said, "Who is your patient, Doctor? A Shinner no doubt?"

"Only a farmer with a laceration," Walsh responded. He was surprised but had never previously been accosted by this new RIC paramilitary force brought over from England. The former Royal Irish Constabulary by this time no longer represented a functioning police force. Ostracized by the general public, they were forced to remain secluded in their barracks fearing attack by the IRA.

The Auxiliary in charge stepped next to Walsh and pushed him away from the man sitting on a gurney. Turning to the patient, he said, "Are you a farmer or IRA? Maybe both?"

The man did not respond. Undoubtedly terrified, the man starred back at the Auxiliary defiantly.

Infuriated, the Auxiliary pulled away the unfinished bandage wrapping, exposing the wound. Clearly, a laceration just sutured. "Get the fuck out of here."

The man looked at Dr. Walsh, who said, 'Go along, Dermot. Keep the bandage clean and return in two weeks so I can remove the sutures."

As the farmer was leaving Agnes Walsh came into the surgery office. "What is going on? What are you doing here?"

The lead Auxiliary said, "Shut your mouth woman! We are here to shut down medical support for IRA murderers. Your son is one of those murderers."

"Are you arresting us?" Dr. Walsh asked.

"You can call it that," the lead Auxiliary said. "Outside, the both of you. You'll be coming with us, Doctor."

The other Auxiliaries grabbed Walsh's parents roughly by their arms and pushed them outside. As they led Dr. Walsh toward one of the lorries, Agnes Walsh screamed insults and started pummeling the Auxiliary holding her arm with her free fist. As she pulled free from his grasp, she fell to the ground. As the Auxiliary reached down to pull her to her feet, she struck him in the nose with her fist.

The blow surprised and infuriated him. In reflex, he swung his revolver striking her hard across the forehead. Falling back, the gash began bleeding profusely. Barely conscious, she remained on the ground breathing heavily.

Seeing what happened, Dr. Walsh attempted to resist but the blow from the butt of a revolver to his head subdued any resistance.

The lead Auxiliary yelled, "Get to it! Burn it to the ground."

Several Auxiliaries carrying jerry cans of petrol entered the house. Minutes later, the building was fully engulfed.

Disoriented and bleeding, Agnes Walsh looked on helplessly unable to get up from the ground. Worse than seeing her home in flames was watching as the Auxiliaries drove off taking her husband.

Dermot O'Connor, the farmer being treated by Dr. Walsh when the Auxiliaries arrived, remained nearby after leaving Walsh's house. Once the Auxiliaries departed, he placed Agnes Walsh in his wagon and set off to his own farm to get help from his wife in treating Agnes Walsh. Not far along the road, he spotted the body of Dr. Walsh by the side of the road.

Murdered by a bullet to the back of the head. A terrible trauma for Agnes Walsh as O'Connor struggled getting the Doctor's body into the wagon. The best he could do was cover the Doctor's head with his coat while his injured wife wept sitting up next to him holding his lifeless hand.

———

Several violent confrontations in November 1920 between the IRA and British Crown forces framed the vicious character of this conflict. This was a challenge to the British Empire. Failure to suppress the insurgency could carry far reaching consequences among other colonies. Although Ireland elected members of Parliament to London, Ireland was nothing more than a mature colonial extension after hundreds of years of British domination.

On the third Sunday of November, the IRA struck a spectacular blow against the British forces in Dublin. The events of *Bloody Sunday* would further harden the violent tactics on both sides.

Michael Collins, the inspirational leader of the IRA, recruited a select team of assassins called the *Squad*. Their purpose was to make clandestine war on British Crown forces operating from Dublin Castle, the seat of British administration in Ireland. On the morning of the 21st, Collins set loose the *Squad* to kill British intelligence agents operating undercover in Dublin. The mission involving coordinated attacks in many different locations proved remarkably successful. Fifteen British agents were killed by gunshot from point blank range.

That afternoon, British forces reacted by surrounding a Gaelic football match in Croke Park. Something provoked the British to open fire with machine guns on players on the pitch. Fourteen players and spectators were killed and another sixty wounded.

Strategically the day's events favored the IRA. British intelligence in Dublin never recovered with covert agents fearing the same fate. The British reprisal against noncombatants further increased IRA support among the Irish population and in America representing a vital source of funding and arms.

Events that Sunday signaled to the IRA the need to escalate direct armed assault on British Crown forces. Make British continued presence in Ireland untenable. The IRA had the Irish population firmly on their side. British public sentiment was turning against the costly conflict in Ireland. Britain could not sustain military operations indefinitely. Greatly increasing British forces necessary to militarily subjugate Ireland was economically and politically unrealistic.

Lacking sufficient weapons and ammunition to arm all IRA members, the leadership fixed on a plan to create active service units, called flying columns. Well-armed small mobile units of fighters intended to harass British security forces. Inflict casualties and seize weapons. Utilize the vast rural countryside of Ireland populated with villages where IRA fighters could obtain support and safe haven. Classical guerrilla warfare tactics.

—

Tom Barry knew Dr. Walsh and his wife Agnes. They saved the lives of many wounded IRA. Losing one son in the Easter Rising of 1916, and their other son Egan now a wanted IRA fighter, Dr. Walsh and his wife now became casualties. Few families gave so much to the cause of Irish Freedom

Before the murder of Dr. Walsh, Barry had already decided to recruit Egan Walsh to join the West Cork flying column and command a section. Walsh displayed exceptional skills in using intelligence for tactical military advantage. In the Tooreen Ambush, Walsh displayed courage and leadership. Barry had in mind another audacious operation to bloody the reviled RIC Auxiliaries. The murder of his father would provide Walsh with the opportunity to transform grief into useful revenge.

Late the night following the murder of Dr. Walsh, Barry approached the home of Dermot O'Connor, the farmer undergoing treatment by Dr. Walsh at the time of the Auxiliaries' raid. Outside the house, ten IRA stood guard. Agnes Walsh was resting peacefully attended by O'Connor's wife Saoirse. Her husband sat with Egan Walsh as a knock on the door startled Walsh from his silent withdrawal. Extracting a revolver from his shoulder holster, Walsh jumped up from his chair.

O'Connor answered the door then ushered Barry into the living room warmed by a fire in the hearth. Walsh lowered his revolver as Barry embraced him.

"How is your mother, Egan?" Barry said.

"Resting. She took a nasty blow to the head. Possible concussion. Dermot was there getting his arm stitched up by my father when the Auxiliaries burst into the surgery. Saoirse says she will recover but needs looking after for a few days. She may never emotionally recover from the death of my father. My older sister in Cork City will look after her."

Barry turned to O'Connor. "What happened?"

O'Connor said, "The bastard in charge accused Dr. Walsh of giving medical aid to the IRA. They let me go after seeing my wound was not from a bullet. When they dragged Dr. Walsh away, Agnes protested and one of them smashed her head with his gun.

"After leaving the house, I walked to my wagon close by. I watched as they hurt Agnes then set fire to the house."

"It was you who found Dr. Walsh?"

O'Connor turned toward Egan. "Aye. As I travelled here to the farm with Agnes in the wagon, I saw Dr. Walsh lying next to the road only a mile further on."

Tears welled up in O'Connor's eyes. "It was something awful. I couldn't leave the Doctor's body out there. Terrible for Agnes her being wounded and now riding in my wagon next to the body of her husband."

Walsh sat down with a vacant look, withdrawing into his despair. Barry pulled up a chair next to him. "Nothing I can say could possibly ease your grief, Egan. Your father and mother have given so much to the cause. Everyone in the Brigade grieves with you."

Walsh looked at Barry without expression.

"You have no choice but to move forward, Egan. The only thing I can offer is for you to join our flying column. I need someone smart like you. You need a way to redirect your grief into action. I can promise you will have the opportunity to strike hard against those responsible for this atrocity against your family."

Walsh remained silent for several moments before nodding his agreement.

The engagement planned by Barry was against the Auxiliary Division of the RIC. The worse perpetrators of British terror in Ireland. Ostensibly a creation to bolster the Royal Irish Constabulary with experienced and trained former British Army officers. However, in practice the Auxiliaries acted independently seeing their mission as one of inflict terror to damage IRA support among the Irish population.

Although former British Army officers with experience in WWI, these were not officers from the traditional British officer corps. Prior to the attrition of the Great War, British officers came from well-connected families, paying for officer commissions. With the carnage of the Western Front, soldiers from the ranks were promoted to fill the ever-increasing demand for replacement officers. Referred in a pejorative sense as *temporary gentlemen*, post-war demobilization found no home for them in the British Army. Instead, having not come from wealth, they faced unemployment in a distressed British economy overwhelmed with returning veterans.

The offer of £7 per week pay provided an attractive inducement to ship out to Ireland for a one-year enlistment in the Auxiliary Division of the RIC. However, there existed no sense of longevity or higher purpose. In practice, higher level command leadership was virtually nonexistent. Individual ADRIC companies were left to operate without restraint with no more motivation than that of mercenaries.

—

The Auxiliaries were chiefly responsible for the reprisal against civilians in Croke Park following Michael Collins' sensational decimation of British intelligence operations in Dublin. Tom Barry therefore thought it appropriate to target the Auxiliaries in County Cork to demonstrate IRA capabilities in the South. Like Collins, Barry intended to inflict serious casualties against this enemy. Engage in repeated small-unit IRA engagements would demonstrate the vulnerability of the Black & Tans and the Auxiliary Division of the Royal Irish Constabulary. By 1920, resignations had depleted the ranks of the original RIC ranks. Those that remained became isolated in their barracks fearing IRA attack and ceased to be an effective counterbalance to the insurgency. What served as policing in Ireland fell to the RIC paramilitary forces of the Black & Tans and Auxiliaries.

By November, the Auxiliaries had been conducting a reign of terror throughout Ireland for several months. Yet the IRA had yet to fire even a shot at them. They represented a formidable mobile strike force with each officer carrying a rifle and two revolvers strapped to each thigh. From their Sam Browne belts hung two Mills grenades. Their mission was to cripple the resistance will of the Irish population. They directed their indiscriminate killings, lootings, and burnings against noncombatant civilians attempting to cut off support to the IRA. Rumors began circulating that the IRA was unable to confront the Auxiliaries. Tom Barry intended to change that impression.

Too exposed for Egan Walsh to remain at the O'Connor residence, Barry took Walsh with him to a safe house. Barry spent the rest of that night explaining his plan of attack to Walsh.

"I have thirty-six men assembled for an ambush. Most are new to the flying column, but all are good lads. I am dividing the raiding party into three sections. I want you to command one of those sections. You did an outstanding job in the Tooreen ambush."

"What is the target?" Walsh asked.

"A contingent of Auxiliaries. From Company C, billeted in Macroom Castle."

Walsh raised his eyebrows. "That is outside the West Cork Brigade operating area."

"Aye, but these are the Auxiliaries responsible for forays to the south. The same command that murdered your father. Come Friday I'm venturing out to select the ambush site. Every day, units of Auxiliaries venture south using the Macroom-Dunmanway Road. Care to come along?"

Walsh nodded. "Where are our men right now?"

"Training. East of Dunmanway. I will take you there tomorrow. I see you already have a revolver."

"It's my brother's Webley. He died in the Easter Rising. Michael Collins returned it to my father. Collins' father and my father were friends and IRB members having grown up not far from each other on the Cork coast."

"I saw you shoot down two Essex soldiers at Tooreen."

Walsh nodded. "My brother Cormac taught me how to shoot. Never thought a time would come when I would use the skill to kill an enemy."

—

At 2:00am on Sunday 28 November, the flying column assembled miles from the ambush site near Kilmichael. A priest arrived an hour later to hear confessions. Individually the men went to him then returned to the ranks. Egan Walsh did not participate. Why should he after Catholic Bishop of Cork, threatened the IRA with excommunication for killing British security forces.

After receiving the priest's blessing, Barry informed them of the mission. They then set out on the long march to Kilmichael avoiding roads. A miserable night with a driving rain drenched the men without relief. They reached the ambush site at 8:00am to a cold winter dawn. The location was a barren countryside interspersed with peat bogs. The position Barry chose was a short stretch of 150 yards where the road abruptly turned west-east before resuming its north-south direction.

The ground rose slightly on the north side of the road with scattered rocks affording limited cover for the waiting IRA. Intelligence reported Auxiliary units passed here every day in a convoy of two or three lorries.

Before allowing the section leaders to deploy their men, Barry addressed the unit. "As you can see, this is not an ideal location for ambush. However, necessity dictates this is where we must make the fight. There is no plan for retirement should the situation turn against us. We shall smash the Auxiliaries or meet our end here. What we do this day is necessary to protect West Cork

13

and show all Ireland that British terror will be met with equal terror.

"It is an honor to fight alongside every one of you this day. God be with us. Now take up your positions."

By 9:00am, everyone deployed to their assigned position. All understood not only their role but the larger picture of the role of each group. The only food available was that offered by the occupants of a lone house nearby along with a bucket of tea. With sodden clothing, the men shivered all day in the cold.

As dusk began to fall at 4:00pm, strategically located scouts signaled movement on the road. As the first lorry arrived at the ambush site, it slowed for the slight bend in the road. At a distance of a hundred yards, they saw a man in military uniform standing in the middle of the road. That was Tom Barry wearing a borrowed IRA tunic with Sam Browne belt and holster. However, with the mixed uniforms of the special RIC British forces, from a distance it was difficult to identify the uniform.

As the lead lorry slowed and came closer, Barry blew a whistle and tossed a Mills grenade. The grenade sailed through the air landing into the driver's seat of the open-topped lorry. The explosion killed the driver causing the lorry to lose control and come to a stop. Rifle and revolver fire erupted from IRA attackers of Section One concealed behind rocks.

Auxiliaries jumped from the lorry and began returning fire. Fighting was at close range and over within a minute. All nine Auxiliaries from the lead lorry lay dead or dying.

The second lorry with another nine Auxiliaries stopped near the bend in the road a hundred yards from the lead lorry involved with the intense firefight. These Auxiliaries dismounted their lorry and began dispersing looking for firing positions.

IRA Section Two consisting of seven men led by Egan Walsh began firing on the Auxiliaries of the second lorry from the north side of the road immediately after it stopped. A third IRA section of six riflemen occupying a chain of rocks south of the road prevented the Auxiliaries from securing cover.

Barry and those that attacked the first lorry now joined in the fight against the Auxiliaries from the second lorry. As the tide of the battle turned in favor of the IRA, Barry called for the Auxiliaries to surrender. A reply came and the IRA temporarily ceased firing. When several IRA stood, several Auxiliaries resumed firing, killing two of the IRA.

Sensing deception, Barry angrily yelled, "Resume firing! Do not stop until ordered!"

An Auxiliary fired two shots from a revolver at Walsh from five yards but missed. Walsh steadied his Webley .455 revolver and shot the officer in the upper chest, following with a second shot hitting him in the left elbow as he spun around from the first round. Yet the man still held his revolver pointing it at Walsh.

Walsh steadied his weapon aiming a kill shot to the head. The man dropped as the large round struck below his left eye.

Walsh looked around at the one-sided carnage. The scattered Auxiliaries from the second lorry were now also dead or dying. The third section took up a position before the bend in the road to deal with a possible third lorry.

Barry saw to the one IRA badly wounded and looked upon the two dead IRA and the greater number of dead Auxiliaries.

Of the eighteen Auxiliaries, one badly wounded man escaped across the barren field finding a house looking for help. Two IRA men unrelated to the ambush were staying at the house and killed the wounded Auxiliary with his own gun then dumped his body in a bog.

While the ambush was a resounding success, the vicious close quarters fighting left the IRA survivors stunned. No one spoke. Many looked upon the scene of carnage expressionless. A couple vomited.

Understanding he must reestablish control, Barry yelled out, "Section leaders, form your men on the road." For twenty minutes, Barry drilled his command, relying on military discipline to refocus his shaken command. They had a long nighttime march ahead of them. No telling the scope of the British response once they discover the bodies of their comrades.

For Tom Barry, the Kilmichael Ambush proved the effectiveness of the IRA in blood. For Egan Walsh he understood this level of violence now represented his life until the British left Ireland, or he died in the attempt.

CHAPTER 2

County Cork, Ireland | 1921

Egan Walsh remained fighting with Tom Barry's West Cork Active Service unit following the Kilmichael Ambush. The fighting between British Crown forces and the IRA intensified with armed confrontations occurring almost daily in the South. On 10 December, British authorities proclaimed martial law in the counties of Cork, Kerry, Limerick, and Tipperary. The following day, the IRA attacked a lorry of Auxiliaries near Dillons Cross. In reprisal, the Auxiliaries went on a rampage setting fire to the commercial center of Cork City, resulting in extensive damage to Ireland's third largest city. The Auxiliaries also engaged in assaulting countless civilians and widespread looting.

Walsh's last participation in a major engagement occurred when the British attempted a massive offensive against the IRA. Obtaining information through torture of a captured IRA member, the British learned that the IRA West Cork Brigade was headquartered in Ballymurphy. Early in the morning of 19 March, the most aggressive of the British forces consisting of 1200 regular army Essex Regiment troops and 120 Auxiliaries from Macroom set out to encircle the IRA. The location was less than fifteen miles from the coastline restricting any IRA retreat only toward the west.

Tom Barry's flying column numbered only 104 men with just 40 rounds of ammunition per weapon. Information on the movement of British forces came too late to allow escape from the overwhelming superiority of the enemy. In danger of encirclement, the IRA could not sustain a protracted fight with their limited ammunition.

Egan Walsh, the intelligence officer for the column, informed Barry that his network of spies reported a British column advancing towards Crossbarry where several roads converged. By the number of lorries observed, it appeared to be a force of similar strength to the IRA.

While seemingly trapped, the location provided ample cover close to the road for the IRA to stage an ambush. At 8:00am, a convoy of a dozen lorries came into view. The concealed IRA engaged at a range of only 5-10 yards on the lead lorries. Walsh commanded the first section to fire on the British. Most of the British causalities fell during the first minutes of the intense firefight. Walsh personally accounted for hitting three of the enemy.

In disarray, several of the unengaged lorries retreated out of the range of fire or sought cover with many of the British fleeing into the fields. As the IRA collected British weapons and ammunition and set fire to abandoned lorries, another column of 200 British attacked from the southwest. The IRA beat back that attack but took casualties. However, the opening allowed the IRA to escape northward. Badly bloodied, the disorganized British did not pursue them. Crossbarry proved another significant IRA victory while avoiding potential destruction of the West Cork Brigade.

———

The war ended for Egan Walsh along with the IRA of the West Cork Brigade with the signing of a negotiated truce effective 11 July 1921. At the time, the flying column was gathered in a training camp in the mountains along the border of Cork and Kerry Counties. Tom Barry was there although his duties had now expanded to that of command of the entire West Cork Brigade.

An early victim of the action at Crossbarry was the much-respected brigade's commanding officer Charlie Hurley. Recovering from a serious wound sustained in February, he became trapped in a remote house and subsequently gunned down by the British as they closed the cordon to entrap the IRA. Barry was the natural choice for election to assume command. Although Barry was younger than a good many of the IRA including Eagan Walsh, he was the most qualified IRA military leader in the field.

The unexpected end of hostilities raised unanswered questions for everyone. For those of Tom Barry's flying column, a welcome relief from living on the run. Yet the future remained uncertain. Could a truce conceivably lead to Irish independence?

Before the unit dispersed to return to their homes and prewar lives, Barry and Walsh spoke.

"You know, this is not the end of the struggle," Barry said. "The British are not ready to grant Irish independence."

"Then we resume the fight?"

Barry nodded. "Seems likely."

Walsh responded, "The British are hoping the Irish people are too exhausted. They will begin negotiations. Drag out talks until the people embrace peace on almost any terms. The war has left many scars in the fabric of Irish society. London will offer something less than independence. We should have ignored the truce and continued the fight. What do you suggest we do, Tom?"

"Keep up morale among the lads. Hide our weapons. The British cannot be trusted. They have over 30,000 well-armed forces in Ireland. Until they withdraw from Ireland this fight is not over."

"You think the Auxiliaries and Black & Tans will honor the truce? Can't see the fuckers staying put inside their barracks."

"We will know soon enough. Keep your revolver on your person, Egan. Like me, you are a marked man. Every Auxiliary would like to put a bullet in your head."

Barry continued, "The British call me ruthless and blood thirsty. The Church even called us murderers. Since the British resorted to murder, torture, and intimidation of civilians, they no longer acted like soldiers. Outnumbered and outgunned, the only

19

way to survive was return their brutality in kind. They'll not be forgetting what we did to them."

Walsh understood Barry was rationalizing the justification of retaliating against terrorism by assassinating the enemy. With the deliberate murder of his father, Walsh was not troubled about going hard against the Auxiliaries or others like the Essex Regiment. "What are you going to do now, Tom?"

Barry smiled. "Getting married I expect. Her name is Leslie Mary Price. A veteran of the GPO in 1916. A senior officer of the Cumann Na mBan. Vowed we would marry when the fighting ended. Even if the truce doesn't hold, it is our time. Will you come to Dublin for the wedding, Egan?"

Walsh embraced Barry, "Of course I will, Tom. Congratulations. I am happy for you both."

"What about you, Egan? Is there someone special waiting for you in Cork?"

Walsh shook his head. "Afraid not. Had a girl before I quit the newspaper and joined the IRA. Unlike your Leslie, she was no republican. Not exactly a unionist but she thought more of a normal life than my going off to be killed or imprisoned."

———

Although relieved with the ending of fighting, Egan Walsh was pessimistic about the future. Personally, as well as that of Ireland. After being on the run for two years, there was no home to return to. When he left his job in Cork to take up arms with the IRA, he moved his meager belongings to his parents' home in Clonakilty. Everything was now gone. His only refuge was his older married sister in Cork where his mother now lived following the death of his father.

His brother-in-law Dr. James Byrne welcomed him to stay in their large home as long as necessary. A full house with two teenage nieces. Walsh's sister, Eleanor and her husband were staunch republicans. Like Walsh's father and mother, they treated wounded IRA and their families without charge during the hostilities.

The environment proved a balm to his damaged psyche. The household went out of their way to comfort him. His nieces treated him as a celebrity. Their school friends knew the names of prominent IRA. That he fought with distinction with Tom Barry's famous flying column made him well known in solidly republican Cork City.

Walsh was welcomed back to the staff of the *Cork Examiner* in late summer of 1921. The editor assigned him to write a continuing column on the peace negotiations with the British government going on in London. Regrettably, the signing of the Anglo-Irish Treaty in December that year brought renewed discord to Ireland.

The agreement did not grant Ireland freedom from the United Kingdom, offering instead self-governing dominion status within the British Commonwealth. The same status as Canada, Australia, New Zealand, and South Africa. The King would remain head of state and Ireland administered through a governor general. The Government of Ireland Act of 1920 previously partitioning Northern Ireland consisting of the northeastern six counties as separate from the rest of Ireland now became official with the 1921 Treaty. The Protestant majority population of Northern Ireland loyal to the British Crown with its largely English-Scots ancestry opted out of joining the Irish Free State comprising the largely Catholic southern twenty-six counties by referendum.

Ireland did not become an independent republic. It further suffered partition with Northern Ireland remaining firmly part of the United Kingdom. For those in the IRA, it was a bitter disappointment. Immediately causing a schism among all levels of the military wing of the rebellion dividing the country. Yet, unlike the overwhelming support of 1918, Irish public sentiment was now split. The Treaty achieved much, including British military personnel leaving Ireland. All domestic functions now fell under the authority of the Provisional Irish Government. This included the courts and the policing functions. Most of all, the Irish people were war-weary, seeing the Treaty as promising a return to normalcy even with its shortcomings.

Like many in the IRA, Egan Walsh felt capitulation to the treaty compromises occurred prematurely. Like Tom Barry, he

21

felt the British were on the ropes with the need to increase military resources if they were to prevail in Ireland by force. However, that was politically untenable among the British population equally weary of war in Ireland.

Tom Barry remained sufficiently militant to consider returning to armed resistance. Joining him were other important rebel leaders such as Éamon de Valera, President of Dáil Éireann and Liam Lynch O/C of the IRA Southern Division. Only Michael Collins, the most prominent individual within the IRA leading the fight against the British upheld the Treaty as the best possible deal achievable.

Unlike Barry, Egan Walsh would not take up arms against the Treaty. That would mean fighting against former IRA comrades not British Crown forces. He argued passionately with Tom Barry and Liam Lynch against renewing of the taking up arms. They were all Cork men having come through the most bitter of the confrontations with British forces. Even Michael Collins, a signatory to the Treaty, was from County Cork. Walsh argued that the British were no longer the oppressing enemy. Armed resistance would result in civil war, Irish against Irish.

Most of the IRA chose to abide by the Treaty. Michael Collins became Commander-in-Chief of the Irish National Forces comprised of former IRA. Armed insurrection against the Treaty meant military confrontation with former comrades. Unlike the war of independence, civil war would divide the Irish and risk destroying the significant gains made by the united rebellion against the British.

The treaty debate ceased in April 1922 when anti-treaty IRA forces occupied the Four Courts complex of buildings in Dublin housing various courts. A standoff ensued after ten weeks before the Irish National Army attacked the Four Courts using artillery to dislodge the occupiers. The bombardment substantially destroyed the buildings. The Battle of Dublin marked the beginning of the Irish Civil War. Fighting then spread to other parts of Dublin and particularly the southern counties.

Tom Barry and other anti-Treaty IRA seized a shipment of arms intended for the Free State police force. While trying to get the arms into the Four Courts, Irish National forces captured Barry, imprisoning him in Mountjoy Prison. Transferred to an internment camp in County Meath, Barry escaped in September making his way south to take command of the IRA Second Southern Division. Reverting to his previous role against the British, Barry assembled a guerrilla unit of 200 IRA as a mobile strike force.

The inspirational leader of the IRA throughout the war, Michael Collins now commanded the Irish National Army. As an instrumental part of the treaty negotiating team for the Irish, he had a personal interest in securing a successful transition for the Irish Free State. In County Cork, anti-Treaty forces ambushed an army convoy assassinating Collins. The death of Collins further hardened the resolve of the National Army to put down anti-Treaty forces organizing in the southwest. Unlike the war for independence, there was little support for civil war among the Irish population.

Regrettably, Egan Walsh's long association with Barry ensnared him in this new conflict. Soon after Barry's escape, a squad of Free State soldiers burst into the newsroom of the *Cork Examiner*.

Entering Walsh's office, an officer Walsh recognized and backed by two soldiers all with drawn revolvers, said, "Sorry to be doing this. Egan Walsh, you're under arrest. Are you armed?"

Walsh now standing opened his jacket revealing his shoulder holster. An old habit of going about armed suggested by Barry now added to his predicament.

"Why am I being arrested?"

"Don't know the details, but my commander said it's about your spying for Tom Barry and Liam Lynch. Something about your intelligence background and being close to Barry."

No point in arguing with this fellow who was only obeying orders. With the polarized environment of the Treaty, it was difficult to appear neutral. Wearing a gun did not help his case. Anti-Treaty activists captured carrying arms were liable for execution.

Interned in the old Cork City Gaol, no one tried to interrogate Walsh or explain the basis for the charges for the three days he spent there. Without explanation, early one morning he was handcuffed and transported under a three-man escort and boarded a train to Dublin.

Walsh asked the same officer in charge of his arrest, why Dublin?"

"Word is there is fear that Barry might make a try to engineer your escape. He's a crafty bastard. Better to lock you away in Mountjoy Gaol in Dublin."

"Who ordered my arrest?"

"The arrest warrant is signed by the Provost Marshal of the Irish National Army. It reads *for suspicion of military action against the Irish Government.*"

———

For several weeks, Walsh endured the indignity of incarceration in Mountjoy Gaol. His attorney told him no evidence existed of his providing information to Barry or any anti-Treaty activists. The case against him was based entirely on his wartime record serving with Barry. Walsh assisted his attorney preparing a defense around his published newspaper columns. He cited consistent content where he repeatedly argued against military response by anti-Treaty factions as disastrous for Ireland.

His attorney remarked, "This is not a normal judicial proceeding. It is a military tribunal just like the British invoked. There is no evidentiary case against you. Just your past association with Barry and your record of intelligence operations in the IRA. Although you publicly warned against taking up arms, there is no question you resent the Treaty. You argued in print that better terms were possible. You had a running public debate with Collins on that issue. Then they arrest you carrying a revolver."

Walsh replied, "How do you intend to make a defense?"

"Since this is not about evidence, your best bet is character references that will provide affidavits attesting that in their opinion you have never engaged in any subversive activities against the Irish government. For that to carry any weight, it must be from those with influence."

Walsh shook his head. "That is not very creative or encouraging, counselor."

Nonetheless, the attorney's efforts paid off. One morning the jailer unlocked Walsh's cell. In walked Richard Mulcahy. Minister of Defense and now commander-in-chief of the Irish National Army following the recent death of Michael Collins.

Walsh stood up from his cot. He knew Mulcahy. Both attended Tom Barry's wedding, as did Michael Collins. A time when the IRA remained militarily unified.

Mulcahy extended his hand that Walsh accepted. "I only recently learned of your arrest, Egan. Been consumed with the chaos following Collins' death. I must ask you as someone I know to be honorable. Have you been secretly helping Barry or Lynch?"

"Absolutely not. Igniting civil war is a terrible mistake. Regardless my disagreement with the terms of the Treaty, I could never take up arms against former IRA comrades."

"I was sure you did not, but I wanted to hear you say it. Why were you carrying a gun then?"

"Old habit. Originally for protection against the Auxiliaries and Black & Tans even after the truce. They never seemed subject to any restraint. Murderous brigands. Didn't relish them waylaying me some dark night. I was told that I had an unofficial bounty on my head. Foolishly kept the weapon on my person. Yet anyone as a former IRA apparently runs a risk. My arrest attests to that. The blokes arresting me said I could be hanged for carrying a weapon. That is the irrationality of civil war. The fighting is hardly over. However, I don't believe I could ever shoot a former comrade even to save myself."

Mulcahy said, "Well, you are free to go. I personally signed the order. The arrest never had merit. However, I suggest you keep a low profile and stay away from anything involving politics. Particularly stay away from Tom Barry. He is headed for a bad end."

———

Walsh immediately returned to Cork. Uncertain what he planned to do, even during the train ride back to Cork he knew that leaving Ireland now became necessary. He was no longer the same person. The arrest and internment reverted his instincts to that of the guerrilla soldier. He now realized he had been no less ruthless than Tom Barry. He did not know how many British he killed or wounded. Yet while Barry and Lynch saw full Irish independence from Britain as the singular objective no matter what it did to Ireland, he saw this glorified ideal in a more complex light.

Even when the civil war ends, the damage to Irish society will linger for generations. He held no interest in reporting on the declining Irish condition as the country fell into anarchy. Only time and distance could alleviate his depressive feelings of profound loss. All the death and misery suffered failed to achieve Irish independence. Ireland now to be torn apart rather than embracing the momentous achievement self-rule and driving British security forces from most of Ireland. Mother was in good hands. His former friends were dead or involved on one side or the other in this civil war. Best to find some peace by leaving Ireland.

From a practical standpoint, Walsh had only modest funds to leave Ireland and start a new life. All he knew was journalism. His editor Albert Fitzgerald regretted his not returning to the *Examiner* after his release from Mountjoy Gaol but understood. Eager to help, Fitzgerald suggested Walsh try Boston. Large ethnic Irish population going back a hundred years.

Fitzgerald said, "I met the former founder and publisher of the *Boston Globe* newspaper on a trip I made before the Great War. My father wanted me to expand my knowledge of running a newspaper in preparation for my succeeding him. I was much impressed with Charles Taylor's far-reaching ideas for managing a major newspaper. A brilliant man. Regrettably, he passed away last year. His son William Taylor is now editor and publisher. The *Boston Globe* covered the Anglo-Irish War extensively catering to their large Irish readership with a predominately republican political viewpoint. The *Globe* is a first-rate newspaper and Boston a first-rate city.

"I can write a letter of recommendation. Might carry some weight. Provide them with your illustrious background. Tell them how you returned to the newspaper after serving in the IRA. Looking to find some peace of mind from this terrible civil war."

"I appreciate that, Albert. Boston might be a good place to re-think my future. Be careful what you say about my service in the IRA, or you'll scare the hell out them."

"There are many in County Cork that appreciate what you did, Egan. The Treaty may hold terms we disagree with, but we still got the bloody crown's forces off our island."

The more he thought about Boston, the more it made sense. He could not bear the thought of remaining in Ireland under current circumstances. America seemed the obvious solution for pursuing his career in journalism.

A few weeks later in October of 1922, Egan Walsh made his way to Southampton in the south of England for steamship passage to Boston. Armed with a couple of new suits and a letter of recommendation along with a generous severance from the *Cork Examiner*, leaving Ireland was still a dispiriting experience.

His brother-in-law generously gave him a Remington portable typewriter as a present. "You often spoke of writing a book, Egan. I discovered this portable machine in an advertisement. Never knew there was such a thing.

"We only heard the undoubtedly censored facts of what went on in the war. You must have a wealth of materials. Telling of your experiences in the war could make for a compelling book for Irish American readers."

As he prepared to board a ferry to make the crossing to Wales, his mother embraced him. "I don't want to think of you being alone. My cousin Trevor lives in Boston. Here is his address. His children Michael and Fiona are your second cousins. Write to me often, Egan. I love you."

CHAPTER 3

Boston, Massachusetts | 1925

It had been almost three years since Egan Walsh left Ireland. Now early autumn in Boston, making it the most glorious time of year. Within weeks, the trees would turn into a pallet of brilliant color. Yet autumn also served as the harbinger of winter. Boston winters could be cruel. Walsh had already suffered through two winters and dreaded another. Ireland was never this cold.

As a reporter for the *Boston Globe*, he spent a good deal of time out and about the city making winter particularly unpleasant. He could manage the cold with proper clothing, but snow and ice posed a challenge for getting around. Walsh liked everything about Boston except its winters.

Apart from seasonal severe weather, living in Boston did not feel totally like exile. This was the most Irish city in America. Leaving the political turmoil of Ireland progressively began healing the emotional scars of the war. Resuming his journalistic career in a place rich in history of rebellion against the British located on the Atlantic seacoast offered a suitable alternative environment.

Boston abounded in speakeasies. Its large Irish American population of South Boston was not about to forego their rich tradition of enjoying beer and whiskey because of ridiculous restrictions imposed by Prohibition. The pub was a social fixture in Ireland. Getting a drink in greater Boston was never a problem with its thousands of speakeasies. Local police never bothered the establishments and often forewarned of federal treasury agent raids. The many Irish pubs offered a familiar social environment for someone newly arrived from Ireland. Journalists liked to drink, affording the perfect environment for developing working relationships at the newspaper.

Discovering his extended family in Boston became the most important social element returning him to a semblance of normal life. Years on the run from British security forces, the murder of his father, the lasting effects on his mother, and deep resentment for his unjust internment after civil war erupted, left scars not easily healed. Yet he followed his mother's admonition and contacted his mother's cousin Trevor Maguire soon after he got settled.

Maguire lived in a predominantly Irish neighborhood of South Boston. In their fifties, Maguire and his wife came to Boston as immigrants thirty years ago from Ireland. The birth of a boy followed a year later and a girl the following year. Working on the docks as a crane operator with his wife working as a cook, they prospered enough to help pay for their children's college education.

On Walsh's first Sunday dinner at the Maguires, he met their daughter Fiona, his second cousin. An attractive woman about his same age. A strong assertive woman who was also a columnist for the venerable monthly magazine *Boston*. Taking a liking to her cousin as something of a celebrity and fellow journalist, she dominated the conversation. Her parents were used to their daughter's exuberant character. Seeing that Walsh was enjoying the intellectual exchange, they let her have her way.

Fiona said, "Your mother wrote to Father saying you were coming to Boston. So sad to hear of the death of your father. She did not provide any details. How did that happen?"

Walsh hesitated preferring not to delve into the ugly details of the Irish War, but this was a logical question. "Murdered. By British assassins. Former British Army officers recruited to support the RIC. Called the Auxiliary Division. Their purpose was to terrorize the Irish population. Murder, torture, destruction of Irish property. Crush support of the IRA. A bad time for all Irish."

The table became quiet, but Fiona wanted to learn more. "Your mother wrote that you were in the IRA. What exactly did you do?"

His deep-seated anger overrode his usual aversion to explaining his role during the War. The Maquires, however, were family and had a right to know. "I was a soldier in the IRA. Part of a mobile strike force of the West Cork Brigade. Guerilla warfare. Hit and run warfare against the superior numbers and better armed British security forces."

She paused for a moment processing his surprising declaration before going on. Not knowing how to phrase the question, "Were you …. involved in the fighting?"

He nodded. "County Cork saw much of the military action during the war of independence. I killed my share of the British enemy. Those British forces engaged in murdering and burning the homes and businesses of Irish civilians. We inflicted our own terror in reprisal."

Fiona's mother interjected, "Fiona, enough for now. Agnes said Egan had many difficult experiences during the war. That's why he is here in Boston. Give him some peace."

Walsh, however, did not mind Fiona's questions. He enjoyed himself immensely that first evening. Here was family even if somewhat removed giving him a sense of belonging.

Before parting that night Fiona asked, "Where are staying, Egan?"

"Since I work in the financial district, I found a room at a boarding house in the North End which is a manageable walk."

"The Italian district. I live not far from there just north of Boston Common. I like Italian food so we must have dinner sometime."

Over the next year, they became close friends, seeing each other often. Fiona was gregarious and often they met for dinner or drinks at a popular speakeasy in South Boston with the feel of an old country pub run by an Irishman with a largely Irish clientele. They became a popular couple when the bartender learned of Walsh's IRA exploits then shared them with the clientele.

Fiona introduced him as her distant cousin from Ireland. Otherwise, they appeared as a close couple. It increasingly felt that way to him. Yet the ever-present circumstance that they were *cousins* always remained. Yet to his thinking, as only *second cousins* should make that acceptable. The definition meant the sharing of one great-grandparent separating the bloodline by three generations. That seemed a sufficiently distant connection that should not prohibit an intimate relationship. However, society and his family might disagree.

———

Since coming to Boston, Walsh consumed his spare time by writing his novel. Autobiographical to the extent that he used events in the Irish War of Independence in which he personally participated as the foundation, he chose to portray the protagonist in fictional terms. This allowed the freedom to construct a plot outside the boundaries of his direct experiences. He could also invest his protagonist with a set of views that might not always align with his. Fiction allowed for crafting scenes where he could exercise dramatic license.

Fiona became deeply invested in Walsh's progress on his novel. His portrayal of his time in the IRA brought them closer. She recognized which of the detailed circumstances likely came from his personal experiences by his vivid word-portrayal of scenes. His writing made the reader feel the sacrifices, the physical suffering of being constantly on the run. The effects of up-close personal violence, witnessing death, and the constant fear of one's own death whether by bullet or British gallows if captured.

He welcomed Fiona's editorial suggestions. After submitting completed chapters to his boss William Taylor, he then passed them to her. As a professional writer, she also possessed a keen sense for literature. Her comments about human behavior sharpened his fictional characters in rewrite.

Fiona was different from any woman Walsh ever met. Self-assured and outspoken, they enjoyed each other's company as if they were brother and sister. She could easily make Walsh blush with her frank comments. The 1920s were a time of great advances in women's rights. He soon learned she was committed to women's rights. He wondered if her activism accounted for her not having a sustaining romantic relationship. Occasionally, she introduced Walsh to a new male friend only for the relationship to soon fall apart.

Walsh completed the first draft of *Price of Freedom* in early summer of 1925. The story set in County Cork used events he either participated in or events gleaned from other IRA comrades. Having lived these events inspired his use of language to convey the fear, the hardships, and the intense comradery. Although infused with his personal views, he attempted to alter the protagonist sufficiently to avoid it being autobiographical. Walsh wanted to avoid any appearance of exaggerating his wartime actions. For actual events, where he portrayed real individuals, he paid great attention to remain faithful to their personalities and to the historical accuracy of events. At least from his perspective. This was not a work of history, but he did not alter facts to fit his plot.

As a journalist, he took great pains to avoid the novel sounding like a reporter's factual account of war. This was about giving his characters life through portraying emotions and perspective, carried along by a dramatic story frequented with realistic violence.

Since joining the newspaper after arriving in Boston in late 1922, the publisher William Taylor personally took a liking to him. Impressed by Walsh's objective reporting of events in Ireland as it descended into civil war where he knew Walsh held strong personal opinions. Learning of Walsh's ambition to write a novel based on his experiences in the war of independence, he also became interested in the project. Over the course of writing the book, Taylor read the manuscript as it progressed, offering editorial comments.

Upon completing the novel and producing a publishable first draft, Taylor surprised Walsh.

"This is a remarkable novel, Egan. *Price of Freedom* needs to be published."

"Thank you, Sir. That is indeed high praise. Not sure how to go about that."

"Let me offer my assistance. I know a senior editor at Charles Scribner & Sons in New York. A classmate of mine at Harvard. Scribner is the premiere publishing house in America. They published Henry James and Edith Wharton. They're always looking for new talent in fiction. I cannot promise they will accept *Price of Freedom*, but I can promise they will give it thorough consideration."

Several weeks after submitting the manuscript, Taylor called Walsh to his office. "I have some exceptionally good news, Egan. Scribner wants to publish *Price of Freedom*. Just got a call from my friend Franklin Meadows. He is to call back in an hour and speak with you."

Walsh could hardly believe the good news. "That is grand news indeed, Mr. Taylor. I cannot find the words to properly thank you for all your help."

"Delighted to be of some assistance in launching your literary career. Now of course there will be talk of money. Publishers offer an advance against future royalties. Since you do not have an agent, I took the liberty of doing some advance negotiation. After Frank expressed genuine enthusiasm for your novel, I told him not to low-ball the amount of the advance just because you are a first-time author."

"Just to see my work in print is the most important."

"Nonetheless, I want you to get a fair deal. I believe you can trust Frank to make you a reasonable offer. You can take the call here in my office. Come back at eleven o'clock."

Taylor stood extending his hand. "Congratulations."

Scribner offered more than a reasonable deal. Not only the advance but also an additional novel commitment to promote the novel surprised even Taylor. Meadows recognized the potential of the vast Irish American population. With establishment of the Irish Free State now the wrenching civil war, the perfect vehicle to promote the book was to make a movie. Scribner therefore offered to attempt to market the movie rights for *Price of Freedom* to a film studio. An adapted script held great potential for the movie screen while promoting book sales.

—

Walsh immediately telephoned Fiona after receiving the call from Scribner. Feeling a part of his success, she was overjoyed.

"We must celebrate. I will make us dinner. Italian. Be at my apartment at six. Perhaps you can find us some Champagne to make this a real celebration."

At his favorite Italian restaurant, they discreetly served wine. As a regular, the owner was pleased to sell him a bottle of prosecco, especially for the offered generous tip.

Arriving at Fiona's apartment, he received more than her usual welcome of a kiss on the cheek. Looking him in the eyes, she said, "I still cannot believe this. You are an amazing man, Egan." She then embraced him kissing him on the mouth, lingering much longer than usual.

Her kiss sent a charged sensation through his body. A feeling not experienced for a very long time. As she disengaged the embrace and took the prosecco, he looked at her with the eye of man appreciating the form of an attractive woman for the first time.

"Take your jacket off. Make yourself comfortable. I will be just a minute."

She returned from the kitchen, setting down two glasses and a bottle of Old Bushmills Irish whiskey on the coffee table. She sat down next to him on the sofa. Close enough for her hip to touch him.

Pouring a whiskey for each, "Here's to the success of Egan Walsh, novelist."

"How did you manage to get a bottle of good Irish whiskey?

She laughed loudly. "Connections. A former gentleman friend had a friend in the bootlegging business. Wanted to impress me by giving me a case of Bushmills since I was Irish."

"Did the gesture suitably impress you?"

"No. I found him lacking in other more important attributes."

She surprised him again by laying her hand on his thigh. "He did not engage me intellectually like you do, Egan. Without that connection, physical attraction diminishes."

Although not experienced with women, he sensed where this might be leaning. Accordingly, he could not contain his arousal.

Setting down her glass after taking another sip of whiskey, she touched his cheek with her other hand. Another kiss left no doubt as to her intentions.

"Hard to put into words how you make me feel, Egan. Different from other men I date. Time that I did something rather than just thinking about you. Can't tell you how many sleepless nights you cause me."

She moved her hand over the obvious bulge of his trousers causing his erection to further respond.

"I want to make love with you, Egan. Seems like you do too."

No question about his state of arousal. "We're cousins, Fiona."

"So what? Besides, we're only second cousins. Come along. Just a man and woman enjoying giving each other pleasure. Dinner can wait."

With that, she pulled him up from the sofa and led him to the bedroom. Fiona demonstrated how much she enjoyed sex by instructing him how best to pleasure her. Much to his delight, he learned techniques that greatly enhanced his own enjoyment.

That first night of intimacy was not to be their last. Fiona made it clear she was not looking for commitment. She had her own career as he did. "We shall simply remain cousins with an unusually intimate relationship. We connect intellectually, why not sexually? Best however to keep that detail from other family members."

——

Several weeks later, Walsh's life would again take a momentous turn. A telegram arrived from Franklin Meadows at Scribner. It read, *Fox Films, Los Angeles seriously interested in film rights Price of Freedom. Telephone William Fox 67-5008 Fort Lee, NJ.*

From the telephone call with the head of Fox Films, Walsh boarded a train to the Bronx in New York City. Fort Lee was just across the Hudson River.

William Fox was an entrepreneur that ultimately found success from hardscrabble beginnings. From a string of nickelodeon storefront venues featuring short motion pictures for five cents admission, Fox founded his own film production company in 1915. Fox recognized motion picture technology would mean large screens in theatrical venues, quickly supplanting the primitive content of nickelodeons. After embarking on investment in theaters it became obvious that also producing feature-length motion picture content could produce another profit stream.

Without preamble, Fox immediately launched into his offer to Walsh. "We produce mostly newsreel films at our studios here in New Jersey. Our feature movies are produced in much larger facilities in Hollywood, California. Hollywood is a district of Los Angeles, about ten miles west of downtown Los Angeles. I believe a movie adaptation of your novel *Price of Freedom* has market potential. We will advertise the movie as starring an all-Irish cast. The director is Irish. You will receive credit for the adapted screenplay. There is a vast population of Irish Americans. The struggle for Irish independence is still fresh and the civil war maintains a tremendous interest in Ireland. We want this film to be an exciting portrayal of the war against the British. To all Americans, the Irish struggle for independence from Britain mirrors the birth of America 150 years ago."

"To see my story come to life on a theater screen is a breathtaking prospect."

Fox nodded. "We are offering $25,000 for the film rights. Additionally, you will receive shared credit for the screenplay. You'll work alongside an experienced screenwriter and director John Ford. Unlike writing a novel, writing a screenplay is a collaborative project. Lots of technical considerations are required for the script to capture the desired effect on film. We are offering $1,000 per week for your work on the screenplay and for acting as technical consultant. It is important that the movie achieves an authentic portrayal of Ireland during the war of independence."

Walsh was stunned. This along with his royalty advance from Scribner provided more money than he ever possessed.

"That is most generous, Mr. Fox."

"What about your job at the newspaper?"

"That should not be a problem. I will ask for a leave of absence."

In truth, he could not overlook the opportunity. This could further his literary career. Leaving eastern winters behind an added bonus. Southern California seemed like an exotic location. Located on the Pacific Ocean with year-round warm weather. Hollywood allowed location filming all year. According to Fox, it had water, desert, and mountains to replicate a variety of locations all within drivable distance.

"Then we have a deal. I have taken the liberty of preparing the necessary contractual documents. My secretary will escort you to an office, giving you the opportunity to review and sign these documents. Advise her if you have any questions. Can you be in Los Angeles in three weeks' time?"

Somewhat overwhelmed, Walsh replied, "Yes. I believe so."

"Excellent. Inform my secretary of the details of your arrival schedule in Los Angeles. She will wire Sol Wurtzel, our head of West Coast production operations. His office is located at the studios on Western Avenue north of Sunset Boulevard. The studio will arrange for hotel accommodations during your engagement with Fox Films."

Walsh left Fox's office with mixed emotions. Asking for a leave of absence from the *Boston Globe* after William Taylor's considerable help in getting him noticed by Scribner felt like ingratitude. Then of course, there was Fiona.

Difficult to characterize their developing romantic relationship. Yet she had a profound effect on him. His first intimate relationship that held more meaning than just the sex. For that matter, there had been only a handful of women with which he ever shared sexual intimacy. He never had intimate relations with Maureen, his first serious relationship before he left to go on the run with the IRA. Fiona struck a responsive chord within him on various levels. From that first night of intimacy, they were practically inseparable, yet they never discussed where it might lead.

While separating from her to the opposite coast would be painful, he had no choice. Then again, it was not an indefinite separation. The following day he broke the news to her at her apartment.

Opening her door, she said, "This is a surprise. Miss me so soon?"

He kissed her. "Some special news I must share. You recall me telling you that my publisher was shopping the movie rights for my novel as a promotional strategy for my novel?"

"Of course. Are you saying that might happen?"

"Not might, it did happen. Just signed a contract with Fox Films."

She embraced him and planted a kiss on his lips. "That is wonderful!"

"Yes, it is. Unfortunately, it means I must leave Boston for Los Angeles. Probably for a few months. Taking a leave from the newspaper. I'm to help with the screenplay and act as technical consultant on the filming."

"Oh my," she said in manner expressing disappointment. "That will be dreadful not seeing you, but I understand. Will you miss me?"

He embraced her. "More than you can imagine."

She touched his cheek. "Me too. How soon must you leave?"

"In two weeks. I need to be in Los Angeles in three weeks. Better part of week's trip by train. Need to get their right after the new year."

She nodded. "Then we must make the most of that time."

After making love that night, she confided as they lay in bed. "I never expected this would go this far. Let my emotions get the better of understanding where this might lead."

"You're not regretting becoming involved with me, are you?"

"Certainly not. Regardless of the complications, you are the one, Egan. You are far more than just someone I screw frequently in secret. You appreciate me for what I am and how I think. We interact as equals. I am thirty-one. Difficult for a woman without a partner to live a fulfilling life as she ages. Now that we have found each other I want us to be together openly. Is that too much to wish for?"

"I want that too. Are you afraid of what your family will think with us being second cousins?"

"Of course. They're not going to understand. We may not give a damn but others in our lives are important to us. My parents' priest will have a shitfit. The Catholic Church does not condone marriage of second cousins. I looked that up. Not likely any more accepting of unmarried cohabitation. Boston Irish are just as conservative as those in Ireland. Family is sacred above all else."

Walsh had no words that might offer comfort. Foolish to believe that their first intimate liaison would not lead to unanticipated consequences.

"We'll find a way. I feel the same way about you, Fiona. I also want us to live openly together."

They fell asleep with the question unresolved. The following morning, they made the best of the situation. The days before his departure passed all too quickly. They took the position that this was a temporary separation for only a few months. Both left unsaid the wider question of the future. How could they make this work?

Regardless the emotional complications caused by Fiona Maguire, she brought him through the difficult transition of leaving Ireland. Turning to writing could easily have resulted in becoming reclusive. She provided balance and a return to the world. Giving him a personal life with emotional meaning. His time in Boston made him realize the depth of his sacrifices during the war in Ireland. Time now to live again.

CHAPTER 4

Los Angeles, California | 1925

Egan Walsh experienced conflicting emotions as he departed Boston for Southern California. The time spent here resurrected his soul from the horrors and deprivations of the Anglo-Irish War. The opportunity to reestablish his journalism career in a different environment while embarking on the start of a literary career presented a future with welcoming possibilities. Standing at his side on the railway station platform was Fiona Maguire, an essential part of that future.

On a cold morning with a biting wind, she was dressed in a stylish fur hat, wool overcoat, and leather calf-length boots. Makeup impeccably in place. The picture intended to leave him with the best possible vision of her. It did that. What should be an exciting moment of embarking on this new chapter in his life, diminished by separating from Fiona. Probably only for a few months, yet that remained uncertain. After completing work on the movie, what then?

What exactly was their relationship? Neither found being second cousins problematic. Perhaps their families but might come around to accepting the relationship. He and Fiona were highly independent people that should be capable of weathering the controversy. They were devoted to each other and comfortable in every aspect of their relationship. However, avoiding discussing

their futures in the context of living as a couple left much unanswered. Perhaps being second cousins held some subconscious ta-
boo even for them.

As his train slowly pulled into the station, he said, "I will call
and write to you, Fiona." He wanted to say more but held back.

Her arm entwined with his, she turned to face him looking
him in the eyes. "I will miss you terribly, Egan. What we have
together might be unusual, but we cannot deny the chemistry.
You turned my life upside down but in a good way. Kiss me now
before I begin to cry."

They kissed a long passionate kiss before Fiona broke her embrace and said, "Goodbye, Egan. Now get on the train." Tears
rolled down her cheek. 'I said I wasn't going to do that. Now go
before I breakdown."

She turned and entered the railway station. He climbed
aboard and found a seat. He looked out the window for Fiona, but
she did not return to the platform to wave goodbye. Adding to
the sadness of leaving Fiona, a gray overcast hung low with a light
snow beginning to fall as the train slowly departed Boston. Little
comfort that he was leaving the cold of another advancing Boston
winter for the warmth and sunshine of California.

—

Fox Films provided Walsh with first-class Pullman railroad
tickets. The Pullman system of carriages afforded sleeping cars, a
dining car, and a facilities car providing a barbershop and bathing
facilities. Nonetheless, Walsh still intended to make a couple of
overnight stops to break up what otherwise was a four-day journey to Los Angeles. A chance to stretch his legs and sleep in a real
bed for a quiet night's rest. He chose the southernmost route
across the country, adding a day to the trip but avoiding possible
severe December weather for the more direct route through Chicago. He wanted to arrive rested and ready to tackle the unknowns of the moviemaking business.

The first leg of his journey took him to New York City where
he transferred to an express train to Atlanta. Spending a night in

Atlanta, he got his first taste of American southern cuisine. The next leg took him through the American South, so different from Ireland or even New England. Proceeding through Texas emphasized the vastness of the United States. The comparative fertility of the South and Eastern Texas gave way to endless barren stretches of landscape as the train ventured into the American Southwest. Three days after leaving Atlanta, he spent the night in Phoenix. Leaving Boston with temperatures close to freezing, Phoenix was seventy degrees in the daytime but dropping into the forties at night. Typical for the low desert according to the hotel clerk.

The topography changed as the train climbed gradually out of the low desert elevations of Phoenix and the Coachella Valley of California. Reaching San Bernardino, he began to see immense stretches of orange groves and the beginning of the Santa Monica Mountains to the north defining the boundary of Southern California. As the train traveled westward entering Los Angeles County, the train progressed through smaller communities surrounding the urban center of the City of Los Angeles.

As the train passed through Santa Fe Springs, a jarring sight of a literal forest of closely spaced towering wooden oil drilling derricks appeared. An ugly eyesore despoiling an otherwise pleasing landscape. Walsh read of the oil exploration boom sparking rampant speculation investment in drilling rights shares.

Traveling the final leg of the trip by the Southern Pacific Railroad, Walsh arrived at the City of Los Angeles Central Station after the seven-hour trip from Phoenix. Located on Central Avenue at 5th Street in downtown Los Angeles meant he must make his way to his hotel in the Hollywood district nine miles to the west. His destination was the Hotel Hollywood on the north side of Hollywood Boulevard at Highland Avenue. Ideally located in proximity to the major movie studios. According to his welcome letter from Sol Wurtzel, the Hotel Hollywood was a favorite residence of those working in the movie industry. *The perfect place from which to acclimate socially to Los Angeles and a new work environment.*

Located at the base of the Hollywood Hills, representing the lower elevations of the Santa Monica Mountains, lemon groves bordered the north side of the hotel with pepper trees lining the south side of Hollywood Boulevard. Surrounding the hotel were three acres of manicured gardens. The location retained the feel of a country resort yet was easily assessable by the trolley system.

It was Tuesday, the 5th of January 1926. Winter in Los Angeles yet the temperature was almost seventy degrees late in the afternoon. No need for his wool overcoat.

Walsh was pleasantly surprised to find Greater Los Angeles well served by a system of electric trolleys and light rail lines. This likely contributed to the rapid growth of an area of hundreds of square miles. Workers had the means of living at some distance from their places of employment with economical means of commuting using public transportation as an alternative to costly automobiles.

Armed with a map of Los Angeles and instructions from a railway clerk, Walsh was amazed with the efficiency of traveling from downtown Los Angeles to his hotel in Hollywood. Much of the distance was covered by light rail service then a short Pacific Electric trolley ride bringing him directly to the hotel. A spectacular orange sunset over the Pacific Ocean fifteen miles to the west greeted his arrival.

Walsh felt as if he travelled to a foreign land after traversing the vast distance from the oceans on each coast of America. Even having just arrived, Los Angeles appeared fundamentally different from Boston. Los Angeles and its surrounding communities covered an immense sprawl from an urban center to suburbs. According to his research, Los Angeles County covered an area as large as his familiar County Cork and County Kerry in Ireland combined.

—

"Good morning, Mr. Walsh. How was your trip from Boston?" Sol Wurtzel said, greeting Walsh at his studio office the following morning. A working office cluttered with piles of what

Walsh assumed were scripts. The walls displayed movie bill-boards of Fox produced movies.

"Exceptionally long but very interesting. America is a vast country."

"Are your accommodations suitable?"

"The Hollywood is a grand hotel, Mr. Wurtzel."

"Wonderful. Movie people from all over like it so you will fit right in. Ready to get started?"

"Absolutely. Looking forward to becoming a part of recreating my story for film."

"Mr. Fox is personally interested in filming *Price of Freedom*. He believes an enthusiastic market exists with the large Irish American population following the Irish struggle for independence as the setting for book. I have read your novel and am equally enthusiastic about the prospects of producing a successful movie. For that matter, John Ford, the director selected to do the film, also read your book. His preliminary ideas for adapting the story to film played a large part in our decision to purchase the film rights and immediately move into production.

"I have arranged for you to meet with your co-screenwriter Raymond Schrock. He collaborated on the script for the highly successful *Phantom of the Opera* starring Lon Chaney released last year. Mr. Schrock has a long list of screenplay credits. Since you have never written a movie script, he will guide you through the process. Without sound for dialog, you can image that it is much different than writing for a live theater play. As a motion picture, *Price of Freedom* is all about the plot and how the actors convey that on screen through facial expression and movement.

"Motion pictures are solely a visual medium so the script must define not only the plot but also emotional subtleties. The minimal dialog appearing on inter-title cards appearing on screen are mere prompts to assist the audience.

"The script frames the scenes more for the actors to interpret their performance for the role and provide them with proper visualization on screen. It also provides a means of determining scene length. Once completing film shooting, secondary editing pares down each scene by discarding certain film footage to craft the finished movie. The storyline must also be shortened to typically around 100 minutes viewing time. It's a complex creative process where the collective contribution of many creative people determines the success of the finished product."

"I understand. I already have a sense of the many moving parts. Especially the technical requirements of camera angles and lighting. I will welcome Mr. Schrock's guidance in drafting the script."

"And that of the director John Ford." Wurtzel pointed to a billboard poster of a native American in feathered headdress looking down from a cliff to a train. "He directed *The Iron Horse*. Released last year. Received critical acclaim. He will work closely with you and Schrock to develop the script that he must bring to life on film."

Walsh remarked, "Without the benefit of sound, it would seem the director has the most difficult task of transforming a collection of ideas and actions into something cohesive and believable. The movie's success rests overwhelmingly on the director's creative guidance."

"Well stated. The actors become the celebrities, but the director is responsible for bringing together everything that makes the movie work. *Price of Freedom* also requires many scenes filmed on a location outside the studio. Since that becomes a significant cost consideration, I too will participate in developing the script. My role is to stay on budget and produce a movie that will generate profits."

"I fully appreciate my role, Mr. Wurtzel. I will follow the lead of all of you that are experienced moviemakers. I understand that the movie script is fundamentally different from my written work. I see my chief contribution is to make the script and the actions appear authentic."

"As an artist, I believe you will enjoy experiencing the unique creative process of making a movie, Mr. Walsh. We use this studio now more for producing our Fox newsreels. Our principal production facilities for producing feature films are located to the west of here on Pico Boulevard. Depending on the requirements for a given scene, *Price of Freedom* will be filmed using studio sets along with external sets on the back lot, and of course likely some location filming elsewhere.

"I'll show you around to give you a sense of the equipment involved in moviemaking. We'll take you down to the Pico Boulevard complex in a couple of days. After lunch, we'll begin work here with Director Ford and Mr. Schrock."

The working areas of the film studio were anything but glamorous. More the appearance of a disorganized warehouse. Large lights suspended on wheeled pedestals everywhere, trailed by great collections of electrical cables. No natural light invaded unless large sliding panels opened to maneuver large sets into place. Wurtzel explained the camera arrangements set into place on certain working sets with some mounted onto carriages able to maneuver the camera position in any direction or height.

Over lunch, Sol Wurtzel asked, "How much of your novel paralleled your actual personal experiences.?"

"With a gun in my hand, I participated in all the major clashes with British forces portrayed in the novel. The only thing I changed was the characterization of the protagonist Brandon Flynn."

"Yes, the big fellow. Son of a blacksmith. We cast that perfectly with veteran actor Victor McLaglen playing the lead as Brandon Flynn. McLaglen is a tall fellow. Former boxer. Seen any of his movies?"

"Afraid not. I've seen only a few movies actually. Mostly since coming to America."

"Well, you'll like Victor. He's paired with a new starlet named Tara Kelly with just a few credits to her name. A tall young woman that will complement McLaglen's stature on film."

As they worked through lunch, Wurtzel became engrossed as Walsh related his many IRA experiences in response to Wurtzel's questions. Egan Walsh was the real thing.

Wurtzel eventually focused on the action sequences from the pragmatic perspective of where best to film these scenes. Most required location filming. "Even though Southern California offers a diverse physical environment that can substitute for a great many locations around the world, duplicating Ireland becomes a challenge. At some point early on in working the script, you, Ford, Schrock, and I will make a journey up the coast to San Luis Obispo County. Preliminary research suggests it might offer the best possibilities for standing in for Ireland. The first task is determining which scenes must be filmed on location."

An enjoyable start for Walsh sensing Wurtzel's enthusiasm for the project.

Returning to the studio, John Ford, Victor McLaglen, and Raymond Schrock were waiting outside Wurtzel's office.

"Sorry to keep you gentlemen waiting. Became carried away listening to Mr. Walsh telling me of his experiences in Ireland. Please introduce yourselves to Mr. Walsh. Together we're going to make a great movie."

Walsh shook hands with everyone. All were of similar age somewhere in their thirties, with McLaglen probably older by a few years. McLaglen stuck out because of his height and physique. Massive hands and a vice-like grip perhaps expected from an ex-professional boxer of some reputation. The others all wore glasses presenting a studious impression.

As they filed into Wurtzel's office, McLaglen said to him, "I read your book, Mr. Walsh. A bloody great story. Look forward to talking to you. I saw service in the Great War, so we have something in common."

As they sat around a large round table, Wurtzel said to Walsh, "The movie business is an informal work environment, Egan. We all use first names, including me. Shall we begin?"

Director John Ford spoke first. "We all read your fine book, Egan. Ray and I have already begun working on blocking out key scenes. Sol and I need to develop a budget. A large part of that is determined by location filming and set requirements."

Walsh said, "Yes, Sol told me about that. Said we need to travel north to examine suitable terrain."

"That's right. Those battles in Tooreen and Kilmichael will make for dramatic scenes, so we need to make them convincing."

Wurtzel added, "Yes, that is high on the agenda. Today I would like to introduce Egan to the hectic business of making movies. Time and schedules are everything. For example, Victor graciously broke out of his busy schedule to join us. He is currently shooting *What Price Glory* for us. Shooting is scheduled for completion by the end of February that fits with the beginning of shooting *Price of Freedom* starting in March. Tara Kelly, Victor's costar as Nora Gallagher could not come today because she is also shooting another movie."

Wurtzel continued, "Constructing the outline of the script is necessary not only for blocking out the scene shooting, but also for casting the supporting characters that make it from novel to the movie. We are somewhat constrained in time because usually we have a script before launching the project. With Raymond's writing experience, John's directional guidance, and your intimacy with the story, we need a first-rate script to capture the essence of your novel for the big screen as soon as possible.

"With that said, I will leave you gentlemen to kick things off by deciding how best to proceed for developing a great script. Stop by my office, Egan, before you leave for the day."

With that, John Ford took the lead. The quality of the movie in all its aspects rested principally with the director. Therefore, he participated in everything from script development, to casting, shooting the film, and then editing to produce the desired effect so essential for refining what will dictate the overall success of the movie.

"Well, as Sol said, "Let's get to it. Why don't you start off, Ray? Because time is critical, Egan, Ray and I also did some preliminary work on thoughts for condensing your story into movie-length. You experienced the events portrayed in the story. That's why we need you as technical consultant. Your credits as scriptwriter, however, are not gratuitous. You are a writer. So don't hesitate to offer ideas or even criticisms. We all have thick skins in this business."

They worked through the afternoon on outlining the script. Walsh was impressed with everyone's familiarity with his book. He also felt encouraged that the shortened screen adaptation preserved the essence of the story. Finding the creative exchanges stimulating, Walsh quickly expelled uncertainties about his contributing value in making the movie. His role as technical consultant promised to place him at the shooting of every scene. As the meeting adjourned for the day, John Ford declared they would resume at 8:00 the next morning.

McLaglen said to Walsh before he left, "I won't be joining you tomorrow. Have a full day of shooting with *What Price Glory*. Besides, writing the script is best left to you blokes. Fascinated by the description of your terrible war against the British made me think I must tell you something up front.

"Fox is billing *Price of Freedom* as an all-Irish cast. From the author of the popular novel and screenplay to cast and director. Ford is not John's real last name. O'Feeny or Ó Fearna or some such. Father came from Galway, he told me. Tara Kelly is pure Irish. Everyone thinks I am Irish because I've played a lot of Irish parts. After your wartime experiences, hope you are not offended to learn I am really British."

Walsh smiled with genuine warmth since he instantly took a liking to McLaglen. "No problem whatsoever, Victor. My fight was against the British government not the British people."

McLaglen returned a large exuberant grin and put his arm around Walsh's shoulder. "We'll make a great movie together, mate. Say, would you like to have dinner with me and my wife Enid tonight? She also read your book and is anxious to meet you. We can get a real drink of good whiskey at the place where we are going for dinner. Good, bonded whiskey not bootlegged crap."

"Sounds good. I would enjoy that, Victor."

"Good. I will pick you up about seven. Where are you staying?"

"The Hollywood Hotel."

"See you later then," as McLaglen slapped him on the back."

As instructed, Walsh stopped at Wurtzel's office before leaving the studio.

Wurtzel said, "How did your afternoon go?"

"Just grand. Fine bunch of fellows. Made me feel part of the team. Have an appreciation where I can best contribute. Looking forward to getting back into it first thing tomorrow morning."

"Wonderful. We will make an important movie together, Egan. I neglected to mention earlier, I have a studio car for your use. You do drive, don't you?"

"Oh yes. While in Boston it did take a while to get used to driving on the right though."

CHAPTER 5

Hollywood, California | 1926

Walsh was waiting in the lobby of the Hollywood Hotel that evening when in walked Victor McLaglen and his wife Enid. He cut an imposing figure with his height and broad shoulders. Enid was tall enough and attractive enough not to be upstaged by the imposing physical presence of her husband.

McLaglen's shook Walsh's hand. "This is my wife, Enid."

Enid offered her hand, "So glad to meet you, Mr. Walsh. I read your book. Both Vic and I can't wait to hear more about your wartime experiences in Ireland."

Walsh smiled. "Please call me Egan. Remember my book is a novel not all of it is autobiographical."

"Just the same, you make the reader feel the details of some horrific events. Much of that must have come from personal experience. The movie promises to be dramatic and exciting. And please call me Enid."

Victor said, "Well, you have the whole evening to chat with Egan, Dear. Right now, let's head to the restaurant. I'm hungry and could use a drink."

Turning to Walsh as they walked to McLaglen's big Packard. "Our favorite restaurant serves the best Italian food in town. Lots of movie folks eat there. The owner Angelo provides an additional inducement for his regulars. In the back, he keeps individual lockers. You bring in your favorite liquor so it's always available for your table. Great for Angelo's business."

"Wonderful. I could use a drink. Why America banned liquor is beyond me. Half the population enjoys some type of alcohol."

"Very strange indeed. But good liquor is not hard to find in Hollywood," McLaglen said. "I can promise you good whiskey. *Trattoria Marchetti* serves wine of course. Not even discreet about it."

Walsh responded, "Excellent. When I lived in Boston, I favored the many good Italian restaurants. Liquor was also plentiful in Boston but mostly at speakeasies. Lots of speakeasies. Is that the same here in Los Angeles?"

"Yup. The police turn a blind eye."

As they drove east along Hollywood Boulevard, Enid McLaglen said, "We just passed another place Vic and I like. It's located on the second floor of a financial building of all things. Called the Montmartre Café. Hollywood's first nightclub. Jazz band with a VIP room in the back serving good liquor."

Walsh added, "As long as the speakeasies pay off the police, it's good business for everyone. However, Prohibition creates official corruption that has wider implications. Creates a perfect illegal enterprise by providing something most everyone wants. A stupid idea that seems so obvious. Wrote a lot about that when I reported for the *Boston Globe*."

All three shared whiskeys before dinner.

Enid said, "May I ask a personal question, Egan?"

"Sure."

"The Nora Gallagher character in your book. Was she patterned after someone in your life?"

Walsh smiled. "Afraid not. I had a girl before I joined the IRA. Might have led to something until I quit my job as a reporter for the *Cork Examiner* to become an IRA fugitive. Decided she wanted nothing to do with my taking up arms against the British. Accused me of forsaking her for politics. I never saw her again after we parted. The Gallagher character is a composite of many women that supported us in the Cumann na mBan. A brave lot they were. The intelligence network comes from my real experience. My first job in the IRA was battalion intelligence officer. I know what those women did risking their lives to support the IRA.

"Of course, I needed a female figure to make my fictional story come alive and show what wives, sisters, and mothers of those openly fighting endured. From my fellow IRA, I heard many heartbreaking stories of their loved ones getting by without them. Life for women in Ireland was difficult enough without losing their man or the family's principal male figure. Mere survival was a struggle for the Irish working class without considering the added difficulties of living under military occupation."

Enid nodded. "Well, you did a bang-up job of creating a strong female character for the movie."

Victor said, "You've not yet met Tara Kelly. Good actress. She played a good part in *Damaged Goods*, a movie I made a couple of years ago in Britain. A pretty young lady."

"Yes, she is, Darling. Maybe ten years younger," Enid said. "How are they going to make you appear closer to your age?"

"The makeup and lighting people do miracles, my dear. They can even make my ugly mug look years younger," Victor said.

Walsh said, "Speaking of your face, Vic, it looks pretty good for an ex-boxer. Read you even went six rounds with Jack Johnson, the heavyweight champion at the time."

"Long time ago when I was in my prime. Johnson never knocked me down ... but he sure beat the livin' be-Jesus out of me. My face looked something awful when it ended."

Walsh replied, "When I went to college in Ireland, I took up real boxing to keep myself in shape. I was a pretty good scrapper when I was young. My older brother taught me how to handle myself against the older toughs picking on me. Schoolyard fighting. When I got into the ring at college, those that knew what they were doing in the ring taught me some painful lessons."

"Did you stay with it?"

"Good enough to compete as a welterweight in college. The training served me well in the war. Especially when forced to resort to street fighting tactics."

"Speaking of war, did you serve in the Great War, Vic?"

"Yep. Served mostly in the Middle East. 10th Battalion, Middlesex Regiment. Wounded twice but no permanent damage. Held the rank of captain when decommissioned at the end of the war."

Turning serious, Walsh asked, "Did my perspective on the conduct of British security forces during the war in Ireland offend you?"

McLaglen shook his head. "No. Hard to imagine British soldiers acting the way you portrayed them in some of the scenes though. I trust what you wrote is what you experienced?"

Walsh nodded. "I did not exaggerate. Remember, these villains I wrote about were just former soldiers. The Black & Tans and Auxiliaries were now acting as mercenaries. Quasi-police taking over from the former Royal Irish Constabulary. Fighting the IRA in an ugly guerilla war where the Irish population despised them.

"You must also appreciate the circumstances for British security forces deployed in Ireland, Vic. This war did not have the clarity of the Great War. They were not fighting for homeland, but instead for what amounted to holding onto a colony. Another rebellion as the Irish periodically did over hundreds of years. This was no different than the American Revolution."

"These Black & Tans and RIC Auxiliaries you portray as monsters. Why did they murder and burn property in Ireland?" Enid asked.

"Can't tell you why men in war sometimes resort to barbarity. Yet for the most part, British regular troops behaved as soldiers. The IRA usually reciprocated in kind. The Black & Tans and the Auxiliaries stand apart as terrorists. Black & Tans were unemployed veterans of the Great War from the ranks. The Auxiliaries unemployed former British Army officers. Economic times in Britain after the war were difficult for all demobilized veterans. Desperate for employment then thrown into circumstances totally different from the Great War."

"For sure," McLaglen said. "The war ruined the economy. Put the country in considerable debt. Not easy to reemploy millions of former soldiers."

"These Black & Tans and Auxiliaries received attractive pay to sign up for a year. As police, not soldiers. They had arrest powers as Royal Irish Constabulary. Perhaps that gave them the feeling they were fighting brigands and criminals. For the Auxiliaries their aggression may have stemmed from difficulties adjusting to loss of status and pay in civilian life. As British officers, most did not come from the moneyed class. Losses by the second year of the Great War demanded Britain fill the need for junior officers by promoting from the ranks. Even referred to these officers by the demeaning term *temporary gentlemen.*"

Victor commented, "I know the term. I was one of those *temporary gentlemen.*"

Walsh continued, "I suspect the average British soldier serving in Ireland did not want to be there. The conflict was unpopular in Britain. Probably the same as those serving King George III in the American colonies a 150 years ago. They also were fighting an unconventional war. The IRA had few men with few weapons and always limited ammunition. Acquiring weapons became the objective of many attacks. That meant fighting a hit and run guerrilla war. Frustrating for conventional troops unable to pin down the enemy."

"Now the Essex Regiment was something different. Why, I can't say. Like the Black & Tans and Auxiliaries, they believed terrorizing the Irish population could break support for the IRA.

"It did not work. The IRA felt the only response to terror was counterterror. The West Cork flying column acted on that strategy. I was part of that. My novel is largely about attacking and evading those British forces engaged in murder, torture, and destruction of property. Fair enough to judge me and those I served for resorting to our own brutal methods.

"Didn't mean to run on about such unpleasantness with my new friends. Please forgive me."

"Nothing to forgive, Egan. Vic and I are not offended," Enid said.

Victor added, "Certainly not. Just glad you don't resent me being a *limey.*"

Walsh laughed. "Publicity portrays you as Irish so that's enough to make you a brother."

After a wonderful dinner with a bottle of wine, Enid asked, "May I ask another personal question, Egan?"

Walsh smiled and nodded.

"Why did you leave Ireland?"

"After fighting the British for two years of bitter fighting with all the death and destruction, Ireland did not achieve independence. The Treaty with Britain made Ireland self-governing like other nations such as Canada, Australia, and New Zealand. Yet not independent. The Treaty also retained the industrialized northern six counties of Ireland as an integral part of the United Kingdom. Ireland therefore was partitioned making eventual independence for the entire island unlikely.

"Regrettably, Ireland remains within the British Empire. A terrible failure for the Irish after suffering so much. I hated the terms of the Treaty as did a good many in the IRA. Unfortunately, many of those anti-Treatyists in the IRA voiced a willingness to continue fighting. With British forces completely leaving Ireland, that meat continued fighting against the new Provisional Irish Government and the National Army. By the rhetoric of certain prominent IRA leaders, I believed the antagonisms might turn the country into civil war.

"The Irish people were tired of war. So was I. My disappointment with the terms of the Treaty could never cause me to take up arms against former comrades. Inevitably the discord descended into a vicious civil war. Irish against Irish. IRA against IRA.

"My former commander Tom Barry, a personal colleague and close friend during the war took an active leadership role with the anti-Treaty rebels. Captured by the Irish Free State National Army, he escaped. I came under immediate suspicion because of my wartime association with Barry's notorious IRA flying column. I was arrested and imprisoned in Dublin's Mountjoy Prison. I faced trial by a military tribunal no different than under British rule.

"Spent two miserable months in confinement. The country became paranoid following the assassination of Michael Collins by anti-Treaty forces. Collins successor in command of the Irish National Army ordered my release since there existed no evidence of my helping the anti-Treaty faction.

"The civil war allowed no middle ground. Impossible to resume my newspaper job with the *Cork Examiner*. Leaving Ireland became my only option.

"The civil war lasted ten months. Its aftermath will affect the Irish psyche for decades. Brothers and friends killing each other as in any civil war. The Irish Free State government proved just as capable of brutality as the British. The British *officially* executed 24 people during the Anglo-Irish War after sentencing by military court martial. The Free State executed 81 in the civil war."

Victor and Enid sat transfixed as Walsh recited his reasons for leaving Ireland. They could see the emotional pain reflected in his face.

"I should not have asked," Enid said.

"Not at all, Enid," Walsh responded laying a hand over hers on the table. "The painful disappointments that compelled my leaving Ireland have receded into memory. My fortunes turned for the better since coming to America."

Changing the subject to more pleasant territory, Victor said, "That it did, Egan. A successful author about to turn his novel into a movie. *Price of Freedom* will become good for both of us."

Walsh replied, "Yes it will. All the better with finding new friends like you and Enid."

———

The script team assembled around a large round table in a conference room at Fox Films. Egan Walsh, John Ford, Raymond Schrock, with Wurtzel's secretary Lilly Romano to take notes. A table in the corner held a coffee urn and a tray of breakfast pastries.

John opened the work session. "Let's start with the opening scene of the movie. For impact, what about the Tooreen Ambush? Strong action and introduces the central character Flynn."

Schrock added, "Starting at that point also allows covering all the dramatic events of the novel with ample development while reducing it closer to 100 or no more than 120 minutes."

Walsh nodded, "That makes sense."

Schrock said, "I made my own list of the most dramatic scenes. Makes for a surprisingly effective sequence of theatrical peaks offering interesting intervening opportunities for building to the next powerful scene."

"Lilly, pass copies to John and Egan."

Ford and Walsh took several moments to scan Schrock's list.

Ford began making notes on the list with a pencil. After a couple of minutes, he said, "If we use this as the production blueprint, a substantial portion of the filming must be on location."

Schrock replied, "Seems that way."

Still thinking out loud, Ford said, "Some of the outdoor close-ups might be staged on the back lot. Need to research these lorries used by British forces to make them accurate."

Turning to his secretary, Ford said, "Lilly, make a note to set up Egan with Jake Lassiter and Evelyn Sullivan." To Walsh, he explained, "Jake is the property master. He needs to start planning for such essentials as these lorries and the various weapons. Evelyn is our head of costume design. Help her get the uniforms and Irish clothing right. They are both located at our main studio complex where we will film the movie. About nine miles southeast of here between Pico Boulevard and Santa Monica Boulevard. Multiple studios and a large back lot. Mr. Fox is still expanding the facility situated on 99 acres.

"Getting back to the location shooting. Makes getting up to San Luis Obispo County soon imperative. Lilly, check my schedule for next week. Need to block out three days to scout possible locations. Need a still photographer to go along. Get Vernon Abernathy. Also Fred Stanton who is to be art director for *Price of Freedom*. Once there, Egan, you need to look for terrain that might serve as suitable locations to duplicate the actual locales in Ireland. Abernathy will then take photos."

Schrock said, "Can we spend the rest of the today working the script?"

Ford nodded. "I blocked out today and tomorrow to work with you and Egan. Want to get a preliminary draft then let you guys flesh out details and define casting requirements."

They made sufficient progress on the script by capturing the principal scenes that defined the story arch. From there they annotated each scene or sequence of scenes with enough production detail to present a preliminary blueprint for the many set requirements, including specifics for the location filming. Walsh was amazed with the pace of the creative process behind the making of a movie.

On Friday, Ford announced to everyone, "Great work everyone. This has the makings for a damn impressive action movie. Next Tuesday morning we head north to San Luis Obispo. Get us train tickets, Lilly. You'll be coming too. Hire two cars in San Luis Obispo. Sturdy cars capable of driving about the back roads looking for location possibilities. Book hotel rooms for three nights for all of us. Fred Stanton and Vernon Abernathy are to meet us here at seven sharp."

Lilly Romano appeared more like a colleague than just administrative help. She reflected an air of confidence. Older than all the men in the room by several years. Her hair was fashioned in a complimentary style. Makeup as if she was auditioning for a movie part. She dressed distinctively as a professional, advertising her equality to her male associates. Attired as neither a flapper nor the buttoned-up style of an earlier time. She wore a white blouse with tailored trousers and fashionable shoes with low heels. Her idea of working clothes.

Even wearing reading glasses, Lilly Romano was uncommonly attractive. Walsh wondered if she might have come to Hollywood as a younger woman looking to be in movies only to become disillusioned with the fierce competition of so many beautiful young women. Obviously intelligent and talented, did she find her niche behind the cameras as making for a more reliable career? Ford and Wurtzel obviously relied on her abilities.

Ford said, "Having read your novel, Egan, we all have a good sense of what was going on in Ireland during the war. We need to put the movie into context for marketing purposes, maybe even an on-screen forward to set the circumstances for the moviegoer. The antagonists are not the British in general. The heart of the story's tension comes from those military forces terrorizing the Irish. The Black & Tans and the Auxiliaries. They are the villains in the movie. Could you draft a forward for a title card explaining the distinction? Very concise with just enough for moviegoers and reviewers to grasp the essence of the story. Framed from the perspective of the Irish protagonists. Just a couple of paragraphs spanning no more than two title cards."

"Certainly. I will work on it this weekend, John," Walsh said.

"Wonderful. Going forward, things likely will become more hectic. Weekends are not sacred in the moviemaking business, Egan."

"Not a problem, John. I am enjoying the creative process immensely."

Ford stood up and stretched. "Now everyone, get out of here and have a relaxing weekend."

For Egan Walsh, he welcomed some alone time. Except for dinner with the McLaglen's, he had been working nonstop since arriving in Hollywood. The weekend presented an opportunity to explore the greater Los Angeles area.

The following morning, he set out driving his studio-supplied 1925 Ford coupe armed with a map and a thermos of coffee. His first destination was Santa Monica.

As he drove west, the endless suburban environs of Los Angeles stretching fifteen miles to the ocean proved an enlightening experience as to what made Los Angeles unique. Unlike Boston, Los Angeles covered an immense geographic area. He made frequent detours exploring the upscale neighborhoods in the Hollywood Hills to the north then the magnificent estates of Beverly Hills further to the west. Many of the biggest movie stars made their home in Beverly Hills. Magnificent mansions set on acres of landscaped grounds.

By the time he arrived in Santa Monica at the famous pier with its rollercoaster, he was hungry. Although few people frequented the pier or the beaches in the winter, he found a lunch counter. In Boston, he acquired the taste for American hotdogs with mustard and ketchup washed down with Coca-Cola.

After lunch, he headed south following the coastline that eventually turned eastward toward Orange County. Orange County was forty miles south of Los Angeles. According to his map, in between was a contiguous suburban expanse of individually named smaller cities. A populated area even greater when considering the communities to the east of Los Angeles that he passed through when arriving by train.

A bright sunny day along the seashore. A modest temperature while most of the country contended with middle of winter weather. The climate alone is understandably reason enough for many people relocating to Southern California.

After passing the port city of Long Beach and turning eastward, he left the spectacular coastline only to be confronted with a jarringly ugly sight. Another expanse of closely spaced towering wooden oil drilling derricks dominated the view. The same spectacle he saw from the train when coming into Los Angeles as they passed through Santa Fe Springs. Driving further along the coastline into Orange County, yet another stand of oil derricks dominated the otherwise pretty beach community of Huntington Beach.

Once beyond the view of the oilrigs he stopped at Newport Beach. Sitting on a bench on the beach and watching the fiery orange hues of the sunset reflecting in the wave sets of the surf lapping the beach made him think of Ireland. The journey back to Hollywood took him through the boundless expanse of orange groves giving Orange County its name.

The day proved a rewarding experience tinged with some melancholy. He missed Fiona. He wrote to her the day after arriving in Los Angeles. Describing the train trip, he avoided making any overt romantic comments, closing the letter by simply saying he missed her.

Ending the letter that way now seemed impersonal. He'll write to her again tomorrow. Tell of his first days working on the movie script and the forthcoming trip next week to scout outdoor filming locations. His emotions dictated he must find a way to express his affection without obligating her to reciprocate. Find a practical solution that will allow them to be together openly.

The next day was Sunday. After breakfast, dark clouds begin rolling in from the ocean. It began to rain. Not unusual since most of Southern California's limited rainfall came during the winter months. A good day to work on the movie forward. Also, the gloomy day complimented his mood for writing another letter to Fiona. Something better expressing his feelings.

My dearest Fiona,

My first days on the job have been most rewarding. I started writing the movie script. Working with director John Ford and an experienced screenwriter Ray Schrock. Met the star, Victor McLaglen. He and his wife took me to dinner. All are wonderful people. Tuesday we will venture north of Los Angeles to scout locations for filming the outdoor scenes. Nothing around Los Angeles looks like County Cork.

Very enthused about working on this project. Just one thing would make it better. Having you here with me. Our relationship has moved far beyond intellectual bonding. I love being with you. Our intimacy makes me feel alive. Do you share that same intensity? If so, we need to discuss how we move forward to be together. We are no longer cousins. We are committed lovers.

Unfortunately, this opportunity has taken me thousands of miles from you. Probably for several months. Los Angeles is an interesting place with better winter weather than Boston. Yet I plan on returning to Boston once I fulfill my obligations working on the movie. After all, it is my movie, but you are in Boston.

Love, Egan

CHAPTER 6

Los Angeles, California | 1903

By 1926, Chadwick Hollister is among the most prominent business figures in Los Angeles. The only son of prominent Wall Street investment banker Franklin Hollister, Chadwick came to Los Angeles in 1903. Twenty-nine at that time, the younger Hollister was the heir apparent to eventually head Hollister Financial. His father was CEO and his uncle Joseph executive vice president. The financial institution founded as a commercial bank by his paternal grandfather in the 1840s evolved into a major Wall Street investment bank under the leadership of his father by 1880. A successful competitor of J.P. Morgan, Hollister Financial specialized in development financing in New York and other major Eastern cities.

In 1903, Franklin Hollister was looking for new investment horizons. The West still represented America's frontier with all the opportunities that accompanied underdeveloped regions. The Great Plains opened to exploitation in the later part of the 19th century with rapid settlement following the subjugation of the native American population. Railroads followed, bringing commerce and the means for people to traverse the vast distance coast to coast. The elder Hollister was also looking for an opportunity to test the entrepreneurial banking acumen of his son, his likely successor to eventually head Hollister Financial.

It was Franklin Hollister's inspiration that moved the bank from its successful but modest commercial New England banking business into investment banking. The clientele changed to large corporations with the magnitude of financial transactions exponentially increasing. Corporations demanded a broader range of services, and competition became more formidable. Although rapidly growing, Southern California was still underdeveloped enough to represent unlimited entrepreneurial financial investment opportunity.

Los Angeles in 1903 had more than doubled its population in the last decade to over 160,000. Los Angeles County was close to 270,000. Indicators forecast the rate of growth to continue accelerating. By 1926, those numbers would grow to a population of 1,000,000 for the City of Los Angeles and 1,700,000 for the county.

In those intervening decades, two factors propelled the extraordinary growth. Additional railroad services into Los Angeles combined with extensive promotion for people to relocate to Southern California. In 1885, the Santa Fe Railroad entered Southern California setting off a rate war with the entrenched Southern Pacific Railroad. Ticket prices dropped to such lows that anyone could afford the fares to travel westward from any part of the United States. This provided the foundation for extensive promotion luring people to come to Southern California, the newest location for economic opportunity.

With the ability to travel west cheaply, promoters published advertisements in Eastern and Midwest newspapers extolling life in southern California. A healthy Mediterranean-type climate with warm winters, unlimited employment opportunities, and abundant fertile farmland. Promotional language made little attempt at adhering to the truth. For example, the land was only conditionally fertile. After all, the Los Angeles basin was climatically classified as high desert. The sandy soil lacked the organic material of the rich Midwest soil. To grow anything in Southern California requires great amounts of water. In a region with comparatively sparse rainfall occurring only in the winter months, sufficient water for agriculture was in chronic short supply. Yet advertisements for agricultural investment ignored those drawbacks, preferring to instead emphasize the extended growing season.

———

Chadwick Hollister, chafing under the yoke of his domineering father, jumped at the chance to get far away from New York. Anxious to get into the speculative business environment of Los Angeles as an opportunity to independently demonstrate his talents. Opening the California branch of Hollister Financial also presented altogether different challenges than New England. Challenges in which his father could not claim superior knowledge. Difficult for his father to interfere with the inability to interact face to face. The slow process of exchanging paperwork worked to his advantage. Communications by telephone put his overbearing father at a decided disadvantage.

Not long after arriving in Los Angeles, Chadwick Hollister understood that resolving the shortage of water was the pivotal factor for sustaining growth in the Los Angeles basin. Regardless of the hyperbolic promotional rhetoric, insufficient water would soon curtail the influx of Americans coming to paradise. Los Angeles' only source of water was the comparatively minor Los Angeles River. Seasonally inconsistent except during the spring when melting snow in the Sierra Nevada often caused damaging flooding.

According to reliable geological reports, the water problem must be solved very soon, or Los Angeles would revert to its origins as a remote Mexican pueblo. For investment opportunities with growth potential to materialize for Hollister Financial, that meant everything hinged on water. Some estimates suggested the Los Angeles River could provide only enough water to support a population of 250,000. Considering the entire County of Los Angeles, the region was already at the limit of sustainability. A sustained period of drought could prove a disaster. Hollister must direct all his attention into determining the viability of existing water planning. If a long-term solution is not developed soon, then the Los Angeles growth boom will collapse. The young

Hollister had no intention of this challenge ending in a failed venture for Hollister Financial. He intended nothing short of achieving success in Southern California. Impress his father and take his rightful place at the helm of the family financial enterprise.

Before heading west, Hollister conducted research to understand the political landscape and business interests of the 20th century phenomenon that was Los Angeles. Transforming from an insignificant Mexican pueblo just fifty years earlier when California became a state presented unlimited banking opportunities for the right person. With sufficient water, Los Angeles investment opportunities became unlimited.

Moral or ethical subtleties never constrained Chadwick Hollister. Raised with wealth, his parents made him believe he was special. Yet where his mother insincerely complimented, his father ruthlessly criticized, expecting his only son to excel with unreasonable expectations. Chadwick applied his intellect to achieving a desired result by ignoring any impediments of conscience. His father was a ruthless autocrat, feared in business dealings. The cause of his son's sociopathic and narcissistic traits once becoming an adult became impossible to separate as genetic or behaviorally programmed.

Chadwick Hollister intended to succeed in Los Angeles. Failure was not an option. Applying that attitude to his research, he understood he must align himself with those in power in Southern California. Whether that meant embracing as allies or getting close to potential rivals. His favored work of classical literature understandably was Niccolò Machiavelli's treatise *The Prince*. A blueprint for ruthlessly managing from a position of power. Applicable in business no different from those of ruling princes. However, Hollister chose to ignore the many underlying logical based aphorisms of Machiavelli's observations about politics and governing. His simplified philosophy reduced to seeking advantage by any means possible and ignoring consequences.

With that mindset, he was interested in learning as much as possible about the character and ambitions of those that might prove helpful in resolving Los Angeles' water shortage. The water problem was reduced to a set of basic elements. Hollister was no geologist therefore any solution must be backed by solid science. In effect, finding sustainable water. If it existed, the problem became how to get it to Los Angeles. That likely meant a great deal of money. It also meant possibly taking water from its current owners. No different from the taking of the great plains from native Americans.

When Hollister arrived in Los Angeles, he came prepared to hit the ground running. Where could additional water come from? Who were the local powerbrokers that recognized the problem? What ideas were under consideration? Who were those with the willingness to do whatever necessary to carry out the *acquisition of water*? That is what investment banks did. Provide funding for ventures with profit potential. If he saw a clear solution, then it was just a matter of teaming with the right people willing to see it through. A worthy challenge for a young New York banker to fund the project providing the foundation for unlimited Southern California investment opportunities.

———

Hollister met with Los Angeles Mayor Meredith Snyder. Introducing himself, "Mr. Mayor, I have come to your city to offer the financial resources of Hollister Financial to the various business interests fueling the region's extraordinary growth. All indications point to the immediate problem of water. Los Angeles cannot continue to grow unless it finds the means of increasing the water supply. What is your view?"

Snyder replied, "Water is truly our most vexing problem. The best person to talk to is my predecessor, Frederick Eaton. He is the foremost alarmist concerning the inadequate supply of water from the Los Angeles River. Eaton is also the former superintending engineer of the Los Angeles City Water Company before it became a public department of the city a few years ago. His protégé William Mulholland is now the superintendent of the Los Angeles Department of Water."

Hollister immediately contacted Fred Eaton. Their first meeting lasted hours. Although self-centered, Hollister could disguise his arrogance and become charming when it suited his purpose. Although naturally inclined to hucksterism, Hollister was an effective salesman. Sensing Eaton's devotion to resolving the Los Angeles water problem, he knew he found the person to pitch his offer of financial assistance for any viable means of securing enough water for Los Angeles.

"As an investment banker, I am looking for new opportunities. Los Angeles is that best opportunity with the fastest population growth rate in the country. However, as my research makes clear, adequate water must be found to sustain that growth."

"You are correct, Mr. Hollister. Very soon, Los Angeles demand will exceed its current source of water. The Los Angeles River originates in the Santa Monica and Santa Susana Mountains. The benefits from snowpack melt are therefore minimal when compared to rivers with head waters in the higher Sierra Nevada Mountains."

"As a newcomer to Southern California, I am sure there are local business interests willing to invest in solutions that will bring continuing prosperity to the region. Seems I have come to the right person to make my offer of financial assistance. If a realistic means of securing an abundant and sustainable new source of water exists, such a project warrants an investment with prospects for significant financial return. I therefore want to make a proposal to you and other likeminded business interests that Hollister Financial stands ready to participate with the necessary capital required to ensure the prosperity of Los Angeles."

Hollister's offer was contingent on making a profit not only from prospective lucrative business opportunities of a thriving Los Angeles, but also in the financing of a viable water project. Such a project would undoubtedly be massive with an investment to match. A municipal project meant suffering the uncertainty of securing public funds with endless red tape. Therefore, investment that might span years must provide commensurate returns.

Fred Eaton already harbored a bold solution. Something germinating for years. Eaton jumped at the opportunity of proposing his idea to someone with deep pockets. The other person critical for transforming his idea into reality was his close associate, William Mulholland.

Eaton paused for several moments before responding. Would this young New York banker be willing to engage in the necessary subterfuge? Regardless, he must seize the opportunity. "Would you be willing to make a difficult journey to the Sierra Nevada Mountains, Mr. Hollister? A week by wagon pulled by a team of mules?"

Caught off balance but quick to realize that Eaton possessed an actual idea for solving the water problem, Hollister replied, "Of course, if you could tell me something of what you have in mind."

"Very well. My solution to Los Angeles' water shortage is to bring water from the Sierra Nevada Mountains. An unlimited source fed by the annual replenishment of the snowpack of these high mountains. A difficult endeavor. The first is acquiring land and therefore the water rights of sizeable tracts of land. Then of course there is the engineering feat of constructing an aqueduct over two hundred miles to bring the water south."

Hollister did not know if what Eaton suggested was engineeringly realistic. Certain to cost millions of dollars. Yet what choice did he have? He must judge for himself. "Sounds like a bold project. A monumental project. If you believe it has possibilities then include me, Mr. Eaton."

Eaton smiled broadly and extended his hand. "Excellent. You appear to be a man of vision, Mr. Hollister. Our trip north will include one additional person. Another hydrology engineer like me. William Mulholland is a rugged fellow I have known for many years. Currently Superintendent of the Los Angeles Water Department."

For Fred Eaton, a remarkable stroke of luck in discovering Chadwick Hollister and convincing him to join with him and William Mulholland in making the exploratory journey. An arduous trek of 250 miles north to the Owens Valley located east of the Sierra Nevada Mountains and north of the Mojave Desert.

After a few days into the trip, Hollister regretted his decision. Although with aspirations to become a rancher, Eaton was a politician and urban creature. Neither he nor the younger Hollister were used to such physical demands traversing such difficult terrain. This was September 1904. Still summer in Southern California and unbearably hot. Hot daytime temperatures plummeted to cold nighttime lows.

In contrast, while the same age as Eaton, William Mulholland was a six-foot well-conditioned man with a bushy mustache accustomed to rough outdoor life. Used to the rigors of working outdoors, Mulholland took charge of making camp each night and cooking simple food. At least they brought along plenty of whiskey to ease their discomforts.

However, for all three the journey proved well worth the physical demands. Runoff from the Sierra Nevada Mountains fed the Owens River providing water for an otherwise arid Owens Valley. Yet agriculture in the valley struggled through lack of an irrigation system for distribution of the plentiful water from the river. Owens Valley was the solution to Los Angeles' water problem. Getting that water south meant constructing a gravity-driven aqueduct. Mulholland said that was technically possible given the elevation of Owens Valley with continuous descent going southward.

The aqueduct was an engineering problem. Acquiring the land was an economic problem. The ranchers and farmers in the valley controlled the water rights. Purchasing enough of the land to control the area's water rights without revealing the purpose was the first obstacle to overcome. Concealing the actual reason for this field trip became essential. Hollister grasped Eaton's concern over the larger problem of concealing the reason for acquiring the land at a price that made the project economically feasible. The otherwise distressed agricultural land value of Owens Valley would immediately inflate if it became known that its value rested with the water rights necessary for supplying water to drought-ridden Los Angeles to the south. The project would then collapse.

They spent a week assisting Mulholland in making a preliminary survey of the area. On the return trip, they spoke about how to go about securing those water rights. Hollister offered that Hollister Financial would provide not only financing for the land purchase but could also conceal the identity of the purchasers. With that offer, Hollister emphasized that multiple purchasers be used to obscure this as a coordinated plan. Everything hinged on purchasing most of the water rights without raising questions about the underlying intent.

—

The trip to Owens Valley afforded the opportunity for Hollister to become an integral member of a highly select group committed to resolving the Los Angeles water problem. Regardless of professed egalitarian motives, each person involved possessed a financial interest. They also understood that achieving success required that their activities remain secret. Certain activities undoubtedly crossed legal lines yet everything they did required elaborate deceit to conceal the true nature of what they were doing. They were playing for big stakes. Any leak outside the circle of conspirators and the project would fall apart.

In learning the names of his other conspirators to the aqueduct project, Hollister understood this went far beyond two water engineering cronies dreaming up a fantastical scheme. The scope of the project had too many facets. It required the will of some of the most powerful business interests in Southern California. People powerful enough to make this happen and weather any backlash.

Eaton and Mulholland eagerly shared the names of these people with Hollister. An offer of financial backing by a large investment bank provided a convincing foundation of the viability of the project.

The names included an impressive list of some of the most powerful local business figures. There was Harrison Otis, the owner of the pro-business *Los Angeles Times*. Otis' son-in-law Harry Chandler who was publisher of the *Los Angeles Times*. E. H. Harriman, President of the Southern Pacific Railroad. Henry E. Huntington, former Vice President of his uncle's Collis' Southern Pacific Railroad and current President of the Pacific Electric Railroad. Both Harriman and Huntington were also members of the San Fernando Syndicate, a secret group of real estate investors.

72

The San Fernando Valley bordered the City of Los Angeles and would become a key recipient of aqueduct water, increasing land values exponentially for inside traders.

Offering vital direct participation for various forms of financial renumeration, there was Moses Sherman, a member of the City of Los Aneles Water Board. Someone with access to confidential public planning related to water management.

Then there was Joseph Lippincott, the Federal Bureau of Reclamation regional engineer. The Bureau was currently exploring plans for building an irrigation system to help Owens Valley agricultural interests utilize the flow of the Owens River to irrigate the otherwise arid environment. Such a federal effort would block any diversion of water to Los Angeles. Lippincott was a close associate of Eaton. He provided invaluable insights into the progress of the potential federal irrigation project while interjecting information to Washington that might add delays.

Lastly, there was California U.S. Senator Frank Flint, a member of the LA Chamber of Commerce and member of the board of directors of two local banks. A strong advocate for Los Angeles economic growth, he would later sponsor a bill in Congress for building the Los Angeles aqueduct across federal lands to facilitate bringing water to Southern California.

Once they returned to Los Angeles, Eaton introduced Hollister to the most important conspirators actively backing the project. New York-based Hollister Financial was well known to financier Edward Harriman. Harriman welcomed the young New York banker's courage to take on a complex risky development of such scope. From a business perspective, Harriman viewed another financing source as good business to hedge his own financial participation. The unknown magnitude of investment required for purchasing the water rights and fronting the financing for the aqueduct presented enormous risk should public funding not materialize. Plenty of profit opportunities existed for sharing investment opportunities. The benefits of hedging rather than assuming the entire financial risk seemed a prudent strategy.

Over the next year, Eaton embarked on a land purchasing spree in Owens Valley. In some cases, he used strawmen to make the purchases to disguise his motives. Simultaneously, he needed to block the Federal Bureau of Reclamation's irrigation planning to assist struggling Owens Valley agriculture. Eaton's close association with the Bureau's regional engineer, Joseph Lippincott, became vital. For a substantial bribe, Lippincott provided confidential information. Going further, Eaton influenced Bureau planning through Lippincott by recommending actions beneficial to a Los Angeles aqueduct.

Encouraging struggling Owens Valley landowners to sell, Eaton offered higher than market prices for the land backed by Hollister Financial funding. The purchasing scheme should prove self-funding with profits expected from future sale of the water rights to the City of Los Angeles, once publicly funded through issuing of municipal bonds.

Once Eaton concluded his purchases, the Los Angeles cartel owned 85% of Owens Valley land with mortgages underwritten by Hollister Financial. With this initial phase of the conspiracy concluded, obtaining public financing for acquiring the water rights and constructing the aqueduct presented the next hurdle. For that to happen, the City must first get federal approval for running the aqueduct through federal land.

The following year Fred Eaton and Chadwick Hollister travelled to Washington. They met with California Senator Frank Flint, a strong supporter of bringing water to Los Angeles. Backed with persuasive economic arguments and substantial political contributions, Flint sponsored a bill granting rights of way through federal lands for the Los Angeles aqueduct.

A further meeting with President Roosevelt succeeded in securing the Owens Valley water for Los Angeles. They made the argument that the economic impact to the fastest growing city in the United States far outweighed the lesser agricultural benefit of the valley without federal funding of an irrigation system. The president agreed, designating the surrounding federal land as a national forest.

Bringing the Owen Valley's water to Southern California required a reservoir terminus once the water arrived in the south. According to William Mulholland, the ideal hydrological solution was to use the aquifer of the San Fernando Valley in Los Angeles County, as a natural reservoir without evaporation loss. Mulholland knowingly mislead the public by underestimating the City of Los Angeles future water demands to counter criticism of the project. Once opened, filling the San Fernando aquifer would consume the majority of available Owens Valley water.

The conspiracy also called for selling the excess water for San Fernando Valley agriculture. With insider information, the conspirators formed the San Fernando Syndicate. Included were Harrison Otis, Henry Huntington, and Chadwick Hollister. In this case, Hollister's investment was personal not a Hollister Financial transaction. Something he withheld from his father. The syndicate purchased substantial tracts of land.

The city charter, however, prohibited the sale or use of city water without two-thirds voter approval. To avoid this, the City of Los Angeles annexed a large portion of the San Fernando Valley with overwhelming voter support in the Valley with the promise of the aqueduct water or the alternative of doing without. The land purchases unified the public behind funding the aqueduct. Those major investors with advance knowledge of the aqueduct saw their land investments increase in value several fold following announcement of the project.

Securing the water rights that emptied the Owens Valley made possible by the Los Angeles Aqueduct proved a remarkable conspiracy for maintaining secrecy with so many individuals involved. The scheme could be attributed to the vision of Fredrick Eaton, made possible by the contributing engineering genius of William Mulholland. Hollister Financial under Chadwick Hollister's leadership made the project possible by underwriting the investment capital required for land acquisition and construction of the aqueduct.

———

The Los Angeles Aqueduct opened ten years after its inception with water flowing from the Owens Valley south into the San Fernando Valley in 1913. All those participating in the illicit conspiracy made out exceedingly well. Fred Eaton accomplished his dream of providing Los Angeles with the water necessary to fulfill its destiny. William Mulholland became a celebrity for successfully supervising the construction of the massive project. For all those making financial investment, the enormous profits justified the risk. Financing for the multi-year project of acquiring land then fronting the construction costs for the aqueduct before repayment by the City of Los Angeles earned extraordinary profits for Hollister Financial through charging front-loaded high interest rates paying dividends during the many years of construction.

Chadwick Hollister successfully executed the challenge of establishing Hollister Financial as a major player in Southern California investment banking. Once lack of water no longer impeded Los Angeles' growth, Hollister began investing heavily in commercial real estate.

Hollister pivotal role in making the Owens Valley scheme possible overshadowed the efforts Eaton and Mulholland. The resounding success made him a powerful player in Southland business and politics. His connections among the region's power brokers opened endless investment banking opportunities. His success also demonstrated to his father his ability to take over the helm of Hollister financial when the time came.

Chadwick Hollister learned a great deal from those early years in the Southland. The astounding success of the aqueduct project fed into his narcissistic character. With bragging rights as the smartest businessman in the Southern California, Hollister felt he finally arrived. Successfully establishing the western branch of Hollister Financial while overcoming difficult obstacles was a singular accomplishment. Exaggerating his contribution to the aqueduct enterprise allowed for comparison to the accomplishments of his father. Rescuing Los Angeles from an uncertain future outweighed anything his father accomplished.

By 1915, Chadwick Hollister was the largest individual owner of Los Angeles downtown commercial real estate. Hollister Financial was on its way to becoming the largest financier of commercial urban real estate development in Greater Los Angeles.

He became a leading fixture in the business and political environment of Los Angeles. He built a magnificent mansion in Beverly Hills on Benedict Canyon Drive on several wooded acres. A fifteen-mile commute to his office in downtown Los Angeles, Beverly Hills afforded a sense of rural living with easy access to Santa Monica on the seashore. For his office, he occupied two adjacent suites, 5B and 5C on the top floor of the Bradbury Building on South Broadway. His office was large, sumptuously decorated in rich mahogany bookcases and furniture with a private bathroom. A conference room adjoined his office. The other suite occupied his staff.

With only five floors, the exterior of the Bradbury was undistinguished. Nothing like the imposing towering buildings of Manhattan. Yet nothing in New York City could match the Bradbury's exquisite interior. Opened before the turn of the century, the interior of the Bradbury overwhelmed Hollister with its sheer beauty.

Walking through the front door, he entered a narrow lobby with a low ceiling. Walking a few steps further brought him into a cathedral-like space reaching up to a skylight illuminating a grand central court infused with natural sunlight. The ever-changing shadows cast accents during the daytime. The interior dazzled the eye with Italian marble and decorative terracotta. Ornamental wrought ironwork offset the polished oak woodwork as you looked up. Wrought iron open *birdcage* elevators added an elegant touch to the Victorian era design.

Having absorbed himself in bringing water to Los Angeles and building the Hollister Financial West brand, Chadwick Hollister was looking for a new challenge. Something lucrative yet exciting. The answer became obvious. Motion pictures.

By 1915, the center for domestic movie making was Hollywood. Gone was the strangle hold on the industry by the Motion Picture Patents Company, commonly known as the Edison Trust. Thomas Edison owned most of the patents related to motion picture filming technology. He established MPPC to enforce use of Edison filming equipment and the exclusively requirement to show only Edison produced films. In the early days of feature film production, New York studios began setting up alternative production facilities in Hollywood, California to circumvent Edison's enforcement of his virtual monopoly that was restricting artistic expression of the new medium.

In so doing, the studios immediately realized the advantages of locating production facilities in Southern California. Not only a climate that afforded year-round exterior filming, but the region afforded access to varied topography. Offering western frontier locations, desert, mountains, and seashore provided backgrounds capable of standing in for all manner of locations demanded for a movie.

By 1915, feature length moviemaking in Hollywood was also becoming a mature industry. Hollister was amazed to learn of the sizeable budgets for producing, promotion, and distributing major feature length movies. It offered short-term financing with large returns depending upon assessing the risks. This was a transient commodity that the public might embrace or flounder at the box office. But the intrinsic allure of movies captivated Hollister the same as viewers from every stratum of the population.

Motion pictures proved transcendent. It took the live stage of theaters in the large cities to every small town in the United States that could offer a venue to project motion films on a screen. Driven by this new technology, motion pictures represented a new art form with universal appeal accessible to everyone.

The slapstick comedies of Roscoe "Fatty" Arbuckle and newcomer Charlie Chaplin became resounding successes in not only America, but also Europe. The American early western films of William S. Hart and Tom Mix created a genre that would dominate motion pictures for decades well into the era of the *talkies*. Newcomer Douglas Fairbanks debuted in the D. W. Griffith production *The Lamb* in 1915, thrilled audiences with his athleticism. The silent era was beginning to mature, exploring more complex themes and applying technology to advance the quality of the viewing experience.

Moviemaking presented an intriguing new business opportunity for Chadwick Hollister. Perfectly situated close to the center of film production in Hollywood. With Hollister Financial's presence in New York he was equally close to corporate head-quarters for several of the major movie studios.

Chapter 7

San Luis Obispo, California | 1926

Taking seats on the train, Ford, Walsh, Schrock, and Lilly Romano sat in four facing seats to discuss how to shoot the film between using studio sets, the back lot, and location filming. The several hours of travel time to San Luis Obispo afforded time to discuss how to shoot the film while in route.

"I was speaking with Sol yesterday. We both have questions about how to film the action scenes of the Kilmichael Ambush. You were there, right?" John Ford said.

Sitting in the passenger seat, Walsh replied, "I commanded IRA Section Two attacking the second lorry of Auxiliaries. The role portrayed by the protagonist Flynn."

"Not sure how to phrase this delicately so I won't make the attempt. In your book, you imply with not too much subtlety that Tom Barry wanted to kill all these Auxiliaries. Is that true?"

Walsh hesitated for a moment. "You must understand the environment, John. The Auxiliaries were conducting a reign of terror. Murdering not only captured IRA but civilians as well. Indiscriminate beatings, torture, and property destruction. Tom Barry ordered retaliation with the same severity to counter their reign of terror. Make them fearful of moving about.

"Everyone volunteering for service in a flying column felt the same way. Take the fight to the enemy. Unable to match the strength in numbers and arms of that enemy, we resorted to using harsh tactics. Often the same methods as used by the enemy. Can't put that all on Tom Barry's doing though. I felt the same way at the time. Did my share of killing the enemy."

Ford remained silent for several moments. "What about the false surrender of the Auxiliaries you wrote about?"

"It happened. Cost the lives of three of our comrades. So, we cut down every one of the bastards."

"Well, here's the thing. That might be possible to explain with the benefit of a novel's written language. The opportunity to explain background and define context. Motion pictures are entirely visual except for occasional title cards. Limited by available screen time. My point is Sol and I agree we need to film the action scenes with all the dramatic violent content while being careful not to portray this as an IRA massacre. We are trying to capture the Irish American audience without introducing a point of controversy."

Walsh tamped down the visceral emotions rising from those memories. He decided it better not to explain the book's scene depicting the murder of Flynn's father as following the actual circumstances surrounding the murder of his own father. No need to justify what he did in the Irish War of Independence.

Walsh instead nodded. "I understand John. The point of the movie is to entertain not attempt to explain controversial actions. I am here to help you make a good movie. Gratified enough to see the script following the story arch much as I wrote it. Should help my book sales."

"Glad you feel that way, Egan."

Ford changed the subject to the reason for this trip to San Luis Obispo. "Ray, have you determined the scenes that require location filming?"

"Yes. Essentially the larger scale combat scenes associated with the ambushes. If we find the right terrain, we can possibly use the same location background footage filmed at different camera angles for other closer filmed scenes that we can replicate on the back lot."

Schrock continued, "Some of the building exteriors we can either contract for shooting in Ireland using distance film footage or create false exteriors on the back lot with the interiors filmed on sets."

He said to Walsh, "Don't suppose you have any photographs of these battle locations do you, Egan?"

Walsh smiled, "No. We were a wee bit busy at the time. I can tell you though that I remember everything about how things looked in sufficient detail. The hills, the roads, the rocks."

Ford said, "It is up to you, Egan, to make our picture appear authentic. You direct Abernathy to take still photos that appear promising and keep a record of our exact location and direction of the shot. Give us an idea how we might be able to take a location and make modifications such as adding fake stonewalls that seem so plentiful in rural Ireland. Use this photographic book I found in a bookstore, *Scenic Ireland*. It will give Fred Stanton a sense of what is required after you describe specific terrain as you remember it."

The rented cars were waiting for them at the train station when they arrived in the town of San Luis Obispo. Population 7,000 and boasting the California Polytechnic State University campus established here at the turn of the century. Ford noted that the town was large enough to probably offer hotel accommodations for the film crew and actors instead of roughing it in tents.

Using a climatic classification reference book of the world from the library, it was Ford that fixed on San Luis Obispo County offering the best possibility for replicating rural locations in Ireland. Both locations are classified as temperate with warm summers. The difference between Ireland and San Luis Obispo was Ireland experienced year-round greater rainfall whereas San Luis Obispo rainfall was restricted primarily to the winter months. Filming in March meant this was the beginning of spring for Southern California, probably the end of the rainy season. Might have to simulate rainfall. There should be enough foliage to allow replicating the countryside of County Cork Ireland. Research also determined suitable locations existed would more likely exist in the coastal regions of San Luis Obispo County. Typical fog in the mornings this time of year could add to the visual impression of County Cork, Ireland.

They would spend the night at San Luis Obispo's largest hotel, setting out early the next morning. After arriving, they spent the afternoon explaining to some locals about filming the movie. San Luis Obispo was to stand in for Ireland. They showed photographs from Ford's book that resembled the terrain of the important action scenes of IRA engaging British forces. The local consensus was the best possibilities lay to the west between the town of San Luis Obispo and the Pacific Ocean. Plenty of open country with dirt roads, most of which were unmarked though.

The only map they possessed was badly outdated. The area suggested showed very few roads. They would probably find roads or perhaps just farm tracks not even charted. This was sparsely populated rural Southern California. Needing help to navigate, for ten dollars a day Ford hired a young man that said he knew the area well to act as a guide.

Ray Schrock and Fred Stanton were familiar with the required production details described in the script. As art director, Fred Stanton explained to everyone, "The three distinct combat events represented the required location filming. Those same locations should also serve for shooting other scenes such as the IRA trekking through the fields. We just shoot from different angles to provide different backgrounds. Therefore, we are looking for terrain with vegetation to mimic the southwest Ireland. Irish buildings of course must be created on the back lot using suitable fake facades to duplicate their distinctive appearance."

John Ford interjected, "That's right. We are targeting Irish American viewers, so we need everything appearing authentic. That's why we have Egan Walsh as our Irish advisor."

The following morning, everyone dressed warmly. This was winter. Probably not much different from Ireland. Armed with field glasses, a good compass, and Vernon Abernathy with a still camera, they set out in the hired automobiles. Ford drove the lead vehicle with Walsh in the passenger seat. In the back seat sat Stanton with Billy the local young man holding the Irish photographic book. Walsh marked the photos that best represented what they were looking for.

That day they bumped along miles of backcountry. Many roads appearing on the map turned out to be nothing more than rutted paths. However, the greenery was promising. The distant hills looking from the coast toward the east could duplicate similar hills in West Cork. There were also lower hills to the southwest right up to the ocean. Abernathy took photos as everyone contributed comments relating to the view as compared to Walsh's recollected descriptions. Stanton noted the locations on the map correlating to Abernathy's shots. Ford looked over the terrain often in silence, occasionally asking questions. Before moving on, Ford made his assessment of the suitability for filming each location. Taking notes, Lilly said to Walsh, "John is visualizing shooting the scene. Deciding if it fits his mental image of the scene."

Returning to the hotel at dusk, Ford said, "Let's convene downstairs in the lounge before dinner. Lilly, did you pack the booze?"

"Of course, John. After bouncing around all day in the cold weather, I assumed liquor was essential. I brought along an ample supply of good quality gin and whiskey. Already tipped the staff to take care of our needs. Also brought plenty of beer and wine for dinner."

For two hours, they drank and talked moviemaking. Dinner followed at the hotel restaurant. With the booze and then the wine, Lilly Romano was feeling the effects of the alcohol. Seated next to Walsh, she was also feeling flirtatious.

"I read your novel. John said much of it was autobiographical. You were really in those battles you described?"

Walsh nodded.

"Must have been something terrible," she said slightly slurring her words.

"That it was. No different from soldiers in war everywhere. War is about killing the enemy while you are trying to stay alive. Can't get more emotionally extreme than that."

Lilly nodded. "God I must look awful. My hair is a mess, and my makeup needs repair."

Walsh smiled. "You look just fine, Lilly."

"Fine? Hope I look a lot better than just fine."

84

Walsh realized she was fishing for a compliment. "For a novelist, a poor choice of words. What I meant was the tough ride all day with the wind from the ocean blowing your hair about did nothing to detract from your beauty. In your present state, you are still an extremely attractive woman, Lilly."

She laid her hand on his thigh. "You mean in my present state of being a bit tipsy."

John Ford seated on her other side heard her. "We all probably have had too much to drink. A very productive day. Early call tomorrow. Going further north out of town toward Morro Bay. Billy says there might be good places there to explore. Let's all call it a night."

Slightly miffed that Ford interrupted her flirtations, she turned to Walsh, "Very well. Since I feel unsteady, would you help me up to my room, Egan?"

Guiding her up the stairs to the second floor, she stopped and looked at Walsh. "I'm not really that drunk you know, Egan. Tell me, do you have a lady friend back in Boston?"

Understanding where she was leading, "Yes there is. Her name is Fiona."

"Are you very close?"

"Very."

She nodded and said, "Oh well. Good for you, not so good for me."

Walsh saw Lilly to her room. Kissing him on the cheek before entering her room, she sighed wistfully, "Good night, Egan."

Walsh went to his room thinking how much he missed Fiona.

—

The following morning, Walsh got up earlier than the rest of the group. At the desk, he asked the clerk to place a long-distance call to Boston. The clerk said he could take the call on the house phone located in a private area off the main lobby.

It was three hours later in Boston. Fiona should be in her office.

"Fiona? This is Egan."

"Oh my God, what a pleasant surprise!"

"I am way north of Los Angeles in the wilds of Southern California. Scouting for possible outdoor filming locations that look like County Cork. Getting ready for another day of driving about with colleagues from the movie studio. Chilly here but probably not like Boston."

"That's an understatement. Well below freezing this morning."

"I'm calling because I have not heard from you since sending you my last letter. I made my feelings clear. Anxious to know your reaction."

She was silent for a moment. He feared the worst in her response.

"I feel the same affection for you, Egan. I did not mean for our relationship to become intimate, but like you said, it was inevitable. I have no regrets whatsoever."

Relieved, he replied, "Yet you sound hesitant. What's wrong?"

"Just not sure how to proceed."

"Because of what your family will think?"

"Partly, I guess. We became the best of friends before becoming intimate. Will all those things we share continue as we go forward as lovers?"

"Why shouldn't everything continue only more closely connected? I have no desire to change your independence. I encourage your career. Neither of us is looking for a conventional relationship with children."

"Will you return to Boston, Egan? It is home. Where I feel most comfortable."

"Of course. Boston is my new home as well. I am not returning to Ireland. Los Angeles is only temporary, especially now that I found you."

"I love you, Egan," she said. He thought he could hear her crying.

"Are you crying?"

"Yes, but only because I am happy."

"I love you too, Fiona.

"How long will you be in California?"

"Not sure. We expect to start filming in early March. Starting with location filming here in San Luis Obispo north of Los Angeles. Lots of moving pieces to making a movie. Once the shooting script is complete, then it will take weeks to construct all the necessary sets. At least the end of April, probably May before completing filming. After that comes editing to produce the finished movie."

Pausing for a moment, he asked, "Might it be possible for you to get away in March or April? Take the train out here. We could be together for a couple of weeks. You'll get to see how a movie is made. The movie version of my novel."

"Oh my, I would love that. But that might prove difficult with my work schedule. My boss just gave me a new assignment. Promoted me to an assistant editor. I am to launch a continuing new feature in the magazine called *Iconic Boston*. Been spending endless hours in the library learning about Boston history. We expect to launch my first piece in April."

"Congratulations. As much as I want to see you, don't let that interfere with this opportunity. After all, that is why I am in Hollywood. If we are to be together each with our own careers, then we must be flexible. What we do professionally enriches our relationship."

They spoke for another few minutes before committing to telephone each other every few days. Each felt overjoyed as they concluded the call.

—

The day proved productive. Within a couple of hours after leaving the hotel on a rutted dirt road different from the prior day, Billy had chosen a route closer to the coast, sandwiched between the hills. Driving along, Walsh looked at the road on his right with the terrain sloping upward from the road. Hills in the distance. He immediately called a halt, exclaiming, "This is the Kilmichael Ambush site!" He jumped out of the car looking in all directions. "Bloody Christ, this is perfect. I can feel that day." Pointing, "Put some rocks along over there above where we stopped the first lorry. Shot down nine Auxiliary constables as they disembarked the lorry."

Walsh stood transfixed for several moments as everyone got out of the vehicles while remaining silent giving way to Walsh's recollections.

As Walsh began walking slowly along the road, John Ford broke the silence, "Vernon, capture Egan's views with still photos. Lilly, stay close to Egan and keep detailed notes. Fred, keep track of where we are on the map. Document the camera angles as Egan points out details as he recalls the gunfight."

Everyone followed close behind Walsh. No one said anything to avoid disrupting Walsh's thoughts. Absorbed in memory, he verbalized the violent engagement recalling that day back County Cork. After moments of silence Walsh turned and said, "Up ahead is a bend in the road. That's where we first glimpsed the British lorries. Tom Barry stood about where I'm standing. He wore an IRA uniform tunic with an officer's cap and Sam Browne belt holstering a sidearm.

"Seeing Barry, the lorry slowed before stopping close in front of him. Barry threw a Mills grenade into the open front of the lorry that exploded seconds later as he blew a whistle.

"Up there was an outcropping of rocks," Walsh pointed. "Perhaps we can reconstruct how it was. Rocks about ten feet higher than the road concealed ten IRA. After only a few minutes, all nine Auxiliaries fell dead or wounded."

After several moments of silent reflection, Walsh resumed walking. Where the road made a bend, he stopped and pointed. "Seven of us comprising Section Two positioned ourselves over there in two rows. The first row behind rocks close to the road with a second row above the first. Intelligence reports said the Auxiliaries always moved in a convoy of two or three vehicles. This position was to take out the second lorry.

"Once the firing began, the second lorry tried reversing but became stuck. However, with more time to react, the Auxiliaries of this lorry had more time to disembark. They scattered trying to find firing positions on the south side of the road."

Lilly stayed close to Walsh scribbling detailed notes in short-hand. Carried away with Walsh's narrative, she asked, "Where were you that day, Egan?"

Pointing, he replied, "Leading this section of IRA fighters from about twenty yards up there. This part of the battle went on much longer. We lost three men. Ended in fierce close-quarter fighting."

"Yet all the Auxiliaries in the second vehicle were also killed?" Lilly asked.

"Yes. The driver managed to escape but killed a distance from here by other IRA."

John Ford asked, "Was the intent of the attack to kill all of them?"

Walsh just looked at Ford and nodded.

They remained at the site for an hour as Stanton directed Abernathy in taking photographs.

Walsh remained silent walking about by himself lost in memory. The others let him be until time for lunch.

Eating his sandwich, Fred Stanton said, "This spot can also fill in for the opening scene of the Toorren Ambush. We just move up the road about a quarter mile and the terrain flattens out. On screen it will appear entirely different."

"What do you think, Egan," Ford asked.

"Maybe. This spot is perfect for Kilmichael if we create the rock outcroppings which figure prominently. After lunch Fred can take us up the road and I'll see if that works for the Tooreen scene."

"Excellent. Billy, next we are looking for a place where several roads come together. Also looking for a road with a bridge crossing a small river. Any ideas?"

Billy took a swig of his Coke and said, "Couple of places we can try. I remember a bridge in that same area. A stone bridge something like one of those in your picture book. Might take some looking for me to find it again."

"Well, that's our mission this afternoon. Find a suitable location for shooting the Crossbarry Ambush."

The afternoon proved equally productive. Billy located a location where three dirt roads converged. They converged from different angles suitable for filming the Crossbarry Ambush. False-front constructed remote sets could provide the necessary Irish buildings. Billy also found the stone bridge crossing a small creek. Note exactly the required appearance, but design technicians could rig a false façade to replicate an Irish stone arch construction. Special effects technicians could then incorporate the false façade with explosives for creating the scene of the IRA blowing the bridge that stopped the pursuing British lorries and allowed for the IRA to escape.

Enthused by their day's success, John Ford said as they piled into their cars to return to town, "Great work everyone. Especially your help, Billy. Tomorrow, we will revisit our selected sites. Rethink their suitability. Get down to mapping out the movement of every member of the cast. Fred and Egan need to determine the necessary props we need to bring on location. Since we have rain in some of the location scenes, we must plan on creating false weather for some of the close-up scenes. Rains all the time in Ireland. Can't rely on that here."

The next day confirmed the prior day's discoveries as appropriate for the location filming. That afternoon, Ford negotiated accommodations at the hotel for the upcoming filming starting the first of March. A good opportunity for the hotel with the slow winter season. He paid Billy a handsome bonus and promised more if he could round up a dozen local men and several trucks to make some extra money for two weeks' work at Los Angeles labor rates. Various manual labor would be needed for transporting and positioning of filming equipment and outdoor sets.

Their last night in San Luis Obispo they celebrated going through the remainder of the liquor and wine. Although Walsh tried to avoid sitting next to Lilly, she was having none of that. She would respect Walsh's declaration of unavailability. However, he was handsome and an interesting diversion. She enjoyed his company and considered subtle flirtation harmless.

The evening wound down as they finished the last of the liquor supply. Attracted to Walsh, Lilly was mindful to constrain her flirtation, respecting his unavailability. While Walsh found Lilly attractive with a vibrant personality, under different circumstances he might easily succumb to her advances. Nevertheless, his feelings for Fiona overcame any such temptations. Parting with a chaste kiss, they retired to their respective rooms for the night.

The success of the trip and the prospect of possibly seeing Fiona put Walsh in a buoyant mood as they returned to Los Angeles the next day. Asking for his room key, the desk clerk at the Hollywood Hotel said, "We have a telegram for you, Mr. Walsh."

Walsh read the telegram. *Initial sales of Price of Freedom are exceeding expectations. Reviews highly favorable New York Times, Chicago Tribune, Los Angeles Times. Forthcoming movie expected to generate increased interest. Congratulations. Charles Scribner II.*

CHAPTER 8

Hollywood, California | 1926

Now that the detailed shooting script was finished and the location filming determined, activities broadened. Walsh began working closely with Fred Stanton the art director to assist in creating the exterior sets. The range of techniques the craftsmen employed in creating visual allusion was remarkable. Wood, cardboard, and plaster could be made to appear as any required material. Construction of the rock outcroppings for the location sets started with a skeleton of sheet metal nailed to a wooden frame. The rocks are created by forming a thin concrete layer into desired shapes and textures then spray painted. Each rock segment designed small enough to allow handling by just a couple of men. The fake rocks repurposed for use in various other scenes.

Building exteriors for the back lot used creative techniques to achieve virtually any required effect. The studio had an impressive library of photographic material at Stanton's disposal to use as a guide. Images of locations of every conceivable type from around the world. Grand stone buildings to primitive village dwellings. Photographs going back to the earliest days of photography. Books with renderings of structures before the advent of photography.

Walsh used the reference library to guide Stanton in creating authentic recreations. What up close appearing as obviously fake allusion looked entirely realistic when viewed through the camera lens. He was immensely enjoying the specialized business of filmmaking.

A week after returning from San Luis Obispo, Walsh was discussing a set drawing with Fred Stanton in the set construction shop. Several carpenters stopped sawing and hammering to look their way.

Walsh and Stanton turned to see John Ford and Victor McLaglen walking with a beautiful woman drawing the workmen's attention.

"Can I borrow Egan for a few moments, Fred?" Ford said. "Egan, let me introduce Miss Tara Kelly. Your character Nora Gallagher."

Kelly was stunning. A bobbed hairstyle with stylish hat and long fur coat.

Kelly extended her hand to Walsh, "So good to meet you, Mr. Walsh. Looking forward to doing *Price of Freedom.* What do you think? Can the makeup and costume people make me look like your vision of Nora Gallagher? I can even do a passible Irish ascent according to Victor. Too bad movies don't yet have sound."

Walsh smiled and laughed, "My idea of Nora Gallagher wasn't someone as attractive as you, Miss Kelly."

"As long as they don't make me look too plain, we'll produce a good picture, Mr. Walsh. Those outfits worn by the women of the Cumann na mBan they showed me are terribly unflattering."

Ford said, "This afternoon, I would like Egan to informally provide us a sense of what it was like for the Irish going through this conflict. It will help you and Victor to imagine the context of your roles."

After Ford departed with McLaglen and Kelly, Stanton took Walsh through the back lot to get a feel for how they duplicated building exteriors.

Walking down a street scene that could stand in for New York or Chicago, Stanton stopped and opened a door. Inside was nothing. Only reinforcing timbers securing walls.

"These are used only for exterior shots. Change the sign and the Italian restaurant becomes a Jewish delicatessen. We create the interiors on studio sets since they are usually movie specific. We have several fake buildings we might be able use to duplicate certain Irish buildings by simply constructing appropriate facades."

Next, they walked through a complete western town of fifty years ago. A working set with cast and crew breaking for lunch as Walsh and Stanton approached. "Look over there," Stanton said, "The fellow in the large white Stetson. That's Tom Mix. Biggest western star in motion pictures. What to meet him?"

"Sure."

Stanton approached Mix who was conversing with someone.

"Mr. Mix, I'd like you to meet someone. This is Egan Walsh. The author of the novel *Price of Freedom*. About the Irish War. He's helping adapt the script. Also acting as technical consultant."

Mix shook hands with Walsh. "Are you new to Hollywood, Mr. Walsh?"

"My first movie."

"What do think about moviemaking?"

"Impressive. Lots of moving parts. People with every imaginable expertise. A complex project to produce what we see on the screen."

"That it is. It can be hard work, sometimes boring, but creativity makes it worthwhile. Like writing a novel, I imagine. By your accent, were you born in Ireland?"

"Born in County Cork. Came to America only a couple of years ago."

Stanton interjected, "Mr. Walsh fought with the IRA during their war of independence."

Mix said, "That was some war. You licked the British pretty good."

"Not good enough to win full independence. That resulted in a nasty civil war. I refused to take up arms against my former IRA colleagues, so I left Ireland."

"You must have some real stories to tell. Come with me. You too Fred. Someone I want both of you to meet. We'll all have lunch together."

Mix led Stanton and Walsh over to an elderly gentleman sitting in a chair smoking a cigar.

"Wyatt, someone I thought you might want to meet. This is Egan Walsh, a veteran of the recent Irish War. Mr. Walsh, this is the celebrated frontier lawman and gunfighter of the real American old west, Wyatt Earp."

Earp stood up. A tall man of impressive height, he stood ramrod straight. In his seventies with thinning white hair and matching white mustache. Dressed in a good three-piece suit, distinguished was the best way to describe Earp's' appearance.

"Pleasure meeting you, Mr. Walsh."

Mix said good naturedly, "Thought we might have lunch together, Wyatt. You and Mr. Walsh can swap stories of your gunfights."

Tom Mix was obviously good friends with Earp. Over lunch he asked Earp, "Getting anywhere with the book, Wyatt?"

"Well Bill is trying to help."

Mix explained to Walsh. "Bill is the big western star, William S. Hart. A good friend of ours. Thought the best way for Wyatt's story to be told was for Bill to help get a movie made. Bill told him to get a writer to first write his biography. Wyatt found a fella named John Flood game enough to take a stab at writing it."

"How's that going?" Mix asked.

"Writing is tedious. I sit there smoking while Flood scribbles away. Josephine is a pain in the ass though. Always trying to twist the story to make it seem something different from what really happened. Whiskey helps me get through our sessions."

Earp looked at Walsh. "All this talk might be confusing to Mr. Walsh. He's from Ireland. Probably wonders who this old geezer is. Why should anyone be interested?"

Walsh smiled. "I've only been in America a couple of years. Afraid I can't say I know your name, Sir."

Mix said, "Of course. I apologize, Mr. Walsh. Over forty years ago, Wyatt Earp was a lawman in Dodge City and Wichita, Kansas, then later in Tombstone, Arizona. Rough frontier towns in the eighteen seventies and eighties. It was in Tombstone that an incident made him famous nationwide. Newspapers called it the Gunfight at the O.K. Corral."

Walsh asked, "What happen there, Mr. Earp?"

Mix interrupted, "Let's head out for lunch then Wyatt can tell you all about it."

All of us piled into Mix's newest car, a cream-colored Duesenberg Model X. He took us to a Mexican restaurant where the proprietor greeted him like royalty. Regardless of federal alcohol restrictions under Prohibition, once seated, a waitress delivered a tray of cold beers.

"Wyatt, tell Mr. Walsh what happened that day in Tombstone, Mix said.

After taking a sip of his beer, Earp said, "It was the afternoon of the 26th of October 1881. My older brother Virgil was city marshal. I was his deputy. Some outlaw cowboys violated the city ordinance about carrying weapons. That morning their drunken leader went about town threatening all the Earp brothers. Along with our younger brother Morgan and a trusted friend, the four of us then went looking to disarm them.

"We found five armed cowboys gathered in a narrow lot at the side of a boardinghouse and a photography shop on Fremont Street. Not even that close to the corral. Guess the newspapers wanted to put a name to the location.

"We recognized all of them. Clantons and McLaurys. Rustlers and generally bad characters. Well, the situation turned ugly. One of the cowboys fired at us then all hell broke out. Bullets flying from both sides. Both my brothers went down wounded. Three cowboys lay dead."

Mix added. "But that wasn't the end of it was it, Wyatt?"

"No. That wasn't the end of the Clantons and McLaurys. My circumstances got worse after that. Public sentiment in Tombstone turned against us. All manner of false stories circulated about how we murdered Billy Clanton, Tom and Frank McLaury. Forced us to move our families into the Cosmopolitan Hotel and hire a couple of men to provide added security.

"Two months later, they ambushed Virgil. Wounded him in the left arm leaving it permanently crippled. Three months after that, they murdered my brother Morgan. Shot him in the back through a window while he was playing pool downstairs at the hotel."

The waitress interrupted Earp's story to bring a fresh round of beers and take their orders.

Earp resumed his story. "Well, the entire family left Tombstone. Too many bad memories. No opportunities remained for us to make a living in Tombstone with hostilities running high. That's the real story of the Gunfight at the O.K. Corral. Not sure why it is remembered as something that special after all these years."

Mix said, "Because you are a legend, Wyatt. And maybe for what happened after the gunfight. The story and legend did not end there did it, Wyatt?"

The memory of the attack on his brothers struck a sensitive chord with Wyatt Earp.

"Unfortunately, not. No possibility existed of seeking a conviction of those everyone knew to be responsible for the murder of Morgan and the attempted murder of Virgil. Law enforcement in Tombstone either sided with the Cowboys or feared any attempt at make arrests. No one serving on a jury would dare find any of the defendants guilty for fear of their lives. The law no longer worked in Tombstone. Forced me to find my own justice. An ugly business where some of those involved came to a bad end. Best I leave it at that. We should enjoy our lunch."

Earp was referring to his legendary and controversial personal vendetta. The outcome of which left an additional four dead *Cowboys* and local arrest warrants issued for Earp, two of his other brothers, and Earp's friend and feared gunfighter Doc Holiday, forcing everyone to leave Arizona Territory.

Tom Mix got the message and changed the subject as lunch came to the table. Wyatt Earp's vendetta remained both a legend and controversial. For a lawman that tried to avoid bloodshed throughout his career, Earp felt compelled to turn vigilante to achieve justice.

Mix said, "Wyatt comes from a different era. What Bill Hart and I try to portray on film. Wyatt offers invaluable advice we can't get anywhere about how things really were during that earlier time."

Returning from lunch with Tom Mix and Wyatt Earp, Walsh walked into John Ford's office. Seated at Ford's round conference table were Victor McLaglen and Tara Kelly.

"Just got back from lunch with Tom Mix and Wyatt Earp," Walsh announced.

"Were you suitably entertained with stories of the old West?" Ford remarked.

"Mr. Earp is quite a character."

McLaglen said, "Earp must have been something when he made his reputation as a young fella. I met Tom last year when I was filming *The Fighting Heart* directed by John. He introduced me to Earp who was consulting on the western Tom was filming. Got talking about boxing when Tom told Earp I used to box professionally. Tom said Earp is remembered as a lawman and gunfighter, but he more often enforced the law with his fists or whacking bad guys in the head with his gun. A tactic called *buffaloing*."

Ford asked, "Did Wyatt tell you about the famous scandal of a big boxing match he refereed in 1915?"

"No."

"Not surprising. Best not to bring up the Fitzsimmons-Sharkey fight in San Francisco. Everyone accused Earp of making a bad call and giving the fight to Sharkey. Anyway, you'll find that Wyatt Earp had a controversial past.

"As for Tom Mix, he can regale you with stories of his own. He doesn't go back as far as Earp, but Tom led a colorful life of his own before coming to Hollywood. He is also a good friend of William S. Hart.

"Bill was the biggest western star before Tom came along. Bill's now getting a little old for the physical demands of Western action films. I hang around these guys mostly because they are interesting company. I have a special affinity for the western genre. Already directed a fair number of westerns. Two starring Tom Mix.

"Now switching the subject to Ireland, I'd like you to give us feel of what it was like during the war of independence, Egan. It affects how Vic and Tara act their roles and how I direct.

"How did you feel? In your view, how did people of every situation feel? How did they get along while the country was in turmoil? What about those like you that took up arms? People favoring the war and those against."

Walsh replied, "Well that's a tall order John. I'll do my best. Let me start by explaining that Irish feelings about British rule go back hundreds of years. The British confiscated Irish land in the 16th and 17th centuries and turned them into Irish plantations owned by settlers from Great Britain. Each Irish generation passes down their experiences for hating British oppression. Periodic Irish attempts at rebellion occurred over hundreds of years.

"The Great Famine however changed everything. The Potato Famine of 1845. Blight destroyed the principal staple of the Irish diet. A million died of starvation and disease. The British government did nothing to alleviate the suffering. Wealthy landowners still shipped grain to Britain while the Irish starved. That was only three generations ago. Emigration to the end of the century dramatically reduced the population of Ireland. You can imagine the bitterness for those that stayed and those forced to leave.

"Then came the European Great War. The British tried to fill ranks depleted from causalities on the Western Front by ordering conscription of Irish males. Most of the Irish population rebelled with collective anger aimed at the British government. I make the point that hatred for British domination became widespread across most segments of the Irish population by 1919.

"Those within the Irish Republican Army that were equipped with arms in County Cork never exceeded more than a few hundred men. Always short of arms and ammunition. We stood against thousands of British Crown forces including 1,500 new Royal Irish Constabulary British recruits known as Black &Tans, five companies of the RIC Auxiliary Division, and eighteen battalions of regular British Army troops. All much better equipped than the IRA with means of mobile transport.

"The IRA became successful only because of widespread support from the citizenry. Non-combatants provided the IRA food, shelter, and intelligence. Every person was mindful of the terrible risk they were taking. Imprisonment, possible torture or even death. The prescribed British penalty for those aiding the IRA was burning of their homes or the means of their livelihood. Everyone lived in fear, but hatred is a good motivator for rebellion. Anti-British sentiment in County Cork historically went back generations. Thousands of regular Irish waged their individual war against the British by actively supporting the IRA."

Ford asked, "What about those that did not support the rebellion?"

"There were those. Most tried to remain neutral. Some actively provided information to the British."

"What happened to those working found secretly working with the British?" McLaglen asked.

"Tried by an IRA military tribunal. Executed if found guilty. Dangerous for those suspected. Difficult to remain neutral. Bad things happened to Irish of both political positions. The IRA also had blood on its hands."

Kelly remarked, "So everyone helping the rebels is scared but brave enough to continue?"

"Most were. For example, the bravery of the character Nora Gallagher you play was common. I knew many women performing such dangerous work. They were soldiers risking imprisonment, torture, rape, or death if caught."

A solemn Tara Kelly replied, "I understand. Living through that must have been something terrifying."

"That it was, Miss Kelly."

McLaglen asked, "I was in the army during the Great War. In all wars, the function of soldiers is to kill the enemy, and sometimes die as well. Your war sounds different. How do I play you on the screen, Egan?"

"The IRA were foremost guerrilla fighters. Everyone was a volunteer. No conscripts. We were few in number and poorly armed. Up against well-armed superior numbers. Everything we did was desperation. The battle scenes in the movie are good examples. The IRA relied on support of the population. Hit the British where they are vulnerable then withdraw. Disappear into the countryside. IRA commanders at every level were elected by IRA members rather than appointed. You play the part of a select volunteer group called a flying column. A mobile strike force organized to bloody the British. The story is about going after those British forces terrorizing the Irish population. Those acting as neither police nor soldiers. The IRA inflicted terror on these murderers as the only means of resisting their brutality."

"Kill as many of these blokes as possible?" McLaglen asked.

"Put that way, yes," Walsh replied.

Ford interjected, "Egan, we spoke about toning down any suggestion that the IRA were assassinating British forces. Even if that occurred at Kilmichael, we agreed not to represent that graphically on film."

Walsh held up his hand. "You are right. Sorry, John. Got carried away. Just wanted to convey the mindset of Vic's character. The Anglo-Irish War lacked much of the clarity of the Great War in which Victor served."

They continued with Walsh citing examples of what it meant to live through those times. To illustrate his portrayal of the Auxiliaries and Black & Tans as unrestrained murderers and arsonists, he recounted incidents in detail. He even explained IRA excesses of killing suspected loyalists of helping the British. Something he did not condone.

All three found themselves enthralled with Walsh's narrative of Irish life during the war.

With everyone emotionally spent, Kelly remarked, "Vic said you left Ireland when the civil war started after the signing of the Treaty with Britain. Why's that?"

"I fought the war against British rule. I disagreed with the terms of the Treaty, but I was not about to fight former IRA comrades."

Ford closed the meeting with, "We all read your book but hearing you talk made it more vivid. I appreciate you taking the time resurrecting difficult memories, Egan. Gives all of us a better sense of how to portray the characters on film."

Kelly said, "I'll do my best to portray the spirit of your character Nora Gallagher. A strong part for me to show my talent."

———

"How are things, Fiona?" Walsh said telephoning her raising his voice to overcome the scratchy long-distance connection.

"Egan, I'm so glad to hear your voice. Working hard. My new column is a real project. Lots of background work. Typing notes from a couple of interviews I did today."

"Kind of late. Did you eat dinner?"

"A sandwich. What are you doing?"

"Like you, working at the typewriter. Scribner sent me a telegram. My book just received several good reviews. Sales are doing well. The movie should prove helpful if it receives good reviews. Spurred me to get serious about developing the subject for my next novel. If I am to be a novelist, I need to always be writing."

"Wonderful. How do you like moviemaking?"

"Fascinating for an outsider like me. Far more complicated than I imagined. Just got back from scouting outdoor locations north of Los Angeles. Stand-in locations for filming scenes of Southern Ireland.

"Thought when I came to Hollywood my credit for the script might have no substance, but it is a real job. Ray Schrock, the experienced screenwriter, and I have completed the initial draft script. There will be continual revisions as the director makes changes as filming progresses, but I made important contributions.

"My role as technical consultant is clearly proving valuable. I'm working closely with the art director to get everything to appear authentic. Enough about my work. Tell me about your project."

"Like your situation, I'm learning about architecture. *Iconic Boston* is best reflected in its architecture. My flat is full of library books giving myself a crash course in Boston architectural history.

"Have interviews lined up for next week. Working right now on developing my questions. I love learning so I'm enjoying the challenge."

"Who are you interviewing?"

"A couple of professors of history, Harvard and Boston University. The staff of the Boston Historical Society & Museum and the Boston Maritime Museum. A journalist at the *Boston Globe* with the title of architectural critic. Been reading some of his past columns to understand how he critiques architecture. Maybe convince him to contribute to my column."

"How's this magazine section going to stand out?"

"Photographs of course. Images dominate magazines. Each issue will cover some part of Boston in depth. Need to present interesting narrative content to accompany the photos. Going to take my own photographs initially. Juxtapose these with older images in some cases. Borrowed a camera from our photography department. A German camera called a Leica just introduced last year. Handheld, easy to work. Uses small 35mm film on a roll. Capable of quickly advancing the film to take multiple exposures of the same shot.

"I'm currently preoccupied with what subject to present in the first issue. I need something to grab our readers' attention. Looking for a suitable image for the magazine front cover announcing the new section."

"You're talented. I have no doubt you will come up with a creative solution. Any further thoughts about coming out to Los Angeles for a week?"

"Lots of thoughts. Think all the time how much I want to be with you. Not going to be possible though until I launch the first issue the first week of April. I need to workday and night to produce content for both the April and May issues by the end of March. That should allow me to escape for a couple of weeks sometime in April."

Further out then he hoped but at least something specific. He could not get away to make the trip to Boston. Besides, that would interfere with Fiona meeting her publication deadline.

"Wish it could be sooner, but at least something to look forward to. I miss you, something awful, Fiona."

"I miss you too. All the more so because things are going well for both of us. We'll just have to share our professional endeavors long distance until we are together again. I love you, Egan."

CHAPTER 9

Los Angeles, California | 1926

In 1926, Chadwick Hollister replaced his uncle suffering increased health problems as Executive Vice President & Chief Operating Officer of Hollister Financial. With Chadwick's successful expansion of the Bank's operations in the West, his anticipated succession to replace his seventy-three-year-old father as CEO was no longer a question.

Spending most of his time in Los Angeles growing the firm's reach in the West, he became a prominent figure in Los Angeles. A wealthy power player in business and politics. Known to everyone. Loathed by many and feared by those who dealt with him in business, Chadwick Hollister possessed no real friends. He held no illusions about how people felt about him, nor did he much care. He measured his life in terms of power and gratification.

His role in the nefarious dealings years earlier in bringing water to Los Angeles by effectively stealing it from Owens Valley agricultural interests became public over time. That it unflatteringly portrayed Hollister as being in the company of the great robber barons of industry and finance of the time pleased him.

His social circle consisted of acquaintances tolerating Hollister for various reasons. Those engaging in personal dealings disliked him or tolerated his arrogance to serve their own interests. Not

105

only ruthless in business, Hollister's unpleasant personality carried over into every aspect of his life.

However, his success since coming to Los Angeles unquestionably transformed Hollister Financial. The venerable Wall Street investment bank had been losing ground to competition since the turn of the century. Having developed the firm from its provincial commercial banking origins forty years earlier, Hollister's father eventually rested on his accomplishments. Acceding to his son's ambitions to exploit Southern California resurrected the firm's stature.

With success in Los Angeles, Chadwick expanded Hollister Financial's reach. From headquarters in Manhattan, with satellite offices in Boston and Philadelphia, he established a presence in other locations in the West and Midwest. Functioning with little interference from his father, Chadwick personally directed all operations outside of the original east coast locations. Headquartered in Los Angeles he now oversaw offices in San Francisco, Seattle, Denver, Chicago, St. Louis, and Houston. Collectively these locations yielded 60% of Hollister Financial profits the previous year.

In Los Angeles Chadwick Hollister moved in the upper strata of business and political influence. He was a member of both the California Club and the Jonathan Club. Harry Chandler, publisher of the *Los Angeles Times* and fellow member of both prestigious organizations remarked to Hollister, "The people that *run* Los Angeles belong to the Jonathan Club. The people that *own* Los Angeles belong to the California Club."

While the Bradbury Building was a uniquely elegant building and although occupying the entire fifth floor, Hollister Financial still needed more space. As a member of the Jonathan Club, Hollister learned of the Club's plans for moving to more elegant accommodations on South Figueroa. Fellow member and longtime acquaintance Harry Huntington and president of the Southern Pacific Railroad owned the club's present building location, the Pacific Electric Building located at 610 S. Main just five blocks from the Bradbury. Huntington readily agreed to lease Hollister the top eighth and nineth floors when the Jonathan Club vacated.

The building sat above the Main Street trolley station serving as the interurban terminal for the city trolley system. The Big Red trolley cars discharged close to 100,000 passengers each workday as many reconnected to travel in all directions. A bustling hub of activity promoted the prominence of Hollister Financial while providing easy accessibility for its growing number of employees.

Although Hollister was part of the Los Angeles elite, he indulged in habits far removed from lavish offices and expensive restaurants. He liked quality liquor, high stakes poker, and women. Not necessarily in that order. Liquor and poker were easy to find. Women not so easy unless your tastes ran to prostitutes.

Unattached women rarely frequented his social circle. The few that did quickly found his egocentric character unappealing. For the occasional mature woman seduced by his money and association with moviemaking, the liaison became short lived.

Common prostitutes were out of the question. However, years earlier, Hollister discovered the means for satisfying his sexual needs. Through his networking, he became associated with Charles H. Crawford, overlord of Los Angeles vice.

However, Charlie Crawford was far more than just involved with illegal vice. Crawford and his associates were known as the *City Hall Gang*. The congenial Crawford developed connections within the city government and police department. Politically savvy, those connections extended from beat cops up to the mayor's office. It provided a cozy arrangement for bribery in exchange for protection for bootlegging, gambling, prostitution, and every conceivable illegal activity. No public sector was immune to the pervasive corruption of Crawford's loose-knit organization.

Crawford developed a reputation for his political shrewdness. His instincts proved so predictive that he could heavily influence contributions from wealthy donors to political candidates and office holders. That gave Crawford the ability to install office holders indebted to his patronage at all levels of city and county government.

Hollister became a confidant of Crawford to enhance his own political influence. He regularly frequented one of Crawford's downtown establishments. The Maple Bar, located at 501 S. Maple just south of Fifth Street, offered a bar with good liquor, poker tables, and slot machines on the ground floor. The second floor offered craps and roulette tables. Crawford made his office on the third floor that also contained five small bedrooms serving as a bordello.

Hollister mostly frequented the establishment's basement. Crates of liquor, barrels of beer, and a gun cabinet occupied much of the space with a single large round table in the center. Crawford ran high stakes poker games here by invitation only. Several well-armed thugs were always in attendance for security.

Crawford's other establishment was the Clover Club, a Victorian mansion among others located in the Bunker Hill neighborhood. Essentially a bordello with nine bedrooms supervised by a madam. While Chadwick Hollister's sexual appetites do not run to common prostitutes.

Charlie Crawford was in the business of serving his clientele whatever they wanted.

In the business of sex trafficking, Crawford diversified to serve a more affluent clientele. Southern California abounded in beautiful young women. Many coming with hopes of becoming movie actresses. Others coming to escape dead end lives from all over the country to a vibrantly growing place in the sun. Crawford found that some of these young women could command astounding fees in exchange for sex to a discriminating wealthy clientele. He therefore created *Los Angeles Business Services*, an innocuous sounding name of his escort service.

Operating out of a small office with no name on the door, the operation consisted of a staff of three women that worked the telephones. Well trained to deflect inquiries related to actual business, they managed arrangements and collected payments. Unlike normal payment in cash prior to sexual services from prostitutes, payment for these call girls was by check mailed to the escort service. For the client, explainable as a legitimate business expense. For Crawford, a way to prevent skimming of profits. Seemingly offering sex on credit, there were never delinquencies in payments. The inherent fear of blackmail ensured prompt payments.

—

Chadwick Hollister exited his Pierce Arrow at the Maple Bar on a Saturday night in early February. Driving the elegant beige with contrasting black fenders luxury touring car was Hollister's bodyguard. Hollister had no need for a bodyguard other than it made him feel important, especially when frequenting Crawford's Maple Bar.

He was here to play poker. Although Crawford's stationed armed thugs to watch over the high stakes games played in the basement, he allowed Hollister's bodyguard to accompany him. Having his own hired muscle provided Hollister with a sense of superiority in this environment of Los Angeles' underbelly

Intimidating-looking Kurt Gerhardt was far more than a bodyguard. His function better described as that of *a fixer*. Hollister needed someone that could get his hands dirty engaging in various illegal activities. Gerhardt served eight years in the U.S. Army, fighting in the Philippine-American War. Leaving the army in 1906, Gerhardt joined the Los Angeles Police Department.

In 1916, Gerhardt caught the attention of Charles Crawford as an ambitious cop that sought out opportunities for engaging in illegal activities for money. Crawford eventually recommended Gerhardt to Hollister. For twice the pay even after considering bribes, Gerhardt left the LAPD.

Both Hollister and Gerhardt approached the front door. Gerhardt knocked and the small peep door opened. Gerhardt simply said, "Mr. Hollister."

The door opened and Gerhardt followed Hollister inside. The stocky fellow opening the door wore a suit that was too tight leaving no question that he carried a gun in a shoulder holster. In contrast, Kurt Gerhardt was tall with a lean but muscular build. He also carried his army issue Colt M1911 .45 semiautomatic in a shoulder holster better concealed under a tailored suit jacket.

"I'll tell Mr. Crawford you are here," the doorman said.

Hollister and Gerhardt found a place at the bar. In the background above the noise of the slots and the din of noisy gamblers, Marcus "Nine Fingers" Jackson played jazz on the piano.

"Good evening, Mr. Hollister. What'll it be?" the bartender asked.

"Your best Scotch. Make it neat with a soda back. What about you, Kurt?"

"A beer," Gerhardt said. After a couple of beers, he would switch to coffee to keep him alert. A long boring night ahead as he watched Hollister play poker.

As the bartender served them their drinks, affable Charles Crawford approached. "Chadwick, good to see you," shaking Hollister hand then Gerhardt's. "Kurt, how are things?"

"Just fine, Mr. Crawford." Crawford might appear good-natured, but Gerhardt knew him to be tough and exceptionally powerful throughout Los Angeles from City Hall to the LAPD, and every corner of the city's underworld.

Turning to Hollister, "Got a good game lined up for you. Four guys from Houston, all in the oil business."

"What's the buy in, Charlie?"

"Twenty grand."

Hollister pulled out a checkbook and scribbled a check handing it to Crawford. He allowed only players he knew that had the ability to cover large amounts to write checks. As the house, he issued each player chips less his ten percent.

"The other four are here already. Come downstairs and I will introduce you."

Hollister knew the names of two of the Texans from recent newspaper articles. Sheridan Lewis and Jacob Berman just bought beleaguered Julian Petroleum last year. The founder C. C. Julian spent years defending legal accusations of selling oversubscribed shares in Southern California oil drilling. Julian finally bowed out by selling his position in the financially troubled company to his Houston partners at a depressed price.

Hollister sat down as Crawford brought him his stack of chips. "How is the oil business, gentlemen?"

Sheridan Lewis said, "California is just getting started. Plenty of reserves. Just need to manage drilling operations more effectively."

Hollister was no expert in oil drilling but understood each oil field could not yield profits infinitely. Oil was not a renewable resource. Newspaper accounts alleged Julian Petroleum engaged in the oversubscription of selling shares. That diluted individual share-yields and promoted over-drilling. Public accusations suggested Julian Petroleum was running a swindle. Something akin to a Ponzi scheme as the sale of new shares paid dividends on early shares. Yet the State of California had yet to file criminal charges. Hollister viewed oil drilling speculation as a sucker investment geared to those uninformed and desperate to make a killing. Yet here were these guys playing high stakes poker when their company was on the verge of insolvency and facing legal problems.

Four hours later, one of the Texans was already down to only a few chips. The Julian Petroleum guys were not much better. None of them were good poker players. Hollister and the remaining Texan had about equal piles of chips. Hollister was an exceptionally good poker player. After the one Scotch when he arrived, he stuck to coffee and mineral water staying focused. The more successful Texan continued to sip Bourbon. By one o'clock in the morning, he was showing the effects. Finally declared he was calling it quits.

The two guys from Julian Petroleum seemed relieved to call it a night and cut their losses. However, the Texan down with his stack of chips wanted to continue. "What the fuck? I need a chance to recoup my losses." Pointing to the other Texan and Hollister, "You two been getting all the best hands."

Hollister responded, "Not better hands, just better played hands."

"Fuck you! Been playing poker all my life. You saying I don't know what I am doing?"

"I'm saying you're not good enough to play against those that are better."

The losing Texan, having also drank a fair amount of Bourbon stood up pushing back his chair.

Bad move. Before one of Crawford's goons could respond, Kurt Gerhardt quickly came alongside the Texan grabbing his arm saying, "Cash in your chips and leave before you do anything stupid."

The Texan pulled away from Gerhardt and swung a misguided left hook directed at Gerhardt's head. Backing away a step, Gerhardt pulled out his .45. The Texan looked at the weapon and took a deep breath but made no further move.

"Easy, Kurt," Hollister said. To Crawford's two men, he said, "Better get Charlie. The game seems to be over."

Hollister thoroughly enjoyed the evening. Leaving as a winner while rewarded with unexpected entertainment made his night.

While the fortunes of Hollister Financial in Los Angeles still derived largely from real estate ventures, Chadwick Hollister began investing in the movie business years earlier. There was a natural bias against banks investing in this new business segment where it was difficult to access financial risk. The movie studios originated predominately by Jewish entrepreneurs having started as nickelodeon proprietors. That business focused on ventures showing minutes-long one-reel films geared to the working class. Hence the name nickelodeon for the five-cent ticket price.

As technology advanced, the industry matured from one-reel of fifteen minutes to lengthy feature movies of multiple reels elaborately staged and displayed on giant screens in specially built theaters. By 1926, there were tens of thousands of movie theaters in the country. Even small towns boasted a theater. No longer catering to poorly produced short curiosities targeting the working class, the middle class demanded sophisticated content. Yet the profit potential of the product rested on the whims of the viewing public. Difficult to predict revenues in advance of totally committing serious capital for production. Each film therefore became a project.

The client base was comparatively small. Five major film studios not only produced 90% of the domestic American movies but also owned 50% of the theaters in the country in 1926. Three other independent studios comprised the remaining share of movie production but did not own theaters. Hollister saw the opportunity years earlier. Local commercial banks shied away from lending to movie studios because of the difficulty in assessing lending risk.

However, the movie business captured Hollister's interest. Beautiful people acting out captivating stories told through spectacular imagery. Domestic movie production was almost exclusively now located in Hollywood. The personal attraction for Hollister was enough to seriously pursue moviemaking financing.

With the ever-expanding western operations of Hollister Financial, Hollister sought to add to his staff someone experienced in financing the entertainment industry. The largest investment banking competitor was Goldman Sachs in New York. Four years earlier on a trip to New York, Hollister successfully pirated a mid-level executive with Goldman Sachs' entertainment business sector. Nathan Schachter was a perfect fit. Harvard degrees in law and finance. Twenty-nine at the time. Intelligent, articulate, young, and ambitious. Schachter jumped at the chance to come to sunny Los Angeles at double his current compensation.

Although Hollister deluded himself into believing the success of the firm's venture into entertainment financing in a big way was due to his efforts, it was the creativity of Schachter. Years earlier, Schachter explained his strategy for developing an entertainment industry clientele for Hollister Financial. "The motion picture industry carries excellent profit potential but with risk more difficult to determine. Funding production expenses is no different from any corporation. What differentiates movie making is the product. Not only does each movie represent a unique product, but one that is produced with the inability to project revenue. A product subject to uncertain demand only after expending substantial production funds. High risk by any definition. Puts off most commercial banking for that reason alone.

"Providing capital therefore becomes largely the domain for larger investment banks. Goldman Sachs and J. P. Morgan & Company are currently the largest players. Between them they finance the Big Five film studios. Bear in mind, these operations also include the distribution channels consisting of thousands of theaters around the country. Obviously, I am most familiar with Goldman Sachs. They fund the two largest of the Big Five."

"Which ones?"

"Metro-Goldwyn-Meyer. Guy with the controlling interest is Marcus Loew. Loew controls budgets and contracts under his from New York based Loews, Inc. that holds controlling interest in MGM. Hollywood operations are run by Louis Meyer. The other is Famous Players-Laskey, better known as Paramount Studios. The Managing partner is Adolph Zukor, also based in New York."

"You know these studio heads personally?"

"Oh yes. As assistant to the entertainment sector manager. The manager was an established executive with Goldman Sachs. Competent fellow with numbers but lacked the skills necessary to close deals. I became the principal client interface. Marcus Loew and Adolph Zukor could not be more different personalities, including their approach to business."

"In what way?"

Schachter gave a short laugh. "Marcus Loew is a low-key thoroughly likeable fellow. Everyone likes him. Loew is an astute businessman, however. In contrast, Adolph Zukor is blunt and ruthless, perhaps a bit paranoid. Those closest to him call him *creepy* behind his back."

Schachter paused to show a smile. "Bitter business rivals yet forced into a personal relationship. By some perverse twist of fate, Zukor's beloved daughter Mildred married Loew's son Arthur."

"You think you can entice these two major studios away from Goldman Sachs?"

"With the right offering, we can make a strong run at them. An offer they must consider. Of course, we must be able to negotiate when Goldman Sachs counters."

Once Hollister got something in his mind, he was tenacious. "Very well, what are you suggesting?"

"First off, pitch this as partly a risk sharing financial participation in their feature films. We offer a conventional credit facility to fund production, overhead, marketing, and distribution for the entire operation with specifically designated films separated out for specific financing. On these selected major projects, the bank shares in 15% of the profits. Over three times the probable interest rate of the credit line. If the movie fails to make a profit, the Bank receives no interest on the loan. We further offer attractive terms of repayment on these selected loan amounts beginning six months after the first draw of funds and payable over twelve months.

Hollister asked, "I imagine movie productions are susceptible to cost overruns. We can't control that so how is that managed?"

"Good question. Costs exceeding the agreed budget become the studios responsibility and become absorbed into general expenses funded through the general credit line."

"How do we select which of these scripts to fund? Not like other investments where benchmarks exist."

"I propose we use experts to advise us on the box office prospects of a given script considering the cast and director. Movie critics perhaps. Not foolproof but it gives us an edge. For those movies they enthusiastically recommend, we can rely on good reviews when the movie is released. For example, I am personally on good terms with the New York Times movie critic. These guys should jump at the opportunity to review scripts in advance."

Hollister offered, "The Los Angeles Time publisher is a friend. I'm sure I can make the same arrangement."

Weeks later Schachter produced the final iteration of a detailed proposal to go after MGM and Paramount. Hollister surprised him instead by asking about the smaller independent studios that did not own distribution.

"Universal is the oldest beginning operations in 1912. United Artists in 1919. Started by the biggest names in the industry. Director D. W. Griffith, Charlie Chaplin, Mary Pickford, and Douglas Fairbanks. The youngest is Columbia Pictures founded just two years ago. All these studios are headquartered locally. None of these own theaters."

"Why not begin with these studios? Might they be not more anxious to share risk and solidify their access to operating capital?"

Schachter didn't think of this first because he wanted to see if he could engineer a coup by unseating Goldman Sachs. He did not realize Hollister's interest transcended mere financial interests. Hollister desperately wanted to become part of moviemaking. Socializing with celebrity stars in a glamorous industry even if it did not prove exceptionally profitable. The ability to see and be seen with them was priceless. A substantial part of the larger corporations' business involved distribution and theaters. No glamour there.

"We can initially pursue them if that's what you wish, Sir. I know enough about MGM and Paramount to understand the risk. I'll need to do more research to understand these other studios in more detail."

"Well, do that, Nate. I'm inclined to start there."

———

Within three years, Schachter made good on capturing a significant segment of major studio financing. First came United Artists. They were the most receptive. The deal removed the constant need for micromanagement of finances by their traditional lenders. Easiest for Hollister Financial to take the plunge with the three highest grossing stars making their own movies thereby reducing investment risk. It also forced producer D. W. Griffith to pay closer attention to budgets and avoid overruns. Next came Columbia Pictures with little financial history, making them eager to find solid financial backing. Lastly Universal also went with the better deal offered by Hollister if for no other reason than to remain competitive.

For the larger players, it took more work. The details for more complicated when assessing the formulas for accounting for the vertical integration of the distribution side of the business. MGM was the first to move from Goldman Sachs. Paramount followed as Zukor saw it as a better deal and forever saw Marcus Loew as his principal competitor.

First National Pictures based in Burbank remained with J. P. Morgan & Company citing they were happy with Morgan's longstanding service.

Fox Films also remained with J.P. Morgan. Schachter was disappointed. At an initial meeting, Schachter and Hollister met face to face with William Fox in Fort Lee, New Jersey. It quickly became clear that Fox did not like Hollister. Subsequent telephone conversations only confirmed there was never going to be a deal.

By 1926, Hollister Financial became the largest financial lender to the movie industry. Profits were steady with the widely distributed risk among many clients and movie projects. More importantly, Chadwick Hollister gained immense stature. Not only was Hollister Financial the largest commercial real estate owner in the City of Los Angeles but became better known for his business patronage of the city's most famous industry, Hollywood. Hollister achieved his personal ambition of becoming an integral part of moviemaking. A perfect environment in which to nurture his vanity by publicly socializing with famous and beautiful movie stars.

CHAPTER 10

Los Angeles, California | 1926

Fiona Maguire finally settled on an idea for creating visual images of her *Iconic Boston* debut section of Boston Magazine. The working title to be, *the dawn of commercial aviation coming to the city.* She wanted to symbolically combine current Boston and its forward-looking energy with its rich history.

Logan Airport came into existence just over two years earlier principally as a military airfield known as Jeffrey Field used by the United States Army Air Corps. From humble beginnings of a 1500-foot cider runway, it now included aircraft service hangers and a passenger terminal. Starting next year, Colonial Air Transport announced scheduled commercial passenger flights between Boston and New York City.

She spent a couple of days photographing aircraft and buildings. Aerial photographs taken from airships existed but nothing recent enough to illustrate the rapid progress. One aerial photo from 1923 taken from high altitude looking east across downtown Boston showed the airport on the other side of Boston Harbor as just a dirty spot in the distance. Interesting if she had a contrasting image of the current airport even though it consisted of only four hangers. She needed a creative angle to present a visually impressive opening article.

While photographing aircraft, she came upon a fellow working on a bright yellow biplane. Stenciled on the side was, *See Boston from the Air.* This was the middle of winter. A man dressed in a fur-lined flight jump suit stood on the bottom wing of the biplane reaching inside the forward cockpit.

Maguire approached and said, "Excuse me. Do you take passengers for flights? I want to take photographs for a magazine."

The man turned and jumped down. Fiona Maguire was also well bundled against the cold.

"That I do. Not much interest during the winter though. It's a lot colder up a couple of thousand feet."

"I still might be interested," she said. "Where would I sit?"

"Well, this is a Curtiss Jenny designed as a trainer. Controls in both cockpits. For taking pictures, best you sit in the rear seat to aim your camera to the side to avoid the struts in your pictures."

"Very well. How much do you charge?"

"Let's talk that over in my office in that hanger over there where its warmer."

Maguire laid out her plan. Take pictures of the airport from low altitude, capturing the East Boston waterfront with the airport in the background. While in the air, circle over downtown Boston and get new aerial shots of some of the older historical buildings from a low altitude.

After settling on a cost, the pilot said. "I can supply you with a warm jumpsuit, but you also need to layer up underneath. Especially your feet and the warmest gloves you can find. Get yourself a knit ski mask. I'll supply goggles. In these temperatures, we'll not last more than one hour. Might want to land and get warm then go up again if you're still game,"

It was Monday, the first day of March. The weather forecast was a high of fifty degrees with sunny skies. Best she could expect for this time of year. After reviewing the locations and the direction for taking each shot marked on the map with the pilot, he said, "Okay. I got it. I'll try first from 2,000 feet. If you want to go lower or higher, just tap my shoulder and signal me with your thumb. No way to speak to each other with the wind and bundled for the cold. Ever been in an airplane?"

119

She shook her head. Looking a little apprehensive, he replied, "You'll be fine once we're in the air. If you want to call it quits at any time, just point down vigorously with your finger."

Once ready to get into the aircraft, she said, "Take a picture of me standing beside the airplane. I'll show you how to work the camera."

Setting the camera and the distance, she changed places with the pilot to stand next to the plane. Dropping the jumpsuit's insulated hood for the close-up photo, she felt the breeze coming off the ocean gently blow her hair for the photo. It felt cold even here on the ground. After the pilot captured her on film, she finished suiting up with ski mask, knit cap, and aviation goggles.

They took off at one o'clock in the afternoon. The cold at altitude was everything the pilot warned about as it seeped into every unsealed gap in her weather gear driven by the rushing air. Approaching the agreed upon one hour to land, she felt optimistic about the photo shoot. Glad though that this part of the ordeal was almost over. Impossible to enjoy the thrill of flying in this damn cold.

The pilot turned around pointing toward the ground. She nodded with relief. Over downtown Boston, she marveled looking down from 1,200 feet according to the altimeter. The plane banked to the right. As the plane leveled out, she could see the airport in the distance across the water.

Suddenly the engine coughed. Moments later, the cough repeated with increased intensity. She could feel the aircraft losing power and the sensation of losing altitude. The altimeter confirmed what she sensed. Then suddenly the engine went quiet, and the propeller ceased rotating.

Leaning forward straining against her shoulder harness, she watched the pilot frantically manipulating controls as their rate of descent increased. The pilot was attempting to make it to the airport by gliding without power after unsuccessfully attempting to restart the engine.

As they came over the water of the harbor, she looked ahead at the docks on the East Boston side. They had nowhere to go and even she could see they were too low. As the pilot tried to level the aircraft for a water landing, Fiona Maguire screamed.

Unable to straighten the yaw angle, the plane hit a swell causing it to cartwheel and come to an abrupt stop. The cartwheeling ripped a wide gash on one side of the fuselage. In less than a minute, it sank below the surface. Neither the pilot nor Fiona Maguire had time to unfasten their seatbelts and escape. At this water temperature, it did not matter. Rescue was impossible before the victims succumbed to hypothermia before drowning.

Witnesses reported the crash identifying the aircraft and pilot. Until divers recovered two bodies strapped into the cockpits, no one knew that Fiona Maguire was aboard.

—

The weekend before the crash, Fox Films Hollywood chief Sol Wurtzel held a kickoff party at the studio for cast and crew of *Price of Freedom*. Victor McLaglen and Tara Kelly spent much of the evening talking with Egan Walsh. Kelly became close to McLaglen while they worked together in London. First a minor role in *Damaged Goods* then a costarring role in 1923 in the *Cornish Coast*.

Although Kelly was free-spirited and sexually liberated, her friendship with McLaglen held no romantic involvement. The gregarious McLaglen was twelve years older and happily married. His mentoring to Kelly contained no ulterior motivation and his wife Enid became Kelly's close friend. The McLaglens' friendship with Walsh was a good way to become familiar with the intriguing Irishman. Walsh was a good-looking guy although with a serious demeanor. Best she behaves herself though. Knowing Kelly's flirtatious reputation, McLaglen sternly warned her that Walsh was serious about a woman in Boston.

"What do you think of the cast, Egan?" McLaglen asked while he sipped a drink. The liquor flowing freely put the party in a celebratory mood. Wurtzel's idea to foster a beginning production comradery. Essential when scenes ran into inevitable snags. John Ford was an outstanding director with a great eye for what worked on film. Yet while dedicated to actors and actresses that he respected, he could be demanding and often prickly. He was just as much an artist as the faces appearing in the film.

Walsh said, "Everyone looks right for the parts. I can imagine their faces once in costume. Good casting."

Sipping champagne, Tara Kelly said, "I joked before about appearing in those awful getups of the Cumann Na mBan. But I'm excited about doing this picture. Nora Gallagher is a gritty part."

Tara Kelly was no vacant-headed actress. Turning serious, she asked, "Is this movie going to portray what it was really like in Ireland during the War, or just made-up Hollywood stuff?"

Walsh replied, "Well, nothing staged can ever completely duplicate real life. However, I've seen what Fred Stanton's people can create. Very impressive. The script follows closely scenes from my book. I think that the recreation will be as believably authentic as possible. Depends of course a lot on you and Vic with John's direction of course."

Kelly smiled. "That's something coming from you, Egan. That afternoon you spent telling us about Ireland during that time was scary."

McLaglen said, "Tara and I will bring your script to life. Tell us if we're not getting the tone right."

Walsh shook his head and smiled as he sipped his whiskey, "I don't think so. That's John's job. He's not the kind to tolerate someone mucking around with his movie."

Filming movie scenes did not follow the script sequence. The filming schedule was about sets and locations. In the case of *Price of Freedom* filming was planned to first begin with the location scenes in San Luis Obispo that required only props rather than sets. Studio and backlot sets were still under construction. Assistant director Joe Collins was in San Luis Obispo supervising the securing of local people for extras and coordinating assembling the necessary props and costumes coming from Los Angeles. The set design people were also on location preparing vehicles to portray British Army lorries and the fake-rocks props transforming San Luis Obispo into rural County Cork.

The costume department already produced the IRA clothing and British uniforms. Much of these were available from the studio's large warehouse stores of clothing and props from prior movies. Seamstresses busily produced additional costuming required by the many extras. The studio armorer already assembled the large number of authentic firearms required for the battle scenes. Walsh and McLaglen were leaving tomorrow for San Luis Obispo with John Ford along with cast members appearing in the location scenes.

Walsh was in a buoyant mood. They will start rehearsing the scenes this week. Anxious to see the result of all the preparation work appear on film. More than that, Fiona telephoned just days earlier that she expected to be able to come out to Los Angeles in a few weeks. Making good progress on her project and the schedule for introducing her new feature section moved out to May. See wanted to see him and decompress from endless hours of nonstop work.

For an outsider, the complex organization of coordinating all the moving parts to moviemaking is impressive to watch. By the second day on location, they began filming the most important action scenes of the Kilmichael Ambush. The appearance of the cast in costume with weapons, and the lorries was astoundingly realistic. Enough to transport Walsh mentally back to that bloody day. He stayed next to John Ford to offer technical comments. Ford delegated him the task of coaching the movement of the extras. By day three, Ford had Walsh in costume as one of the IRA to provide a focal point for the cast extras to follow during the action sequences.

Unable to reach Fiona by telephone that night dampened his enthusiasm for sharing the day's events. He tried unsuccessfully early the next morning before heading out to the shoot, then again after returning to the hotel that evening. By the end of the week, he became concerned.

By Saturday, Walsh could not contain his anxiety any longer. He placed a long-distance telephone call to Trevor Maguire, Fiona's father.

"Hello."

"Is this Trevor Maguire?" Walsh said.

"Yes. Who's calling?"

"It's Egan Walsh, Trevor."

The unexpected silence caused him to say, "I was calling because I've not been able to reach Fiona for several days."

"Ah Christ, Egan," Maguire said with unmistakable hurt in his voice. "You'll not be knowing then."

"Know what? What's wrong?"

"Fiona is dead," then her father broke down weeping."

"No!" Walsh replied in pain. "How? What happened?"

Recovering his composure, her father said, "She died in an airplane crash. Happened Monday. No one knew she was a passenger on a small two-seat plane until divers discovered two bodies the following day. The plane went down in Boston Harbor."

"Why was she on an airplane?"

"Her boss the magazine's editor thinks she was taking photographs. Drivers recovered her body still holding a small camera in her hand."

"The funeral?"

"We are laying her to rest on Monday. Where are you calling from, Egan?"

"California. Impossible for me to get to Boston by then," breaking down himself with tears flowing unchecked as he absorbed the news. Recovering sufficiently after a couple of moments, "God be with you and your family in her loss, Trevor. I became close to Fiona. I am more than heartbroken. I shall write to my mother and tell her of your tragedy." With nothing more to say he rang off with, "Goodbye, Trevor."

———

Although preferring to withdraw into his grief, he was to have dinner with McLaglen and Ford that night. Couldn't very well conceal what was affecting him so he immediately found them chatting in the hotel bar drinking from the liquor inventory provided by the studio. Pulling them aside, he told them of the bad news he had just received. Both insisted he sit down.

Ford said, "Nothing can take away the hurt. Since you cannot attend her services of course makes it even worse. I grew up in the

Irish neighborhood of Munjoy Hill in Portland, Maine. I remember my parents attending wakes for friends. Not being particularly religious, I always thought that was an enlightened way of paying respects to the departed. Make it a time of joyous remembrance. Tonight, the three of us will have our own wake for your Fiona."

Reluctantly, Walsh agreed. These were good friends that wanted to help. He found himself easing into speaking of the emotional affect Fiona had on him. "A magnificent woman. Intelligent. A fiery Irish lass. Loved everything about her." He stopped short of revealing their relationship as second cousins. Cast and crew had Sunday off before resuming filming in San Luis Obispo. All three got drunk that night.

———

He appreciated everyone being solicitous and wanting to make helpful gestures. Yet in many ways it made dealing with his grief more difficult. His inclination was to suffer in seclusion. Circumstances dictated otherwise. While in emotional pain, that remaining week in San Luis Obispo afforded him the diversion of engrossing his attention in fulfilling his filming responsibilities. Intense work, especially through repeated retakes under the demanding direction of John Ford, provided a diversion to his grief.

Everyone including Walsh was pleased with the location filming. Traveling back to Los Angeles, he realized he must endure another round of condolences. But reminding himself that came with having so many new friends brought him a measure of comfort.

The shooting schedule commenced immediately upon returning from San Luis Obispo. The majority of the sets by now completed with only some back lot work remaining. Walsh welcomed the demanding work to absorb his depressive thoughts.

As expected, everyone he counted among his friends shared his grief. His new women friends Enid McLaglen, Tara Kelly, and Lilly Romano wept as if they knew Fiona. Tears also filled the eyes of his other male associates and friends. Tears even welled in the

125

eyes of Tom Mix and Wyatt Earp. All had taken a particular liking and professional respect for Egan Walsh.

Weeks later, Walsh received a package at the hotel. Addressed from Boston. Once inside his room he anxiously opened it. Inside he found a letter, an issue of the *Boston Globe*, and a framed photograph. He looked at the photograph. The shock hit him like a fist. It showed Fiona standing next to an airplane. An enlargement captured her face with a confident smile. The image brought a fresh round of tears.

The newspaper ran a column on the front page. The headline read:

Boston Magazine Journalist Dies in Plane Crash.

Divers recovered the bodies of Fiona Maguire, senior writer for the magazine *Boston* and pilot Jeffrey Scott from Boston Harbor following the crash of a small airplane on Tuesday. The cause of the crash remains undetermined pending further examination of the recovered aircraft. Scott was an experienced pilot …

A captioned photograph of a ship hoisting the biplane from the water by a crane appeared within the column.

It took several minutes before sufficiently recovering from seeing Fiona's face in the enlargement before opening the letter. It was from Fiona's mother.

Dearest Egan,

When the divers recovered Fiona's body from the wreckage of the airplane, they discovered her camera. We developed the film. Mostly images of Boston she took that day from the airplane for her new magazine section.

Someone took this picture of her before taking off. It is our last picture of Fiona.

We discovered your letters as we sorted through her apartment. Fiona never told us how deeply you cared for each other. Perhaps she was uncertain how we might feel since you were second cousins. Only right that you should have her last picture.

God bless you Egan Walsh. You will survive this just as Trevor and I must. May your life eventually find joy once again after suffering this terrible loss.

Siobhan Maguire

CHAPTER 11

Hollywood, California | 1926

The loss of Fiona brought Egan Walsh to the brink of despair. She brought something into his life never experienced before. A bonding that transcended his natural tendency toward introspection. He also had no one close after leaving Ireland. The murder of his father left him wounded and instilled a terrible need to exact revenge. That rage fixed on the perpetrators dominated all emotion as he fought the British. By the end of the war, Egan Walsh was no longer the same person that originally took up the cause of Irish independence by joining the IRA. Not only had he killed his share of British, he did so efficiently and without remorse. That hardened him emotionally. Fiona did much to reshape his humanity.

His mind now became divided. Moviemaking still engrossed his interest but without the same enthusiasm. Depression never far from consuming him. Intellectually knowing the intensity of grief would eventually subside brought no comfort. To be replaced with what? A pervasive sadness? The loss felt more deeply for their time together being so brief.

Yet the unrelenting violence of living the war also left him emotionally calloused to personal loss. As in war, the only choice was to force himself to move forward. Take what pleasures he could find in life and relegate tragedy to memory.

Egan Walsh sat next to John Ford as he directed shooting scenes number 8 and 9 on back lot sets. This represented the day's shooting schedule.

Fake building fronts when viewed through the camera lens convincingly reproduced city streets of Cork, Ireland. Amazing how the set construction and artistic people employed various techniques to make stone from painted plaster of Paris, with still backgrounds of painted canvas. Structures in the distance reproduced in smaller scale to replicate perspective.

Scene 8 was a sequence of closely connected segments as the character Nora Gallagher made her rounds among her intelligence network on a bicycle. Tara told Walsh she had practiced riding the bicycle around the studio parking lot for days. She had not been on a bicycle for years. Scenes 8 and 9 featured her character Nora Gallagher providing sustained dramatic screen-time for Kelly. The script read:

```
8. EXT. NORA GALLAGHER'S IRA INTELLIGENCE NETWORK
     (Back lot filming)
     EXT. Different repetitive scenes:
     Gallagher bicycling with stops to
     pass and receive information ver-
     bally, then receiving some papers
     from a shopkeeper. She unfastens a
     couple of buttons on her blouse and
     stuffs them inside.

     I/E. Concluding scene with Gal-
     lagher riding with a farmer in a
     typical Irish two-wheel horse drawn
     cart delivering food to IRA hiding
     in a barn. Flynn is there along
     with the flying column O/C Tom
     Barry.
     (Back lot & Studio filming)
```

McLaglen playing the lead character Brandon Flynn and the supporting actor portraying the IRA commander Tom Barry joined Kelly for the final sequence. Ford devoted the afternoon to shooting the tense dramatic scene 9. This following scene

provided Kelly with close ups with the intensity of her character
Nora Gallagher facing real danger.

9. EXT. NORA GALLAGHER ACCOUSTED BY BLACK & TANS
   Back lot filming)
   Depict Gallagher after hiding information for the IRA in her clothing. Riding her bicycle, three
   drunken Black & Tans stopped her
   toppling her to the ground. They
   make lewd remarks as she gets up.
   One pushes her about, tearing her
   dress and she retaliates by hitting
   him with her fists. As the altercation escalates, his two colleagues
   stop the assailant short of committing sexual assault. Her unexpected
   response distracts them from
   searching her, saving her from arrest by discovery of the papers
   concealed under her blouse.

What intrigued Walsh more than the actors' performances
were the believable backgrounds created from the sets, props,
lighting, and camera angles. The transformation once committed
to film was remarkable as everyone viewed that day's developed
film footage the following day. His first experience in seeing the
raw film footage was the location shooting in San Luis Obispo.
These studio sets gave him another level of appreciation of the
artistic techniques in creating believable scenes from scratch. Even
without sound, watching Tara Kelly and the cast perform within
these sets combined to bring alive the experience when captured
on film.

That and John Ford's directing. Just capturing a scene of a couple of minutes often required several takes. A good deal of the
developed film eventually ended up discarded during the editing
process. He watched the cast perform while occasionally observing the expression on Ford's face to gauge his reaction to the take.

Filming did not usually follow the scene chronology. The
schedule involved optimizing the use of sets used for multiple

scenes and utilization of the cast. The location scenes being a good example. With the location filming completed, a good deal of the movie footage was already in the can using the industry expression. Victor McLaglen dominated those scenes playing the Brandon Flynn character. They involved the battles with British security forces where the Kelly character did not appear therefore, she did not go to San Luis Obispo.

In all, Kelly's character was to appear in ten of the thirty major scenes. Good exposure, especially if *Price of Freedom* did well at the box office.

As filming progressed, Walsh settled into a routine. Interesting work with creative people, yet evenings alone with his thoughts remained difficult. His writing stalled. His dark mood overshadowed efforts to fix on a story for a new novel. His editor at Scribner even called encouraging him to devote his time to writing was the best therapy for managing grief. Perhaps so, but he found it difficult to turn his thoughts toward writing.

Watching the filming of scenes 17 and 18 affected him more than anticipated. It was one thing to write about the murder of the Brandon Flynn character's father, quite different to see it portrayed by actors on a set. The dramatic scene paralleled what he envisioned of his own father's murder made it emotionally jarring for Walsh. The set he helped create reminded him of his father's own surgery. The casting was perfect. The direction and acting delivered a sustained performance of outrage and pathos.

```
17. I/E. MURDER OF DR. FLYNN
    (Studio filming)
    INT. Nora Gallagher is visiting
    Flynn's parents. Scene is set in-
    side Dr. Flynn's examining room
    on the ground floor of the large
    two-story house with Dr. Flynn
    and his wife Agnes. It is after
    dusk as headlights shine into the
    windows.
    (Studio filming)
```

EXT. A lorry with a squad of eight Auxiliaries comes to a halt in the gravel driveway and they jump from the lorry. Four approach the front door with drawn revolvers. The officer in charge begins pounding on the door with his fist.
(Back lot filming)

INT. All three inside the house observe the armed Auxiliaries disembarking the lorry. Agnes Flynn grabs Nora's arm and points for her to go upstairs.
(Studio filming)

Title Card: Agnes Flynn says, "The RIC, Nora! Probably because of Brandon. Go upstairs and hide yourself."

INT. Dr. Flynn opens the door and an Auxiliary violently pushes him back inside. A verbal altercation ensues and soon after the Auxil- iaries roughly push the doctor and his wife outside.
(Studio filming)

EXT. Auxiliaries force the doctor and his wife to their knees on the ground. Camera moves to a close- up of the Auxiliary leader asking Dr. Flynn questions. A change of his expression appears before he shoots Dr. Flynn in the back of the head while the camera remains on the killer's face. Exhibiting anger and disgust, the killer im- mediately swipes the barrel of

his revolver viciously across the side of Agnes Flynn's head knocking her to the ground.
(Back lot filming)

INT. Through an upstairs window, Nora Gallagher observes the horrible scene covering her mouth with her hand.
(Studio filming)

EXT. The Auxiliary leader orders the house burned. His men gather cans of petrol from the lorry and douse the exterior perimeter of the house setting it ablaze.
(Back lot filming)

INT. Gallagher observes the Auxiliaries departing. Smelling the smoke, she makes her way down the staircase.
Studio filming)

Trying all the doors, she is blocked by the fire raging from all sides of the house. In desperation, she sees an opening outside a large window where the flames appear less intense. She smashes the window with an armchair and successfully climbs outside covering her shoulders with a rug to protect her from the heat of the flames.

18. EXT. GALLAGHER ATTENDS TO FLYNN'S MOTHER
    (Back lot filming)
    Gallagher is confronted with the horrible scene of DR. Flynn lying face down with blood soaking the

133

```
ground from the exit wound of the
shot to the back of the head. Mer-
cifully, she cannot see his face.
Agnes Flynn is barely conscious,
bleeding profusely from a large
gash to the side of her forehead,
she tries to crawl closer to her
dead husband as Gallagher gently
restrains her. Gallagher tears a
portion of her slip into a make-
shift    bandage   to   bind   Agnes
Flynn's    head    to    staunch    the
bleeding. Scene is filmed against
the   background   of   the   burning
house.
```

When director John Ford said, 'That's a wrap' as filming concluded on the closing scene of *Price of Freedom* with the fire consuming the set façade of the Flynn house at twilight, cast and crew applauded. Ford was the first to embrace Kelly. "Outstanding performance, Tara."

Everyone was shaking hands and hugging Kelly. Arm in arm with Victor McLaglen, she made her way over to Walsh. Walsh gave her a hug. "Marvelous, Tara. That was a moving performance. On the big screen it will be even better."

Walsh did not share just how deeply the scene affected him. There was no Nora Gallagher to minister to his mother. Just Dermot O'Conner and his wife Saoirse Agnes. All the time Agnes Walsh remained inconsolable over the murder of her husband.

Kelly replied, "You and Ray wrote a great script."

McLaglen said, "This'll be a good movie, Egan. Not official yet but Sol is already considering the idea of filming a sequel. Starring me and Tara again."

Walsh nodded, "Yes, I know. Sol already floated the idea with me. You and Tara are to portray the same characters now caught up in the Irish Civil War."

"With you to write the script and make the technical stuff authentic, it can't miss."

Walsh replied, "Not that easy to frame a story set during the Irish Civil War. The war of independence was black and white. The civil war carried only shades of gray. Former IRA comrades killing each other because of differing views of the terms of the treaty with Britain. The script needs to find some common ground or risk offending those politically on one side or the other."

"Well, if anyone can write that script it is you," Tara said. "Let's pick up Enid and all have dinner together."

Tara Kelly was becoming a much sought after woman. She was twenty-eight and beautiful enough to compete for roles against even younger starlets. Her film credits provided enough experience to understand how the movie industry operated. Enough experience to access her bargaining leverage in salary negotiations. Street smart while retaining her femininity. Enough experience in life to sidestep unwanted male advances by male stars or studio execs. She acquired a reputation for dating men outside the industry. Little material for Hollywood gossip columns.

However, her obvious liking for Egan Walsh did not extend toward romance. She found true friends in Victor and Enid McLaglen and seemed to place Walsh in that same context. Older, more experienced friends with their own lives. As for Walsh, he never made an advance toward her or even flirted good-naturedly because she knew of his relationship with Fiona in Boston. That did not change after his personal loss of Fiona. Kelly felt secure around McLaglen and Walsh. More like brothers where she could seek refuge from the pressures of Hollywood.

Walsh was a mysterious foreigner with a colorful past. Handsome and articulate with a successful novel to his credit. His recalling of experiences during the Anglo-Irish War intrigued her. Admitted to having killed many British enemies, but never made himself out as a hero. He spoke of those times reluctantly and then only to coach her and McLaglen. Obviously introspective, she commented once to him good naturedly, "Do you ever smile, Egan? Why so serious?" She found Egan Walsh a fascinating enigma and a trusted friend with no romantic motives. The effect of Fiona's death on him profoundly distressed her.

Everyone offered that the grief would progressively subside. No telling how long that might take. Having seen the filming of what could have been his father's murder only added to his feeling of being alone. His mother never recovered emotionally from the murder of his father. Cared for by his only sister, she never regained her former vibrant personality. Fiona's unexpected death added yet another personal loss. His few new friends since coming to Hollywood substituted for family. Yet those friendships came about because of this moviemaking project which might prove only temporary. Would he now remain in Southern California?

Although introspective by nature, he still felt a void when returning each night to his hotel room each evening. Unanchored was the best word to describe his feelings. He was thirty-three years old. Both his professional and personal life were uncertain.

—

Filming concluded by the middle of April and editing by early May. Premier releases in major cities of *Price of Freedom* opened to enthusiastic audiences accompanied with favorable reviews. Early box office indications projected exceptional financial success. Trade publications cited favorable antidotal comments by Irish American organizations and confirmed by attendance in the heavily Irish northeastern markets.

All this solidified William Fox's decision to produce a sequel. Production costs were projected at less than *Price of Freedom* since many of the sets and props could be used for the sequel. Victor McLaglen and Tara Kelly to be cast in their roles as Brandon Flynn and Nora Gallagher. John Ford would again direct. Egan Walsh and Ray Schrock would co-write the script. Walsh again was to act as technical consultant.

Walsh understood the Irish Civil War from his unfortunate experience of internment by the newly establish Irish national government. He understood both sides of the Treaty debate. Knew all the key players. Reported extensively in the *Boston Globe* about the civil war as it tore apart Ireland for a year.

Yet writing a movie script without it being provocative was a daunting challenge. It was about a civil war. Impossible to find a middle ground from which to base a story. No way to shy away from the politics intimately understood by Irish Americans.

Yet he agreed to remain in Hollywood and work on this movie. He enjoyed his circle of friends and had no alternative plans. Finding a worthy subject for another novel still eluded him. Returning to journalism at the *Boston Globe* might be possible, except for Boston's weather and too many memories. Remaining in Southern California seemed the right choice for the moment.

The success of *Price of Freedom* proved good for the careers of both Victor McLaglen and Tara Kelly. While committed to starring in the sequel, other offers began coming in. Although not in the top tier of movie stars, they were generating exceptional reviews in the trade publications along with the success of *Price of Freedom*.

———

Walsh was in a studio conference room of the Fox studio on Western huddled with John Ford and Ray Schrock debating possible thematic ideas for *Dying for Ireland*. The working title and setting were the only established elements of the sequel. Walsh outlined the challenge for doing a picture about the Irish Civil War resulting from with the unsatisfactory terms awarding only limited independence for Ireland. How to make a commercially successful movie about a controversial subject without alienating part of the public and providing material for movie reviewers to criticize must be resolved before everything else. Walsh could provide them with plenty of material to make a dramatic movie with action scenes. They could introduce new characters in the form of the opposing military leaders of the civil war, particularly Michael Collins and Liam Lynch.

When they broke for lunch, William Fox was stepping out of Sol Wurtzel's office.

"How's it going guys?" Fox said addressing all three of them.

Ford replied, "Making progress, Mr. Fox. Trying to find the right note to make a good movie without offending those Irish in America that did not favor the treaty that ended the war with the British. Mr. Walsh tells us he did not agree with the treaty terms but chose not to take up arms against his fellow countrymen, so he understands both sides fighting the civil war."

"Excellent. I'm sure you fellas will figure it out," Fox said.

From behind William Fox, Victor McLaglen, Tara Kelly, and Sol Wurtzel joined Fox. Walsh, Ford, Schrock, and Romano had just left the conference room. To everyone, Wurtzel announced, "We just signed the contracts for Victor and Tara to do *Dying for Ireland.*"

Tara Kelly grabbed Walsh and McLaglen on each arm and said, "Let's go have lunch and celebrate."

Walsh looked at John Ford who smiled and motioned with his head for Walsh to go along.

At lunch, Kelly said, "Victor and I are invited to a grand party Saturday night. Hosted by that banker Hollister who is a big deal in financing most of the studios. All the biggest stars are coming. Chaplin and Valentino. Pickford and Fairbanks."

"Where's this party?" Walsh asked.

"At Chadwick Hollister's house in Beverly Hills. He likes entertaining with movie people as his guests. Everyone says it's a grand mansion. Victor isn't going so I don't have an escort for the evening."

McLaglen said, "Not my sort of party. Enid and I already have plans to go to the Hollywood Bowl. The Los Angeles Philharmonic is performing. Enid got me interested in classical music. A nice spring evening under the stars is more to my liking than listening to a bunch of drunken movie people."

Kelly said, "Well, I'm going. Spending an evening with gorgeous men like Charlie Chaplin and Rudolph Valentino is *my idea* of a good time."

Looking at Walsh, she said, "I don't want to go alone though. Maybe you could come as my escort?"

Walsh smiled but shook his head. "No. I can't do that, Tara. I wasn't invited and not someone prominent in the business. Not my kind of evening either. You'll just have to go by yourself. I'm sure those handsome male movie stars won't ignore you. Just behave yourself and don't drink too much."

CHAPTER 12

Hollywood, California | 1926

Walsh came down for breakfast at the hotel before heading out to the studio to resume work on the script for *Dying for Ireland*. As usual, a waiter brought him coffee and the *Los Angeles Times*. The bizarre saga of the popular evangelist Aimee Semple McPherson's alleged kidnapping again made for that day's front-page headline. Yet Walsh's attention immediately went to the right-hand column. It read:

Actress Tara Kelly Found Dead

Hollywood, CA - The body of film star Tara Kelly was discovered this morning at her bungalow on North Serrano Avenue. Kelly recently starred in the successful movie *Price of Freedom*. According to police, Kelly's housekeeper discovered Kelly dead in her bed yesterday morning. Police believe Kelly had been dead for several days. Police refused to provide any further information about a possible cause of the actress' death until the Los

Angeles County Coroner's office
performs an autopsy.

Walsh sat at the table processing the shock. Losing his young friend just as her acting career began flourishing was yet another personal tragedy. Coming only months since the untimely death of Fiona Maguire, the news was even more distressing. He immediately telephoned Victor McLaglen.

Enid McLaglen answered the telephone. "Enid, this is Egan. Have you seen the newspaper this morning?"

"Not yet. We just woke up. Making coffee. Vic is shaving. What is it?"

"It's about Tara Kelly. She was found dead at her home."

"Oh god no! What happened?" Enid liked Kelly and the two women became close as Kelly worked on two pictures with her husband. "Vic, come here quickly!"

Enid was crying when her husband came into the kitchen with shaving cream still on his face. "What's wrong?"

Through her tears she handed the phone to him, "It's Egan. More bad news."

"What is it, Egan?"

"It's about Tara. In this morning's newspaper. She was found dead at her home by her cleaning woman."

"How did she die?"

"The police don't say. Only that she was found in her bed. Waiting for an autopsy."

"Bloody hell! Goddammit! Such a wonderful girl. I am going to the studio. Come with me?"

"Of course."

"I'll be at your hotel in twenty minutes," McLaglen said.

They went to Sol Wurtzel's office at the Western Avenue studio. When they arrived, a visibly upset Lilly Romano said, "Sol already knows about Tara Kelly. He's talking to Mr. Fox on the telephone right now. When he's done you can go in."

Walsh said to Lilly, "The newspaper didn't give much detail. Do you know anything more?"

"No. Just read it in the *Times* like you did. When Sol arrived, he already knew."

Wurtzel was just as upset. "Not sure what this means about going forward with *Dying for Ireland*. Without Tara, that changes things without her character. We'll sort that out later. Right now, I'm concerned more about how she died. Hope this does not turn out to be another Hollywood scandal. Both of you were close to her. Any idea what could have happened?"

Both shook their heads. Walsh volunteered, "Vic and I saw her last Friday. She looked fine. In a great mood."

McLaglen said, "Tara and I were invited to a party at the home of that bigwig banker Hollister last Saturday. She was excited since major stars like Chaplin and Valentino might be there. Not my kind of thing. Enid and I went to the Hollywood Bowl that night."

"She tried to entice me to escort her, but I also begged off. Told her I wasn't invited," Walsh said.

Wurtzel said, "Unfortunately we don't know the cause of her death. She appeared young and healthy. Any reason to believe drugs might be involved?"

McLaglen spoke up immediately, "Can't be drugs. Working with her on two movies, I never saw any indications, Sol. She also never drank too much. Never seemed down. Always confident, making wisecracks."

Walsh was at a loss as to what to do. He didn't want to be around studio employees speculating endlessly about what might have happened. The longer this went on without knowing more facts, rumors would start to proliferate.

———

Hollywood could not bear another scandal. Even those incidents clouded by mysterious circumstances grew out of proportion through endless speculation. The public gravitated to the titillation surrounding the demise of the beautiful and famous. None more so than movie stars. Like watching a train wreck on film.

Almost every year for the past few years a spectacular scandal tarnished the public image of the movie industry. This put the movie industry under attack by moralizing reformist groups for portraying inappropriate subject matter. As celebrities, published accounts of the personal lives of movie stars frequently focused on unflattering behavior, often at odds with their on-screen characters. By 1926, the public generally viewed those in the movie industry as leading hedonistic lifestyles.

Many cities and even states actively talked about passing censorship laws. Reports of the debauched lifestyles of certain movie celebrities continually added to pressure from conservative Christian organizations. Many of the same women's organizations and outspoken evangelizing Christian preachers that brought about the passing of the 18th Amendment to the U.S. Constitution bringing about Prohibition made the largest noise for advocating government censorship of the new entertainment medium.

Largely through the efforts of Paramount head Adolph Zukor, former postmaster general William Hayes became Chairman of the Motion Picture Producers and Distributors of America. The studio heads lead by Zukor tasked Hayes with using the MPA as the platform from which to preempt government censorship. He was to use the organization to find the means of satisfying the militant critics through industry self-imposed censorship. Continuation of successive movie industry scandals could undermine that effort.

Yet movies with implied sexual content, indelicate social issues, and graphic violence were often among the most successful at the box office. Studio executives wanted to find some common ground to retain freedom of creative control over movie content without oversight from organizations of moralistic crusading old ladies and religious leaders.

Tara Kelly's death therefore provoked considerable concern if her death came about from anything other than natural causes. Along with every other studio executive in the movie industry, Zukor and Hayes learned about Kelly's death the same day that it became public. So did Chadwick Hollister.

Zukor called Hollister immediately knowing the banker's extensive connections in Los Angeles. "What do you know about this actress's death, Chadwick?"

"Nothing more than what appeared in the newspapers this morning. I already placed a call to my source within the LAPD. An assistant chief. I expect to hear from him soon with the details of her death. What the LAPD knows but are withholding from the public could give us time to prepare if it is something presenting a problem for the industry. I will let you know as soon as I hear more."

"Christ, we cannot afford another scandal at this time. Should this somehow involve drugs, we need to pull out all the stops to manage the fallout. That includes City Hall, the LAPD, and the media."

"I understand, Adolph. There are things I can do with the government sector, but the media is not so easy. I am friends with *Los Angeles Times* publisher, Harry Chandler. A strong advocate for promoting Los Angeles. However, William Hearst of the *Examiner* is a sensationalist and cannot be counted on to tamp down injurious details. I'll get back to you as soon as I know more."

Hollister would postpone acknowledging Kelly presence at his party on Saturday. That was four days before the discovery of her body. The police already revealed she died days earlier. His party would soon come under scrutiny. With so many celebrities in attendance, that alone will prompt a media feeding frenzy for salacious detail to feed the newspapers and trade magazines. Managing the crisis will be a personal challenge.

———

After a miserable day, Egan Walsh returned to his hotel. The desk clerk handed him a message. It read, *Call me as soon as you can. Tom.* From Tom Mix, likely about Tara.

"Do you know any more than what the newspapers reported?" Mix said.

"No. I've been huddled with Vic and Sol most of the day.

"Did you know Tara went to that big party at that banker Hollister's house on Saturday?"

"Yeah. She told Vic and I. Vic was invited but didn't go."

Mix said, "Well, I was invited, and I went. Everyone was there. Chaplin and Valentino. Mary Pickford and Douglas Fairbanks. Lots of beautiful actresses. Clara Bow, Gloria Swanson. Norma Shearer. Tara comes in on the arm of that young English actor Leslie Fenton that played with Vic in *What Price Glory*. Believe me she turned heads. Dressed in a sexy tight-fitting blue dress."

"What happened at the party? How did she seem?"

"Fine. Happy. I can tell you that Chaplin and Valentino both took a shine to her. Hollister also spent a lot of time hanging around her. I left early, maybe two hours after she arrived. Party was still in full swing."

"Was she drinking?"

"I suppose so, but I didn't pay that close of attention."

"Did you see anything unusual about Tara's behavior?"

"Not exactly. Although just before I left, there seemed to be some falling-out between her and Fenton. Couldn't hear what was going on because I was on the other side of the room. Anyway, Fenton left looking pissed off."

"Any idea what might have happened?"

"Maybe upset about her ignoring him. Pretty obvious that Chaplin and Valentino were competing for Tara's attention. Obvious to several of the other women by their expressions. Probably didn't like being ignored by this newcomer."

"Interesting. Wonder how Tara got home if Fenton left. What time did you leave, Tom?"

"Probably about ten. Had to be up early Sunday."

Walsh called McLaglen and explained what Mix told him. McLaglen tracked down Fenton. Sounding upset on the telephone, Fenton said, "How about I meet you at the Montmartre Café. Been a rough day after learning about Tara. Need to talk to a friendly face and get a couple of drinks. What a bloody fucking shock."

In the rear of the Montmartre was a speakeasy haunt reserved for the movie set.

Fenton found McLaglen sitting with Walsh.

"Leslie, this is Egan Walsh. *Price of Freedom* was his story. A good friend of Tara's."

Fenton replied, "So sorry for both of you. I know you worked with Tara. Anything more about how she died?"

Walsh replied, "Not yet. That's why we wanted to talk to you. Newspapers place her time of death last Saturday or Sunday. Tell us about what went on at the party, Mr. Fenton."

"Well, Tara asked me to go as her escort. As it turned out, she didn't need an escort."

"What do you mean?" Walsh asked.

"All these famous beautiful actresses and Tara upstaged them by capturing the attention of those big-name actors. After a couple of hours, it became obvious to everyone."

"Including you?" Walsh said.

"Yeah. It ticked me off. She abandoned me after an hour. Felt out of place by myself among all these famous movie stars."

"Anyone in particular occupying her attention?"

"Oh yes. Charlie Chaplin and Rudolph Valentino. Everyone knows Chaplin's reputation with women. Then later, the host Mr. Hollister took an interest and seemed to hover close to her."

"Was she drinking heavily?"

"Didn't think so, but maybe too much. As time wore on, she became more .... not sure of the word... animated is the best way I describe her behavior. Smoked a lot of cigarettes using a long cigarette holder that women like to use."

"What happened then?"

"I finally had enough. Pulled her aside and said I was calling it a night and leaving."

"What did she say about that?"

"She wasn't angry, just said she had no intention of leaving. Having too much fun. She said, with all these big stars here, how can I leave? I replied that everyone notices you are taking advantage of that. With that, she became miffed. Told me to just leave. She'd get a ride home or take a taxi. So, I left."

Essentially what Tom Mix described. So how did Tara Kelly get home? Did someone from the party take her?

———

The following Monday's addition of the *Los Angeles Times* printed another column on page one announcing Tara Kelly's cause of death. Hearst's *Los Angeles Examiner* however carried it as its headline reading: *Another Drug Tragedy in Hollywood*.

Hollister was successful in getting *Los Angeles Times* publisher Harry Chandler to avoid making it the headline, yet it still became a front-page story.

Actress Tara Kelly Found Dead

Hollywood, CA. - LAPD Assistant Police Chief James Fletcher released the results of the autopsy on actress Tara Kelly. Fletcher said, "Tara Kelly's housekeeper found her body last Wednesday. According to the autopsy performed by senior medical examiner pathologist Dr. Louis Richardson, Kelly died from a lethal overdose of cocaine ingested accidentally."

Further details provided by Chief Fletcher stated that responding police officers found Kelly dead in her bed dressed in a nightgown. A quantity of cocaine was found at the residence. Investigators determined Kelly lived alone with the residence securely locked with no evidence of forced entry. Both LAPD investigators and the Los Angeles County Coroner's Office found no evidence suggesting foul

play. The state of the decease's remains indicated death occurred 48-
72 hours prior to discovery of the
body.

Funeral services for Tara Kelly
will take place at 1:00pm this Thurs-
day, July 15 at St. Vincent De Paul
Catholic Church at 621 W. Adams
Boulevard. Interment will follow at
Hollywood Memorial Park on
Santa Monica Boulevard.

———

Hundreds of people attended Tara Kelly's funeral. Hollywood celebrities made a particularly large showing along with be-
hind-the-camera studio personnel that worked on Kelly's movies.
Fox Studios was well represented including William Fox, Sol
Wurtzel, and the entire cast and crew of *Price of Freedom.*

Walsh felt something was terribly out of place about Tara
Kelly's death. A drug overdose did not seem to fit. Both Victor
and Enid McLaglen felt that way also. Might she have gotten carried away and did something foolish at that party? If so, how did
she get home? Then what happened? The newspapers mentioned
nothing about attending this party along with some of Hollywood's biggest celebrities. Did the LAPD investigate her actions
around the time the coroner suggested as the time of death? Any
competent reporter would ask the police that question. The media
attention will not die down. Too many people know of the party.
Once some enterprising reporter latches onto that, the story will
become self-perpetuating. When revealed that Kelly was partying
with the likes of Hollywood royalty like Chaplin, Valentino, Pickford, and Fairbanks around the time of her death, that becomes a
story in itself. The taint of cocaine involvement will make this the
latest Hollywood scandal.

Kelly's untimely and questionable death only plunged Walsh
further toward depression. The last six years of his life a continual

148

struggle for survival. The bitter violence and despair of the war. The murder of his father perhaps because of his actions. The false imprisonment following the signing of the Treaty. Self-exile to America brought safety but loneliness leaving friends and family in Ireland.

The period of recovery by returning to journalism and writing fiction provided a gradual return to normalcy. Then finding Fiona changed his life. Their relationship became so much more as they fell in love. Coming to California provided a challenging diversion while promoting commercial success of his writing. The promise of a stable parallel career in journalism opened a bright future. Far from recovery over the tragedy of Fiona's death, he now suffered the tragic loss of this young woman friend. While not romantically involved, he felt protective of her and considered her a friend. That it left a great deal of unanswered questions was disturbing.

His friend Tom Mix attending the same party as Kelly gave an account of her demeanor at the party. Leslie Fenton, her escort that evening, portrayed Kelly as enjoying herself. According to Fenton, she became the center of attention of Charlie Chaplin and Rudolph Valentino. Nothing to make Walsh understand a drug overdose as the cause of death even accidentally. Walsh did not believe Kelly used drugs. Did someone give her drugs? Did she appear under the influence of drugs at the party? Did she take the drugs knowingly? How did she get home?

For his own state of mind, he cannot leave the questions surrounding her death unresolved. As a matter of personal responsibility and to satisfy his journalistic instincts, there must be more to her death than explained simply as an accidental drug overdose.

If the Los Angeles newspapers declined to further investigate the story beyond the police statement, then he would. He still had his accredited press credentials with the *Boston Globe*.

CHAPTER 13

Los Angeles, California | 1926

Using his accreditation as a reporter for the *Boston Globe*, Walsh telephoned the reporters for the *Los Angeles Times* and *Los Angeles Examiner* reporting on Kelly's death.

To the *Times* reporter, he said, "I just happen to be in Los Angeles on vacation, but the death of another Hollywood actress fresh off the success of *Price of Freedom* is national news. What did the police say about the circumstances surrounding the discovery of Kelly's body?"

"Nothing more than what we published."

"That statement from the assistant police chief provided no details. Did someone question the lead investigator at the scene?

"Tried but told that all information must come through Assistant Chief Fletcher's office. The reason given was because the deceased was a celebrity, the LAPD must be careful not to encourage rumor. They said the matter seems straightforward. Another Hollywood star succumbs to drugs."

"Who did you speak to at the LAPD?"

"Lieutenant Dekker from the Hollywood Division. The precinct station is located on North Wilcox. Dekker was in charge of the investigation after discovery of the body by the cleaning woman."

"What's the name of the cleaning woman?"

"Her name is Wanda Hernandez."

"Do you have an address?"

"What's the difference? She's just an old lady that discovered Kelly dead in bed."

"Did anyone from the newspaper speak to her?"

"Not that I know of."

"Why not? Seems like any good reporter would follow up with interviewing her. What was Kelly's condition? What did the surroundings in the room look like? What did she know about Kelly's habits?"

"Listen, we would have except word came down from upstairs not to pursue the story further. My editor said *it's just another Hollywood drug tragedy. Another scandal is bad for the movie industry. Bad for Los Angeles.*"

The reporter sounded irritated by management's censorship. After a pause, he said, "Wanda Hernandez's address is 336 West Third. Apartment 204. Good luck." The reporter hung up.

Walsh got similar treatment from the *Examiner* reporter. The guy said, "Can't help you pal. The story is off limits for some reason. Boss said move on. Why should a Boston newspaper give a shit? Nobody in LA does."

Pissed off, Walsh responded, "Because Tara Kelly was Irish and so am I. Lot of Irish in America. Those assholes in the LAPD should do your jobs. You guys should also do your jobs. I already know more than you printed." This time Walsh hung up.

While the *Los Angeles Times* and Hearst's *Examiner* maintained a low interest in Kelly's death, the *Pasadena Star-News* chose to publish a follow up piece. Reporter Benjamin Zimmerman's byline cited Kelly's attendance at a lavish party around the time the coroner identified as the time of death.

New Information Concerning Deceased Actress Tara Kelly

Pasadena, CA. - Benjamin Zimmerman: This newspaper has obtained new information concerning circumstances surrounding the death of movie actress Tara Kelly over a week ago. The coroner pronounced her death as accidental resulting from a cocaine overdose. To understand Kelly's movements and state of mind, the LAPD has provided no answers to questions related to the decedent's whereabouts prior to the established time of death. On the Saturday prior to the discovery of her body on the following Wednesday, Tara Kelly attended a lavish party along with some of the biggest names in Hollywood. Saturday falls within the window for the estimated time of death of Kelly by the medical examiner.

Movie celebrities attending the party on that Saturday night represented the major Hollywood movie studios. Clara Bow, Harold Lloyd, Gloria Swanson, and director/producer Cecil B. DeMille from Paramount. From MGM, Norma Shearer, Greta Garbo, John Gilbert, Buster Keaton, producer Irving Thalberg, and producer Samuel Goldwyn. From United Artists, Charlie Chaplin, Rudolph Valentino, Mary Pickford, Douglas Fairbanks, and director D. W. Griffith. From Fox, Tom Mix and Tara Kelly. A who's who of Hollywood. As a rising star, Kelly received praise for her starring role in the recent film *Price of Freedom*.

Hosting the party was financier Chadwick Hollister at his mansion on Benedict Canyon Drive in Beverly Hills. Hollister Financial is among the largest financial institutions providing financing for the movie industry.

Many questions remain surrounding the circumstances of Tara Kelly's death by accidental cocaine overdose. Sources close to the young actress deny she was a user of drugs. Los Angeles Police Department responses to our inquiries do not shed further light on a possible explanation for this tragedy. This reporter has independent information confirming LAPD investigators have not yet interviewed any of the celebrity guests. Given that Tara Kelly's death may have occurred around the time of the party on the prior Saturday night makes everyone attending as potentially possessing information that might establish Kelly's state of mind. Obtaining essential basic information would seem standard practice under the circumstances of a high-profile death. When did Kelly leave the Hollister residence on Benedict Canyon in Beverly Hills? How did she return to her bungalow on Serrano Avenue nine miles away in Hollywood since she had no car? Did anyone leave with her?

The opening salvo of the sensationalist media followed soon after. The monthly Hollywood tabloid *Look-See Magazine* featured Kelly on its cover. The magazine fed on unsubstantiated rumor, sensationalized without attempting verification of facts. *Look-See* raised yellow journalism to the level of farce with its typically lurid fictionalized stories contrived from fabricated embellishments. No matter how outlandish and clearly speculative the gossip, *Look-See Magazine* maintained a profitable circulation. The public gravitated to reading titillating stories and many loyal readers believed the articles to be factual.

In this issue, *Look-See* correctly revealed Kelly attending the party of movie industry financier Chadwick Hollister's along with a complete list of the famous stars at the gala industry event. The remaining content then departed into speculative nonsense.

Look-See Magazine was just an example of the fringe media. Kelly's death however began its ascent to full-blown scandal. Every studio head could only watch in horror. Paramount head Adolph Zukor feared the worst. Always seeking advantage by going on the offensive, he was a tenacious competitor. Ruthless and bad tempered, his universal dislike was well earned. He immediately called every studio head badgering them to counsel those actors and directors that attended Hollister's party to say nothing to the media, and as little as possible to the police. *It is vital that the LAPD does not find reason to continue investigating the circumstances of her death. She died of an accidental cocaine overdose. A terrible tragedy, nothing more. Let that be everyone's reply.*

The piece in the *Pasadena Star-News* gave encouragement to Walsh that the circumstances surrounding Kelly's death were not a closed issued. The LAPD was obviously treating her death with alarming indifference. From his journalist experience that meant powerful interests were probably involved. Those interests most likely the motion picture industry and the identification of Hollywood as the iconic symbol of Los Angeles.

Walsh needed to understand why the LAPD appeared indifferent to further investigating of circumstances surrounding Kelly's death. How could the coroner rule her overdose was accidental or self-induced without a thorough report of everything

154

about the scene where responding police found the body? Were any reporters asking these same questions? Regardless, he would start by contacting LAPD Lieutenant Dekker.

It took some doing but eventually his call was put through to Dekker. This time only by misleading the receptionist after repeated calls giving his name as a journalist for an eastern newspaper did not produce results.

"I need to speak to Lieutenant Dekker."

"Who's calling?"

"Rather not say. I have some information for Lieutenant Dekker regarding the death of Tara Kelly."

After a long pause, "This is Dekker. Who is calling?"

"My name is Walsh. *Boston Globe*."

"You're the sonofabitch that keeps calling. What do you want?"

"Simple question. Is the LAPD investigating a party that Tara Kelly attended the night of her death?"

"Thought we made it clear that all press inquiries and responses must go through Chief Fletcher's office. There is nothing further I can provide than the information already released. This is nothing more than a drug overdose. Just because she is a movie actress doesn't make things different."

"I keep hearing that shit from everyone I talk to. The LAPD should do a proper job of investigation. Makes the LAPD appear complicit in obstruction by refusing to investigate relevant information. The press will not relent." Walsh abruptly hung up.

It became clear that the Los Angeles power structure feared another scandal. The spectacular growth of Los Angeles translated to wealth. Although skeptical, Walsh could not rule out that Tara Kelly's death might have resulted from personal bad choices. If so, that should be explained by facts rather than conjecture. Walsh could not rest without finding the truth. That meant he would take up his own investigation. Approach this as a reporter.

In a telephone conversation, Walsh's former boss William Taylor publisher of the *Boston Globe* said he would gladly accept his submissions for continued reporting on the death of Tara Kelly. It was just as newsworthy in Boston as in Los Angeles.

Unlike those with vested interests in Hollywood fearing another scandal, the *Boston Globe* had no such concerns. If Walsh could provide evidence of an official cover up, that alone would become a major newsworthy story even if Kelly's death proved to be an accidental drug overdose.

Along with the local *Pasadena Star-News*, Walsh would try to raise an outcry nationwide and ensure Kelly's death remained in the news. With the movie *Dying for Ireland* on hold, he could devote his full attention to investigative journalism.

His first thought was to contact the Pasadena reporter Benjamin Zimmerman. A possible ally with local connections. From his time at the *Boston Globe*, Walsh understood the power of the American free press. From 1916 through the Anglo-Irish War, the republican-leaning *Cork Examiner* came under intense British censorship and contributed to his eventual decision to join the IRA.

———

Sitting in his office, Hollister's secretary buzzed his intercom, "Police Chief Fletcher is calling." Thinking, what the hell now? "Put him through."

"Good morning, Chief. What can I do for you?"

"Wanted to tell you that a fellow named Egan Walsh, a newspaper reporter for the *Boston Globe,* is asking questions. Called the lieutenant in charge of investigating the actress's death. Asked if we were investigating your party on that Saturday night."

"What did the lieutenant tell him?"

"Nothing. Told Walsh that all information regarding the death of Tara Kelly must come through my office. Explained as a celebrity death, it was receiving special attention. Walsh became angry saying the LAPD was obstructing further investigation. He's called my office repeatedly."

"A Boston newspaper? Who is the guy?"

"A reporter, currently on a leave of absence. Spent a couple of years with the *Boston Globe* after coming from Ireland. That's where his background becomes interesting. Walsh fought for the

IRA during the war for Irish independence. British even put a price on his head."

"What's his connection to Tara Kelly?"

"While working at the *Globe* he wrote a novel. That novel became the source for the recent movie *Price of Freedom*. Fox Films bought the film rights, hiring Walsh to write the script and act as technical consultant. That's how he came to know Kelly. Walsh and Kelly were also to work on a sequel to *Price of Freedom*."

"What was Kelly to Walsh?"

"Don't know. Could just be friends. Might be more than friends. Walsh suffered the loss of a woman in Boston that died in an accident earlier this year. Whatever his motivation, maybe he knows she did not use drugs. Without more information, he's suspicious. Perhaps just the instincts of a reporter. Whatever his reason, doesn't look like he is going away."

Hollister remained silent for a moment. An unexpected loose end. "Thank you, Chief. Anything I can do for you, Chief?"

"No. I'm fine."

Fletcher should be fine. He owned Fletcher after years of keeping him on the *payroll* as Fletcher rose from captain to commander to assistant chief. Fletcher was an investment that paid off. His interceding with the coroner's office immediately following Tara Kelly's death earned him an extraordinary bonus. Hollister explained her death as an indiscretion by someone very important that turned into tragedy but did not provide Fletcher any specifics.

This new problem of Walsh however required employing private investigative resources to monitor Walsh's progress. Pressing the intercom, "Evelyn, have Mr. Schachter come to my office."

"Take a seat, Nate. This matter of that actress's unfortunate death is becoming another scandal for the film industry. It's always about drugs. Yet someone out there insists on making this something larger. The matter indirectly involves us since I threw that party for Hollywood big-name celebrities. Since Tara Kelly attended the party, the press might attempt to connect the party with her death creating a damaging scandal. Hurting us in the process and our studio clients."

"Who is this problem, Sir?"

"His name is Egan Walsh. Worked on that picture *Price of Freedom* with Kelly. Maybe sexually involved with her. For whatever reason, he's pissed off about her death enough to make waves. What we need to know is what Walsh is doing. I want you to hire a private investigative firm to follow Walsh round the clock. They are to report to you daily on his activities. Select an agency with a reputable background and enough manpower to do the surveillance. Cost is not a consideration."

"I'll get on it immediately."

———

Walsh waited several hours before Wanda Hernandez returned to her apartment. A woman in her sixties. Walking with a slight limp, she climbed the external stairs carefully carrying a bag of groceries in one arm holding onto the railing with her other hand. He gave her a couple of minutes before knocking on her door and removing his hat.

Opening the door a crack, she said, "*Si?*"

"Are you Wanda Hernandez?"

In broken English with concern in her voice, "Who are you?"

"My name is Egan Walsh. I worked with Tara Kelly on the movie *Price of Freedom*. She was a good friend and good person. Helped me when I suffered a personal loss. I just have a few questions. May I come in?"

Hernandez hesitated a moment but then let him into the apartment.

"Please sit down, Señor Walsh."

He sat down on a well-worn sofa, and she sat on a chair opposite.

"I do not believe Tara used drugs. Did you ever see anything like that in her home?"

Hernandez shook her head.

"Did you ever see her ... acting oddly?

Again, Hernandez shook her head.

"Now this is difficult to ask, but can you tell me how Tara looked when you found her?"

Hernandez pulled a handkerchief from her pocket and dabbed her eyes. "After I unlocked the front door and came in, I called out for her, but she did not answer. I went into her bedroom and saw her lying on the bed. Thought she was asleep, so I touched her hand. That was terrible!" Hernandez made the sign of the cross. "Her hand was cold. I tried to lift her hand, but her arm was stiff. I knew then she was dead and called the police."

After dabbing her eyes and composing herself, Walsh asked, "What was Tara wearing?"

"Wearing? She was wearing a nightgown of course."

"Did she have her makeup on?"

Hernandez looked puzzled for a moment then replied, "Yes. I can picture her face. Still had lipstick and eye makeup on."

"Did you see a blue dress lying about?" Tom Mix had told him Kelly wore a tightfitting blue dress to the party.

"No."

"Any clothes or shoes lying about as if she returned from a party and undressed hurriedly?"

"No."

"Did you ever find men's clothing in Tara's home?"

Offended by the question, she replied adamantly, "No, never."

"Did you see anything like pills or alcohol on a table next to her bed?"

"Hernandez just shook her head."

"Wanda, do you believe Tara used cocaine?"

"No! Tara would never do such a thing. She was a beautiful and kind person."

Nothing Wanda Hernandez told him specifically contradicted the coroner's conclusion of accidental cocaine overdose. Yet too many circumstances remained unexplained. How did she get home from the party since her escort left earlier? Did someone drive her home? When did she ingest cocaine? Did she acquire the cocaine, or did someone give it to her? Could she have been too high to undress for bed before becoming unconscious? Did she hang up the blue dress in the closet while strung out on the drugs? Was the dress still there? The housekeeper confirmed she had been dead for some time by describing rigor mortis. Then again, what if none of this had anything to do with the party? What if she died Sunday or even Monday?

Regardless that he might be making more of the inaction of the LAPD than just sloppy investigation, he must see this through. If Tara made a foolish mistake and tried cocaine which cost her life, then so be it. That meant resolving the many unanswered questions of circumstances surrounding the determined time of death window.

Did the LAPD interview Tara's neighbors? Even if they did, he would conduct his own interviews. He harbored no expectations about learning anything of importance, but he must make the attempt.

Kelly's bungalow community consisted of six modest size single-level homes occupying a corner of a block bounded by North Serrano Avenue and Sunset Boulevard. All six homes faced an inner green courtyard with well-lighted walkways. The rear of the homes faced the streets surrounded by eight-foot block walls. Resident garages occupied the end of the development on the Serrano Avenue side. Each home was separated by a six-foot high block wall from its adjacent neighbor. A secluded, quiet setting. Tara Kelly's home was in the middle of one row.

Walsh canvased the small neighborhood one evening hoping to catch people at home. No one answered the door at the first house adjacent to Kelly's. At the second, a man answered the door. Walsh identified himself as a reporter. Asked if he saw Tara Kelly that particular weekend? The reply, no. Did the LAPD question him as to anything he knew about his neighbor Tara Kelly? Again, no. The man volunteered that he knew his neighbor was a movie actress, but he rarely saw her. Never saw her with a man.

Next was the house directly across from Kelly's.

"Good evening, mam. I am a newspaper reporter. Covering the story of Tara Kelly's death for the *Boston Globe*. Boston being heavily Irish American, Miss Kelly's unfortunate death is newsworthy nationally."

The woman was in her sixties, nicely dressed holding a tea-cup. "About time someone came around to ask if any of us saw anything."

"The police have never questioned you?"

"Nope. Lazy bunch I'd say, though enough of them were here the morning the housekeeper discovered Tara's body. Tara and I shared the same housekeeper. Comes in every other week. I saw Wanda standing outside so I went over to her. She was very upset and crying."

"I spoke with Wanda Hernandez yesterday. What did she tell you?"

"Wanda told me she found Tara lying in her bed. Not breathing. The body was cold to her touch. I read in the *Los Angeles Times* that Tara died of a drug overdose. Never would have guessed she used drugs."

"She didn't. I'm sure of it. I'm a reporter but I also worked as a technical consultant with Tara on her last movie, *Price of Freedom*. Her death is personal for me. That's why I'm asking questions the police should have asked you."

"I see. Then please come in, Mr. Walsh. I have something important to tell you."

Once inside, she said, "My name is Constance Lawson. My late husband was a movie director. My beloved Paul died far too early of cancer. I worked in costume design for MGM until retiring last year. Being movie people, Tara and I talked occasionally. I can tell you that she was not a drug user. I would know. Been around enough actors that abused morphine or cocaine or drank too much.

"Oh, I'm sorry. Place sit down and make yourself comfortable. Would you like some tea? Have a pot already brewed. Tea is my vice at night. Helps me relax and sleep."

"Yes, a cup of tea would be nice."

Once she returned with the tea, she sat down. "Been following the newspaper accounts of Tara's death which didn't say very much. It did say the medical examiner placed her time of death as probably several days prior from when they discovered her body on that Wednesday. That could mean the weekend. Then someone I know told me the Pasadena newspaper reported Tara attended a big party with many Hollywood stars on the previous Saturday night."

Walsh said, "Yes, I am aware of that party. I also tied calling the LAPD to find out if they were investigating for any connection to Tara's death. Been unsuccessful so far in getting them to respond. The Los Angeles newspapers made no mention of a party in connection with Tara's death."

Lawson replied, "However, I made that connection. I usually read before going to bed to help fall asleep. That Saturday night, reading wasn't doing the trick. I decided I might as well make some tea. It was around one o'clock on what would be Sunday morning. I went into the kitchen and put the kettle on then walked back into the living room to wait for the water to boil. Sat right in this chair but didn't turn on the light. Looking out the front window toward Tara's, I saw that her lights were on. Thought to myself, if she was up maybe she might like a late-night cup of tea. So, I went back to the kitchen to make the tea. When I returned about to go over to Tara's, that's when I saw him?"

"What? Saw who?"

"A man leaving Tara's house by the front door. The lights in her house were now dark."

"But you saw a man?"

"Yes. Look out the front window toward her house. Notice how the landscape lights provide enough light to see someone."

Walsh turned around and looked at Tara's darkened home with the front lit by the exterior lighting. "Can you describe the man?"

"Tall. Average build. Dressed in a dark suit and tie. Wore a hat."

"Could you recognize him if you saw him again?"

"Afraid not. Light wasn't that good, and neither are my eyes."

Constance Lawson provided Egan Walsh with sufficient reason to press forward. This was immensely important information. Was the man a guest at the party who brought Kelly home?

The fact that a neighbor observed a man leaving Tara Kelly's house at one o'clock Sunday morning added a relevant unexplained circumstance. The police having never questioned any of the neighbors only added to the suspicion that some individual or group was stonewalling a thorough investigation. That suggested a motive more sinister than avoiding bad publicity for the movie industry. Somebody important felt at risk. That pointed to Hollywood celebrities.

The Pasadena reporter Benjamin Zimmerman seemed sufficiently interested to pursue the story by raising questions about the party. With Walsh's additional material, Zimmerman's newspaper might be willing to cooperate with his efforts to continue investigating.

In a lengthy telephone conversation with Zimmerman, he explained his interest in the matter. Zimmerman agreed to meet for lunch the following day in Pasadena.

———

Walsh met Benjamin Zimmerman at an Italian eatery on Colorado Boulevard a couple of blocks west of the offices of the *Pasadena Star-News* located at the corner of South Oakland Avenue. Seated at a front table near the front windows, Walsh recognized Zimmerman by the description he provided. The balding older guy with glasses, smoking a pipe with today's edition of the newspaper on the table having a glass of wine.

He stood to shake hands as Walsh approached the table.

"Care for a glass of Chianti? Like Los Angeles, Pasadena ignores Prohibition."

Walsh smiled, "Sounds good, especially with Italian food. Got to like Italian cuisine during my years in Boston. More creative cuisine than Irish fare."

Zimmerman raised his hand getting the attention of the waitress for another glass of wine.

"You said on the phone you knew Tara Kelly while working with her on the movie *Price of Freedom*. But you're also a reporter for the *Boston Globe*? Would you mind explaining the connection?"

"Certainly. While working for the *Globe* I also wrote a novel, *Price of Freedom.* My publisher arranged selling the movie rights as a way of promoting the book. As things turned out, Fox Films wanted to do the movie. As part of the deal, I co-wrote the movie script and served as technical consultant on the filming."

"Technical consultant? You have moviemaking experience?"

"Did you happen to see the movie?"

"As a matter of fact, I did. Damn good movie. You wrote that?"

"Yes. It was adapted from my novel. The movie script was a team effort. My most important contribution came from my background. You see I came to Boston only four years ago. The movie paralleled events in which I participated. I fought with the IRA. Before that I worked as a reporter for the *Cork Examiner.*"

"Well, I'll be damned. You personally participated in those actual events portrayed in the movie?"

Walsh nodded.

Zimmerman paused for a sip of wine. "Now this tragedy of Tara Kelly's death. As a friend with the instincts of a reporter you smell something fishy?"

"That about summons it up."

"Got to ask this, Mr. Walsh. Were you romantically involved with Miss Kelly?"

Walsh shook his head, "No. Just good friends. I became good friends with her costar Victor McLaglen and his wife Enid. All three of us kind of treated Tara like a younger sister. We felt protective of a young woman making her way in the tough movie business. I will be honest with you, Mr. Zimmerman, I feel a measure of responsibility for not looking out for her better. You see, she asked if I would escort her to that Beverly Hills party. I declined, explaining to her I was not invited. Besides, everyone there was a celebrity actor, director, or producer so I didn't fit in."

"Had you gone with her, how might that have changed things?"

"Because I believe something happened at the party or is connected in some way. I also discovered information through my own efforts that has not yet been made public. Someone else escorted Tara to the party but left early without her. How did she get home that Saturday night? Did someone take her home? These become unanswered questions that the LAPD seems to be avoiding investigating."

"Who escorted her to the party?"

"A young British actor named Leslie Fenton."

"How is it that you know this?"

"I am also friends with the western actor Tom Mix. He told me about Fenton taking Kelly to the party and seeing Fenton leave the party without Tara. Seems Fenton became irritated that Charlie Chaplin and Rudolph Valentino dominated her attentions."

"Have you approached Fenton?"

"Yes. He recounted substantially what Tom Mix told me."

"Might Fenton somehow be involved with giving Kelly cocaine?"

Walsh made a gesture with his hands suggesting he did not know. "A possibility, but I don't think so."

As the waitress approached, Zimmerman said, "How about we interrupt our discussion to order some lunch. I highly recommend the spaghetti carbonara."

After placing their food orders and getting refills on the wine, Walsh continued. "As I told you, I spoke with a LAPD Lieutenant Dekker of the Hollywood Division. The supervising officer of the investigation after the housekeeper discovered Tara's body. Dekker gave me nothing. Said because it involved a celebrity, all public comments must come from Assistant Chief Fletcher's office. Been unable to reach Fletcher to discuss why the LAPD is not investigating the circumstances of the Beverly Hills party since it occurred within the medical examiner's estimated time range of death."

"My experience as well when I tried Fletcher's office," Zimmerman offered.

"However, I discovered something that might be significant," Walsh said. "The police never interviewed Kelly's neighbors. Therefore, I did. Found something possibly relevant to Kelly's death. If true of course. Woman by the name of Constance Lawson. Lives across a common area from Kelly's house. She couldn't sleep that Saturday night. Got up to make a pot of tea and noticed the lights on in Kelly's house through her front window. She and Kelly were on friendly terms, so she thought about walking over to Kelly's to share teas with her."

"What time of the night was this?"

"One in the morning."

"Lawson then told me she was about to walk over to Kelly's when she saw a tall man leaving Kelly's house through the front door. The house lights now turned off."

"This is the middle of the night. How is she able to see this man?"

"I was at her house after dark. Landscape lights provide enough light to see somebody. Probably only a hundred feet between their houses. Said the man wore a hat, dark suit, and tie."

"Is this woman credible?"

"I believe so."

"Got a theory what might have happened?"

Walsh said, "No. Not enough information. The only apparent certain thing is someone with a lot of influence wants Tara Kelly's death buried as nothing more than an accidental overdose. That leaves the unsaid possibility of suicide. Knowing Kelly, I don't believe that either. Don't even believe she would knowingly experiment with cocaine, but all that is still a possibility. What I want is to simply know the truth of why she died."

As their food came, they broke off further discussion until finished eating.

Walsh said, "That was exceptional spaghetti, Mr. Zimmerman."

"Glad you liked it. If we are going to collaborate, call me Benny."

"Then would you be willing to share what we each find? Collaborate on the story with the *Boston Globe*?"

"Why not? On opposite coasts we're not exactly competing. Gives the story more legs with broader coverage."

Walsh nodded. "Thanks, Benny. I need a local ally that is willing to stand up to whoever is stonewalling further investigation of Tara Kelly's death. Also, call me Egan."

"What's your next move, Egan?"

Walsh already knew the answer. "Without the LAPD willing to discuss details, I am going to try the Los Angeles County Coroner's office. I want to understand details about the overdose. How was it ingested? How much? What was the condition of her body when the police arrived at her house? Any forensic details discovered through the autopsy more than the limited explanation given out by Chief Fletcher?"

Zimmerman shook his head. "The pathologist is not going to talk to a reporter."

Walsh grinned. "Reporter? I am an attorney from New York representing the deceased's family. Easy enough to print business cards and type up a letter retaining my services."

Zimmerman smiled broadly. "I like your style, Egan."

———

Nathan Schachter knocked on Hollister's office door and approached Hollister seated at his desk, "The private investigator, Aaron Ginsberg called in his report this morning. His operatives observed Walsh having lunch in Pasadena with a reporter named Benjamin Zimmerman of the *Pasadena Star-News*. They spent two hours at an Italian restaurant."

"Sonofabitch! That's the reporter that named those attending the party in his column. The only fucking newspaper that printed the names of my guests that evening.'

"Not the only newspaper, Sir. Walsh's former newspaper, the *Boston Globe*, also ran the same story. Looks like Walsh and Zimmerman are teaming to make Kelly's death a continuing national story. After all, if it concerns Hollywood, it becomes news. Both newspapers fall outside the span of influence for our ability to suppress. Even Hearst is careful about printing negative material about Hollywood in his rag the *Examiner*.

"Walsh appears to be returning to newspaper reporting. Probably because this is personal. First harassing calls to the local precinct followed by trying to get to Chief Fletcher. Then he visits the home of Tara Kelly's housekeeper. Walsh is an aggressive journalist. If he keeps this up, the matter could evolve into a major scandal, Mr. Hollister."

CHAPTER 14

Los Angeles, California | 1926

With the uncertainty of proceeding with a sequel to *Price of Freedom*, Walsh consumed his time with investigating Tara Kelly's death. He saw very little of his movie friends, all of which were involved in new movie projects. He did, however, keep them informed about his discoveries despite a lack of response by the LAPD. He shared with them his belief that someone with influence wanted to prevent further inquiries surrounding the Beverly Hills party. With all the movie celebrities attending that party, sensitivity to bad publicity was understandable. However, that could also serve to cloak complicity in some wrongdoing related to Kelly's death.

He did spend time with Wyatt Earp. He found Earp's perspective particularly inciteful as he drew parallels from his own experiences. Recounting his frustrations about Kelly's death, Earp remarked, "Know how you must feel, Egan. My experience in Tombstone over forty years ago was much the same as Los Angeles today. Moneyed interests protected the outlaws and controlled law enforcement. I think Los Angeles might be worse than Tombstone. Los Angeles is the last of the western boomtowns. Now appearing all grown up but a place full of crooked businessmen and politicians.

"Moviemaking is among those economic interests important to Los Angeles. Sounds like the police are taking orders from

169

somebody with a lot of influence. Hiding something that he wants to make go away. You're bucking powerful interests. Watch your back, Egan."

Obtaining interviews from those that attended the party was the next logical step. Even with Benny Zimmerman's assistance that was a tall order. These were among Hollywood's biggest stars. The studios were overprotective of their prime assets. Getting close to them would be difficult. Yet that seemed the only way to establish how Tara got home and obtain observations of what was going on at the party. Not likely any of these people, including the host Chadwick Hollister, would consent to interviews unless forced by legal or public pressure.

It was weeks since Tara Kelly's funeral when Sol Wurtzel called him. "Have some good news, Egan. Mr. Fox has decided to proceed with *Dying for Ireland,* provided you and Ray can come up with a compelling script. The timing is critical to build on the success of *Price of Freedom.* The first task is again to create the arch of the story set during the Irish Civil War. We had anticipated a continuation of the principal characters of Brandon Flynn and Nora Gallagher. Now we need a different leading female role to give the movie balance by adding another dramatic element. Any thoughts?"

"Nothing specific. Yet to link *Dying for Ireland* to *Price of Freedom* we must deal directly with what happened to the Nora Gallagher character. Perhaps a dramatic opening scene depicting Gallagher's violent death following on the closing scene of *Price of Freedom.* Filmed in some way not requiring Tara's image. Weave a new female character into the fabric of the story in some way. As to a female leading part, we must be careful. Any romantic involvement with the Flynn character might be out of place for moviegoers to accept after we kill off Gallagher in the opening scene."

"I see what you mean, Egan. Can you come to my office tomorrow? John and Ray will be here. We need to pick up where we left off. Time of course becomes critical to take advantage of the popularity generated by *Price of Freedom.* More demanding because *Dying for Ireland* requires creating an original story not an adaptation from a novel."

Good that Walsh now had something to occupy his attention and keep his investigation of Kelly's death in perspective. Reengaging with his friends might brighten his outlook. He still intended to find out what happened to Tara Kelly, yet he also needed to move on with his life. He must return to writing. Developing the script for *Dying for Ireland* became a step in that direction. However, movie scripts did not satisfy his literary aspirations. Until movies included sound and therefore dialog, they remained solely a visual medium only. As a novelist with one success to his credit, he needed to settle on a subject with a plot sufficient to challenge his creativity. A story populated with characters compelling enough to commit himself to the lengthy process of writing a novel.

———

"Egan, so good to see you," Lilly Romano said coming from around her desk embracing him and kissing him on the cheek. "Where have you been hiding?"

He had not seen her since Kelly's funeral.

"Good to see you too, Lilly. Should have called you. Been too absorbed in trying to find out more details surrounding Tara's death. Obsessed by so many unanswered questions. Coming soon after Fiona's death makes it emotionally difficult. Need to work off my pain and frustrations by trying to find answers. Been ignoring my friends for too long. I apologize for not coming around to see you, Lilly."

"I understand, but now I'll be seeing you regularly with *Dying for Ireland* back on the schedule. Anxious to begin working with you on the script."

Walsh smiled. Lilly was back to flirting if he read her facial expression correctly.

"That's the plan. I look forward to that also, Lilly."

He found Lilly Romano an extraordinary woman. Attractive and intelligent with a confident manner that people found naturally engaging. Time that he devoted more attention to his personal life rather than wallowing in self-pity. Fiona taught him that by how she enriched his life. Thinking about what to do for the remainder of life could also include becoming open to another romantic relationship. Remembering Lilly's unrestrained interest when they were in San Luis Obispo, why not ask her to dinner?

"I've not been idle these past several months since we completed *Price of Freedom*. Troubled by the uncertainty of so many unexplained circumstances surrounding Tara's death, I began conducting my own investigation. I'd like to share that with you Lilly. I also need to make up for ignoring you. Would you have dinner with me tonight?"

Surprise registered on her face before breaking out into a large smile. She stepped closer and gave him a kiss on the lips. "I'd love that, Egan." Pausing as she remained standing close and looking intently into his eyes for a moment, "Now back to business. Everyone is in Sol's office." Taking him by the arm, she led him to Sol Wurtzel's office and opened the door. Before closing the door behind Walsh, she gave his arm a squeeze.

Walsh shook hands with everyone.

Wurtzel said, "Ray's done some research on the Irish civil war, but we want to hear how you explain what went on, Egan. Next step is to define the major segments to put on film. I already told John and Ray your idea about how to segue from *Price of Freedom* to *Dying for Ireland* with the loss of the Nora Gallagher character."

Director John Ford said, "Yes. Opening with a funeral scene sounds perfect. All we need to do is explain her death in a believable manner that plays into the script of *Dying for Ireland*."

Walsh added, "We should make it part of the story. Been thinking about that. What about this? First of all, we must establish where the Brandon Flynn character falls on the controversial treaty signed with the British. Like almost all the IRA, we hated that the treaty did not provide for full Irish independence. I felt it was a failure. We should have continued the fight. The British could not sustain the fight indefinitely. However, the country was tired of war fought among our homes and businesses. Complete withdrawal of all British security forces and relinquishing control of the police proved too overwhelming. More than that, Michael

Collins the inspirational IRA leader and no one more aggressive was a signatory to the Treaty with the British.

"As for me, I knew that civil war might become a possibility. Every member of the IRA was forced to take sides. I refused to take up arms against my fellow comrades and left Ireland. *Dying for Ireland* must have a point of view. I suggest Brandon Flynn take the side of the pro-treaty faction. Joins with Michael Collins who should become a central character in the movie. Although Flynn is dissatisfied with the terms of the Treaty, the hated British security forces left the Southern twenty-six counties of Ireland and relinquished control of the RIC. Because of his exploits during the war of independence he is made a colonel in the newly formed Irish National Army."

"How does the death of Nora Gallagher come about?" Ford asked.

"There was an actual incident months after the signing of the Treaty but before the full measure of civil war broke out. A National Army brigadier-general was shot dead under suspicious circumstances attributed as an anti-Treaty IRA assassination. We create a similar incident as the opening scene of *Dying for Ireland* with Flynn the intended target of some anti-Treaty IRA faction. We temper that later by showing it was an unsanctioned renegade action.

"Flynn is from County Cork where anti-treaty sentiment ran high. My old comrade Tom Barry reluctantly took that side. The most aggressive IRA commander during the war of independence now became a dangerous anti-treaty figure. Therefore, it makes sense for Michael Collins, now commanding the National Army, to send Flynn to Cork to negotiate with the IRA anti-treaty leadership to avoid taking up arms. Flynn's attempts to dissuade Tom Barry and the most outspoken IRA militant, Liam Lynch. Both of which become the movie's antagonists to Flynn character."

"That's a perfect opening," Ray Schrock commented. "How then do we explain Nora Gallagher losing her life?"

"How do we film that without Tara Kelly?" Ford asked.

Walsh replied, "Flynn is driving a car down a street to visit his sister who cares for his mother. Nora Gallagher is in the passenger seat. A stand-in actress viewed indistinctly by the camera through the windscreen, or from the rear window. Flynn is dressed in his National Army uniform. Sam Browne belt and holster, armed with his Webley service revolver.

"Rifle fire shatters the windscreen of the car. The car runs off the road coming to a stop. Unharmed, Flynn exits with his revolver drawn while trying to pull Nora across the driver's seat to take cover with him behind the side of the car. A dramatic camera shot shows her arm hanging from the car seat with blood dripping from her fingers."

"Sonofabitch! I love it," Ford said slamming his palm on the table. "Egan's a born director, Sol."

Schrock added, "Then a title card comes on screen, *As a ranking officer with the Irish National Army, Brandon Flynn's negotiation mission with anti-Treatyists fails. His beloved Nora Gallagher has given her life for Ireland.*"

Wurtzel said, "I like Egan's concept. Ties together the two movies. Got any ideas for the central premise of the movie, Egan?"

"Nothing specific. If Flynn becomes a senior officer in the National Army, this becomes a war movie. Yet fundamentally different from the IRA guerrilla war against British security forces during the war of independence. The anti-Treaty militants of the civil war did not enjoy widespread popular support. Remember, they are taking up arms against fellow Irish and former IRA comrades. Flynn is now sided with the new Provisional government. Better armed and enjoying greater popular support. Ireland is exhausted from years of war. This becomes the movie's backdrop. The anti-Treatyists therefore become the antagonists. However, we should portray them sympathetically. Irish patriots that fought to free Ireland. Not supported by the Irish population but still former Irish patriots. Living in Boston, I can tell you there remains support for those IRA that took up arms against the Treaty. Not unlike sentiment for Confederate soldiers of the American Civil War."

"What about a female leading role?" Wurtzel asked.

"I suggest a role other than a romantic interest of Flynn. Fans still identify with the Nora Gallagher character," Schrock commented.

Walsh offered, "The most vocal women sided with those condemning the Treaty. A possibility occurred to me. Why not give Flynn a sister? A family member that remains a staunch Republican working secretly against him. It epitomizes the cruelty of a civil war tearing apart families. Make her a counterpoint to Flynn becoming a soldier in the National Army. Give her a background as an active participant for the IRA during the war of independence the same as Nora Gallagher. A climactic personal blow to Flynn toward the end of the movie when her actions become exposed. Flynn and his sister each feel betrayed, further depicting the tragic nature of civil war."

Around the table the others silently absorbed how that might come together to provide a more complex theme. Walsh summarized, "The sister becomes the center of a countervailing dramatic thread. The combat scenes dominated by the National Army featuring the Flynn character interspersed with scenes of the parallel story of the clandestine activities featuring the sister."

Ford eventually nodded, "That could work. Allows the movie to play to each side in the civil war while enriching the story with a parallel subplot."

Schrock said, "I can see how we can weave together a script with good visuals and strong dramatic content. The sister adds the right antagonistic conflict with a tragic personal twist."

Wurtzel said, "I agree. That will be our initial outline. Can you fellows prepare a preliminary synopsis before the end of the day? I want to telephone Mr. Fox and tell him we have the story for *Dying for Ireland*."

"Can we borrow Lilly for transcription as we brainstorm the plot?" Walsh asked Wurtzel.

"She's all yours, Gentlemen."

———

They worked through the day and had lunch delivered. With the experience of *Price of Freedom*, the creative effort of constructing the story for *Dying for Ireland* progressed with remarkable speed. Ford and Schrock treated Walsh now as a gifted professional. Everyone was impressed by his inspired plot concept for *Dying for Ireland* that offered a perfect extension to *Price of Freedom* while remaining a distinctly different story.

What was surprising was Lilly Romano's contribution to the back and forth. More than just transcribing their discussion ideas, she actively participated by contributing useful comments. Known by Ford and Schrock as a forceful personality with a good mind, they readily considered her inputs. Walsh sensed she had done this before. He found her comments particularly insightful for constructing the subversive role of the sister sympathetically.

Walsh contributed by suggesting authentic action scenes and using them to provide the backbone arch for the movie. Following the opening scene of the death of Nora Gallagher, the story would begin with the anti-Treaty IRA occupation of the Four Courts buildings in Dublin in April. This then building with the stunning visual effect of the National Army forced to dislodge the rebels using artillery marking the definitive start of the civil war in June 1922. Several possibilities for Flynn's participation in military actions against the rebels in July and August with Tom Barry featured as his adversary. The assassination of Michael Collins in August by anti-Treaty rebels turned public sentiment further against the rebels. The killing of the fanatical anti-Treaty IRA commander Liam Lynch in early April 1923, followed by the ending of hostilities in May providing a fitting conclusion of the action elements of the movie.

Walsh said, "To condense the history, we might wish to restrict the military action scenes to devout to developing the dramatic story of the sister's clandestine activities in support of the now hopeless rebel cause with scenes portrayed from that perspective. The movie ending in personal tragedy with Flynn's discovery of his sister's treachery."

By late in the afternoon, they collectively assembled their fragmented notes into a preliminary script. Reading the synopsis, a delighted Sol Wurtzel said, "Excellent. We'll go with this. Since it's Friday and we made such progress, everyone go have a relaxing weekend. John is otherwise committed next week but Egan and Ray should resume working on the script here Monday."

Walsh asked, "Can Lilly also work with us next week? Her contributions have proved invaluable."

Lilly gave him a smile.

"Sure. I'll make do without her valuable assistance," Wurtzel said.

As Ford and Schrock left and Wurtzel returned to his office, he turned to Lilly. "I know you must have things piled up on your desk, Lilly. You get out of here too. Been a long day for all of us. I'm going to call Mr. Fox right now. First thing Monday mail him a copy of the synopsis."

Standing together after Wurtzel returned to his office, Walsh said to Lilly, "Still up for dinner?"

She smiled mischievously, "Absolutely. Besides, I want to hear what you've been up to these past weeks. Haven't seen much of you since San Luis Obispo. I've missed you, Egan."

"Do you know Trattoria Marchetti on Hollywood Boulevard?"

"Oh yes. One of my favorites. How about you follow me home? Let me change and touch up my makeup. I have a small bungalow in the Los Feliz district just north of here."

Her house was no more than a mile north climbing into the hills above Hollywood. Exiting their cars, Walsh remarked, "This is a lovely location."

"I thought so. Bought it three years ago."

Entering the Spanish style single level bungalow, Walsh was equally impressed with Lilly's decorating tastes. Terracotta tile flooring with tasteful area rugs complemented heavy wooden furniture upholstered in fabric or leather. Carefully selected artwork adorned the white uneven adobe texture plastered walls with pleasing contrasting effects.

"Beautifully decorated. Very impressive."

"Thank you. Called Southwestern style. Care for a drink while I get ready? There's whiskey and gin over there on the drink bar."

"How about for you?"

"Sure. Fix me a gin and tonic if you don't mind chipping some ice from the ice box."

Walsh made her drink and settled in the living area with a decent Scotch. A remarkable multi-talented woman. He looked forward to the evening.

Even more so as Lilly came out of the bedroom twenty minutes later. Always put together, she transformed from fashionable work attire to understated elegance. A figure-hugging white knit dress wrapped at the waist with a belt accentuated her breasts and revealed cleavage. A flaring hemline at the knee gave the dress a modern look. White pumps complimented her outfit. Given the warm summer evening, she daringly forwent nylons in favor of bare legs. With her light olive skin, dark hair, and dark eyes, the white ensemble provided perfect contrast.

Lilly shunned the current shapeless female fashion that attempted a radical departure from the turn of the 20th century's first decade known as the Edwardian era. From decades even earlier, feminine attire was characterized by constricting undergarments seeking to reshape the female form by artificial means. Twenties-fashion sought to free women's bodies from the uncomfortable constraints of earlier era foundation undergarments. It attempted to introduce a new sexuality by shorting shirts and revealing legs. It went further by seeking to deemphasize female breasts even to the extent of flattening those amply endowed. While shortening the hems of shirts and dresses thereby revealing legs below the knee, it also dropped waistlines to the hips. This deemphasized the classic hourglass female form previously exaggerated by corsets or girdles.

She hated the frumpy look calling it tasteless and sexless fashion. Sacks with stupid-looking hats. She had good breasts accentuated by a narrow waistline, flaring to well-proportioned hips. She knew she had a good body and intended to display it in her own expressive manner of dress. Working in the movie industry, she adored the bare-shouldered gowns emphasizing the showing of cleavage portrayed in period movies. With her friend Evelyn Sullivan Fox Films' head of costume design, she developed her own individualized sense of fashion. Long hair sometimes worn pulled up, shunning the short, bobbed hairstyle in vogue, and avoiding hats unless required for a formal occasion. Lilly Romano did things her way.

Walsh grinned and stood up. "My, my. You are one grand looking woman, Lilly Romano."

"Thank you, Egan. Haven't been to dinner with a handsome man since… since San Luis Obispo with you. Tonight, I shall watch how much I drink. I have missed you terribly. Now sit down and we'll finish our drinks then be off."

Sitting down with her drink, she said, "You said you've been investigating the circumstances surrounding Tara Kelly's death. What is it about her death that you question?"

"I don't believe Tara used cocaine. She also went to a Hollywood celebrity party Saturday night before her death. I knew she did because I had dinner with Tara and Victor McLaglen and his wife a couple of nights before the party. Victor was also invited but he chose not to go. He and Enid went instead to the Hollywood Bowl. Without Victor, she did not want to go alone so she asked me. I begged off. This was for Hollywood celebrities. I learned later that an actor named Leslie Fenton took her to the party. My friend Tom Mix also attended and later told me he saw Tara at the party and that Fenton left early without her.

"I wonder if things might have turned out differently had I gone with Tara. My instincts say the circumstances are not consistent with a finding of accidental drug overdose. Inexplicably, the Los Angeles police are not investigating any further."

Lilly was a silent for a moment before asking, "Were you romantically involved with Tara?"

Walsh looked up surprised. "What? Definitely not. Never had any such thoughts. Victor and I became her friends from working together on the movie. Tara and Enid McLaglen were good friends from meeting when she worked with Vic on a previous movie.

"I am troubled by many unexplained circumstances surrounding her death. The LAPD refuses to investigate further. Therefore, I am. Already discovered some disturbing things that make me think someone influential wants to prevent further inquiry. As a former newspaper reporter, I can't let it go until I become convinced her death came about as a result of some foolish accident."

Lilly set down her drink and came over to him taking his hand. "I'm sorry. Not my place to ask you such a personal question. Let's go to dinner. I want to hear more why you think there is something more to Tara's death than reported in the newspapers."

At the restaurant, Lilly surprised him again by speaking to owner Angelo Marchetti in Italian. She discussed how they prepared certain items on the menu and talked knowledgeably about wine. Angelo treated her as if she was movie royalty. She did look the part.

Lilly became enthralled and equally troubled about Kelly's death as Walsh recounted what he discovered and the unexpected obstacles to getting answers to what he deemed as fundamental questions. He explained teaming with reporter Benny Zimmerman of the *Pasadena Star-News* who also remained critical of the LAPD's treatment of Kelly's death.

He concluded his narrative with his interview of Kelly's neighbor Constance Lawson seeing a man outside Tara's door at one o'clock Sunday morning. "The pressing question becomes the Beverly Hills party which plays into this because it occurred within the time frame of her death as determined by the county medical examiner. I know that Leslie Fenton left the party early without Tara. Disgusted by her preoccupation with Charlie Chaplin and Rudolph Valentino. How did she get home? Did someone drive her home? How was the cocaine ingested? Questions the police should routinely determine."

As dinner came out, Walsh said, "No more about of the sad circumstances of Tara's death tonight. Let's enjoy our dinner. I want to hear about you, Lilly. All I know is that someone said you came to Los Angeles from New York."

They enjoyed a special pasta dish Angelo prepared just for them after much back and forth with Lilly in Italian. Paired with an exceptional northern Italian wine, Walsh became absorbed in listening to Lilly.

"I was born in Milano, Italy. Emigrated to New York with my parents when I was one year old. My father was educated at the Politecnico di Milano as a structural engineer. He worked in railroad construction for the Società per le Strade Ferrate dell'Alta Italia, the Upper Italian Railways Society. We came to New York in 1900 for the opportunity for Father to work on New York City's first subway. Now you know that I am thirty-seven.

Lilly smiled mischievously. She was confident about how she looked regardless of age. Walsh just shrugged communicating it was irrelevant.

"Mother taught English at the university where she met my father."

"When did you come to Los Angeles?"

"In 1917. I came out when William Fox sent Sol to oversee Fox Film's west coast studio operations. At the time, I was working at Fox Films headquarters in Fort Lee, New Jersey just across the Hudson River from upper Manhattan.

"I grew up in Greenwich Village which included a lot of Italian immigrants. My first job was at the *New York Times*. Working nights while attending City College."

"What was your field of study?"

"Journalism."

"Interesting. What attracted you to journalism?"

"After my first year at college, I took a job at the *Times*. Just a clerical job in the archive department. Not reporting or anything close. Anyway, I became interested enough to change my major in history to journalism. When I graduated college in 1910, the newspaper promoted me out of archives to obituaries."

When the waiter inquired about dessert, both declined. Lilly then said, "How about a digestif? Ever had Italian grappa?"

"Oh yes. When I lived in Boston."

To the waiter, she said, "*Due grappe per favore, signore.*"

"After three years in obituaries then doing human interest pieces, I realized that as a woman I would not likely ever make it as a reporter doing real journalism. At least at the *Times*. Saw a listing in the classified section for an executive assistant at Fox Films. I loved movies so I applied.

"Although the job turned out to be largely secretarial, I soon became involved in all sorts of interesting movie work. From the beginning, I liked working for Sol Wurtzel and Mr. Fox. They recognized my abilities early by giving me challenging work. Never mattered that I was a woman."

"I can see that by how much everyone respects you as part of the management team. After ten years, how do you feel about your career move?"

"No regrets. I like Hollywood and the movie business. I like the people I work with. Paid very well." Laying her hand over his on the table, "How about a nightcap at my place?"

He smiled thinking there was perhaps more to the rest of the evening than just a nightcap. The way she dressed tonight admittedly aroused him. About time he abandoned his depressive thoughts. Attracted to Lilly Romano, this might be a beginning.

It was only a short ride to her house. As he turned into her driveway, she reached over and touched his cheek with the back of her hand. "I had a wonderful time at dinner, Egan. Thank you for asking me out."

"Thank you, Lilly. I enjoyed being with you immensely.

She smiled and nodded. "Me too, Egan."

She handed him her key. He opened the door and stepped inside. She followed and he closed the door. She was standing next to him as he turned toward her.

Putting her arms over his shoulders she moved against him making sure he felt her breasts on his chest. "We can have a drink later. I wanted you each night when we were in San Luis Obispo. Respected you though for being faithful to Fiona and resisting my advances. But you never left my thoughts. Will you make love to me now?"

He kissed her and pulled her closer.

After several moments locked in a kiss while caressing each other with their hands, they pulled apart and walked toward the bedroom.

He quickly removed his suit coat and pulled off his tie then sat on the bed to untie his shoes. Looking toward Lilly. She had removed only her shoes. She grinned at him as she pulled off her earrings. "Continue taking off the rest of your clothes."

He obeyed while all the time looking at her. Down to his underpants, she said, "Take them off too."

Doing so exposed his full erection.

"That looks inviting. Let me see if I can arouse you even more."

She removed her belt then unbuttoned the wrapped dress. Shedding it, she draped it over her dressing table chair allowing him to look her over.

He was delighted that she wore no slip, revealing only brassier and silk knickers. His immediate thought was she planned her ensemble tonight with the intention of easy disrobing.

She smiled seductively while reaching behind her back to unclasp the brassier. Slowly she pulled it off, revealing her bare breasts. Taking two steps, she stood in front of him still seated on the edge of the bed.

"Thought you might like to pull off my knickers."

With a hand on both her hips at the elastic band, he slowly pulled down the garment exposing her dark pubic hair.

Stepping out of her knickers, "Do you like what you see?"

He reached his hands to cup both breasts and began kissing her midsection.

She bent forward and held his erection in her hand. Touching between her legs, he felt the wet from her arousal.

After pleasuring each other, they fell back on the bed. Breathing heavily, she rolled on her back and gasped, "Get inside me now!"

Both tried to forestall orgasm as long as possible. When she eventually arched her back while making sounds of pleasure, he felt her begin climaxing and allowed himself to release in an equally intense orgasm.

They remained locked together savoring the experience for several moments before he lowered onto his elbows to kiss her.

Eventually, he rolled off her and laid next to her. After enjoying post-coital contentment in silence for some minutes, she got out of bed. Putting on his shirt, she did not button it, leaving her breasts exposed. She knew she looked good naked.

He retrieved his underwear from the floor. It was a warm night with the windows open.

"Care for that drink now?" Lilly said as they both went to the living room.

"Sounds good. I need reviving."

"You may need it. We have the whole night ahead of us. You will stay the night won't you, Egan?"

He smiled broadly. "Of course. Could not think of anything I'd like more."

"Wonderful. Then we can spend the entire weekend together making love. Maybe take a break to go to the beach."

CHAPTER 15

Los Angeles, California | 1926

Come Monday morning, Egan Walsh felt like a new person. Spending the weekend with Lilly Romano changed his outlook. She provided the means to escape his self-absorbed brooding. Pursuing Tara Kelly's death became obsessive as means of coping with his own loss of Fiona. He intended his investigation to continue vigorously but now more as a journalist committed to discovering the truth. The relationship with Lilly might not prove sustaining, but they both seemed sufficiently invested in each other to let things develop naturally.

They spoke about that frankly after making love Sunday afternoon. Both related their past relationships. Since his experiences with women were limited, he understood only that Lilly was unique and complex.

His romantic partners were few. His first was Maureen, meeting her while both were students at the University of Cork. She became his first sexual experience. That occurred only after many months of seeing each other, then only after becoming engaged. Both raised Catholic, neither attended mass. Both wanted to avoid being trapped in a conventional life dominated by children. It created friction between both their families. Maureen continued pursuing her legal studies, aspiring to become a barrister, a rarity in Ireland. He took a reporting position at the *Cork Examiner*.

He failed to understand the depth of her loyalist political sentiments with Britian until the 1916 failed Easter Rising rebellion. That became a contentious issue between them. At the time, he thought the rebellion was foolishly ill-conceived and blamed the Irish Republican Brotherhood leadership for the death of his older brother. For her, the rebellion was simply treasonous. Yet events that followed brought him to believe with conviction that for the first time in hundreds of years there existed the possibility of freeing Ireland from British colonial rule. He joined the IRA and soon left his job at the *Cork Examiner*. Maureen wanted no part of a life with someone willing to risk their life in a rebellion that she and her family opposed.

No chance for finding romance while on the run for two years during the war for independence. After coming to Boston there was a brief affair with a secretary at the *Boston Globe* that went nowhere before discovering Fiona.

A somewhat different background for Lilly Romano. She never married but had several past romantic relationships. During the weekend, she candidly related her reasons for never marrying. Generally, she spoke in complimentary terms about her past lovers. "All these relationships ended mostly because of my intransigence to compromise on issues I found fundamental to my sense of self. I feel compelled to dictate my life. Too strong willed I suppose. I believe I scare men. That is why I do not have a partner."

"Obviously you like men physically," he teased.

"Just because we have great sex doesn't mean I chose you because you are good in bed. I also find you somewhat interesting." Kissing him to make sure he understood she was joking, she said seriously, "I also don't seem to scare you."

No illusions on his part that the weekend was primarily about sex. Lilly obviously had more partners during her lifetime than he did. Likely, more than the ones she mentioned. With her looks, finding willing sexual partners could never be a problem. Impossible to intellectualize why two people become deeply attracted. He believed Lilly shared the same feelings he did.

He may have anticipated where Friday night might lead, but it materialized only because of Lilly's less than subtle seduction. Fine by him. He seemed to gravitate to strong women that viewed their lives outside the conventional role prescribed by society. First Maureen, then Fiona, now Lilly. Maybe his aversion to accepting stereotypical gender norms. Women were unfathomable. Fine by him. He felt no need to compete and certainly did not want to dominate a woman. He relished the equality status of Fiona that seemed to also be Lilly's view of life. Regardless, if his relationship with Lilly deepened further it would be because their emotional bond complemented their individual desires.

Monday morning, he showed up at the studio offices on Western Avenue. Displaying a wide grin, "Good morning, Lilly. Did you have a good weekend?"

She replied with her own coquettish expression, "Oh, I had a marvelous weekend. Now I have the pleasure of collaborating with you this week in writing *Dying for Ireland*. Thought about that all weekend. Ray's already here. Ready to get started?"

A productive day notwithstanding the distraction of repeated eye contact with Lilly and seeing her conspiratorial smile. By late afternoon, the three of them hammered out a sufficiently detailed outline they felt achieved the dramatic arch of the story. Sitting down with Sol Wurtzel before calling it a day, Schrock said, "Take a look at this, boss," as Lilly handed Wurtzel several typed pages.

Wurtzel read through the outline without making a comment. "Very good. Hits all the dramatic points we discussed. Did you mail Mr. Fox our notes from last week, Lilly?"

"Yes, first thing this morning."

"Okay. Let's hold off sending further details until we develop the first draft of a complete working script. Can we target that by the end of the week?"

Everyone nodded except Walsh who replied, "I have some personal business I must attend to tomorrow. Can't make it until around noon. I can work as late as necessary tomorrow though."

"Not a problem. Let's pick it up tomorrow right after lunch then, "Wurtzel said.

Walsh stood next to Lilly's desk after Schrock left for the day and Wurtzel returned to his office. She asked, "What are your plans for this evening?"

"No plans."

"How about I cook us dinner?"

He smiled. "That sounds inviting."

"You can become addictive for a lonely woman, Mr. Walsh."

He laughed. "I don't think you are ever lonely, Lilly."

Again, that Lilly skewed smile. "How about seven? Need to stop at the market. By the way, what is that personal business occupying you tomorrow morning?"

"I'll tell you tonight."

———

As Walsh watched Lilly prepare dinner, and he prepared drinks, she asked, "Okay, what are you doing tomorrow morning?"

"The next logical step in my investigation of Tara's death. A visit to the coroner's office. Interview the pathologist that performed the autopsy. How much cocaine did Kelly ingest? Any way to determine how she ingested it? Did cocaine trigger a bad reaction because of some other physical condition? What about the amount of alcohol in her body?"

"The pathologist is not going to talk to just anyone. Especially not a reporter from an eastern newspaper."

"How about if he believes me to be an attorney from New York representing the deceased's family? If I need to press the matter, I tell him I'm prepared to go to the state attorney general's office and take legal action if necessary. I believe the LAPD has not properly investigated circumstances surrounding her death. Specifically, the movie celebrity party in Beverly Hills."

Lilly turned from tossing a salad to look at him. "Christ, you're serious. Impersonate an attorney? Could get your ass in legal trouble."

"Maybe. Not sure what I'm doing is illegal, but it doesn't matter. If arrested, I can turn that into a headline for the newspapers.

188

I have at least one reporter whose local newspaper is willing to join me in pursuing what more and more looks like an official cover up."

"What newspaper is that?"

"The *Pasadena Star-News*. A reporter by the name of Benjamin Zimmerman was the first to mention the Beverly Hills party and publish the names of the movie celebrities. I met with him a week ago. Told him everything I've discovered. Also told him my next move was the coroner's office."

"What did he say?"

Walsh grunted, "Much like your reaction. Anyway, I already prepared for tomorrow. All the medical examiner can do is refuse to discuss the matter. Therefore, at nine in the morning Allen Campbell, attorney at law with the New York law firm of Cadwalader, Wickersham & Taft will appear at the new Hall of Justice located at 211 West Temple, room 100. The location of the Los Angeles County Department of Medical Examiner-Coroner. According to my research, the facility is fully equipped for scientifically processing human remains. Refrigerated storage, autopsy tables, and viewing room for identification so I expect the pathologists are also at this location."

"You made up this factious lawyer?"

He smiled, "Oh, no. There is a real Allen Campbell at Cadwalader. Old law firm in New York City. I did a story once when I was at the *Boston Globe*. Campbell represented some guy in a big embezzlement case. I even printed business cards."

Lilly burst out laughing. "You are one ballsy sonofabitch."

After dinner, they shared a bottle of wine and chatted until about ten o'clock sitting together on the sofa.

"I suppose you must get back to the hotel tonight."

"I must shower and shave. Need my best suit and lawyer tie to get into the Campbell character. Irish name so my accent fits."

"I guess I'll let you out of my clutches. Besides, we both had too much to drink tonight. Tell you what. You can tell me about how Mr. Campbell made out tomorrow morning. How about I spend tomorrow night with you at the hotel? They also have a good restaurant there."

"Perfect idea."

"As she embraced and kissed him at the door, she said, "You are becoming a pleasant habit. Now get out of here before I pull you into the bedroom."

———

At nine o'clock Monday morning, Walsh entered the Hall of Justice and made his way to the Medical Examiner-Coroner's office. There was a small waiting room with a sliding glass window in the wall. To the middle-aged woman seated behind the glass partition, he said. "I am here to see Dr. Louis Richardson. I am an attorney representing the family of someone deceased.

The woman looked at him with an uncomfortable expression. "Please sign the register. Give me a few moments."

He watched her leave her chair and hurriedly leave her cubicle through an inside door. He signed the ledger as Allen Campbell then sat down placing his briefcase on the floor.

Five minutes later a door opened and a man in a white physician's jacket approached him. Are you the attorney asking for Dr. Richardson?"

Walsh stood up. "Yes. Allen Campbell."

"I am Dr. Sullivan. I regret to inform you that Dr. Richardson died a week ago."

Walsh stood there dumbfounded. "Died? What happened?"

"A terrible traffic accident. Struck down while entering his car. Circumstances are unclear. It was dark and the vehicle that hit him left the scene. Please come into my office and I will try to assist you."

Walsh followed Sullivan down a hallway to a small conference room.

Once seated, Sullivan said, "What did you wish to see Dr. Richardson about?"

Walsh handed Sullivan a business card and opened his briefcase removing a folder. "I am here concerning the death of the actress Tara Kelly. I represent her family in Brooklyn, New York. There seems to be unanswered questions about certain circumstances surrounding her death. The Los Angeles police have been unhelpful. I am referring to a party the deceased attended consistent with the estimated time of death. You see, the family is certain that Kelly was not a drug user. However, they might not have known and wished to think otherwise. Nonetheless, they deserve better answers."

Walsh extracted a single typed sheet of paper from the folder. Along with printing business cards, Walsh had a ream of paper printed with the colorful Seal of the City of Los Angeles.

"I made myself a persistent nuisance at LAPD headquarters until I obtained a meeting with Assistant Chief James Fletcher. Fletcher is personally managing the Kelly case if you can call what they are *not doing* an investigation. The newspapers have reported the names of some of the biggest movie stars that attended that lavish party in Beverly Hills. Fletcher told me there is concern that the death of Tara Kelly does not escalate to become another major scandal for the movie industry. He says Kelly's death was a straightforward case of a drug overdose. As the drug of choice for casual users, cocaine is easily ingested by inhaling the powder.

"I insisted on seeing the official autopsy report or I would petition the California State Attorney General's office to look into the matter. My law firm has significant clout."

Of course, Walsh never spoke to Fletcher much less ever met with him. The fabrication was meant only to pressure Sullivan into cooperating.

Sullivan read Walsh's fake letter. Under the printed seal appeared the header, *Office of Assistant Chief of the Los Angeles Police Department James R. Fletcher.* Addressed to *Dr. Louis Richardson, senior pathologist at the Los Angeles County Department of Medical Examiner-Coroner.* The content read: *Attorney at Law Allen Campbell representing the family of the decedent Tara Francis Kelly is hereby granted access to view the official autopsy report and any accompanying information from the Medical Examiner-Coroner records. Signed James R. Fletcher, Assistant Chief Los Angeles Police Department.*

Sullivan's demeanor instantly turned anxious. "I knew from the start this would get worse." Letting out a deep sigh, "Wait here a moment. I'll get the file from the vault."

Walsh just nodded while avoiding asking Sullivan what he meant. Gratified that Sullivan did not notice the header on the forged Fletcher letter was typed rather than printed along with the colorful seal of Los Angeles appearing as a facsimile of official LAPD stationery. Walsh could not very well have the printer prepare stationary for a LAPD police chief without providing an explanation and probably requiring authorization.

Returning, Sullivan sat back down, placing a folder on the conference table. Walsh sat across from him. Sullivan extracted the autopsy report. Before handing it to Walsh, he began reading it. After several moments his eyes opened wide in surprise before uttering, "What the hell!"

Walsh watched as Sullivan thumbed through several pages. "This is bullshit! Not what Richardson and I observed. Richardson was the attending pathologist. Why did he report incomplete findings? The summary makes no mention of relevant specific observations Richardson discovered and which I observed."

"May I see the report?" Walsh said.

Sullivan handed Walsh the autopsy. Reading through the report, Walsh failed to understand why Sullivan was upset. To Walsh, it confirmed the publicly released conclusions. His questions concerned only cocaine levels and how it may have been introduced into Kelly's body.

"I don't understand, Doctor. Why do call this report false?"

Sullivan composed himself. "Soon after Kelly's body arrived, Chief Fletcher arrived. He and Dr. Richardson spent maybe a half an hour in this very room. Whatever was going on it was loud."

"What do you mean?"

"From the hallway I could hear what sounded like arguing. Couldn't hear what they were saying though. Anyway, Chief Fletcher leaves and Dr. Richardson comes storming down the hall mad as all hell. Told me to come with him.

"We end up in the morgue where we keep the bodies under refrigeration prior to autopsy. We find the label marked Tara Kelly and pull out the drawer. Pulling away the sheet, we look at the body. She'd been dead for days. Not so pretty anymore. First noticeable thing was the bruising."

"Bruising? Where on the body?"

"Upper arms. Neck. Then on the thighs after Dr. Richardson pulled up her nightgown. Pulling on rubber gloves, Richardson then examined the vagina. Moments later, he turned to me and said *I observe extensive vaginal damage.* I then did the same and concurred with his findings. The body was in advanced rigor mortis but we both concluded she was sexually assaulted."

The admission stunned Walsh.

Sullivan continued. "Richardson altered his autopsy schedule to begin on Kelly immediately. Two hours later he called me back to the autopsy room. He had already removed tissue samples for toxicology testing but wanted me to look at the surgically exposed vaginal area. I concurred that the evidence confirmed she suffered sexual assault. Richardson then went on to explain that Chief Fletcher forewarned him that Kelly may have been sexually assaulted but needed to withhold that information until the LAPD concluded their investigation.

"According to Richardson, Fletcher told him, *many big stars attended a party Kelly attended making them possible suspects or witnesses. Important for the moment this appears as an accidental cocaine overdose even though evidence at Kelly's home suggested she overdosed intentionally. The LAPD will release a statement indicating the cause of death was accidental cocaine overdose without any further detail. This had all the makings of another major Hollywood scandal. The LAPD had to get this right and find the person responsible for the assault.* I expected to find the official report stating Richardson's clinical conclusions as he verbally explained them to me." In disgust, Sullivan pushed the folder aside. "I watched Richardson take many photographs of the bruising on the corpse and the surgical examination of the vaginal area as standard practice when such evidence might be required for a criminal investigation. Those photographs are missing from the file."

"If she was assaulted, did you test for semen?" Walsh asked.

"Not possible. She had been dead too long."

"What about the amount of cocaine found in her body?"

Opening the folder and extracting a report Sullivan said, "Quite substantial according to this lab report. Enough to kill most anybody, certainly a 115-pound woman. No needle marks on the body, so not taken intravenously. Evident in the nasal cavity, lung tissue, and intestinal tract. That's a little unusual."

"What do you mean?"

"Most users do not ingest cocaine orally. Much quicker to achieve more immediate effects by snorting it directly up the nose or smoking it. Gets into the bloodstream quicker."

"What is the significance of cocaine being found in the stomach?"

Sullivan replied, "Suggests possible suicide or even homicide."

"Any idea why Dr. Richardson became complicit in this deceit?" Walsh asked.

Sullivan shook his head. "Louis was a good pathologist and a good guy. He remained upset and remote after that day. We never discussed it further. I assumed he agreed to keep quiet, and the police would release a sanitized autopsy conclusion. Never believed Richardson might actually go further and create a totally false autopsy report. He would have made notes on his observations. They are also missing along with the autopsy photos. Nothing in this file is consistent with what I myself observed when we examined the body together."

Why Dr. Louis Richardson went along with this conspiracy deepened the mystery of Tara Kelly's death. Could it have been for money or out of fear? Might dying in an unexplained automobile accident been the work of someone removing the threat of a possible witness? If so, considering the complicity of LAPD brass, that someone wields enormous power.

Walsh leaned forward, "Listen to me, Dr. Sullivan. I suggest you not tell anyone what you just told me. What if Dr. Richardson's death was not an accident? If you tell anyone, you might not be safe in Los Angeles."

"Jesus Christ! Are you saying someone murdered Dr. Richardson?"

"After what you told me then showing me a fictitious autopsy signed by Richardson, followed by his untimely death that becomes a distinct possibility."

194

"What do you mean?"

"Because Richardson was the only witness to this conspiracy. Except of course you that nobody but me knows about. Keep it that way. I assure you that I will not reveal your name to anyone."

"What are you going to do with this information?" Sullivan asked.

"Not sure. There is no evidence to support what you told me. Nothing enough to force exhumation of her body. I imagine that would also do no good after the passage of so much time. Neither one of us can make this right without evidence, Doctor."

Sullivan sat in silence contemplating Walsh's comments.

"The LAPD wants Kelly's death to fade away. Police Chief Fletcher's interference makes that clear. The LAPD is not going to aggressively pursue what possibly happened among the rich and famous movie crowd that Saturday night. Too much money is at stake. I will simply tell Kelly's family I could find no evidence of foul play."

Walsh got up and shook hands with a numb Dr. Sullivan. "Mind what I say, Dr. Sullivan and keep quiet." Walsh retrieved his fake Fletcher letter and left the building.

———

Schachter delivered the private investigator's report to Chadwick Hollister the following morning. "Ginsberg reported Walsh entered the Los Angeles Hall of Justice building at 9:00am yesterday morning. One of his operatives followed Walsh inside and observed him entering the offices of the Los Angeles County Medical Examiner-Coroner. The operative did not follow inside to avoid being spotted by the subject. Walsh remained inside for eighty minutes then left and drove back to the Fox Films offices on Western Avenue in Hollywood."

Hollister said, "Thank you, Nathan." As soon as Schachter left his office and closed the door, Hollister called Chief Fletcher's direct telephone number bypassing the LAPD headquarters switchboard.

"This is Chadwick Hollister, Chief. Got more bad news concerning this Walsh character. My private investigative sources report that Walsh visited the county medical examiner's office yesterday. What the fuck could he be looking for there?"

"Probably wanted to see the autopsy report. As a reporter, they would not release it without police authorization. Besides, the autopsy is irrelevant."

"What do you mean irrelevant?"

"Because it simply supports what we publicly released. Tara Kelly died of an accidental cocaine overdose. Nothing more. That was part of my arrangement with Dr. Richardson. $50,000 for creating a false autopsy report and keeping his mouth shut. I made sure of that by personally looking at the autopsy report and everything in the file. Seems like that was not enough though for whomever you are protecting, Mr. Hollister."

Fletcher knew Hollister was complicit in whatever happened to Tara Kelly. Called him that Wednesday morning at around the time her body was discovered. Told him a story about a famous actor took a liking to the pretty actress. Declined to identify the famous actor's name.

Hollister told Chief Fletcher that this famous guy and Kelly disappeared upstairs for a long time. This unnamed famous guy comes downstairs and tells Hollister that Kelly passed out drunk in one of the bedrooms. After all the guests left, Hollister said he had his bodyguard Kurt Gerhardt drive Kelly home. Hollister sounded upset on the telephone. Fletcher does not necessarily believe Hollister's story. The telephone call alone means Hollister knows more than he is revealing. That is clearly evident by the staggering amount of money Hollister paid him to contain the fallout from Tara Kelly's death.

Fletcher soon regretted his involvement when Hollister called on him to strong arm the pathologist Richardson. Hollister possibly became paranoid after he relayed Richardson's reaction. Hollister may have removed the doctor as a potential threat fearing the hush money might not prove sufficient.

"Come now, Chief. Richardson was getting into his car parked on Temple Street as it ran downhill from the Hall of Justice building. Working late that night. According to LAPD reports in the newspaper, a truck going too fast probably struck Richardson. Someone with maybe too much to drink that was not about to stay at the accident site."

Fletcher suspected it was no accident but was not about to confront his benefactor. "My point being there is nothing Walsh can gain by a visit to the medical examiner's office. Just a frustrated reporter grasping for information."

"Just the same, I have every studio head calling me about what can be done to tamp down the bad press associated with Kelly's death. They are hypersensitive about threats of governmental censorship on the movie industry. That in turn affects Hollister Financial with its substantial involvement in financing the industry. The studio execs think I have pull with various local government offices, so they come to me."

Fletcher thought Hollister's interest might be more self-serving. He hosted this party at his house, so it was not just about the reputations of movie stars.

"Is there not some way to prevent Walsh from making more noise? What about arresting him on some charge? Perhaps dealing in cocaine? He was friendly with Tara Kelly. Maybe he was her drug dealer?"

"No. Taking direct action against Walsh would be unwise. It would indicate that Walsh was onto something. Walsh is also a reporter. No evidence exists of Tara Kelly's sexual assault. She died of an accidental overdose of cocaine. I personally examined Richardson's autopsy report. Richardson is no longer a threat. The matter is closed, Mr. Hollister." His tone left no doubt as to his meaning.

Fletcher believed Richardson's death was not an accident. Far too convenient. Probably the work of Hollister's bodyguard Kurt Gerhardt. Fletcher knew Gerhardt's background as Hollister's fixer with connections to Charlie Crawford and the Los Angeles underworld. Money corrupted James Fletcher. Taking money for looking the other way and greasing the wheels of those with money was the extent of his corruption. He admitted to himself that he went too far in covering up for what happened to Tara

Kelly. Too many years compromised by Hollister left him little choice. However, he was not about to let Hollister draw him deeper into this dangerous conspiracy without knowing full details.

Chapter 16

Los Angeles, California | 1926

Walsh showed up at the Fox offices immediately after leaving the medical examiner's office. What he learned from Dr. Sullivan confirmed his fears that Tara Kelly's death involved more than a drug overdose. Yet he was no closer to learning what really happened. Nor any closer to identifying suspects that might have assaulted her and caused her death. With the extensive efforts to cover up the crime, this confirmed that someone with exceptional reach was behind the cover up conspiracy.

Ray Schrock and Lilly Romano were in the conference room when he arrived. Knowing where he went this morning, Lilly would be anxious to hear what happened. However, he needed to relate the staggering news to her privately. Walking in on them, "Good morning. You two making progress?"

Schrock replied, "I think so. Worked around those areas needing your input. By the end of the day, I think we can show good progress. If you'll excuse me, I need to use the facilities. Be back in a bit."

As Schrock got up and went to the toilet, Walsh said to Lilly, "I could use some coffee. How about you?"

"Good idea." They went to the small kitchen area with a commercial coffee urn. Out of earshot to anyone in the office, she said, "Well, did you get anywhere?"

"More than I could have expected. The short version is the LAPD press release about the cause of Tara's death is intentionally misleading. Tara Kelly did die of a cocaine overdose but maybe not of her own doing. She was sexually assaulted."

Romano gasped. "You're saying she was raped?"

"Yes. I'll tell you more details later when we're alone. I spoke with one of the pathologists that examined Kelly's body. He spoke candidly after the shock of what he found in the official file. He was a colleague of the certifying pathologist that performed the autopsy but who died days later in an automobile accident. I find the circumstances suspicious but maybe I'm just becoming paranoid."

"What's this mean, Egan?"

"Not sure, but it means Tara did not die accidentally. We'll talk about it tonight. I also need to bring the reporter Zimmerman up to speed. Decide how to proceed. We agreed to work together and pool our information. He will report locally for the *Pasadena Star-News*, and I will publish on the east coast with my former employer the *Boston Globe*. I'll call him when we break for lunch and see if he is free to meet tonight. Care to join me?"

"Absolutely. My god I can't believe this has turned so ugly. You are doing the right thing by continuing to pursue this, Egan."

Schrock stuck his head into the kitchenette area, "You guys ready to get back to the script?"

They spent another hour working on *Dying for Ireland* before breaking for lunch. Walsh and Lilly could not just break away alone without Schrock so all three went to a diner close by. Both reconciled to concentrating on the script as difficult as that may be given this startling news that Walsh discovered. He was anxious to discuss with Lilly and Zimmerman to get their thoughts on where to go next with this independent investigation.

While they ordered lunch, Walsh used a payphone to call Zimmerman.

"My alter ego Allen Campbell, attorney for the family of deceased movie star Tara Kelly showed up at the Los Angeles County Medical examiner's office this morning, Benny. Found out that the pathologist Dr. Louis Richardson died in an automobile accident within a week after discovery of Kelly's body. Talked with another pathologist. Learned more than I could have expected. Better not discuss it on the phone. Are you available tonight?"

"Of course."

"How about that Italian place where we had lunch? Around seven? I'll buy you dinner and a drink. You'll need the drink."

———

On the drive to Pasadena, Walsh shared with Lilly what transpired at the medical examiner's office that morning. While knowing Tara Kelly only professionally, what befell the rising actress was still deeply troubling for Lilly Romano.

"You were right about her death being all wrong," she said. "She had a head on her shoulders. Not the type to do something stupid like trying cocaine. What next? If the Los Angeles Police are part of a cover up, where can you go?"

"I don't know, Lilly. There is nothing to corroborate what Dr. Sullivan told me. I promised not to reveal any of what he told me to anyone. Clearly too dangerous. It contradicts the official autopsy report signed by Richardson, now conveniently dead. We can't trust the LAPD. Could jeopardize Sullivan's career or maybe put him in harm's way. I believe someone killed Dr. Richardson.

"Perhaps Benny Zimmerman might have a suggestion what we should do. Apart from Sullivan's information, we don't have any evidence of wrongdoing, much less any idea who might have assaulted Tara."

Walsh found a table in the back of the restaurant where they could talk out of earshot.

A waitress came over. Walsh asked for three glasses of Chianti."

Romano raised her eyebrows.

"Zimmerman knows this place. Not only is the food good but the wine flows without question."

Minutes later Zimmerman spotted him and came to the table.

"Benny, this is Lilly Romano. I work with her at Fox Films. She and a couple of other friends have been helping investigate Tara Kelly's death.

"Glad to meet you, Miss Romano."

"Thought you might like some wine, Benny. After you hear what I discovered you'll want something stronger."

Walsh launched into the full narrative of his experience at the medical examiner's office. Zimmerman took out a pen and note-pad from his jacket pocket taking notes once Walsh said that the pathologist Dr. Richardson was dead.

"An automobile accident you say?" Zimmerman said. "Must have not noticed it or not made the connection."

"Neither did I. Probably buried on the inside pages or the ob-its. My guess is LAPD Assistant Chief James Fletcher issued the public statement on Richardson's death without mentioning his connection to Tara Kelly's autopsy. Anyway, Richardson's death sounds far too convenient for whomever is behind this cover up."

Walsh then explained his conversation with Dr. Sullivan, a colleague of Richardson. "After explaining the reason for my be-ing there while posing as Allen Campbell a New York attorney, Sullivan immediately turned uncomfortable and said, *I knew this would get worse*. When he retrieved the autopsy report, he was shocked by what he found in the file. It got a whole lot worse.

"According to Sullivan, LAPD Chief Fletcher showed up at the morgue shortly after Kelly's body arrived. Told of a loud ar-gument between Fletcher and Richardson behind closed doors. When Fletcher left, Richardson had Sullivan accompany him to the morgue freezer where they looked at Kelly's body. That's when both the pathologists discovered heavy bruising and clear forensic evidence of sexual assault."

Zimmerman reacted with, "Holy shit! She was raped?"

"Maybe even murdered," Walsh said. "She still died of co-caine overdose, yet how did that happen?"

"Wait, go back," Zimmerman interrupted. "You say this was after Chief Fletcher had this argument with Dr. Richardson, and before Richardson had actually examined the body?"

Walsh nodded.

"That means that the perpetrator or someone protecting him forewarned Fletcher. Rumor has it that Fletcher is the most corrupt of among LAPD brass. This probably confirms he is a crooked sonofabitch."

Walsh went on describing every detailed scrap of information imparted by Dr. Sullivan, including the toxicology results and the significance of cocaine in the intestinal tract.

After more wine, they broke off from discussing the matter at hand as the waitress returned to take their dinner orders.

Waiting for their food, Zimmerman said, "As you said, Egan, we have no evidence. The LAPD is complicit in the cover up. Too premature to go to the district attorney. Difficult to tell how far this conspiracy of silence goes. Even if Sullivan were to testify, there is no corroborating evidence. Nothing even to petition for exhumation which would probably be forensically inconclusive anyway. The attorney general will not open an investigation without tangible evidence of a crime being committed. Nothing we have supports an allegation of LAPD obstruction of justice."

Walsh said, "I agree. Yet we now know that Kelly was sexually assaulted that Saturday night. That strongly points to someone attending Hollister's party. Somebody prominent with enough influence and money to prevent a normal investigation. Goes as high as bribing or threatening the pathologist Richardson by LAPD Assistant Chief Fletcher. Possibly goes higher and wider, including perhaps the DA's office. The perpetrator of the assault might be a major movie star or studio executive. Someone at that party saw something useful that evening. To shake that tree and force the celebrity attendees to submit to interviews, we must find something that scares the shit out of them on a personal level. So where do we go from here, Benny?"

"Keep up the pressure. Keep repeating the circumstances surrounding Tara Kelly's death in the news. The person responsible for committing this crime has exceptional influence to get the LAPD to participate in a cover up. However, this is Hollywood. The lives and tragedies of movie stars are exceptionally newsworthy. If we keep the unexplained circumstances surrounding Kelly's death in the news, public pressure might eventually yield something. Conspiracies fall apart because of too many people involved, each with their own motivations.

"I agree with you that the Beverly Hills party is connected in some way to Kelly's death. We can only hope those celebrities will feel the pressure and come forward with information that might prove useful. If they and the studios continue to stonewall the public's right to know, there could be public blowback if we get enough reporting and editorials willing to stay the course. The perpetrator might eventually feel the matter is not going away and do something foolish bringing attention to himself."

"Very well. Knowing what we know, as journalists we have no choice but to continue. Our next pieces however must hit harder," Walsh said.

Lilly offered, "I can offer to help. I am friends with Rachel Jankowski of *Motion Picture Magazine*. She shies away from reporting rumors and engaging in speculation like the shills for the Hearst publications Louella Parsons and Adela Rodgers St. Johns. Thinks of herself as a journalist not a gossip columnist. Perhaps her column might be used in goading those celebrity attendees of the party to become more forthcoming. Egan said his friend Tom Mix is not shy about discussing what he observed at the party."

Walsh added, "Lilly worked for the New York Times early in her career, so she understands journalism. She also knows her way around Hollywood."

Lilly added, "Besides Jankowski, I have many contacts in the front offices of other studios. I can begin a whispering campaign that might add to pressure of those celebrity attendees of the Hollister party to become forthcoming. Tom Mix and Leslie Fenton have made public statements. Why are the others remaining silent?"

Zimmerman smiled and nodded. "Welcome aboard, Miss Romano."

"Call me Lilly, Benny."

Walsh said, "How about this, Benny? We each draft our next column for our respective newspapers since we know the background details. Then let Lilly act as editor by contributing an independent view. I know I am getting too close to this so I could benefit by an objective perspective."

"Excellent idea," Zimmerman said. "Christ, after hearing the fruits of Egan's masterful investigating efforts, I could now use a real drink. I know a place around the corner. You guys care to join me?"

"Lead the way, Benny," Lilly said.

———

The three of them worked the next two nights at Lilly's house in the Hollywood Hills. Picking up takeout food after leaving the studio, Zimmerman brought wine. Walsh wanted to hit harder than Zimmerman while Lilly provided editorial compromise. Just like her contributions to the *Dying for Ireland* script, Lilly possessed a writer's talent to hit the right notes for achieve the desired objective.

Benny Zimmerman published the following in the *Pasadena Star-News*. It served notice to those attempting to cover up the death of Tara Kelly that the matter was nowhere near settled. The *Boston Globe* published essentially the identical article. Already the matter was taking on the mantle as the next Hollywood scandal with the serialized newspaper reporting of Tara Kelly's death captivating audiences nationwide.

Actress Tara Kelly Death Remains Unresolved.

Pasadena, CA: Benjamin Zimmerman:

The death weeks ago of actress Tara Kelly remains burden with many unexplained circumstances. A mystery largely because the Los Angeles Police Department refuses to thoroughly investigate potentially relevant circumstances surrounding her death. Circumstances that could either corroborate the official cause of death as an accidental cocaine overdose or suggest the possibility of foul play. After multiple attempts to acquire more information, the LAPD refuses to adequately explain their lack of interest in pursuing obviously troubling inconsistencies in Tara Kelly's death. All public comments are restricted to coming only from the office of Assistant Chief James R. Fletcher. The lack of any ongoing investigation while important questions remain unanswered suggests the LAPD is participating in a cover up. Who is behind this obstruction of justice conspiracy?

The LAPD states the cause of death was accidental cocaine overdose. Yet the medical examiner gave the estimate of time of death around the time Kelly attended a Hollywood party along with many leading movie stars and studio executives. According to our inquiries, the LAPD has not interviewed any of these celebrity attendees. So far, only a couple have offered public statements about their observations that Saturday night.

The prominent western actor Tom Mix was more forthcoming, describing seeing Kelly at the party as she arrived with actor Leslie Fenton, even describing her wearing a stunning blue evening gown. Mix said he saw Fenton leaving without Kelly. Mr. Fenton confirmed he did leave without Kelly explaining that he argued with Kelly. Both Mix and Fenton commented on what appeared obvious to many of the guests, that Kelly was enthralled by the attentions of Charlie Chaplin, Rudolph Valentino, and the party's host Mr. Chadwick Hollister. This appears the likely reason for Fenton leaving the party early without Kelly. The relevance of this is how did Tara Kelly get home that night? Did she leave with someone at the party?

The financier Chadwick Hollister hosted the party at his estate in Benedict Canyon. By the statements of Mix and Fenton, Hollister was very much engaged with Kelly during the party. Neither he nor his office at Hollister Financial has responded to our inquiries, nor issued any sort of public comment. Why this collective secrecy surrounding the death of this young actress?

Mr. Egan Walsh, a former reporter for the *Boston Globe* and acquaintance of Miss Kelly has been independently investigating. Walsh co-authored the script for *Price of Freedom* adapted from his novel and became acquainted with Miss Kelly professionally. Walsh reported a neighbor of Tara Kelly saw a man leaving Kelly's home at one o'clock in the morning the night of the party. The LAPD has never interviewed this person or others in the neighboring bungalows.

Walsh also interviewed Kelly's cleaning woman who discovered Kelly dead lying in bed at her home dressed in a nightgown. The woman reported never seeing drugs in Kelly's house. The housekeeper said she did not see a blue gown. Why has the LAPD not been forthcoming with the full extent of what they found when her body was discovered? Where is the blue dress? Those details could go toward explaining Kelly's state of mind that night. Did she ingest cocaine to experience its euphoric effects, or the opposite of knowingly committing suicide perhaps induced by depression?

Just days ago, an anonymous caller telephoned the newspaper saying they had reason to believe that Kelly suffered some sort of assault the night of the party. Unfortunately, the caller offered no further details. For this reason, we bring up the question of the blue dress that could be evidence of foul play.

The only public comments of most of the party's attendees have come through studio press releases, none of which provide any insights to the many unanswered questions surrounding the death of Tara Kelly. Prominent movie stars and producers from MGM, Paramount, and United Artists attended the party yet there has been no reporting of what they saw other than from Tom Mix and Leslie Fenton. Did Kelly ingest cocaine at the party? Who then provided the drug? How did she get home that night? Did someone take her? Who was the man seen leaving her home after midnight the night of the party? Where is the blue dress? Did someone assault her?

Too many unexplained circumstances exist to leave Kelly's death explained simply as an accidental drug overdose. Adding to that is the unfortunate and inconvenient death of the pathologist that performed the autopsy on Tara Kelly. That death weeks ago did not at the time prompt questions in connection with Kelly's death. The death of Dr. Louis Richardson is explained only as an unresolved a hit and run accident. For those impeding the investigation into Kelly's death, the inability to question Dr. Richardson in further detail is all too convenient. Perhaps the pathologist might have observed something on her remains that could be significant. Might the doctor's death have been murder? The

LAPD declares that Richardson was struck by a hit and run driver as he was entering his car parked near the medical examiner's office one night. Because of the extensive damage done to Richardson's vehicle, authorities believe he was struck by a truck. No one has been charged in that incident. The anonymous caller cast doubts on the thoroughness of the autopsy findings which now might connect both deaths.

Why are these movie stars and studio executives reluctant to speak about what they observed at the Beverly Hills party? The public demands a full and transparent investigation be conducted into the death of Tara Kelly. With the LAPD refusing to investigate further, perhaps the matter should be turned over to the California Attorney General's office?

Uncorroborated by any tangible evidence, it was premature to publish the explosive revelations made by the pathologist Dr. Sullivan. Both Zimmerman and Walsh were responsible journalists. The reference to possible foul play in their respective reporting was as far as they could go.

CHAPTER 17

Los Angeles, California | 1926

Chadwick Hollister read Zimmerman's column the following morning. Since the *Pasadena Star-News* was the leading local newspaper pursuing the death of Tara Kelly he received it daily. He also received the *Boston Globe* daily by airmail two days after publication. Walsh reported essentially the same article as Zimmerman. From Hollister's many contacts in New York City, he learned made the major newspapers picked up Walsh published articles in the *Boston Globe*. The story was gaining traction nationwide. Even Hollister's father telephoned him rebuking him for the negative publicity reflected on Hollister Financial. What was he doing to mitigate the growing scandal?

That telephone call ended in an argument. Telephone calls followed later that morning from Adolph Zukor from Paramount, Marcus Loew from MGM, and Joseph Schenck, president of United Artists. All had movie stars, directors, and producers that attended the infamous Hollister party. Like his father, all were looking to him to do something. Hollister Financial was the largest financial institution funding the movie industry. Chadwick Hollister was its most active political lobbyist in local affairs. Well known as a powerful figure with influence in every aspect of Los Angeles County, he was often called on to *fix* problems. The Kelly affair was fast becoming a serious problem.

Hollister attempted to explain to these studio executives that the LAPD was cooperating by not adding to the press feeding frenzy. However, many questioned the strategy of the attendees to his party continuing to remain silent which seemed to further accusations of a cover up.

The abrasive Adolph Zukor pointedly asked, "What the hell really happened at your party, Hollister?"

"As I told you, Adolph, the actress got drunk and fell asleep in one of the upstairs bedrooms. We called her a taxi and sent her off by herself. When she left my house, she was embarrassed but sufficiently sober. She did not want any of the other guests to see her, so my bodyguard bundled her in the taxi at the rear of the house out of sight. She left alone."

"What about all this extraneous bullshit this reporter is citing? Are you withholding something that happen at the party?"

"No, I am not, Adolph. If something happened to the actress, it didn't happen at my home. If one of the guests did something, it happened elsewhere. But I still see no reason to even assume something happened other than the young woman simply overdosed on cocaine.

"That's what the autopsy concluded and the reason the LAPD is not pursuing the matter further. I know Chief Fletcher. Have spoken to him several times on this matter. The real troublemaker here is this fellow Egan Walsh."

"The guy named in the Pasadena newspaper?" Zukor asked.

"Yes. He's also a journalist. Fletcher says Walsh is conducting his own investigation. Been harassing the LAPD. Fletcher believes Walsh may have been romantically involved with Kelly. Possibly the person responsible for providing her with cocaine. Remember, the medical examiner only concluded accidental death. No way to know if she overdosed intentionally."

"You mean suicide?"

"Why not? Could be something related to her involvement with Walsh."

"Then why is Walsh so vigorously pursuing this in the newspapers?"

"Well, he's a reporter turned novelist. The reporter Zimmerman is probably doing this to sell newspapers. Maybe Walsh is preparing to write a new book. A fictional account of the actress being murdered perhaps."

"Christ. The longer this goes on, the more harm is done. If not resolved, every screwball theory perpetuates this like some terrible serial. Worse than the murder of William Desmond Taylor four years ago. That still has not entirely subsided."

"I understand, Adolph. My best advice is for everyone to sit tight and ride out the storm. It cannot go on indefinitely."

Hollister was not about to admit to Zukor or any of the movie people that he knew of the sexual assault on Tara Kelly or that his bodyguard Kurt Gerhardt drove her home that night unseen by any of the other guests. Unfortunately, Gerhardt was seen by Kelly's neighbor according to the newspaper account.

The other telephone calls went no better. By midday, Hollister made up his mind. There was no way he was going to let this obsessed foreigner continue his newspaper attacks. Buzzing his secretary, "Find Gerhardt and have him come to my office immediately."

Chadwick Hollister could be impulsive. He hated inaction and hated even more anyone getting in his way. The studios had circled the wagons around their stars. The LAPD was cooperating. He removed the threat of the only direct evidence of a crime by Fletcher and Gerhardt dealing with the pathologist Dr. Richardson. Walsh remained the problem. He was the one providing information to the reporter Zimmerman and picked up by the wire services from his articles in the *Boston Globe*. Remove Walsh and the story would eventually cease to be newsworthy.

Once Gerhardt arrived, an agitated Hollister immediately launched into describing his course of action. "The time has come to remove this nuisance Walsh who continues to make dangerous allegations concerning the death of that actress. Can't very well have you dump him off a pier in San Pedro, but I'm sure you can arrange something that will put him in the hospital."

"Won't that make matters worse, Sir?"

213

"Not if you can arrange it to appear it was the Los Angeles police that beat the shit out of him. He and that Pasadena reporter have been smearing the LAPD viciously. What do you think?"

"Must be careful not to piss off the LAPD. Assistant Chief Fletcher is in this too deeply, but we must consider the new Chief of Police James Davis. A real piece of work. Nicknamed Two-gun Davis because he's trying to make a name for himself by going after the bootleggers. Already giving Charlie Crawford problems. Making it harder to pay off lower-level officers essential for running booze and allowing speakeasies to do business.

"If you want to do this though, I know three cops that should be up to this for a price. Not shy about breaking heads. Crawford uses them from time to time. They could beat Walsh badly enough to put him in the hospital. Leave his face untouched so the press cannot print pictures to make a big deal out of what can be downplayed as just a mugging. Have these cops then pass the word throughout the police department that Walsh got what he had coming for publicly attacking the LAPD. Still a risk that the Pasadena reporter might portray this for what it really is and make matters worse."

Hollister grinned. "Fuck the Pasadena reporter. I'll take the risk. Leaves Walsh with no doubt about the consequences of continuing his crusade. The LAPD is happy to have Walsh off their back. Even Chief Davis might not be interested in investigating the incident further. This is what I pay you for, Kurt. Creative solutions to fix awkward problems. How much do we pay these dirty cops?"

"$1,000 each plus a $2,000 commission to Crawford should be enough."

Hollister nodded. "Make it happen, Kurt. Pay more if necessary. I'd like this sonofabitch Walsh put in a casket, but I'll settle for a cast."

"One more thing, Sir. Call off the private investigator. Don't want one of his operatives witnessing the attack on Walsh."

"I'll have Schachter take of that. Either this ends Walsh's meddling, or we resort to something more permanent."

Gerhardt knew the three LAPD officers intimately from his time with the LAPD. They usually worked through underworld kingpin Charles Crawford. Best to use Crawford to contract their services, keeping this at arm's length from Hollister.

"Mr. Hollister needs to fix a problem, Mr. Crawford," Gerhardt said as he sat with Crawford in his office on the third floor of the Maple Bar. The third floor provided bedrooms for prostitutes, a water closet, and Crawford's corner office.

For someone as powerful within both city hall and the Los Angeles underworld, Crawford's office was exceedingly small. It accommodated only a small desk and chair, a safe, and a single chair opposite the desk where Gerhardt sat. The walls were decorated with nude photographs of women. This was Crawford's secondary office from where he conducted much of his illegal endeavors. His more public office was located on Sunset Boulevard in Hollywood, professionally decorated as befitting his influence with Los Angeles political affairs.

Everything about Charles Crawford was incongruous. Although only forty-seven, he looked ten years older. An imposing physical figure with his height and physical stature, his gray hair earned him the label the *Gray Wolf of Spring Street*. To most he appeared an affable grandfatherly-type, quick with a smile and a soft voice. For those that knew him, his physical appearance was at odds with his notorious reputation for viciousness and cunning. He not only possessed extraordinary political savvy, but that same talent applied to his ability to ruthlessly manipulate the diverse Los Angeles underworld to his advantage.

Crawford gave Gerhardt his signature smile. "Something to do with the bad press over the death of that actress? Hollister's name keeps coming up about her attending a party at his home the night of her death."

Gerhardt merely nodded. "Mr. Hollister believes this fellow Walsh has some personal motivation to keep up his newspaper attack. He is a former reporter from Boston, conducting his own investigation. Claims there is more to the woman's death then the official pronouncement that she died of an overdose of cocaine. He has no evidence for making allegations, so he chooses to go after the LAPD for not investigating further. He's manufacturing a scandal which hurts the movie industry."

"And Chadwick Hollister finances the movie industry," Crawford offered. "What does your boss have in mind, Kurt?"

"Convince Walsh to stop his attacks in the press. Locally, only the Pasadena newspaper continues publishing these articles based on Walsh's continued agitation. Without Walsh there is no story. The issue goes away. I was thinking perhaps those three cops known for using physical persuasion as a sideline might be of use."

"How far do you want them to go in working over Walsh?"

"Enough to put him in the hospital. Tell them the reason for this is to stop Walsh's inquiries. Afterwards, they are to circulate the rumor that the police cannot put up with this kind of slandering of the LAPD. They're to lay off Walsh's face though. No photographic evidence of a beating for the newspapers to publish and portray this other than just a mugging."

"How much are you offering for the job?"

"$1,000 for each of the three cops. $2,000 for your fee."

Crawford let out a short laugh. "Ordinarily, a fair price. However, considering this has now become a larger issue, I believe my fee should be three thousand. As for the cops, I'll tell them your offer and you can settle with them when you meet them."

Gerhardt nodded. "That will be acceptable, Mr. Crawford. "Mr. Hollister wants this to happen soon. What should I tell him?"

"Be downstairs in the bar tomorrow night at seven. I'll have those cops here and you can make the arrangements with them. I'll take my fee now."

"Yes, Sir." Gerhardt reached into his jacket pocket and pulled out a stack of $100-bills, counting out $3,000.

"Tell your boss to tread carefully. Physically attacking a member of the press can backfire, making the matter worse. I'll let you explain to these cops how far you want them to go. I'll tell them you are offering $1,000 a piece, but they may want to negotiate. Bring enough cash. They'll expect payment in advance."

Kurt Gerhardt knocked on the entrance door to the Maple Bar promptly at seven o'clock. The large fellow manning the door recognizing Gerhardt said, "Three guys downstairs in the basement are expecting you."

Three off-duty cops dressed in cheap civilian suits sat at the round poker table.

"Did Mr. Crawford explain what I need done?" Gerhardt asked.

Two of the men were stout barrel-chested guys pushing two hundred pounds. The taller, slender third cop responded, "Yeah. Who's the mark?"

"A reporter by the name of Walsh. Working with another reporter in Pasadena but it is Walsh that's making a stink over the drug overdose death of that actress. Making the LAPD look bad in the process."

The taller cop said, "Crawford said you wanted this guy worked over pretty good. How bad?"

"Enough to put him in the hospital. Important though you do not touch his face. We don't want any photographs appearing in the newspapers. When you are through, tell him this is just a warning. Next time it'll be his girlfriend.

"This will likely make the newspapers. When it does, spread the word throughout the department that's what happens to reporters that attack the LAPD."

Tall cop asked, "Who's paying for this?"

"Does it matter?"

"Not really. Crawford said a $1,000 each. We'll do it for $1,500 each," Tall cop said.

Gerhardt nodded. "Agreed. Walsh resides at the Hollywood Hotel on Hollywood Boulevard. Currently spends most of the day at the Fox Film studio on Western near Sunset. Involved with a woman working at Fox by the name of Lillian Romano. She has a house in the Los Feliz district. Address is 2406 North Catalina Street."

The tall cop said, "We need to do surveillance and pick a location. We'll do this within three days. Give me a number and I'll call you after it happens."

"Just let Crawford know. He'll get word to me."

———

Walsh told Lilly he was meeting with Zimmerman that evening. Zimmerman called him explaining he received a call from Rachel Jankowski, the columnist from *Motion Picture Magazine*. "Jankowski said Lilly explained what was going on but without revealing anything not already published. Jankowski sounds like a real journalist not some gossip columnist like Louella Parsons or Adela Rodgers St. Johns. I looked at some of her articles. Writes more about the business side of the movie industry not the nonsense rumors about the love lives of the stars. Anyway, she already identified the death of Tara Kelly as the next Hollywood scandal. Seems we made a good public case painting the LAPD as involved in a cover up which gives the story its mystery. Told me she was already preparing a piece in her next column coming out in a week. Wants to meet with us to review our material in more detail. Interested?"

"Absolutely. How about I come to your office tomorrow night? Discuss how Jankowski might be helpful."

"See you about six then," Zimmerman said.

Leaving the studio with Lilly, Walsh said to her, "Rachel Jankowski contacted Benny after you called her. Wants to know more about what we uncovered concerning Kelly's death. Going to meet with Benny tonight to strategize how much to share with her and assess if she might be a useful ally. Not sure how long I will be. I'll see you back here tomorrow morning. Tell you about what Benny and I are planning to do next over dinner tomorrow night. I'll plan on spending the night at you place if you like."

Standing in the parking lot, she looked around making sure no one was watching. Embracing and giving him a long kiss, "Of course I like that. Call me when you get back to the hotel tonight and tell me how it went with Benny."

Walsh made the sixteen-mile drive north through Glassell Park to Eagle Rock to pick up Colorado Boulevard running east to Pasadena and Zimmerman's office on North Lake. Absorbed in his thoughts, he did not notice a Ford sedan following at a discreet distance. After huddling with Zimmerman for ninety minutes, it was dark when he returned to his car to make the trip back to the Hollywood Hotel. As he pulled away from the curb, the Ford sedan parked several car-lengths away did the same.

Thirty minutes later, Walsh parked in his usual space near the back entrance to the hotel. As he walked toward the hotel, two well-built men exited a Ford nearby. Stopping to light cigarettes, they let Walsh walk ahead of them.

Close to the hotel entrance stood a tall man staring at him intently. Walsh approached and said, "Good evening."

The man replied, "Are you Egan Walsh?"

Surprised and wary, "Yes. Who are you?"

The man pulled a revolver from a shoulder holster under his suit jacket. Motioning with the gun, "Walk back toward the parking lot."

Walsh turned around and began walking joined by the two stocky men at each side.

The man holding the gun said, "Follow my associates to that Ford over there. We're going for a ride, Mr. Walsh."

Reverting to his instincts from the war, Walsh knew that if captured, never allow the British to take you away. As the war progressed, capture likely meant death by hanging for anyone known as an IRA gunman. Almost certainly it meant rough treatment and probably some form torture if taken by the Auxiliaries or certain other security forces inclined to maltreatment. His advice to the men he commanded was look for the first opportunity and attack your captors. Do not think, just act. Your best chance occurred immediately when under the least control of the enemy. Once they took you away all chance became lost.

Walsh had no intention of leaving with these three thugs. Whatever they intended would happen right here. As they approached the Ford, the tall man holding the gun said to one stocky cop, "Handcuff him."

As the stocky man extracted handcuffs from his pocket, Walsh swung his briefcase while pivoting, knocking the tall guy's gun from his hand then stepping closer into him. Raising his right leg, he came down with all his force, landing his heel into the man's left knee.

An audible sound damage came from the man's knee accompanied by a loud gasp of pain.

Turning around to confront the other two assailants, Walsh stepped into the stocky man coming at him. They met chest to chest allowing him to contain the assailant's attempt to land a blow to his face. Evading the blow allowed Walsh to smash the heel of his palm into the man's nose.

The tactic learned from his early teen years in street fighting proved a useful tactic in taking your opponent out of the fight.

Walsh's success was short lived as the second stocky man now came at him with a leather covered sap known as a blackjack. A flat spoon-shaped heavy lead core wrapped in leather was useful for inflicting pain with the ability to avoid breaking bones. Used by police as a non-lethal method of containing a violent suspect, it also saw use in beating out confessions.

The man caught Walsh from behind and began laying into his upper arms. Walsh could not land a punch without suffering blackjack blows to his arms.

The guy with the broken nose then joined the fight grabbing Walsh and throwing him to the ground. Blood pouring from his nose, the enraged cop began kicking Walsh with his heavy brogans while the assailant with the blackjack kept up a continuous assault landing blows to Walsh's back and midsection while avoiding the head.

This went on for a sustained amount of time until both assailants paused to catch their breath. The tall guy managed to get to his feet with some difficulty because of his damaged knee. After retrieving his gun, he hobbled closer. Although his badly damaged knee caused considerable pain, he was overcome with rage. "Turn the sonofabitch on his back. We're not through with him yet."

The two stocky men rolled Walsh over. The one bleeding profusely stood over him covering him in dripping blood.

The tall guy said, "Work on his midsection and thighs."

With blackjack and shoes, another session of abuse began until the tall man eventually called a halt, "That's enough."

Walsh was groaning from intense pain coming from every part of his body. Barely conscious, he found it difficult to focus.

The tall man apparently in charge said, "No more newspaper columns criticizing the LAPD about that actress that overdosed. Tell that Pasadena reporter he could be next. If that is not enough, there's always your girlfriend. You don't want to see her going through this.

"Understand what I'm saying? How you doing so far?"

Walsh only grunted.

"Well, I guess we need to press our point more forcefully."

Nodding to his colleagues, the beating resumed.

As the blows continued battering him, he eventually lapsed into unconsciousness. The beating stopped as the assailants made sure Walsh was still alive. After a minute, Walsh recovered consciousness and began coughing up blood.

The tall man motioned with his head for them to leave. The assailant with the blackjack helped the tall guy who was unable to put weight on this injured knee.

"How's the leg, Sarge?"

"Christ, what do'ya think you dumb shit! Just help me to the fucking car. Get Ziegler and me to a goddamn hospital. Any questions, we had an auto accident. Hit and run driver."

———

Walsh lay in the hotel parking lot unable to move for close to an hour before another guest discovered him. It was after nine o'clock when the ambulance delivered him to the Queen of Angels-Hollywood Presbyterian Medical Center on North Vermont Avenue in East Hollywood. As they wheeled him into the emergency room and before sedating him, he demanded they call Lilly Romano. Her number was in his wallet. A nurse removed his wallet and found Lilly Romano's business card and scribbled home phone number. The nurse nodded to him before another nurse stuck a needle in his arm as he quickly passed into a sedated state.

Coincidentally, this same emergency room treated two injured police officers earlier. One was still here awaiting surgery on a damaged knee sustained in an automobile accident.

CHAPTER 18

Hollywood, California | 1926

Egan Walsh awoke as daylight filtered through the window blinds of his hospital room the morning following the attack the previous night. A nurse checked his IV and noticed his eyelids fluttering as the sedation wore off. He let out a gasp as pain took hold.

"Mr. Walsh, how bad is the pain?"

"Something bloody awful. How bad am I hurt?"

"The worst is three cracked ribs on your left side. One punctured your lung. Required immediate surgery last night to stabilize the ribs and repair the tissue damage to the lung. You are also passing blood in your urine. Need to keep an eye on that to see if you suffered any kidney or other organ damage.

"Other than that, your body is a mass of deep contusions starting to turn dark purple like your arms. I'm afraid you look an awful sight. The superficial effects and swelling must subside before we can fully assess for any more serious damage to muscles and tendons in the extremities. At least whoever did this did not touch your face. Do you want more pain medication now?"

Just then he noticed Lilly Romano standing behind the nurse. "Not now, nurse. Want to stay awake and talk to the pretty lady."

The nurse smiled. "Of course. Day shift is coming on duty soon and they will check in on you regularly. The doctor will also be in to see you this morning."

"Hospital called you last night?" he said to Lilly as the nurse left.

"Yes. Got here when you were in surgery. They were good enough to allow me to stay. Fell asleep in that chair a couple of hours ago. Nurse even brought me some coffee before you awoke."

She touched his cheek with the back of her hand and broke down in tears. He attempted to lift his arm to touch her hand resting on the railing of the bed, but a sharp pain caused him to instead grunt.

"Don't try to move, Egan. My god what did they do to you? The nurse said your whole body is a mass of bruises just like your arms."

"Worked me over good with their feet and a blackjack, a mean sort of small lead club. Used by muggers and police. Three guys. Did this as a warning to lay off investigating Tara Kelly's death. Got the impression they might have been police dressed in civilian suits. Warned me about attacking the LAPD in the newspapers. Thinking I was unconscious when they left me, one of them addressed another as *Sarge*.

"What happened?" Lilly asked.

"They jumped me after I parked the car around eight-thirty last night. Wanted to take me somewhere in a car. From my times as a fugitive in Ireland, I learned never to be captured by the British. These blokes looked to be the same kind of nasty lot.

"Took the first opportunity to counterattack. Did enough damage to two of the bastards to prevent them taking me to somewhere and doing God knows what."

Resting her hand against his cheek as the only place that did not cause pain, she felt somewhat comforted that he was not more seriously injured. "Besides Sol and Ray, who do you want me to call?"

"Benny. Warn him he might be a target next." He must consider that Lilly might also be targeted if he continued, but that was a matter he would take up with Lilly later. "Vic and Enid. John Ford of course. My pals Tom Mix and Wyatt Earp. You have Mix's number of course. Have Tom call Wyatt."

"Okay. They will all want to see you. You up to it?"

"Sure. The pain is something awful, but the pain killers put me out. I'd rather just use medication when I need to sleep. I want to think clearly."

"You're not going to give this up, are you?"

"Not a chance. This has gone beyond a cover up. I'll give them a war if that's what they want. Confirms a crime was committed. Nobody goes to this extreme over bad publicity. Someone is protecting the man that raped Tara. Somebody with a lot of local influence. I want the sonofabitch that raped and maybe murdered Tara."

"I understand. I'm going downstairs and get some more coffee and something for breakfast then make the calls."

"After that, you need to go home and get some rest, Lilly."

"I'll rest tonight. I want to be here when the doctor comes in. Need to hear what he says. You will need care to recover. You don't look even capable of feeding yourself."

"Thanks, Lilly."

"You've become very special to me. By the way, are all your vital parts still in working order?"

Catching her meaning, he attempted to laugh, but it hurt too much. "They left my balls intact if that's what you mean."

"Well, that is the most important part, but I'm also glad they did not spoil your good looks."

Smiling he said, "Wonderful seeing you when I first woke up, Lilly. Now go get yourself some breakfast."

Sol Wurtzel and Ray Schrock came to the hospital immediately following Lilly's call.
They arrived as Lilly was feeding him breakfast with sips of coffee since he could not raise his arms or even work his hands.

After Walsh provided a brief accounting of the prior night's events, Wurtzel said, "After Lilly called to explain what happened, I called Mr. Fox. He said he fully supports what you are doing. He read the newspaper accounts you published in the

Boston Globe. He is disgusted with the official handling of Tara Kelly's unfortunate death. She was part of our moviemaking family. If her death involved foul play, it must be exposed. Said to tell you to keep at your efforts to get to the truth."

"Thanks, Sol."

"Mr. Fox also said he still wants to produce *Dying for Ireland.* You up to continuing working on the script?"

"Of course. Going to be laid up here for a time. Waiting to hear what the doctor says."

At that moment, the doctor entered the room. "Excuse me gentlemen. I am Dr. Blaine. Operated on Mr. Walsh last night. Need to see how he is doing now that he is awake. Can everyone give us a few minutes?"

Walsh said, "I'm okay with everyone staying, Doctor."

"Very good. The nurse says you are refusing the pain medication. No need to suffer."

"Morphine puts me to sleep. I prefer to remain alert. Besides morphine is habit forming."

"Your choice. Use it for sleep though. You need rest to heal properly. Our immediate concerns are healing of the ribs. The 5th, 6th, and 7th ribs on your left side all suffered fractures. The uppermost rib totally separated and punctured three centimeters into the middle lobe of your left lung. The surgery repaired the damage to the lung we made other repairs to the damaged musculature around the ribs. Since we cannot fully immobilize the ribs like an arm or leg, we must rely on the surrounding soft tissue to stabilize the ribs to heal correctly, therefore the uncomfortable restrictive binding about your chest.

"You are passing blood in the urine. We need to monitor that for a couple of days to assess for kidney damage. The soft tissue of almost every part of your body suffered extensive trauma. That is probably the source of the greatest pain right now. Other than passing blood and the damage to your lung, there are no indications of injury to other organs. All your vital signs are within range."

"How long before I can leave the hospital?"

"Probably a week. Depends on your mobility. By then, the bruising to the musculature should have subsided measurably. The biggest concern is keeping your midsection tightly wrapped to keep the ribs immobilized. I'd say about six weeks before the ribs sufficiently heal. Still going to suffer various degrees of discomfort from the extensive soft tissue trauma. Hell of a beating these thugs inflicted."

"Well, I guess I'll live to fight another day," Walsh said as the doctor left. To Sol he said, "If Ray and Lilly are willing, we can resume work on the script from my hospital room if you can get the hospital staff to agree."

"If you're up to it, that works," Sol said.

"We might even be able to finish in a week's time, Sol. Especially with Lilly's help."

Sol smiled. "Seems like she has found a new calling in screenwriting. The studio will muddle along somehow without Lilly's invaluable management of the front office."

The developing relationship between Lilly Romano and Walsh was not lost on Sol Wurtzel. A good match. Walsh possessed real substance of character. A better fit for the intelligent and complex Lilly falling for him instead of one of those handsome actors she occasionally dated.

Later that morning, Victor and Enid showed up.

Looking at Walsh's exposed arms as he lay slightly propped up in bed, Victor McLaglen recoiled in surprise saying, "Bloody hell! Somebody did a right nasty job of beating the bejesus out of you, boyo."

Enid approached and gasped as she looked at the deep purple coloration on both forearms and upper arms. "Oh my god!"

"Not as bad as it looks, Enid. The broken ribs are far more serious. But I'll live."

Benny Zimmerman arrived a short time later followed by Tom Mix and Wyatt Earp. Walsh felt a surge of emotion with the concern of his newfound circle of friends.

As the room filled with people, a nurse and two male orderlies came in. The nurse parted through the visitors to the bedside. We are relocating you a larger room, Mr. Walsh. Mr. Wurtzel made arrangements with the hospital director. Seems you are a VIP. I can see the need for more space. You're going to the top floor with a nice view of the mountains."

The new room was much larger with several comfortable chairs. The view indeed was special. Once resettled, Walsh launched into repeating the details of the attack.

Victor McLaglen asked, "What happened when you refused to be taken away?"

"I didn't say anything but wasn't about to be taken away. Surprised the guy with the gun. Broke his knee with my foot. Moved on one of the others and broke his nose. The third guy laid into me with a blackjack. Couldn't do much to defend against the blows. Then the guy with the broken nose weighed in. Once on the ground, they kept at me kicking and working me over with the blackjack.

"I believe they were police officers in civilian suits. Warned me about attacking the LAPD in the newspapers. One of them called the fellow with the gun *Sarge*. Warned that the Pasadena reporter was next unless we ceased agitating about the Kelly murder. You need to vigilant, Benny."

Walsh thought about the threat made to Lilly. They knew about her because they obviously had him under surveillance. He must warn her and find a way to protect her.

Elderly Wyatt Earp listened to Walsh's narrative. He moved next to the bedside and placed his large hands on the railing. "I know something about being stuck in a position where criminals controlled local law enforcement. Told you to watch your back. Los Angeles is a mean place. Has a lot in common with Tombstone over forty years ago. Do you have gun, Egan?"

"Yes. My service revolver from the war with the British."

"I read your book so I know that you can use a handgun. You might think about keeping it handy."

"Can't legally carry a sidearm in Los Angeles. It's the twentieth century, Wyatt."

"You can if you have a concealed weapons permit." To make his point, Earp opened his suit jacket to reveal a holstered Colt.

"Why should the LAPD issue me a permit?"

"Probably not the LAPD, but maybe the Los Angeles Sheriff's Department. They have the same authority. You've good reason to carry a weapon for protection. These fellows that did this are professionals. Avoided harming your face to prevent sympathetic photographs from appearing in Mr. Zimmerman's newspaper. The assault issued as a warning. If these were Los Angeles police officers, somebody very powerful is behind this. Keep up your investigation and the violence may not end. I have an acquaintance. A captain in the sheriff's department. What about I bring him up to see you?"

Everyone looked at Earp then Walsh. The death of Tara Kelly had moved to a new level of drama with the threat of continued violence feeling uncomfortably close.

"Sure thing. That might be a good idea, Wyatt."

The gathering broke up with nothing more to say. Everyone was shaken by seeing Walsh incapacitated not by an accident but by a deliberate act of premeditated violence. Everyone except Lilly Romano and Benny Zimmerman left the hospital room promising to visit again.

"Listen, Benny, these thugs also threatened you. Hold off publishing anything further on Tara Kelly until we think this through. We struck a nerve, but we are no closer to getting answers unless someone comes forward with new information. I'm also worried about Lilly's safety."

"I hear you. Egan. However, I'm a journalist. Your beating is news. Christ the LAPD has not even followed up by questioning you. They should be here interviewing you about identifying your assailants. I checked before coming up. The hospital duly reported your admission into the hospital to the LAPD as a criminal assault. The bad guys are expecting to see something in the papers. I'll come short of alleging the assailants as being police officers because we cannot corroborate that. That it ties in with the other compounding circumstances of the Kelly affair however cannot be ignored."

"Okay, Benny. Just be careful not to fan the flames too strongly."

"I'll be constrained. Yet somehow, we need to learn what the attendees at the party know. If the LAPD was not complicit in this cover up, they would already have interviewed everyone at Hollister's house that night as a matter of routine. You and I discussed that at length an hour before those goons beat the shit out of you. Jankowski can apply pressure, maybe even directly on certain actors that attended the party. She has a good reputation and might uncover something."

Walsh responded, "Even if she does, we will never discover the truth by journalistic investigation alone. Unless law enforcement becomes involved, we can only continue to inflame public pressure."

"Nonetheless, I think we should enlist Jankowski's help," Zimmerman said. She adds another resource. Whoever is behind this can't go after every reporter. They targeted you because you obviously are the source behind the published pieces. The bigger the scandal becomes prevents those behind this from repeating something so brazen as what they did to you."

"I agree. Let Jankowski apply pressure but hold off raising more of a stink beyond writing about that happened to me. Don't want you to end up like this.

Walsh looked at Lilly, "The guys that did this not only threatened you Benny but also *my girlfriend* if I didn't back off. Can't risk that. I need to get back on my feet and rethink this before proceeding further."

Lilly came to his side and stroked his cheek. "So, you're admitting that I'm your girl?

"Did you harbor any doubts?"

She kissed him on the lips. "Never. Just like hearing you say it."

Zimmerman said, "You're in Lilly's capable hands, Egan. Get on with your recovery. Brought you some medicine that might help with the pain."

From his jacket pocket he extracted a pint of Irish whiskey and handed it to Lilly. "I'll be in touch."

After Zimmerman left, Walsh said to Lilly. "You need to go home. Get some rest."

Lilly nodded and took his head in both hands and kissed him with passion.

The following day, Lilly returned with Ray Schrock. She went to the bedside, kissed Walsh and asked, "How are you feeling this morning?"

"Got some sleep. Had some breakfast. Could use some more coffee though. Surprisingly, the pain is less intense. Able to raise my legs and arms if I'm careful. Asked the nurse when I could get out of bed. She told me when I feel up to it. Maybe in another day. Wheelchair of course to avoid reinjuring the ribs."

Schrock said, "Sol called me before I left this morning. They signed Colleen Moore for the *Dying for Ireland* role of Brendan Flynn's sister Noreen. Told me to tell you and Lilly he's expecting us to deliver a powerful script. He and Mr. Fox want to get into production as soon as possible. You up to working, Egan?"

"You bet. Can't do much else lying here."

—

The following day Lilly was sitting in front of a typewriter at a round table with scattered papers and a stack of folders. Ray Schrock sat across from Lilly. Walsh felt good enough to be propped up to better interact with Lilly and Schrock. On a chest of drawers sat a coffee urn requisitioned by Lilly from the cafeteria. Script writing required a constant source of hot coffee.

A couple of hours later, Wyatt Earp and a tall lanky police officer came into Walsh's room.

Walsh said, "Good morning, Wyatt. Always good to see you."

"Am I interrupting?"

"God lord no, Mr. Earp," Lilly said. "Egan needs a break. We're writing a movie script. A sequel to *Price of Freedom*. Stars Victor McLaglen again. We're writing a new female part as his character's sister. A tribute to Tara Kelly as the movie opens on her character's funeral."

Earp nodded. "Excellent. Life goes on. This is Captain Timothy O'Keefe of the Los Angeles County Sheriff's Department. A

231

watch commander at the West Hollywood station. I spoke to Tim about your circumstances, Egan."

"I'm Lillian Romano and this is Ray Schrock. And of course, our colleague the wounded Egan Walsh over there."

O'Keefe shook hands then approached Walsh's bed. Walsh raised his right hand as O'Keefe's big hand hesitated as he saw the bruising of Walsh's entire arm. Carefully he took Walsh's hand giving it a slight squeeze.

"Sonofabitch. Excuse my language, mam. Never seen somebody so black and blue. Wyatt said your whole body is a mass of bruising. Broken ribs. Glad they didn't touch your face."

"Whoever ordered this didn't want pictures appearing in the newspapers making the assault newsworthy," Earp said.

O'Keefe said, "Wyatt thought legally carrying a gun for protection was a necessary precaution. From what he told me, I couldn't agree more. This was not a robbery. The threat remains when you get out of here and you continue kicking the anthill. If anyone needs a concealed carry permit it is you, Mr. Walsh. Came prepared to execute the paperwork right here."

O'Keefe reached into a leather portfolio and took out a file folder and a fingerprinting ink pad. Lilly moved next to him and said, "Let me fill this out for Egan. Difficult for him to use his hands."

"Thank you, mam."

Once the three-part carbon application was completed, Lilly held it for Walsh to sign then O'Keefe carefully applied Walsh's thumb print to all the copies then signed and dated the document. He handed Lilly Walsh's copy. "All set, Mr. Walsh. Wyatt said you know firearms, but just the same, remember you are still just a citizen not a peace officer."

"I understand, Captain. I appreciate you and Wyatt taking the time to do this for me."

"Not at all, Mr. Walsh. Glad to help a fellow Irishman and an Irish patriot. Wyatt loaned me your book. Then I saw the movie *Price of Freedom*. Wyatt said you were in those fights during the Irish War of Independence you wrote about."

"Yes, I was. Just as bad as it looked in the movie. War is like that."

"I have family still in Ireland. County Kerry. All republicans there. Thank you for your service to the Irish Republic, Mr. Walsh."

Earp then stood up, "Well, we'll be letting you folks get back to work. Captain O'Keefe offered to buy me lunch before taking me home. Mind my words to watch your back when you get out of here, Egan. Good day Miss Romano and to you Mr. Schrock."

"Well, I'll be damned," Schrock said. "Wyatt Earp. Famous lawman and gunfighter. Still looking pretty good for his age. How old is he Egan?"

"Seventy-eight he says."

"It's his eyes," Lilly said. "Blue like yours Egan. Both of you have intense eyes."

—

Four days later after some long hours, they finished the first draft of the script for *Dying for Ireland* on a Saturday. The next day Sol Wurtzel along with director John Ford, Ray Schrock, Lilly Romano, and Victor McLaglen held a mini celebration in Walsh's hospital room. Champagne and catered brunch. Politically astute, Lilly arranged for the hospital director, Dr. Blaine, and the various attending nurses to join the celebration since they were violating hospital protocols, not to mention Prohibition laws. Blaine also announced that Walsh's progress suggested he could leave the hospital in another two days. He would need outpatient nursing care for therapy and managing his hygiene needs probably for at least a week. The healing of the ribs remained the pacing factor.

Monday morning, he missed Lilly's presence throughout the day as she returned to the office, Restless and bored, he felt recovered enough to move about in a wheelchair if assisted out of the bed by a nurse. The muscles remained sore but improved each day, enough for his arms to slowly propel the wheelchair.

At noon, Benny Zimmerman came into the room and found Walsh eating lunch at the table while sitting in a wheelchair. "Benny, good to see you."

"You're not going to believe what just fell into our laps. Look at this."

Zimmerman handed him a folder with a stack of papers. The top document said it all. The autopsy report of Tara Kelly. Not the autopsy Dr. Sullivan retrieved from the medical examiner files, but the factual autopsy findings Sullivan described verbally to Walsh.

This autopsy summary read: *The cause of death was conclusively cocaine overdose based on tissue toxicology and the absence of any other possible cause. Physical damage to the vagina and associated contusions are consistent with violent sexual assault occurring no more than 2-3 hours prior to death. The cocaine was introduced by both inhalation and ingestion into the gastrointestinal track. There was no indication of intravenous injection. Forensically this meant the victim smoked or inhaled the cocaine directly. Finding cocaine in the gastrointestinal track is unusual since the euphoric effects are delayed by the digestive process as compared to inhalation or intravenous injection which reach the circulatory system more rapidly.*

While the cocaine overdose could have been intentional, the evidence is not consistent with concluding the cocaine ingestion as accidental. Therefore, the postmortem evidence suggests either suicide or the possibility of homicide in association with the closely time related violent sexual assault which from the tissue damage rules out having occurred from consensual intercourse. Signed Dr. Louis C. Richardson MD.

Walsh reread the summary before looking at the other pages. These consisted of typed observational notes, many accompanied by graphic close-up photographs, and a toxicology report.

After several minutes digesting the material, Walsh let out a sigh. "Now we know why the cover up. How did you come by this?"

"Richardson's widow, Edith. She called me first thing this morning. Asked if I was the reporter writing those articles about the death of the actress Tara Kelly. Said she had something I must see. Skeptical of course but I agreed to see her if she wanted to come to the newspaper office. You can imagine my shock when she presented this."

"How'd she come by it?"

"Told me she finally forced herself to go through her husband's belongings. Found this in an envelope inside a shoe box tucked at the back of her husband's closet shelf. Along with the autopsy was this."

Zimmerman handed Walsh a bank deposit account passbook from Great Western Savings & Loan. Inside was a deposit entry for $50,000. Walsh recognized the date as a few days before Richardson died in the hit and run incident. Another entry showed a withdrawal just last Friday for $50,000 closing the account.

"Not their regular bank. She knew nothing about this money. Told me she took the money out because this passbook might become evidence. Seems she has been following my newspaper columns on Kelly's death. From which she knew your name. Read my piece about your assault. When she found this material, she put two and two together. Scared the hell out of her.

"She went on to tell me how much her husband was upset starting the day he performed the autopsy on Tara Kelly."

"The same day Dr. Richardson got that visit from LAPD Assistant Chief Fletcher and what Dr. Sullivan related to me," Walsh said.

"Anyway, she figures this was hush money. Said her husband was a good man, a good doctor. Doubted he would certify to a false autopsy for money. Said she became physically ill after seeing the postmortem photos. Realized her husband's death was maybe not an accident. The same people that did this to the actress possibly killed him. The same people that put you in the hospital."

"Why did she come to you?"

"Scared. She did not dare take this to the police after what I wrote about the LAPD covering up Kelly's death. Scared for her life but wasn't going to let those behind this get away with possibly murdering her husband to cover up another crime. Said the bank deposit book was evidence but the money was hers.

"Edith Richardson is a smart woman. She protects herself by making it my problem while doing the right thing. I told her to keep the money. Put it somewhere safe. The question is what do we do with this?"

"Unfortunately, this only confirms that a crime was committed then intentionally covered up by bribing a public official who is now dead. Doesn't get us any closer to identifying who is behind this. Doesn't even implicate Assistant Chief Fletcher who seems to be the front man in the LAPD's complicity in the conspiracy. As you pointed out, our independent investigative efforts probably will never lead to identifying the perpetrator behind all this. What we do have is sufficient evidence to take to the California Attorney General as you suggested in your column."

Zimmerman said, "Maybe this bank book will lead to whoever is behind this. Always follow the money. Unless they gave Richardson $50,000 in cash which seems unlikely, someone probably opened this bank account in his name and deposited the hush money by a bank-to-bank transfer. If that's the case, there is a paper trail."

Walsh said, "Although this doesn't point to who raped Kelly, it should be enough to force the California Attorney General to instigate an investigation. I'm not a lawyer but this should constitute evidence of possible public corruption and possibly a conspiracy to obstruct justice associated with a violent crime."

"I agree. Yet we must consider the possibility of this conspiracy reaching all the way to Sacramento," Zimmerman said.

Walsh replied, "Well, if it does, we won't give Attorney General Webb any choice."

Zimmerman added, "Webb does have a legacy to protect. Christ, he's been attorney general since 1902 and still going strong. At least the Governor will not interfere. Losing his own party's primary nomination, he's a lame duck with little popular support."

"To hell with politics, legitimate or corrupt, Benny. We give Sacramento no choice by first publishing this authentic autopsy report. Once in the public domain, neither the governor nor the attorney general will be able to avoid the public outcry for justice." Walsh turned to Lilly. "Ready to contribute editorial comment to our drafting of columns in the *Pasadena Star-News* and the *Boston Globe*?"

Romano said, "Absolutely. Whoever raped and murdered Tara will no longer be able to suppress a real investigation. This will make front-page headlines nationwide. Regrettably, it may shake the very foundation of Hollywood."

Chapter 19

Los Angeles, California | Spring 1926

Months earlier after Victor McLaglen and Egan Walsh declined to escort Tara Kelly to the gala Hollywood party in Beverly Hills, she approached the young British actor, Leslie Fenton. She knew Fenton from when he appeared with McLaglen in *What Price Glory*. Fenton jumped at the chance to escort her. Just like Kelly, this presented an opportunity to rub shoulders with the Hollywood elite, including major producers and directors. Hollister's invitation surprised Kelly. Both her and McLaglen undoubtedly were included because of the box office success of *Price of Freedom*.

Arriving in Fenton's modest Ford coup, they parked at the end of a long line of flashier automobiles on that Saturday night in early May. Chadwick Hollister's estate sat on several acres on Benedict Canyon Road in the hills above Beverly Hills. The long driveway snaked through the beautifully landscaped front lawn after passing through the wrought iron gates of the eight-foot block wall surrounding the grounds. The driveway formed a large circle in front of the main entrance to the sixteen-room mansion. Branching off from the circular driveway a segment extended toward the rear of the property to a multi-car garage with a carriage house on a second story. This served as apartments for live-in household staff.

As Kelly and Fenton walked up the drive, standing next to the many parked luxury automobiles uniformed drivers chatted and smoked cigarettes. It was seven-thirty with a brilliant sunset visible to the west over the Pacific Ocean.

A uniformed black butler greeted them at the front door. Inside a maid took Kelly's light coat. She was dressed in a shimmering blue gown purchased especially for this evening. Tight fitting with a slit exposing one leg, the top of the gown exposed her shoulders and neck featuring her prized large gold necklace with matching earrings. Her hair grown long for the filming of *Price of Freedom* now restyled in a trendy bob. As she and Fenton entered the large living room, heads turned.

Looking about the room filled with famous actresses, a confident Tara Kelly knew her beauty was a match for any of them.

The host Chadwick Hollister came up to her immediately. "Welcome, Miss Kelly. You look stunning. Congratulations on your remarkable performance in *Price of Freedom*."

Kelly offered her gloved hand that Hollister took then bent slightly to brush a kiss to the back of her hand.

Kelly said, "This is Leslie Fenton. Good enough to be my escort since Victor McLaglen had a schedule conflict."

Fenton offered his hand which Hollister shook and said, "Yes. You appeared in *What Price Glory*. Correct?"

"Yes. Good of you to remember, Mr. Hollister. I'm just standing in for Mr. McLaglen.

Kelly remarked, "What a grand residence you have, Mr. Hollister."

"Thank you. Let me introduce you around. I am sure you will recognize most of the guests."

Chadwick Hollister was a large man in his early fifties. Thinning hair but still handsome in a distinguished way. He looked like a successful banker.

With Fenton following, Hollister led Kelly on his arm toward a group of four men standing together. They had already spotted Kelly as Hollister brought her closer. "Gentlemen, may I present the lovely Miss Tara Kelly fresh from her success in *Price of*

Freedom, and her escort this evening Leslie Fenton from *What Price Glory*."

These men represented some of Hollywood's most famous producers and directors. "MGM is well represented this evening with Mr. Cecil B. DeMille. Mr. Samuel Goldwyn, and Mr. Irving Thalberg."

DeMille and Goldwyn were in their forties, looking older because of their baldness. In contrast, Thalberg was Kelly's age with the looks of a movie star. The fourth gentleman was the tall austere looking acclaimed director D. W. Griffith, the oldest of the group but strikingly handsome with his patrician Roman nose.

"And this is Mr. D. W. Griffith. One of the most influential figures in creating the American motion picture industry as we know it with his many iconic films."

Hollister motioned to a waiter in white coat balancing a silver tray of glasses of champagne followed by a waitress with a tray of canapés. Both Kelly and Fenton took a glass of champagne ignoring the food until introduced to the other guests. Somewhat awkward shaking hands with both hands occupied. They did not want to draw unwanted attention considering such a celebrity gathering. By comparison, Kelly and Fenton were Hollywood newcomers. This was an opportunity to network and be seen by important people.

The party had been underway for well over an hour when Kelly and Fenton arrived. By now the guests had separated into distinct groups or individual pairings that typically occur at such gatherings. In the formal living room, the queen of Hollywood society Mary Pickford sat on a sofa with her equally famous husband Douglas Fairbanks, the swashbuckling star of popular period-based action films. Seated across from them were Gloria Swanson and her third husband Henry de La Falaise married just the prior year. La Falaise was a French aristocrat and decorated hero of WWI, translator, sometime director, producer, and with exceptional good looks, an occasional actor. Yet he was best known as Swanson's third husband.

This group also included two other celebrated scene actresses. Norma Shearer was the protégé rumored to be the romantic interest of producer Irving Thalberg. Clara Bow, escorted by the ruggedly handsome young Latin actor, Gilbert Roland, represented the sex symbol personification of the Roaring Twenties. The expressive-faced comedic stars Harold Lloyd and Buster Keaton offset the dazzling elegant beauty of the other stars.

Even the host Chadwick Hollister held local celebrity status. Everyone in the business knew his New York investment bank Hollister Financial was the principal source of funding for the motion picture industry. As a prominent Los Angeles figure, Hollister's name appeared frequently in the local press and movie trade magazines.

Hollister introduced Kelly and Fenton around to this impressive body of Hollywood aristocracy, all of which offered congratulations on Kelly's performance in *Price of Freedom*.

Douglas Fairbanks said, "You were a perfect complement to Victor McLaglen. Great job. Word is Fox Films is going to cast you and McLaglen in a sequel. That true?"

"Yes. I believe so. Thank you for complimenting me on my work in *Price of Freedom*. I so love your action movies and your wife's wonderful films."

While possessing movie -quality good looks, twenty-four-year-old British actor Leslie Fenton was little-known. He had few acting credits, mostly in minor roles. Hollister however graciously introduced him as having a supporting part in the acclaimed movie *What Price Glory.*

Hollister then led them to a large room he called the conservatory and library. At one end of the room was a grand piano set into a round turret dominated by large glass windows extending upward two stories. A bass player and a clarinet player stood to either side of a grand piano accompanying the black pianist at the keyboard.

"The young piano player is Earl Hines. Up and coming jazz pianist with his own unique style. Brought him out from Chicago just for the weekend. Heard his recordings on the radio and tracked him down. By the way, if either of you want something stronger than champagne, please just ask a waiter. I have a better bar than any speakeasy."

At the other end of the spacious room lit by two crystal chandeliers was the library portion of the room. The twelve-foot ceiling was lined on three sides by bookshelves with the top shelves assessable by a moveable ladder. The books were all leather-bound with small brass plaques identifying genres, subjects, or authors.

"Over there on that pedestal is my prized possession. It's called the *Ellesmere Chaucer*, or *Ellesmere Manuscript*. Hand-written in the 15th century with exquisite illustrations of Geoffrey Chaucer's *Canterbury Tales*. My good friend railroad magnet Henry Huntington has offered me a small fortune to acquire it for his library and art gallery in Pasadena. Now let me make the last of the introductions to these illustrious movie celebrities."

Seated or gathered among the comfortable leather upholstered reading chairs with side tables, this smaller group was no less famous. Kelly knew the current biggest star of westerns, Tom Mix, because of his friendship with her costar Victor McLaglen. Then recognizable by any woman, the Italian actor Rudolph Valentino. The big screen captured his dark piercing sultry eyes perfectly conveying unquestionable appeal to the opposite sex. That sex appeal and his portrayals in movies set in exotic foreign locations produced consistent box office success. While male moviegoers gravitated more to the masculinity expressed by Douglas Fairbanks, Valentino's suggested seductiveness appealed to females of all ages.

Valentino was five foot-nine in height. Standing next to him was diminutive Charlie Chaplin, five inches shorter. Yet Chaplin was exceptionally handsome. A transformation once he removed his signature toothbrush-shaped mustache and shabby clothing of his beloved *Little Tramp* character portrayed on screen. With curly hair and blue eyes, his reputation as a womanizer attested to his ability to seduce women regardless of his short stature.

The woman occupying Chaplin's attention was the young Swedish star, Greta Garbo. She was seated next to her latest handsome leading man John Gilbert. Gilbert had the great good looks of Valentino with an onscreen presence that also made him a romantic leading man. Garbo was fresh from her recent starring role in the MGM success in *Flesh and the Devil* costarring Gilbert. Louis B. Meyer escorted her to the party this evening even though she and Gilbert had an off-again on-again romantic relationship. Louis Meyer found Garbo's somber facial expression particularly suited to dramatic roles.

Attesting to Kelly's looks and dressed in the figure hugging tight blue evening gown, everyone turned toward her as she approached. Hollister introduced her and Fenton first to Greta Garbo seated next to John Gilbert. "Miss Garbo and Mr. Gilbert of course stared in the recent hit movie *Flesh and the Devil*."

Coming to where Valentino was standing, Hollister said, "Let me introduce Miss Tara Kelly and Leslie Fenton to these two gentlemen that need no introduction.

Kelly exclaimed, "Hardly. Everyone recognizes Mr. Valentino and Mr. Chaplin. Even without your screen mustache, Mr. Chaplin, you are recognizable. I adore the movies of both of you. Honored to be invited by Mr. Hollister to such an exclusive party of so many great actors and actresses."

Chaplin took the initiative by taking Kelly's hand then offering, "I saw *Price of Freedom*, Miss Kelly. You delivered a remarkable performance. I venture we'll be seeing much more of you work."

Not be outdone, Valentino did the same, saying in his Italian accent, "I also saw your movie. For such an elegant, beautiful woman you made a most believable Irish rebel."

Many of the guests were smoking and Kelly asked Fenton for a cigarette. Placing it in a white cigarette holder, Chaplin was quicker than Fenton to offer a light from a gold lighter.

Poor Fenton soon realized he already lost Kelly to the attentions of Chaplin and Valentino. She could not very well refuse the seat offered by Chaplin who took the seat next to her. The sheer elegance of the room with it architectural appeal, with jazz in the background while surrounded by famous glamourous men, made Kelly feel she had professionally arrived.

Not long after sitting down, Hollister returned as he walked among his guests striking his champagne glass with a knife to get everyone's attention. "Instead of a formal dinner, I thought a sumptuous buffet to be a better option. Everyone can roam into the dining room to make a selection from a wide assortment of food or stay seated and resume enjoying the opportunity to relax among your fellow artists. Staff will serve you where you choose. Just signal a waiter who will explain the menu items and he will bring it to you. Small folding tables are available as required."

Hollister treated Kelly with particular attention. "Shall I summon a waiter, Miss Kelly?"

"Yes, thank you. I like the idea of eating right here. Such a wonderful room and I love the music. You have a spectacular home, Mr. Hollister."

Kelly had a waiter bring her a selection of seafood and a salad. Fenton found the opportunity to engage with her as the other celebrities went about getting something to eat. However, Kelly was distracted by the conversations of the three biggest and the most attractive male stars in Hollywood. She picked at her food enough to satisfy her hunger then got into the spirit of the party.

Hailing a waiter, "Would you get me a gimlet please? With crushed ice and easy on the lime juice."

Kelly enjoyed a stiff drink. A gimlet consisted of predominately gin with fresh lime juice and simple syrup suited to the individual's taste. It went down easier than martinis yet with the equivalent alcohol content.

Instead of the waiter returning, Hollister himself presented her with her drink in a cocktail glass. "As you ordered, Miss Kelly."

"Why thank you, Mr. Hollister."

Hollister replied, "Care for a cigarette, Miss Kelly?"

"Yes, I would. Please call me Tara."

Hollister reached into his inside left tuxedo jacket and took out a cigarette case. "I smoke French Gauloises. They're on the strong side. Made from dark Middle East tobaccos. But I see you use a long cigarette holder which will smooth the flavor. A good compliment to someone who enjoys strong liquor."

Kelly took the cigarette and fitted it into her holder with Hollister ready with his lighter. Kelly inhaled the smoke cautiously. The tobacco was strong, but she liked the distinctive flavor. By the time she finished and crushed out the cigarette she felt a wave of euphoria. Slow down on the gimlets she told herself. Important that she make a good impression with this rare opportunity to socialize with Hollywood royalty.

Hollister moved on to mingle with other guests. With Garbo engaging with John Gilbert seated next to her, Charlie Chaplin saw the chance to reengage with Kelly as the other beautiful woman in close proximity.

"Is the sequel planned for *Price of Freedom* going to be just as good?" Chaplin asked.

"I hope so. Same writers. One of them is the novelist who wrote the book. He personally fought against the British in the Irish War of Independence. Oh my! I didn't mean to offend you, Mr. Chaplin since you are British."

"Not at all. I side with the Irish to be free of British rule. A checkered history of British treatment as a colony for hundreds of years. Can I fetch you another drink? I might try one of those gimlets myself."

When Chaplin returned with drinks, Hollister had already moved into his spot and was engaging with Kelly.

"Can I perhaps have another one of your cigarettes, Mr. Hollister? They are very distinctive."

"Why of course. My pleasure," he said presenting his opened cigarette case for her to select another.

"These are wonderful. Where can I get them?"

"I have them shipped from New York from an importing distributor. Not sure if they are generally available in Los Angeles I will send some to your home."

What Kelly was enjoying was not the rich dark tobacco taste but the effects of cocaine. A cocaine user himself, Hollister preferred occasionally lacing his cigarettes rather than inhaling the powder directly into the nostrils.

Hollister smiled at Chaplin and said to Kelly, "Excuse me once again, Miss Kelly. As the host, obligations once again call me away."

As Hollister walked away, Chaplin moved in, giving Kelly her drink and sipping at his own gimlet. Having been thoroughly ignored, Fenton finally had enough. Standing in the background, he came over to Kelly. "Can I see you for a moment, Tara?"

Looking at him annoyed, she nodded. Turning to Chaplin, "Please excuse me a for a moment, Mr. Chaplin. I'll be right back."

Walking with Fenton to the other end of the room, Kelly stopped him by placing her hand on his arm. "What is it, Leslie? That is rude pulling me away like that."

"Rude? It is you who are being rude. I was good enough to escort you here tonight then you abandon me to cozy up to Chaplin and Valentino. The new darling of Hollywood."

With the music disguising their voices, Kelly responded angrily. "Christ, Leslie, you sound jealous. It's not like we are dating. I can't help it if men find me attractive."

"Especially in that tight blue dress cut down the front to the waist."

"Listen, Leslie. I don't want to hurt you, but tonight is important to me. Besides, I'm having a fun time. If you want to leave, go ahead. I'll take a taxi home."

Fenton said angrily, "Fine by me."

He was so pissed off that he left without even saying anything to the host. The episode was not lost on either Chaplin or Hollister. Both observed the obviously disagreeable exchange between Kelly and Fenton from a distance. As Kelly returned to her seat next to Chaplin, she said, "I can't believe I'm sitting here talking with the most recognizable movie actor, the great Charlie Chaplin."

"You make me sound ancient," Chaplin said with a big grin.

"Oh no. It's all about your beloved character, the *Tramp* that you created. An iconic masterpiece of acting. A perfect mix of comedy with pathos. Your success with *The Gold Rush* last year shows your popularity is greater than ever. Are you planning another movie featuring the *Tramp*?"

"But of course. I love the character as much as my fans. Working on some new ideas."

Chaplin was a masterful seducer of women. Preferably younger woman. Although Kelly was twenty-eight, still young enough and certainly pretty enough. Chaplin compensated for his

246

short stature by being famous, handsome, smart, witty, and making a woman feel his genuine interest in the moment.

While Kelly may have sensed Chaplin's motives, she could not help reveling in the attention. Part of that was a cocaine induced euphoria that reduced inhibitions and counteracted the effects of probably too much alcohol. She knew she also caught the eye of Rudolph Valentino who Chaplin deftly outmaneuvered. Although not mingling as much as she wanted for professional reasons, Kelly enjoyed being the subject in this male competition.

Hollister surprised her by laying a hand on her shoulder. "I am going to go out in the back garden for a breath of air. A perfect night for a stroll. Care to join me?"

Preferring to stay put but coming from the host, she could not politely refuse. Although older, Hollister was also obviously competing in the seduction game. Once outside he offered her another cigarette. Walking together in the garden, she looked back on the mansion illuminated by lights and suddenly began to feel inexplicably strange. By now she had ingested a considerable amount of cocaine.

Not realizing how this might be affecting someone new to the drug, Hollister lit her another doctored cigarette. As they walked back toward the house, a wave of anxiety suddenly overcame Kelly. Feeling nauseous, she wondered if it was the alcohol or maybe the rich seafood. She just wanted to lie down.

Hollister noted she was breathing heavily and walking a little unsteadily. "Are you feeling alright, Tara?"

"Just feeling a bit odd. Need to sit down. Maybe somewhere away from the other guests. I feel a little embarrassed. Maybe too much alcohol."

"Perfectly understandable, Tara. I'll take you to one of the guest bedrooms. Rest for a while then come down after it passes."

Hollister had to help her navigate up the stairs. He showed her into a bedroom. "Just lay there. Prop yourself up. I'll turn off the lights except for this reading lamp by the chair in the corner. Take your time. I'll check back in a while and see how you're doing."

Once Hollister left, Kelly became concerned. She'd had too much to drink on enough occasions to realize this was different. Her heart was pounding. Finding it difficult to focus, she felt faint, wanting to just lie back and go to sleep. At least she was not making a scene and ruining Hollister's party.

———

Hollister returned to his guests. Noting Charlie Chaplin's interest in Kelly, he pulled him aside. "I took Miss Kelly for some air in the garden. She looked like she was not feeling well. Probably too much alcohol. She asked if there was somewhere to lie down, so I let her use one of the guest bedrooms. Embarrassed for the other guests to see her not her usual vibrant self. If anyone asks, maybe cover for her. I'm sure she will appreciate your discretion."

"Of course, Chadwick. Young women don't know how to hold their liquor."

"But we can't do without them can we, Charlie?"

Chaplin just smiled. Was Hollister being a smartass directing that comment to him?

Only fifteen minutes after leaving Kelly, he returned and opened the bedroom door quietly. Kelly was lying on her side with her knees drawn up into a fetal position. She was breathing deeply, appearing to be asleep.

Laying a hand on her shoulder Hollister said, "Tara. Are you okay?"

She groaned but her eyes remained closed as she rolled over further burying herself face in the pillow. Her gown revealed her bare back down to the waist. He touched her skin which felt hot. Having also ingested cocaine, his thinking was not fully rational. With the heightened sexual arousal effects induced by the cocaine, he cast off normal caution. Then again, Chadwick Hollister did not observe limits that constrained most people.

He pulled the grown off her shoulders. Having gone this far, there was no turning back. Turning Kelly onto her back, she remained unconscious. Removing the blue gown still did not wake her. Nor the removal of her undergarments.

Hollister abandoned all restraint as he looked at Tara Kelly fully naked.

———

Twenty minutes later, Hollister sat in the armchair in the bedroom. The effects of cocaine diminishing with the surge of adrenalin from what just transpired. Now becoming fully aware of his irrational sexual attack on Kelly, his immediate thoughts turned to self-preservation. Breathing rapidly from an overwhelming sense of fear, he forced himself to calm down as the enormity of what he just did took hold.

He got up and went to Kelly laying there. He was not sure if she was breathing even after laying his hand between her breasts. Touching her neck to feel for a pulse also proved inconclusive in his agitated state. He could only feel the pounding of his own heartbeat.

Composing himself, it took several minutes to fix his tuxedo back to a presentable state. He must get to Kurt Gerhardt immediately while acting completely normal to his guests, prepared with some explanation for his absence from the party.

Gerhardt was his fixer for circumstances arising from Chadwick Hollister's darker inclinations. Whatever it cost, Gerhardt must find a way to fix what just happened.

Chapter 20

Los Angeles, California | Spring 1926

Shaken and thinking of only how to escape the consequences of his lapse of giving way to his impulsive sexual instincts, Chadwick Hollister willed himself to appear the gracious host.

Throughout his life of privilege, he observed few boundaries. While successfully managing his use of cocaine, sex was another matter. Even during his teenage years growing up in New York he engaged in risky behavior. Father's money covered up problematic situations and shielded his deviant exploits from his mother. Yet there was nothing in his troubled history comparable to this.

Hollister looked around for Chaplin. He would be the first person to inquire about the absence of Tara Kelly. If anything, Hollister was a survivor of overcoming the consequences of his base instincts. He was smart, ruthless, and clever when it came to serving his purpose. Using Chaplin as the means for subtly explaining Kelly's absence should anyone ask about her allowed him to focus on fixing the problem.

"Charlie, got a moment?" Hollister asked as he guided Chaplin to a quiet area out of earshot.

"Checked on Kelly a short time ago. Not just sleeping but passed out. Couldn't even wake her. Might be hours before she wakes up. Going to give it an hour then have my driver Gerhardt drive her home. Don't want her waking up here in the morning hungover. If anyone asks about her absence, please explain."

The more people Chaplin told, the better for the cover story forming in Hollister's mind.

Hollister located Kurt Gerhardt eating in the kitchen as the catering staff were cleaning up the food and preparing to serve dessert. He motioned with his head for Gerhardt to come with him.

"We have a problem, Kurt. Upstairs in one of the guest bedrooms."

"What kind of problem, Sir?"

"A serious problem. Let me show you."

Entering the bedroom, Hollister switched on the ceiling light illuminating the room. Gerhardt looked at the nude body of Tara Kelly lying on her back in the bed.

Gerhardt went to the bedside and reached down touching Kelly's neck. In so doing he saw deep red marks on her neck. There was a weak pulse. Surveying the body, he saw blood staining the bed between Kelly's thighs. Gerhardt knew what happened.

Gerhardt shook Kelly then slapped her cheeks. No response.

"Too much alcohol?" Gerhardt asked.

"Probably, but also cocaine," Hollister said.

"Cocaine? You gave her cocaine?" Gerhardt knew Hollister used cocaine because he procured it for him.

"How much?"

"Hard to say. She had maybe four of my laced cigarettes."

Gerhardt knew that Hollister preferred ingesting cocaine in his cigarettes. Hollister understood his limits, but Kelly may not have known she was smoking cocaine. No way to tell how much she ingested. Hollister probably did not measure the amount of cocaine he introduced into each cigarette.

"Do you have smelling salts in the house?" he asked Hollister.

"Maybe. There is a first aid kit in the kitchen."

"Go check. Need to see if we can revive her."

Hollister hurried downstairs.

Gerhardt knew what happened. Hollister raped Kelly. Probably so high on cocaine she barely understood what was happen-

251

ing. May already be beyond medical help. In her condition, calling for an ambulance does not become an option for Hollister. Gerhardt knows what must be done.

Hollister returned handing Gerhardt the smelling salts. Smelling salts release ammonia gas irritating the membranes of the nose and lungs causing the muscles that control breathing to react and revive a fainting victim.

Gerhardt wrapped Kelly in the bedding to avoid panic if she revived and found herself naked. He then broke the seal on the vial of smelling salts and held it under Kelly's nose. Her head involuntarily thrashed about trying to avoid the pungent ammonia smell but failing to restore her to a fully conscious state.

"I believe she might be suffering a lethal overdose of cocaine. Maybe contributed by alcohol. You can't call an ambulance without being charged with a serious crime, Sir."

Hollister shook his head unable to contemplate such a fate. "Can't you just get her out of here? Take her home? Put her in her own bed?"

"What if she does not die?" Gerhardt replied.

Hollister understood what Gerhardt was implying. "Then it's better if she is dead?"

Gerhardt just looked at Hollister. After several moments, Gerhardt said, "Get me some cocaine. I'll get some fruit juice from the kitchen.

When Gerhardt returned, he found Hollister seated in the reading chair in the bedroom holding his head with his elbows supported on each thigh. Without saying anything, he looked up and handed Gerhardt a packet of cocaine. Exhaustion began setting in as he came down from his cocaine high coupled with the rush of adrenaline dissipating. He had never done something this reckless.

Gerhardt brought a glass of orange juice and a spoon from the kitchen. He unfolded the wax paper packet of cocaine then dumped the contents into the orange juice. The amount of cocaine appeared to be several ounces. A lethal dosage for even an addict with a high tolerance. Stirring the mixture, he said, "She may die from an overdose from the quantity she already ingested. We can't rely on that. Better if she is dead than alive to tell what happened. This makes sure she does not recover."

"What do we need to do?" Hollister was sweating and breathing deeply trying to overcome his anxiety.

"Just help me. I'll explain later why this is your best chance for getting out of this. Get that other vial of smelling salts. I'll sit her up and hold her while you try to revive her. Then you try to get her to swallow as much of the orange juice as possible. Do it slowly in small amounts to let her swallow repeatedly."

Hollister hesitated.

Gerhardt said, "Do it, Sir. You have no choice. I can't do this alone. I'll then get you out of this mess."

Hollister responded as Gerhardt raised Kelly fully upright so as not to choke on the orange juice. He broke the vial waving it under her nose while turning his head away from the pungent ammonia fumes.

Kelly again moved her head about and took several deep breaths once Hollister removed the smelling salts. Hollister carefully put the glass to her lips then eased a measured among of orange juice into her mouth. Although still not fully conscious, Kelly responded as Hollister allowed her to swallow before introducing more orange juice. After several repetitions Kelly became nonresponsive to his further attempts to open her mouth.

"That's enough," Gerhardt said as he laid Kelly back down.

"Now what?"

"We wait until we're sure she is dead."

With Hollister looking as though he might collapse, Gerhardt led him back to the armchair. "You need to go back to your guests. Put some cold water on your face. Take a shot of whiskey. You must appear normal. In no hurry for anyone to leave. To anyone asking, Kelly is awake but repeatedly throwing up. You gave her something to settle her stomach, but we all know that only a good night's sleep will make you feel better after too much to drink.

"I will stay up here and make sure things go according to plan. Then I will come down and tell Matty and Angela to call it a night and take tomorrow off since we arranged for a cleaning service to come in and clean up from the party. Give it your best performance, Sir. There's a lot at stake. Once everyone is gone, I'll tell you what comes next."

Hollister did his best to put on the proper face of a concerned host managing an awkward situation. Although late, several guests remained. Many of the Hollywood crowd partied hard.

Gerhardt fixed the covers over Kelly as if she was sleeping should anyone become inquisitive. He then sat down to think through the next steps to cover up this disaster.

After twenty minutes he checked on Kelly. Convinced there was no pulse, he left the bedroom, closing the door and went downstairs. Hollister was seated talking to several studio executives that remained. Catching his eye, Gerhardt just nodded and went off to the kitchen.

"Call it a night, ladies. Mr. Hollister said for both of you to take tomorrow off. We have a cleaning service coming to do a thorough cleanup from tonight's party."

Once the cook and housekeeper retired to their quarters over the garage, Gerhardt made a pot of coffee. A long night ahead of him. Fix this mess and Hollister would richly compensate him. No longer just a hired hand. He'd come a long way from the small money he made as a dirty Los Angeles cop.

After the last guest left, an exhausted Chadwick Hollister walked into the kitchen and sat down at the small table with Gerhardt.

"Now what?"

"I remove the body. Drive it to her house. I have her address and housekey from her purse. I dress her in a nightgown and tuck her into bed. On a nightstand I will set a glass of water or soda. Mix in some cocaine. Leave the remaining quantity in the packet next to the glass so even a dumb cop will put two and two together as the scene of a suicide. I'll wipe off any of my fingerprints and leave her house locking the door behind me using her house key. I'll assume she has another spare key inside somewhere. No forced entry. Whoever did this is someone she knows.

"After I leave, gather up the bedding and tell the cleaning people tomorrow to dispose of it. Tell them a guest spilled wine then vomited. Get rid of the woman's clothing by concealing it a trash bid someplace far from the house."

Hollister sighed heavily. "Won't it become evident she was sexually assaulted?"

"No doubt about that. There will be an autopsy. Can't cover that up. There was blood on the bedding. You're a big man. Looks like you were a bit rough. Bruising will begin showing on her arms and elsewhere."

"Then how do we play that?"

"The police will find out about her attending this party. They'll want to interview everyone in the house."

Hollister turned pale at the magnitude of the scandal. Even if he escaped criminal responsibility, it would ruin everything he built since coming to Los Angeles. Interviewing of famous movie stars and studio executives by police will create a press feeding frenzy unequalled by any prior Hollywood scandal. Sex, drugs, and murder. Continuing police investigations will turn this into a never-ending story. Unresolved it will go on indefinitely with speculation only adding to the mystery.

"You have only one opportunity to contain this, Boss. Get to Assistant Chief Fletcher immediately after someone discovers Kelly dead in her own bed. All the better if that discovery takes a couple of days to complicate the autopsy results regarding the time of death. It will cost you, but Fletcher is your only option. He can control the scope of the investigation. Tell him there is no reason to suspect the assailant was someone from attending the party. There will be no evidence that it did not happen elsewhere, including her own house. If necessary, we can see that Fletcher is steered toward other possible suspects."

Gerhardt knew Assistant Chief James Fletcher was Hollister's highest-ranking source in the LAPD. Hollister paid Fletcher a substantial monthly retainer hidden in the form of rent payments collected by Hollister Financial's real estate management firm. Hollister used the firm as a means for laundering illegal money transactions such as bribes.

Gerhardt looked at Hollister saying nothing. However, Hollister seemed to be processing what Gerhardt was saying. "If you spread enough money about, it might even be possible for Fletcher to conceal the fact that Kelly was raped. Keep it simply that she died of a cocaine overdose which will be the cause of death concluded by the autopsy. He needs only to arrange for sanitizing the autopsy to remove any reference to other damage found on the body."

"How can Fletcher cover up the … sexual angle?"

With a tone of exasperation, "Payoff the pathologist with a lot of money. Backed it up by the threat of losing his position. Powerful interests want that detail hushed up. Let Fletcher figure that out. That's what you pay him to do."

Hollister nodded with an expression that he understood. "How will we know when her body is discovered?"

"I'll return here and report how things went. Let anybody still here see me. After a couple of hours, I'll drive back and set up a stakeout close enough to watch her place until someone enters her house and calls the police.

"I'll remain in the neighborhood until that happens. Might be days. I'll need to periodically leave for an hour or so to use a toilet and get something to eat. But I'll know in enough time to call you to get in touch immediately with Fletcher once the police arrive at her house. You must convince Fletcher to take charge of the investigation before it spreads out and includes more than just the responding police officers. He needs to control all public communications. Be prepared with a story you tell him."

"What if this doesn't work? If Fletcher refuses to cooperate or is unable to hide the sexual stuff?"

"Then you are still in a better position than having a young woman dead from a drug overdose found in a bedroom in your house after being raped. Getting her back into her own house puts you at enough distance. Makes setting this up to appear as a suicide more plausible without directly pointing to you. Besides, there are a lot of famous Hollywood celebrities that might come under suspicion to muddy the possibilities of suspects further. Somebody maybe followed her home."

———

Hollister and Gerhardt returned to the bedroom. Finding a blanket in the closet, Gerhardt spread it on the floor. Turning to Hollister, "Help me lift her onto the blanket. Take her feet."

As Gerhardt took her weight by lifting Kelly's body from under her arms, Hollister grabbed each ankle. Once situated to one edge of the blanket, Gerhardt said, "Now help me roll her in the blanket. Then we carry her downstairs and put her in the backseat of my car."

Although Kelly probably weighed no more than 115 pounds, navigating the stairs was still awkward with the body wrapped in the blanket and difficult to get a firm hold.

Setting the body down, Gerhardt left to open the rear door of his Ford sedan parked in the driveway. No lights appeared in the household staff apartments above the garage. Returning to the main house, he switched off all interior and external lights. Under cover of darkness, they secured the body in the back seat, then returned to the main house.

Once inside, Gerhardt said, "I will call you here at the house once I observe anyone entering Kelly's house. Stay close to the phone. Might take a day or two. Prepare what you are going to say to Fletcher. Your best tactic is to imply that someone famous may have sexually molested a young actress at your party Saturday night.

"Say something like, *I had my bodyguard Gerhardt drive the actress home and watch over the house to make sure this famous person did not return since he left the party drunk. The actress appeared under the influence of drugs or too much alcohol. She was distraught. I was concerned that this might blow up into something serious. Gerhardt reported LAPD officers arriving at her house and called me. Something very serious obviously happened.*"

Gerhardt put coffee into a thermos. Took a bottle of brandy from the bar and bagged a couple of apples. A long night ahead of him and no telling how long before someone discovered the body.

Hollister was nearing collapse from exhaustion. Separating the bloodstained sheet, he stripped the remaining bedding,

257

throwing it on the floor for laundering by the cleaning people. The bloodstained sheet needed disposal far from the house. As for the blue dress and Kelly's undergarments, he is uncertain. Holding it in his hands he could smell Kelly's perfume. The scent brought forth mixed emotions as he replayed what happened. Explain this irrational excess of lust on the effects of cocaine. He was not out of the woods yet by any means. Put his mind to managing the problem of avoiding the consequences. Perhaps curtail smoking cocaine?

—

It was not until the following Wednesday when Gerhardt called Hollister early in the morning. Gerhardt had maintained surveillance on Kelly's house since Sunday morning.

"It just happened. A woman just arrived. Opened Kelly's front door with a key. Looks like maybe her housekeeper. I'm parked close by. Once I see cops arriving, I'll call again. Then you make that call to Fletcher."

"Got it. I appreciate what you're doing, Kurt. You will be paid handsomely."

Hollister went downstairs in his bathrobe. He needed coffee before calling Fletcher.

"Good morning, ladies." Matty and Angela were already in the kitchen. "Didn't Kurt tell you to take the day off? The cleaning service is coming today to clean up from last night's party."

"Yes, Sir. Thank you." Matty the cook, said, "We just wanted to make sure the caterers didn't rearrange the kitchen. Can we get you anything?"

"Thank you. Just make me a pot of coffee then go have a nice day."

With coffee in hand, the telephone rang twenty minutes later. Before he could say hello, Gerhardt said, "Two LAPD police cars just arrived. Call Fletcher."

Calling Fletcher at home at this hour might catch him before he left for headquarters.

"Fletcher residence," a maid answered.

Telling the woman his name and saying it was urgent, Fletcher came on the line within moments. "Mr. Hollister. Is everything alright?"

"No. In fact I have something of an emergency. More like a fucking disaster that I need your help in containing. Last night I hosted a party. The guests included many of Hollywood's biggest movie actors and top studio executives. Too much booze and people letting their hair down. Anyway, a couple of these actors got into a competition over who could bed a beautiful young actress attending the party. The actress enjoyed the attention, becoming flirtatious. She was probably a little drunk and I think she might have been high on drugs by her behavior."

Anxious for Hollister to get to the point of what he called a disaster, Fletcher said, "What happened?"

"Hard to say. One of my staff took me aside and said I must come upstairs. Said there is a naked woman lying in a guest bedroom sobbing saying someone raped her."

I rushed upstairs and confirmed what the housekeeper reported. "I believe one of these actors might have molested the actress, or maybe things just got out of hand."

"Who are these actors?"

"I'd rather not say, Chief. I don't know if it was even one of them. Could be someone else at the party."

"Okay, then what's the woman's name?"

"Tara Kelly. The female lead in the recent movie *Price of Freedom*."

"What happened after you found her in the bedroom?"

"She was inconsolable, kept crying and started acting erratic. Wouldn't even cover herself. It was then I thought her problem was probably drugs more than alcohol. Had my housekeeper stay with her to try to calm her down."

"Did she come to the party with anyone?"

"Yes. Another male actor. He left the party earlier without her. Someone commented that it was because she was paying too much attention to these big-name actors that were all over her."

"And he left before this incident upstairs?"

"Yes."

"What is it you want me to do?"

"Here's the troubling part. My housekeeper eventually came down and said the young woman fell asleep in the bedroom. Sometime later I went to check on her. She seemed sound asleep. I tried waking her, but she just murmured and fell back asleep. Like someone passed out. Wanting to save her from embarrassment, I arranged for my bodyguard Kurt Gerhardt to drive her home.

"With assistance, my housekeeper aroused her with smelling salts then helped her get dressed. Although unsteady, they guided her out a back door to where Gerhardt's car was parked in the upper driveway, so no one observed her leaving."

Exasperated, Fletcher said, "You still have not said what you want me to do."

"Sorry, but it was necessary to explain the background. Anyway, I was worried that Kelly might be upset enough to make trouble. Start telling people she was raped by whoever might have had sex with her. Could become another Roscoe Arbuckle scandal. I told Gerhardt to stay and keep watch on her house until the following day. Did she leave or did anyone come to her house?

"Gerhardt kept watch all the next day. That was Sunday. She didn't leave nor did anyone enter the house. I tried calling her repeatedly but got no answer. Repeated this Monday and yesterday. Sent Gerhardt back to her house early this morning to knock on her door. He just called. Said the LAPD just arrived.

"If the police are there then something bad must have happened. I need you to take personal charge of whatever this is and contain the fallout as much as possible. Call me back when know what the hell is going on, Chief."

"Stay by your phone. You'll hear from me soon," Fletcher said and disconnected the call.

An hour later Fletcher called. "As bad as it gets, Mr. Hollister. Tara Kelly is dead."

"Oh no! My god. How?"

"The supervising officer at the scene says most likely a cocaine overdose. They found a quantity of cocaine by her bedside. Might be accidental or even suicide. The victim was dressed in a nightgown. Dead for some time. Maybe days. Rigor mortis well advanced. However, I'm told they observed bruising on her neck and upper arms. Maybe indicative of sexual assault."

"What happens next?"

"They are processing the scene right now then the body will be taken to the county morgue. The county medical examiner's office will perform an autopsy. He'll determine the cause of death and comment on any evidence suggesting a crime."

"If the cause of death is determined as cocaine overdose, can you keep a lid on the other salacious details about sexual assault? That will just inflame the tone of the newspaper coverage. Drug use is a known problem in Hollywood."

"I can't control what the medical examiner pathologist will determine. They're not part of the Los Angeles Police Department "

"I understand, Chief. Let me be very crass about this situation. This is a terrible tragedy losing this young actress. However, there are larger financial consequences for the movie industry with a scandal of this magnitude at this time. Image not only an upcoming actress dying from a drug overdose, but raped possibly by someone famous? It could literally tear apart the movie industry. I'm offering you $50,000 if you can officially contain Tara Kelly's cause of death as nothing more than an *accidental* cocaine overdose."

Fletcher paused for a moment considering what Hollister just offered. He also knew the sonofabitch knew far more than he was saying. He knew exactly who raped the victim. Regardless, he was offering a staggering amount of money. Hollister's bribery was also well concealed by complex transactions under the control of his bank. The $50,000 bribe therefore held little risk of discovery for Fletcher.

"I will do what I can, but if the pathologist concludes there was a sexual assault, I will need some very compelling leverage for him to omit any reference to sexual assault."

"Listen, Chief. You now understand the importance of this. A lot of money is riding on making a satisfactory outcome to an otherwise disastrous problem. Offer the pathologist whatever it takes to persuade him to cooperate. If that is not enough, suggest that

261

his job might be in jeopardy unless he delivers a sanitized autopsy report."

"I will keep you advised as to my progress, Mr. Hollister."

CHAPTER 21

Los Angeles, California | 1926

Discovery of the original autopsy report and hush-money pay-off concluded that Tara Kelly was sexually assaulted prior to her death. It also provided documented evidence of a conspiracy to cover up the matter, implicating the Los Angeles Police Department as complicit in the conspiracy for egregious failure to perform even basic investigative requirements.

For Egan Walsh and Benny Zimmerman, it was time to go public. No longer just publishing circumstantial evidence of a cover up, but now irrefutable evidence that Tara Kelly was the victim of a serious crime. Raped and possibly murdered. With no evidence of using drugs prior to attending the Hollister party, her death by cocaine overdose likely became murder staged to appear as suicide.

Instantly this would elevate to the latest Hollywood scandal. The evidence would leave the California Attorney General no choice but to open an investigation. One that would investigate Tara Kelly as a victim of a violent crime, and a criminal conspiracy involving members of the LAPD and unknown others to protect the perpetrator. Assistant Chief James R. Fletcher's active involvement with the case would come under intense independent scrutiny. This might also force high-profile law and order-crusading LAPD Chief of Police James Davis to act on police corruption.

Once the story breaks in the newspapers, it should generate a public outcry for those Hollywood celebrities attending the Hollister party to come forward and tell what they know. To preserve their reputations, there will be no cover hiding behind lawyers or studio spokespersons. Walsh also wondered if at some point this might prompt investigation into the questionable death of Dr. Richardson. Perhaps it might even encourage Dr. Sullivan to come forward with what transpired after Kelly's body arrived at the county morgue.

An energized Egan Walsh said, "We need to get on this immediately. Starting tomorrow. I've had enough of being couped up in this hospital. The doctor spoke of releasing me tomorrow. I'll make sure that happens first thing in the morning. Can you come and pick me up, Lilly?"

"Absolutely. It will do you good to start moving about. You up to that?"

"I think so. Even though I still hurt all over, it's about the ribs. Still need a couple of weeks to make sure those fractures heal. When I move wrong, I'm sharply reminded by the surrounding muscles which take longer to mend. Comforting to know those two cops I damaged are also going through painful recovery."

———

Lilly arrived at the hospital early that morning. Walking was easy enough but getting into her car took some maneuvering. Even with the stiff binding of his midsection, any twisting of his upper body brought stabs of pain.

After stopping at the hotel, Walsh waited in the car. Lilly explained to the hotel manager that Mr. Walsh was recovering nicely from his automobile accident, the reason she communicated to him after the incident. "Just released this morning from the hospital. I'm going to look after him for a few days at my house until he recovers. Need to pick up some clothing and shave things. Please keep his room. He'll be returning." Given their developing relationship that may not be necessary, but she did not want to be presumptuous.

"Of course, Miss Romano. When you are ready, just ring the desk and I'll send a bellboy to assist you. Most distressing news when you telephoned a week ago. Please extend the hotel's wishes to Mr. Walsh for his speedy recovery."

Back in the car, Walsh said, got everything?"

"Everything in the room. Clothing, shoes, toiletries, type-writer. You do travel light."

In anticipation of his release Lilly took the liberty of purchasing a new outfit of trousers, belt, shirt, socks, shoes, and underwear. Buying men's clothing was a new experience. Egan Walsh was a welcomed new experience.

He smiled at her and touched her cheek. "You're a wonder, Lilly. My gun and shoulder holster?"

"In the suitcase. Are you really going to carry it?"

"For certain. What we're about to publish will kickover a hornets' nest. No longer about the bad guys trying to silence my investigations. Yet whoever is behind this might go over the edge. Perhaps irrational or vindictive enough to come after me as the source of his current predicament which just became worse."

Arriving at her house and once out of the car standing upright, he navigated the few steps up the inclined sidewalk to the front door with a little difficulty. Once inside a feeling of wellbeing overtook him. Gratified for having escaped permanent injury and the comfort of being under Lilly's care.

After she carried in his suitcase and typewriter, she said, "Sol gave me the day off to get you settled. Tomorrow I must get back to the office and get things organized. Sol says he cannot do without me. He's right about that. I'm the engine that keeps the ship afloat. But today I will devote to taking care of you."

She guided him into the kitchen. "I'll put some coffee on. How about some breakfast?"

"Sounds wonderful."

After enjoying eggs, bacon, and toast he remarked, "Feel like a new man after surviving on hospital food."

"How about a decent shower? Sponge baths in your bed can't be satisfactory. I think you're in need of a good scrub and shampooing your hair. Are your ribs up to standing in the tub?"

"I think so. A shower will do me good."

Lilly gave him a long kiss then said, "Let's get to it then."

She led him to the bedroom, sitting him on the bed. While he began removing his shirt, she removed his shoes and socks. He was moving well enough to stand up and unbuckle his belt and drop his pants to the floor."

Lilly then began to unwrap the tight bandage from his midsection. "I'll go run the water to get it hot."

He walked into the bathroom and Lilly turned. "All set." Pulling down his underwear, she surveyed his naked body. Large areas of dark purple bruises now turning yellow still remained. The sutured long red scar from the surgery to repair the ribs made her shudder. "Hold on to my shoulder as you step inside the tub."

He stepped on the footstool while holding her shoulder, then carefully stepped into the bathtub. The movement caused him to wince from a spasm of pain.

Standing on the footstool, she began shampooing his hair. After rinsing his hair, he reached for a long-handled bath brush.

"No need for that. You just stand there. I'll wash you. You go moving around and you risk opening the stitches."

With a soaped washcloth she began gently bathing him. Cautious with applying too much pressure on the worst of the bruised areas.

She left his genital area for the last. Washing him there would likely arouse him. That was her intention. She laid the washcloth on the edge of the tub and soaped her hands. As she touched him, she could immediately feel his erection growing.

"When the nurses washed you, did they arouse you like this?"

Quickly becoming fully erect, he made a sound of pleasure before answering, "Never. They didn't look like you."

She stopped what she was doing with her hands for a moment and reached for a towel.

"You could just keep that up," he said expressing disappointment by her stopping.

"Oh, I intend to. I'm first going to get into the shower with you. Thought that might arouse you further."

She removed her clothing as he watched. Joining him in the shower she picked up the washcloth and began washing her arms and legs. He began soaping his hands and washing her breasts, quickly moving down her belly then between her legs.

After rinsing off and turning off the water, she began toweling him off.

"You up to lovemaking?"

Thoroughly aroused, he wondered if he could manage that with his ribs. "I want you as you can see. I'll just have to be careful."

After helping him from the bathtub, they stood and kissed, stroking each other's bodies for several moments before walking into the bedroom.

Lilly pulled back the bedspread and sat him gently on the edge of the bed. Grabbing a pillow, she placed it on the floor. Holding his erect cock in her hand, she looked up into his eyes with a smile before bending down and taking him into her mouth.

After several minutes of pleasuring him, she stood up. "Now that I got you good and aroused, I want you to lay back." As he struggled situating himself on the bed in anticipation, she said, "Let me help you."

She lifted his legs onto the bed. "Slide over toward the center of the bed. I need a little room. Just lay back and relax. Don't move. Let me do everything."

With that she climbed onto the bed. Positioning herself on her knees, she threw one leg over to straddle him. Guided his erection inside of her caused a gasp of pleasure from each of them.

As she increased the pace of her hip movements, she said in a throaty voice, "I like being on top in control," just before they each climaxed.

Although it was October, in Southern California that was still summer. A warm breeze from the open window wafted over them as they lay on the bed basking in postcoital contentment. Propping up on one elbow Lilly looked into his eyes, "You're the one, Egan."

"The one?"

"Yes. I never felt this way about a man before. Guess that means I'm in love with you."

He looked at her with a serious expression. "I am in love with you, Lilly. We're right for each other."

———

For the next two days, Benny Zimmerman worked with Walsh during the day at Lilly's house. In the evening, Lilly made dinner then provided editing changes to the material for publication in their respective newspapers. They simultaneously prepared the package to be sent to the State of California Attorney General, Ulysses Sigel Webb. It documented every detail of what they learned in their independent investigations. Information about the Beverly Hills party that Saturday night that fit within the time period of Tara Kelly's death according to the medical examiner. They identified their sources. Information about the party and the celebrity attendees was provided by Tom Mix and Leslie Fenton. The neighbor Constance Lawson's sighting a man leaving Kelly's home late the night of the party.

The material included Walsh's statement about attempting to obtain information from the LAPD supervising officer that responded to the call from Kelly's housekeeper. Zimmerman put together newspaper clippings about every statement and comment issued by LAPD Assistant Chief Fletcher. The only thing not revealed was what Dr. Sullivan told Walsh. Walsh instead wrote a statement that he had information provided from an anonymous source that Chief Fletcher visited the Los Angeles County Medical Examiner-Coroner office shortly after Tara Kelly's body arrived at the morgue.

Lastly, Zimmerman photographed the original autopsy report, associated notes, and autopsy photographs. He made additional sets of enlargements for himself, Walsh and the *Boston Globe*. Zimmerman kept one copy in his office safe, another in a personal safety deposit box, and gave Walsh two sets. The *Pasadena Star-News* and *Boston Globe* headline stories would be published by the time the original documents provided by Edith

Richardson arrived in Sacramento. This left the Attorney General no choice but to pursue the matter.

Coordinating with their respective publishers, Walsh and Zimmerman submitted their columns in order that the story broke for the Sunday newspaper additions. Both newspapers planned to run this as the headline story. The content of both stories was essentially identical except for specific comments attributed to Walsh or Zimmerman. The *Pasadena Star-News* ran the headline:

NEW SCANDAL ROCKS HOLLYWOOD
Actress Tara Kelly Was Raped

Pasadena, CA: Benjamin Zimmerman:

This and other newspapers around the country have for weeks published repeated stories related to unexplained circumstances surrounding the death of movie actress Tara Kelly. Kelly's housekeeper discovered her dead in her bed at her home in Hollywood on Wednesday June 16. The preliminary report issued by the Los Angeles Police Department stated that her death appeared possibly a drug overdose with cocaine found at the scene. A subsequent medical examiner's autopsy report concluded cause of death was by accidental cocaine overdose.

That became the basis for an acquaintance of Miss Kelly working with Kelly on her latest movie *Price of Freedom* to pursue his own investigation. Egan Walsh is a journalist on leave of absence from the *Boston Globe*, and cowriter of the movie's

269

script adaptation from his bestselling novel. Mr. Walsh does not believe Tara Kelly used drugs. Furthermore, the autopsy placed her death as 3-4 days earlier. Walsh knew that Kelly attended a lavish party of movie celebrities and studio executives at the Beverly Hills estate of movie industry financier Chadwick Hollister the prior Saturday. Making inquiries, Walsh learned that the LAPD was not pursuing further investigation of the actress's death. They considered the matter closed based on what has now been discovered as a falsified autopsy finding of accidental death.

Walsh uncovered a multitude of unexplained circumstances that bear directly on Kelly's death. These include no explanation of how Kelly got home from the Beverly Hills party since she had no car. How then did she get home? Did someone take her? Walsh also interviewed a neighbor who claimed seeing a man leave Kelly's home in the early morning hours of Sunday following the Saturday night party. Inexplicably, the Los Angeles Police Department has repeatedly refused to investigate further. This and other inconsistences led Walsh and this reporter to conclude that a highly orchestrated conspiracy was attempting to suppress important relevant information surrounding

Kelly's death. Walsh's inquiries resulted in a personal brutal assault by three as assailants just a week ago. He suffered serious injuries requiring a week in the hospital. Walsh claims his assailants were likely off duty LAPD officers. With new evidence recently provided to this newspaper, that accusation now carries sufficient weight to warrant investigation.

The headline does not exaggerate. The allegation that Tara Kelly was violently sexually assaulted prior to her death by cocaine overdose is a statement of fact. If the reader turns to the center section of pages 4 and 5, we have reprinted a photograph of the original autopsy report and the addendum notes by the certifying pathologist Dr. Louis Richardson. The entire autopsy file also included postmortem photographs taken at the time of the autopsy but are too graphic for public presentation.

Edith Richardson, the widow of pathologist Dr. Richardson found these materials hidden away in a shoe box as she sorted her through her deceased husband's belongings. Note on page 5 a photograph of a bank deposit account passbook showing an entry for $50,000. Mrs. Richardson knew nothing of the account. The implications seem obvious that this was intended as a bribe to falsify the autopsy by sanitizing any reference of the sexual assault. Since Richardson died in an unresolved hit and run accident just days after performing the autopsy, this might suggest that Richardson was threaten with physical harm to suppress his actual autopsy findings. That Dr. Richardson kept his truthful original may attest to guilt for succumbing to intimidation. It further raises the question stated in Dr. Richardson's original autopsy summary that Kelly's death might also be murder. The summary reads: *Therefore, the postmortem evidence suggests either suicide or the possibility of homicide with the closely related associated sexual assault to the victim. Signed Dr. Louis C. Richardson MD.*

An unnamed source reported that LAPD Assistant Chief James R. Fletcher visited the County Medical Examiner-Coroner's office shortly after the morgue received Tara Kelly's body and spoke with Dr. Richardson. The substance of their conversation is not known. Suspiciously, all public communications concerning Tara Kelly's death immediately became exclusively restricted to Chief Fletcher's office.

This unusual interest by Fletcher along with the LAPD's refusal to pursue investigating Kelly's death further causes us to present this newly discovered and suppressed evidence to the office of California State Attorney General Webb's office. The Attorney General received the entire original autopsy file yesterday. This newspaper and the public demand the California Attorney General take charge of investing Tara Kelly's death as a violent crime. The Los Angeles Police Department has violated the public trust.

Essentially the same story ran in the *Boston Globe* under Egan Walsh's byline: The *Globe's* front page headline read: **MOVIELAND TRAGEDY EXPOSED**, with the column headline reading: **Actress Tara Kelly Raped Before Dying of Cocaine Overdose.** At the end of Walsh's column, the *Boston Globe* published his photograph along with that of Tara Kelly.

Editor and publisher William Taylor added a lengthy editorial section concluding with:

The story of Tara Kelly's death extends well beyond the violent act of sexual assault and perhaps even murder. Egan Walsh exhibits the best in journalism for pursuing this story on his own initiative. He was a friend to Tara Kelly and committed to finding justice for her. Doing so at obvious considerable personal risk given the grievous assault he suffered at the hands of powerful and influential individuals behind this cover up. If such influence extends into determining the Los Angeles Police Department as complicit in a violent crime that will

273

prove an even greater injustice. Mr. Walsh's efforts are a remarkable example of the power of the Constitution's First Amendment that affords a free press to present the truth to the public and thereby hold public officials to account.

The *Boston Globe* will continue to pursue this story to its conclusion.

Monday editions throughout the country carried the Tara Kelly story on their front page. Every newspaper in Southern California could no longer avoid addressing the information published by the *Pasadena Star-News*. Since they only had the information found in the *Pasadena Star-News* and *Boston Globe* most newspapers resorted to resurrecting the major Hollywood scandals of recent years. Although damaging to the movie industry everyone went to the movies and this latest scandal was good for newspaper circulation.

With the identification of rape, most focused on the immediate parallel to the demise of the popular comedic actor Roscoe "Fatty" Arbuckle. An intimate liaison between the rotund Arbuckle and the diminutive aspiring actress Virginia Rappe was alleged to have caused her death. Arbuckle was charged with rape and manslaughter in 1921. Yet there no physical evidence of rape existed. The cause of her death ultimately determined as peritonitis from a ruptured bladder. Although acquitted of both criminal charges, Arbuckle became toxic because of moralistic critics of not only objectionable movie content, but also the personal lives of the actors.

Many newspapers went further to portray Hollywood as a hedonistic community. Almost every year, Hollywood suffers a new scandal. With the maturing of moviemaking, the first such incident involving a movie star occurred in 1920 with the horrific suicide death of actress Olive Thomas in Paris. Because Thomas was married to superstar Mary Pickford's brother, the lurid details of

274

her horrific death became a major headline. After returning to her hotel with her husband, the intoxicated Thomas swallowed a caustic solution of mercury bichloride used to externally treat her husband's chronic syphilis. Sexually transmitted disease and alcohol intoxication painted a debauched lifestyle of the rich and famous. It mattered little that the circumstances were different from the Kelly tragedy, it served to illustrate the alien social conventions of people in the moviemaking business.

The next scandal to rivet Hollywood was the murder of William Desmond Taylor in 1922. The popular and successful producer was shot to death by a single bullet at point-blank range in his home and remains unsolved. Among the suspects were three young actresses, ruining their careers. The mystery of Taylor's death continues to foster unfounded speculation.

The handsome actor Wallace Reid's morphine addiction was well known. Following an injury sustained in a train accident, he became addicted to morphine. The drug proved necessary to manage constant pain while performing physically demanding scenes in a series of hectic movie production schedules. Rehabilitation programs were nonexistent at the time. Reid eventually collapsed on the set. Taken to a sanitarium because of his weaken condition, Reid died in 1923. Technically the cause of death came from influenza compounded by his morphine addiction aggravated by alcohol use.

The mysterious death of Thomas Ince in 1924 riveted the public because of the many celebrity names associated with the famous filmmaker's death. In that sense, the parallels to Kelly's death did have some parallels. Newspaper magnate William Randolph Hearst was negotiating with Ince for Hearst's *Cosmopoliton Productions* to use Ince's studio. Hearst created *Cosmopolitan* to produce movies for Hearst's mistress, actress Marion Davies. Hearst invited Ince for a weekend cruise on his yacht to finalize details.

Aboard Hearst's yacht *Oneida,* Ince fell ill from food and drink aggravating his chronic digestive condition of peptic ulcers. Taken off the yacht to a hospital in Del Mar, Ince suffered a heart attack and died. The mystery of death derived entirely from unsubstantiated rumors that he was shot on board the yacht and died of a gunshot wound to the head. The invented story behind the rumor was that Hearst had mistaken Ince for actor Charlie Chaplin. As a guest also on the yacht, rumor alleged Chaplin was the intended victim of a jealous act by Hearst suspecting him of attempting to seduce Hearst's mistress Marion Davies. The invented story was complete nonsense.

Ince lived in Beverly Hills on an estate he named *Dias Dorados* located at 1051 Benedict Canyon Drive. Some publications made absurd reference to the proximity of Chadwick Hollister's located just one mile north of the Ince estate.

Although ignoring the violent rape associated with Tara Kelly's death, the notoriously flamboyant Hollywood party girl Barbara La Marr's death just months earlier drew erroneous comparisons. La Marr died of tuberculosis exacerbated by years of living a dissipated life of little sleep, booze, with a long-standing cocaine and heroin addiction.

There existed no common thread with Tara Kelly's death and these other tragic deaths of Hollywood celebrities. The true significance of the unresolved mystery surrounding the death of Tara Kelly was its profound impact as the latest in a series of Hollywood scandals. Moralizing critics already hounding the movie industry now possessed another incident from which to launch a new round of attacks.

———

The following weekend, Lilly drove Walsh to the Fox production studios on Pico Boulevard to meet with director John Ford and the cast and crew preparing to begin filming *Dying for Ireland*. Victor McLaglen, the star of the forthcoming movie, was there with his wife Enid. It was his first introduction to Colleen Moore cast as the female lead to play the sister of McLaglen's character. "Victor told me about what happened. That it was because you were investigating Tara Kelly's death is a frightening thought."

McLaglen remarked to Walsh as he delicately put his hand on his shoulder. "How's the mend coming along?"

"Much better. Still stiff but every day is better. Being careful to make sure the ribs heal. Damn tired of being bound tight with an elastic bandage. Must have been real torture for women to endure corsets around the turn of the century."

Lilly arranged for the rest of Walsh's other close friends Tom Mix and Wyatt Earp to also be there. They had not seen Walsh since he left the hospital. After the production kickoff of *Dying for Ireland* at the studio, Lilly made dinner reservations at the Montmartre Café on Hollywood Boulevard.

Everyone accepted Lilly and Egan as a couple. Out of deference to the elderly Wyatt Earp, Lilly seated him next to Walsh. After dinner Earp said, "You armed?"

"Not tonight, Wyatt. Are you?"

Earp's blue eyes lit up as he reached inside his suit jacket pocket pulling out the butt of a Colt revolver enough to show Walsh. "Learned it best to be armed in case some bad character from my past caught up with me. You need to wear a gun, Egan. That's why I got you a concealed permit."

"Lilly thinks it's foolish and a little scary."

Earp leaned behind Walsh to speak directly to Lilly seated on Walsh's left.

"Miss Romano, Egan should carry a sidearm. This thing will never be over until the person who harmed the actress is brought to justice. That is somebody with a lot of influence. If Egan is right, he has the Los Angeles Police in his pocket. Already tried warning Egan off."

Turning to Walsh, Earp said, "Until that happens, you're not safe, Egan. Today's Los Angeles is not much better than what I faced after that famous gunfight in Tombstone over forty years ago. Los Angeles is another boomtown going through growing pains no different than back then.

"Everyone now knows that someone assaulted Tara Kelly, maybe murdered her. You and that reporter Zimmerman outmaneuvered the culprit and upped the stakes. But your enemy still has influence and money. Don't count on the attorney general getting to the bottom of this. Whoever is behind this does not often lose. Might just get it into his mind to take revenge on you as the

277

cause of his troubles. Revenge is a powerful motivation. Wear the gun, Egan."

"I see your point, Wyatt. You're a good friend and if anyone knows about this sort of thing it is Wyatt Earp. I'll take your advice."

Chapter 22

Los Angeles, California | 1926

The public clamor led by the *Pasadena Star-News* and the *Boston Globe* made the speculations and accusations impossible for the media of any political bent to ignore. Even the conservative *Los Angeles Times*, well established as a key component for collectively protecting the region's economic interests, felt compelled to weigh on the side of pursuing further investigation into the death of Tara Kelly. William Randolph Hearst's sensationalist *Los Angeles Examiner*, which had been unusually constrained in commenting on the anomalies raised by Walsh and Zimmerman, did an about face by coming out vigorously in support of looking to identify Kelly's assailant.

The public accusations of complicity in covering up the circumstances of Tara Kelly's death dealt a particularly embarrassing blow to newly appointed Los Angeles Police Chief James E. Davis. As an assistant chief heading up the LAPD's vice squad since the enactment of Prohibition, the bombastic Davis already earned the label of *Two-Gun Davis* for his advocating using force to go after bootleggers. Even though the Volstead Act made trafficking in alcohol a federal crime, Davis claimed bootlegging to be the principal cause of violent crime in Los Angeles. Upon appointment as chief of police, he set out to not only arm the department but to also establish an aggressive posture of using force against criminals. Davis publicly declared; *The LAPD would hold court on gunmen in the Los Angeles streets. I want them brought in dead, not alive and will reprimand any officer who shows the least mercy to a criminal.* Yet Chief Davis inherited a police department riddled with corruption. Much of that was associated with bribes from the very criminal elements cited by the new chief.

Davis ignored several key challenges for making a name as the new face of Los Angeles law and order. That the population overwhelmingly resented being denied alcohol presented the foremost obstacle. While the Volstead Act enforced the 18th Amendment to the U.S. Constitution, it only banned the manufacture, sale, and distribution of alcohol for the purpose of drinking. The drinking public could therefore imbibe alcohol without legal penalty if they could obtain it. Trafficking in alcoholic beverages became more profitable than prostitution, gambling, or drugs. The profit potential resulted in unprecedented violence between competing criminal factions.

Prohibition also corrupted law enforcement. From the street-level police ranks to higher command, district attorney offices, to judges, bribery became an endemic problem for every municipality from small towns to the largest cities. Los Angeles was no different.

An entrenched well-organized influential powerbase controlled both city and county affairs in Los Angeles. Charles Crawford was among those that controlled the economic interests of the Southland. While loosely controlling Los Angeles vice, he exercised considerable influence over local government as a conduit for corruption. The Los Angeles power base was collectively protective of anything that might economically harm its reputation whether from a crusading police chief or a scandal in the movie industry presenting a broader threat. The collectivism of Los Angeles rested upon the region's spectacular growth. Petroleum and real estate speculation, the center of the emerging aircraft manufacturing industry, and Hollywood as the center of moviemaking translated into wealth.

The uproar over revelations surrounding the death of Tara Kelly was the latest expression of organized denial. That the cover up began unraveling became another inconvenient issue confronting the newly appointed LAPD chief. As a former colleague of Assistant Chief Fletcher in the LAPD command structure, he must now deal with Fletcher's mishandling of the Tara Kelly affair. A political animal, Fletcher had powerful support within City Hall. That meant he enjoyed support from Charlie Crawford and his loosely organized criminal syndicate known as the *City Hall Gang*, including a lawyer by the name of Kent Kane. Parrot efforts got current Los Angeles Mayor George E. Cryer elected. Known as the *De facto mayor of LA*, Parrot was considered the real *boss* of municipal politics in Los Angeles politics.

Chief Davis could do little except fume over the embarrassment of the state attorney general removing control of the investigation into Kelly's death out of his hands. He suspected Assistant Chief Fletcher of doing the bidding of some powerful interest but found it impossible to move against a subordinate that well-connected.

As pressure mounted on the California Attorney General Webb, the week following publication of the original autopsy report, Webb announced the appointment of a special investigator to head the investigation of the death of Tara Kelly. His public comments elaborated on the scope of the investigation which included surrounding circumstances connected the rape and possible murder of Kelly, to the death of pathologist Dr. Richardson, and allegations of a broad criminal conspiracy to obstruct justice. Unfortunately for Chief Davis, Attorney General Webb concluded his public statement with the implied threat that he expected full cooperation from local Los Angeles public officials including law enforcement. *Prima facie evidence exists of the involvement of public corruption in the mishandling of relevant circumstances that dictated criminal investigation.*

Chief Davis would essentially become subordinate to Assistant Attorney General Albert Curry and his small team of investigators from the AG's office and several state police officers. Worse yet, these jurisdictional usurpers would be looking into the internal workings of the LAPD.

The LAPD could no longer shield the celebrities that attended Hollister's party from questioning. Failure to voluntarily submit to depositions would result in subpoenas and a worsening of bad press. Chadwick Hollister, Kurt Gerhardt, and Hollister's household staff included.

Hollister therefore became immediately concerned about his constructed narrative about Kelly falling asleep drunk. What did he say to the guests to account for Kelly's absence from the party? He recalled telling Charlie Chaplin that his housekeeper was watching over Kelly vomiting upstairs from too much liquor. That meant preparing a response should Chaplin tell that to an investigator. Sure to be questioned, the housekeeper would deny any involvement with Kelly.

Gerhardt was even more exposed since he took Kelly home and could testify to her condition and state of mind when he helped her into her house. They needed to get out in front of the observation by Kelly's neighbor of seeing a man leaving Kelly's house at one in the morning. Obviously, that was Gerhardt. Although circumstantially that made him a potential suspect, no physical evidence existed pointing to him as the rapist or connecting him with providing Kelly cocaine.

Hollister and Gerhardt would be questioned about any indication that Kelly was sexually assaulted either by visible evidence or her behavior. Their agreed upon position centered around maintaining the position that no sexual assault took place at the party. Kelly appeared drunk which was consistent with her drinking champagne and gimlet cocktails. As for any effects of cocaine, they had no way to judge as being distinct from someone intoxicated with alcohol.

With the investigation taken over by Sacramento, LAPD Assistant Chief Fletcher would also come under intense scrutiny. Hollister was careful to lay enough groundwork with Fletcher to convince him that Kelly was molested by someone very famous. An unfortunate circumstance but extraordinary economic repercussions were at risk should the identity of the perpetrator be exposed. The existing scandal was damaging enough but a charge of rape against this famous actor would have unimaginable implications.

"That was the source of your healthy renumeration to contain the fallout, Chief," Hollister said as they lunched at a small diner outside the city. Both thought it prudent to avoid being seen together. "Which I might add has been exceptional. No way you could anticipate Dr. Richardson getting a conscience and keeping that damning autopsy for his wife to discover."

Fletcher was upset at the time when he learned of Richardson's death. He suspected Hollister was behind that. Most likely that piece of work he employed as his bodyguard Kurt Gerhardt arranged for the *accident*.

Now of course that helped Fletcher's position. He could deny any knowledge of the hush money paid to Richardson to falsify the autopsy. Stick to his story that with the cause of death certified by Richardson as accidental cocaine overdose, there was no crime to investigate. Controlling public comment justified to protect unnecessary harassment of celebrity movie stars. Nothing pointed directly to any connection to those attending the Beverly Hills party with the actress's death.

Fletcher said, "I'm about to have a bunch of assholes grilling me about my actions related to this Kelly affair. That prick Davis will make no effort to shield me. Are you sure the paper trail on my fees is bulletproof if these Sacramento investigators look deeper?"

"Don't worry, Chief. Your monthly retainer coming from SoCal Management Services has an audit trail supporting your regular payments as net rental proceeds from your ownership position in various commercial properties, backed with documentation. I control this third-party legal entity. I use it exclusively for managing Hollister Financial's real estate holdings."

Hollister did far more than control SoCal Management Services. Nathan Schachter personally managed the shell company's off-books transactions running accounting transactions through Hollister Financial, obscuring the audit trail where necessary by altering bank entries.

"As for the large commission paid for your services in the Kelly matter that can be explained by the sale of your equity position in a property. If necessary, I can produce the necessary documentation supporting a complex sequence of falsified transactions that launders the source of the money."

Satisfied, Fletcher returned to the immediate problem. "Do you know who raped the actress?"

Hollister replied, "I think so."

"Someone important enough to continue protecting him?"

"Yes. Should he even become identified as a suspect, the damage would be unimaginable. Economically, it is worth keeping the circumstances surrounding Kelly's death unresolved. As damaging as the current bad press is, it cannot go on indefinitely. The public is fickle and easily moves on to the next train wreck.

"Besides, I can't be positive it was him. There is no evidence anything happened at my home that night. The rape could have happened at Kelly's house later that night or even the following day. The perpetrator might also be someone entirely unexpected. Possibly someone not even associated with motion pictures. Just keep to your story, Chief. You are covered personally. You also have powerful friends with a shared interest."

———

Assistant Attorney General Albert Curry was a bookish-looking man in his mid-forties. Although not experienced in prosecuting violent crimes, Curry was smart and tenacious. His underwhelming physical appearance belied his strong track record of successful prosecutions of complex litigations against corporate defendants.

Curry intended to personally handle the most important interrogations. Other investigators on his team visited Kelly's home. They then concluded interviews with the LAPD responding officers and Hollywood precinct supervising officer Lieutenant Dekker. The investigators concluded that the LAPD made only a perfunctory examination of Kelly's residence. Finding a quantity of cocaine by the bed, they treated this as just a routine drug overdose death. Thoroughly searching Kelly's residence and interviewing the housekeeper produced nothing of significance.

Curry's first interview was with Edith Richardson, the deceased pathologist's wife. "Tell me about your husband's state of mind when he came home after conducting the autopsy on Tara Kelly."

"He was very upset but wouldn't tell me why. Locked himself away in his study and did not even eat dinner."

"Was this unusual?"

"This seemed different. It was his job to examine dead bodies. He took his responsibilities seriously, but I never saw him this disturbed. Later when I found the original autopsy hidden away with that bank deposit book, and followed what the newspapers were suggesting, I realized what happened."

"And what did you think happened, Mrs. Richardson?"

"Louis was a good man. We have been married twenty-four years. Never had children so we were very close. I could not believe that Louis would sacrifice his integrity for money. We were well off. Money was never an important issue."

"Why do you think he falsified the autopsy?"

"Must have been out of fear. Whoever deposited that money must have threatened to harm me if he did not do as they wanted. Falsifying the autopsy would have gone against his ethics. He could only have done that to protect me."

For Curry's investigation, Richardson's motivation was not material. His investigators examined the records of Great Western Savings & Loan. On the surface it appeared legitimate. However, Great Western's records indicated the deposit consisted of bearer bonds. A notorious vehicle for laundering money. Edith Richardson withdrew the funds and closed the account. "Curry showed her the deposit slip and asked, "Is this your husband's signature?"

Looking at the carbon copy, she replied, "Heavens no. Looks nothing like Louis' signature."

"And you know nothing about your husband possessing such a large sum of bearer bonds?"

"No. I don't even know what a bearer bond is. Does this mean that Louis did not open this bank account, Mr. Curry?"

"Would seem that way."

"Then someone very powerful and wealthy is behind whatever is going on about this actress's death. Does this mean that my husband's accident might have been murder?"

"That is a possibility that we are also looking into. I am very sorry for your loss, Mrs. Richardson."

Curry then moved onto LAPD Assistant Chief James Fletcher. Seated in Fletcher's office at LAPD headquarters, Curry opened with, "Please explain your interest in personally controlling official public comments in the matter of Tara Kelly's death."

"Quite simply to tamp down expected rampant speculation since she was a movie star. There was nothing to suggest any crime had been committed. LAPD responding officers found nothing at her home where her body was discovered to indicate anything beyond an overdose of cocaine. A quantity of cocaine was found beside her bed.

"The autopsy confirmed accidental cocaine overdose as the cause of death. Case closed. Nothing further to investigate. The muckraking speculation in certain newspapers did not change any of that."

"Of course, you now know of the extenuating circumstances that indicate a crime was committed in the form of a violent sexual assault. That of course opens the possibility that her death might also be murder. At the very least it strongly suggests the overdose was not accidental. What is your position on this matter now, Chief Fletcher?"

"My conclusion is that someone very powerful is behind covering up the crime. Powerful enough to bribe the attending medical examiner pathologist to falsify the autopsy."

"Some accuse the LAPD and you in particular as participating in that cover up. How do you explain your unusually rigid control of information related to the Kelly natter?"

"I believe I already explained, Mr. Curry. Had the Attorney General not assumed control of the investigation, I would have formed an LAPD task force of detectives to open an investigation."

"One newspaper account alleges you visited the morgue shortly after Kelly's body was brought in. Why was that?

"I did visit the medical examiner's office, but only after the autopsy. I wanted to personally speak with the pathologist knowing there would be intense public interest in the death of a movie actress."

"You spoke with Dr. Richardson?"

"Yes. He told me only that Kelly died of an overdose of cocaine. No forensic evidence existed that it was anything but accidental or possibly intentional."

Having deflected Curry's questions, Fletcher then went on the offensive. "Let me also point out that so much press attention has been focused on Kelly attending a party in Beverly Hills with many leading movie stars the Saturday prior to discovery of the actress's body the following Wednesday. According to the pathology, she might have died within a period extending as much as twenty-four hours or more after that party. Newspapers gravitate to the salacious interest that this is the latest scandal to hit Hollywood. Leaping to speculate that the perpetrator might be a famous movie star. No evidence points to any suspects at this time."

"Well, that's what I am charged with investigating. Thank you for your time Chief Fletcher."

Fletcher was smooth under fire but unconvincing to Curry. He was holding back. Los Angeles had a reputation as a tightly controlled city by powerful business interests and s cooperating municipal government. That obviously included the police. Curry's background information on Fletcher confirmed that Fletcher enjoyed powerful connections in City Hall and the Los Angeles Board of Police Commissioners. As for powerful local business interests, none was more influential than its highest public profile business sector, Hollywood moviemaking.

———

Next on Curry's list was Chadwick Hollister, his bodyguard Kurt Gerhardt, and Hollister's household staff. In view of the conspiracy to obscure evidence associated with Tara Kelly's death involving a criminal act, the party at the Hollister residence becomes a circumstance central to the investigation.

Curry arrived with his lead investigator State Police Lieutenant Duncan Townsend. Unlike Curry, Townsend had extensive experience investigating violent crimes. Curry planned to interview Hollister while Townsend simultaneously interviewed Kurt Gerhardt and the resident household staff.

Seated in Chadwick Hollister's large conservatory and library room, Curry began. "I have seen the list of Hollywood celebrities attending your party in June. Quite impressive. Was there any methodology to selecting these attendees?"

"Only to the extent I wanted to include people associated with all the major studios. You see, most of the studios are my clients. Didn't want to appear slighting any studio. I also consider a number of studio executives among my closest friends."

"Most of the guests and producers invited were among the most famous motion picture names. Tara Kelly was not exactly in that category. Why was she invited?"

I wanted Fox Films to be represented. I invited Tom Mix the current leading western actor and Victor McLaglen with his two back-to-back successful movies, *What Price Glory* and *Price of Freedom* in which Kelly played the female lead. Mix attended but McLaglen did not."

"What about this British actor Leslie Fenton that arrived with Kelly?"

"Fenton had a lesser role in *What Price Glory*. While not a leading man, I am a conscientious host and tried to make him feel welcome among the glitterati."

"Why did he leave early without Kelly?"

"I'm not sure. Didn't notice until much later when someone mentioned it."

"Fenton told my investigators he was upset that Kelly was ignoring him. Said she was enamored by the attention that Charlie Chaplin and Rudolf Valentino were lavishing on her. Tom Mix recounted observing the same behavior. What did you observe?"

"Well, I'm not a good judge of that. I spent much of my time mingling among the guests spread out here and in the living room. Didn't stay put very long with any particular group."

"My people have spoken with several of your guests. Several concur that Kelly seemed always with a glass of champagne or cocktail. Eating very little and smoking."

"I couldn't say. However, that may account for her looking a little pale causing me to ask if she might like a breath of fresh air."

"Is that when you took her outside?"

Tread lightly from here on out, Hollister thought. Some guests may have seen more than he thought. "Why yes. I needed a break as well. Some fresh air free of all the cigarette smoke. Anyway, once outside as we walked along the rear garden paths, she appeared to become visibly sick. You know the look when someone has had too much to drink. The look that says they are about to throw up."

"What did you do then?"

"She expressed embarrassment. Said the alcohol must be getting to her. Was there somewhere she could lie down without anyone noticing? I said I would take her to one of the guest bedrooms upstairs. I took her to a quest bedroom where no one would disturb her. Then I closed the door and returned to my guests."

"Did Mr. Chaplin ask where Kelly was?"

"As a matter of fact, he did. I told him she had too much to drink and wanted to rest for a while. She was embarrassed. Told him my housekeeper would look in on her."

"Did she?"

"No. I could not locate her. Located my bodyguard instead and asked him to look in on Miss Kelly. A short time later he returned downstairs and took me aside. Told me that Kelly was hanging over the toilet repeatedly vomiting. Nothing he could do so he closed the bathroom door and came to get me.

"Made my apologies to a couple of guests saying I needed to attend to something. Then I went upstairs with Gerhardt. We entered the bedroom to find the room lit only by the open bathroom light revealing Kelly on the bed lying on her side. A disgusting pool of vomit close by her head on the bedspread. The smell was terrible."

"What did you and Gerhardt do then?"

"I told him that he must plan on driving her home when the alcohol wears off and she wakes up. I'm going to return to the remaining guests. I recall telling Mr. Chaplin that Kelly was not just asleep but passed out. To keep it low key, I left it to Mr. Chaplin to explain Kelly's absence to anyone that asked."

"Tell me about what you and Gerhardt did to get her home. Was she awake? Able to walk?"

"Eventually we got her awake. Still not feeling well but at least it looked as if her vomiting was under control. We helped her down the rear staircase. There were still a few guests remaining, so I thought it best to shield her from embarrassment."

"Then what?"

"We bundled her into Gerhardt's car."

"So, Gerhardt drove her home?"

"We thought about calling a taxi, but I thought better of it after seeing she might be a handful in her condition. I felt better about Gerhardt being able to manage any difficulties."

"What time did Gerhardt leave with Kelly?"

"Sometime around midnight as I recall."

"What did you do then?"

"Rejoined my few remaining guests."

"When did Gerhardt return?"

"About an hour later. Couldn't tell you the exact time but I know it was before two o'clock. That's when the last guests left."

"Which guests were that?"

"Mr. Chaplin and Mr. Valentino. They became friends I am told after Chaplin and Douglas Fairbanks urged Valentino to join their United Artists studio."

"What did Gerhardt tell you about Kelly's condition after arriving at her bungalow?"

"Kurt told me she sobered up considerably during the drive while he kept the windows open for fresh air. Still looked pale with her hair disheveled from her drunken ordeal, but she was able to walk to her front door. Good enough that she thanked him then closed her front door. He heard her lock the door."

"This fellow Walsh that seems to be responsible for haranguing in the Pasadena newspaper about a cover up over the actress's death. Why has Walsh singled out your party for particular attention?"

"I have no idea. His persistence seems obsessive. Of course, he knew Tara Kelly. Spent time with her during the filming of the movie *Price of Freedom* I am told. Wrote the movie script adapted from his novel. Perhaps he has personal reasons. Maybe they were more than just friends."

"However, his persistence apparently paid off. Turns out Kelly's death is far more complicated than a case of accidental cocaine overdose. Was cocaine present at your party?"

"Good heavens no. My guests are all prominent movie stars or studio executives. They may drink too much, but they don't do drugs."

———

In a separate room Lieutenant Townsend simultaneously interviewed Kurt Gerhardt. He knew Gerhardt was a former cop that may have accounted for his surly demeanor at being questioned.

"When Mr. Hollister brought you into the bedroom, what did you see?"

"A woman in a blue dress lying on the bed. Smelled vomit so I turned on the light. A fuckin' mess on the bed. Mr. Hollister said to let her sleep it off. I was to check on her every fifteen minutes."

"What about when Mr. Hollister told you to drive her home?"

"She eventually woke up. Looked awful. Like anyone having a hangover after too much drinking. Unsteady, but we helped her downstairs and into my car. She wanted to lie down in the backseat, but I insisted she sit in the passenger seat. Didn't want her getting sick and making another mess."

"How long did it take to drive her home?"

"Twenty or thirty minutes."

"Then what?"

"Then I walked her to the front door. Helped her unlock the door."

"Did you go inside with her?"

"No."

"Did she say anything?"

"She just thanked me and went inside. Closed the door. Heard her lock it."

"Then what?"

"Christ, I drove back here. What do you think? It was late and I was pissed off about having to nursemaid a drunken actress."

Back in the car outside Hollister's home, Curry and Townsend compared notes. Hollister's and Gerhardt's stories matched. After comparing notes, Curry remarked, "Sounds like they rehearsed the script."

Townsend added, "Gerhardt knows more than he's telling. As the last person to see Kelly alive, he must remain a suspect. Don't think we're going to learn much from either Hollister or Gerhardt unless we turn up something to shake them up. Then again, maybe the sexual assault happened the following day. Maybe nothing to do with anyone at Hollister's party."

"That's possible. But someone with a lot of clout and money is either the perpetrator or is covering for the perpetrator," Curry said. "Kelly was a movie actress, but did she socialize with the Hollywood movie crowd? Let's see how the rest of the team is progressing with talking to the Hollywood crowd attending the party. Then we move on to reconstructing Tara Kelly's life. I want you to start by interviewing Egan Walsh. Interesting background. He not only started this crusade in conjunction with the Pasadena reporter, but he also knew Kelly from working with her on her last movie."

Townsend replied, "What if Walsh had more than a professional relationship with Kelly?"

"Interesting that you mention that. Hollister suggested something along those lines. Probably just resents Walsh dragging him into this mess. However, you need to find out Walsh's connection to Kelly. Right now, we have no strong suspects and far too many possibilities. The money paid to the pathologist is the strongest indicator pointing to the stature of the person that assaulted and probably murdered Kelly. Find out if Walsh has access to that kind of money?"

"Townsend said, "Hollister does. Makes Gerhardt even more a suspect. He had opportunity and no real alibi other than his boss."

"Therefore, we move forward keeping an open mind," Curry said, "By the autopsy findings both the original and the falsified version, Kelly died somewhere between Saturday night the last time seen alive and possibly as late as early Monday. Forty-eight hours. Most likely the sexual assault happened at either Hollister's house on Saturday, or Kelly's house sometime later within that time window. What did the LAPD investigative report say about the circumstances at her house after finding the body?"

"Very little. Just the obvious fact of finding cocaine near the bed. The house was locked when the housekeeper unlocked the front door with her key on that Wednesday. The dead actress found in her bed dressed in a nightgown."

"What about the clothing Kelly was wearing to the Party? The blue dress?"

"No mention of the blue dress in the LAPD report. Seems like the LAPD concluded this was a simple drug overdose and made no attempt at a thorough search."

"Therefore, do you agree that Kelly was most likely assaulted and ingested a lethal quantity of cocaine at either Hollister's or Kelly's residence?"

"Yes, Sir. Unless we discover something different."

"Then get your team over to Kelly's house and see what you can find."

CHAPTER 23

Los Angeles, California | 1926

With Tara Kelly's death just a few months earlier, another ca-
tastrophe of seismic proportions rocked Hollywood. Rudolph Valentino the male sex symbol dubbed the Latin Lover entered a Manhattan hospital in mid-August. Misdiagnosed as suffering from appendicitis, surgery was performed. Following surgery, Valentino developed peritonitis. His condition worsened
with a severe case of pleuritis developing rapidly in his left lung.
He then contracted sepsis from his weakened condition. Screen
heartthrob Rudolph Valentino died unexpectedly eight days later
at the age of thirty-one. The cause of death subsequently determined as perforated ulcers mimicking the symptoms of appendicitis. However, for the week of his illness, the entire country was
riveted by yet another mysterious death befalling Hollywood.

Valentino's funeral became a spectacle worthy of an epic period movie. 100,000 people lined Manhattan streets to pay their
respects at the funeral home. A riot erupted among fans trying to
gain entry to the funeral home requiring over 100 NYPD mounted
police to restore order.

In Hollywood, California, Valentino's death did not deter State Police Lieutenant Townsend and two of his team from showing up at LAPD Hollywood Division to pursue the Tara Kelly matter. They told the desk Sergeant they wished to see Lieutenant Dekker.

Escorted to Dekker's office, Townsend introduced himself. "We need to search Tara Kelly's residence. Do you have a key?"

"I can't give you the key without clearance from Assistant Chief Fletcher's office."

"You don't seem to understand, Lieutenant. I'm here on orders from the state attorney general. I don't need your approval or that of a fucking Los Angeles assistant police chief. My being here is just professional courtesy. Either give me the key or we'll just break down the door and charge you with obstruction."

Dekker turned over the key.

Townsend and his team spent two hours at Kelly's residence. No way to tell but it seemed to Townsend that there was not even a perfunctory search conducted by the LAPD. All the drawers in the bedroom appeared undisturbed. A thorough search turned up no cocaine hidden away. The only anomaly was not finding the blue dress and matching heels described by Leslie Fenton and others as worn by Kelly to the Hollister party. Lack of finding the dress suggested the rapist was also a murderer.

Not finding the dress added to the mystery. Perhaps torn, or revealing physical evidence of sexual assault, its absence made finding her dressed in a nightgown suspicious. Her assailant could have staged the scene to look as if she overdosed either accidentally or intentionally. Townsend's findings added to a probable case for homicide and the incompetence or culpability of the LAPD to cover up. However, it did nothing to get closer to identifying the perpetrator.

While Dr. Richardson's original autopsy revealed that Kelly suffered a sexual assault, it only determined she died by cocaine overdose. It provided no indication if ingested accidentally, intentionally from despair after suffering a violent rape, or by the rapist poisoning her. Contradictory autopsy reports signed by the deceased pathologist and a secret payment of hush money only made clear that someone powerful is behind a cover up.

State Police Lieutenant Duncan Townsend researched Egan Walsh's background before interviewing him. He found Walsh forthright and believable. Asking Walsh directly if he had a romantic relationship with Tara Kelly, Walsh responded, "No. I came to know her through Victor McLaglen and his wife Enid. Kelly previously costarred with McLaglen. Met her when I began working on the script for *Price of Freedom*. The McLaglens adopted her like a younger sister. For that matter, they adopted me as an outsider coming to work in Hollywood.

"Tara was focused on her career. I was in a relationship with someone back in Boston at the time. Tara and I just became good friends and occasionally socialized together with the McLaglens. Tara never spoke about being in a regular relationship with anyone."

"How come she did not ask you to escort her Hollister's party?" Townsend asked.

"She did. After Victor McLaglen declined to accompany her since he was also invited. Seemed the party was a gathering for movie stars and a few rising stars like Kelly. I begged off. I was not an actor. Just came to Hollywood as part of deal made by my publisher to promote my book. They sold the film rights to Fox Films. Didn't want to appear as a party crasher looking to network with Hollywood celebrities. That's why she recruited the actor Leslie Fenton as her escort that evening."

"What do you know about Fenton?"

"Nothing. Never met him until interviewing him after Tara's death. Poor fellow has had a bad time of it in the press. I'm sorry about that. He seems to have been forthright in explaining about that night. Some newspapers accuse him unfairly of stranding Kelly at the party."

"Who do you think raped Tara Kelly?"

"I have no idea. As far as this party is concerned, I only accused the LAPD of not investigating an obviously relevant circumstance surrounding the time determined when she died. That is among other gross investigative omissions by the LAPD. Only now becoming clear that closing the case prematurely was part of a broader conspiracy to cover up a crime. Someone with influence paid a great deal of money to falsify the autopsy. I personally believe that payment was arranged by someone high up in the LAPD with money provided by involved with the movie industry."

"Assistant Chief Fletcher?"

"Possibly, but I have no proof to make that accusation. I only criticized Fletcher of malfeasance by not properly pursuing the death of Kelly."

After Townsend reported his results of interviewing the McLaglens, John Ford, and Tom Mix, he was convinced that Walsh was not romantically involved with Tara Kelly. All of them told of the depression Walsh suffered after the untimely accidental death of Fiona McGuire in Boston. Learning too late of McGuire's death did not allow time for him to attend the funeral in Boston. Walsh remained in California finishing the filming of *Price of Freedom.* Kelly was supportive toward helping Walsh recover, but never exhibited any romantic inclinations between them.

Assistant Attorney General **Curry** became convinced that **Walsh was not a suspect. His** crusading efforts toward seeking a fuller explanation for what he thought was a questionable explanation of Kelly's death appeared consistent with his relationship to the actress. Walsh's entire background portrayed him as someone of strong ethical character, not likely to act irrationally. As a journalist, pursuing the story on his own was an understandable motivation. Walsh also did not possess the financial resources or influential connections necessary to bribe public servants.

The hush money was central to the investigation. The $50,000 paid to Dr. Richardson was likely not the only money paid to cover up Kelly's rape and probably murder. A staggering amount of money. It pointed directly to the perpetrator or someone protecting him as a person of considerable means. Yet there was no trail with which to pursue the money. The deposit made by someone unknown to the bank, forging the name on the account to then deposit non-traceable negotiable bearer bonds.

As for Egan Walsh, he could do nothing more now that the investigation was in the hands of the state attorney general. As a responsible journalist, he found satisfaction that his efforts at least produced official action. Regrettably newspaper coverage proved disappointing with the absence of any progress by law enforcement. What passed as news in many newspaper columns was nothing more than editorial conjecture. He reserved his submissions to the *Boston Globe* to straight reporting pieces of occasional factual material related to the Kelly affair as it was now called. Most of his time became occupied with his role as technical consultant for *Dying for Ireland* preparing to go into production.

Instigating official investigation into Tara Kelly's death and his relationship with Lilly Romano produced a sense of peace for the first time since arriving in Southern California. Yet still troubling that the person responsible for Tara Kelly's death was still out there. The newly opened investigation might never uncover the identity of the perpetrator.

While the perpetrator must now be feeling increased pressure, the matter was never going to go away, or far from Walsh's thoughts. Although fully recovered from the vicious beating, Walsh was a realist. Whoever ordered those off-duty cops to beat him remained at large. Perhaps irrational and bent on revenge for the person responsible for his continuing troubles. He did as his friend Wyatt Earp instructed, much to Lilly Romano's dismay. When out and about, he went armed. The weapon close at hand when they slept. His weapon was a newly acquired Colt Police Positive Special .38 caliber revolver with a four-inch barrel. A common police weapon recommended by his benefactor Captain O'Keefe of the Sheriff's Department who provided him with the concealed weapons permit. The Colt weighing 23 ounces was far more practical to conceal in his shoulder holster than his much heavier British Webley service revolver at 39 ounces.

———

Egan Walsh threw himself into his role as technical consultant as Fox Films began filming *Dying for Ireland*. The industry trades

298

were already using Fox publicity information promoting the forthcoming sequel to the successful *Price of Freedom*. The movie would again star Victor McLaglen in the role of Brandan Flynn. The promo material openly revealed that the producers were honoring the memory of Tara Kelly by retiring her role in the opening scene of her funeral. Her character Nora Gallagher having died in a valiant death in the final days of the Irish War of Independence portrayed in *Price of Freedom*.

Irish American moviegoers embraced *Price of Freedom*. The unanswered questions surrounding the death of Tara Kelly kept her name in the public eye. That she died the victim of a repugnant crime brought advance interest for a sequel. *Dying for Ireland* would follow Brandan Flynn through the contentious aftermath following the treaty with Britain giving Ireland limited freedom but not full independence. Civil war erupted into open violence initiated by anti-Treaty factions of the former Irish Republican Army. A large number of former IRA supporting the new Irish Free State joined to form the Irish National Army. Unlike the war for independence, an overwhelming majority of the Irish population supported the new Irish state and the end to the brutal war with Britain.

Filming began at the Fox studios lot on Pico Boulevard. Walsh was not only again technical consultant, but he could claim the script as again largely his creation. For ethnic Irish in America, there were undoubtedly mixed views about the civil war. Walsh's thoughts that the movie provide a sympathetic portrayal of the victorious pro-Treaty Irish government prevailed. Events since the end of the Irish Civil War three years earlier proved that was the right course based on prevailing sentiments of Irish Americans. Through the protagonist Brandon Flynn, he attempted to treat the complex feelings of the Irish by using his own feelings of resentment for some of the terms of the Treaty while rejecting taking up arms against former comrades.

John Ford was again directing, which was a delight. Colleen Moore was perfectly cast for the role conceived by Walsh for Flynn's sister Noreen secretly working against her brother now a senior officer in the Irish National Army. He hoped the script succeeded in portraying the wrenching emotions of families pulled apart by civil war rather than a betrayal of her brother.

Filming started in early November. While Walsh spent his days on the set and backlot of the Pico studios, Lilly Romano spent most of her time at the Western Avenue offices. Her work on the scripts of both *Price of Freedom* and *Dying for Ireland* greatly impressed Sol Wurtzel and William Fox. Promoted with a new title of Executive Script Manager, her principal function became the previewing of all script submittals to look for viable opportunities. She would also play a role that variously might involve script contribution, editing, or *fixing* a script. Wurtzel relied heavily on her artistic opinions. Instead of replacing her former role, he paid her more and told her to develop a staff and supervise her former organizational duties.

In the evenings, they enjoyed the ability to talk shop together. Shortly after being released from the hospital, Walsh moved in with Romano at her insistence. As she reiterated, he *was the one*. They quickly adapted together domestically as if they had been together for a year. For Walsh, life took on new meaning after finding Lilly Romano. Painful memories of the last several years no longer dominated his thoughts.

While the mystery of who harmed Tara Kelly persisted, Walsh was satisfied that he did everything possible to find her justice. The horrific assault inflicted on him proved that. Yet whoever raped and murdered Tara Kelly remained at large. There seemed no further reason for Walsh to remain a target but until brought to justice, he would remain vigilant.

As the climate of Southern California moved into early winter, this marked the Southland's short rainy season. Director John Ford took the opportunity for location shooting to bring the production crew back north into San Louis Obispo County after Thanksgiving.

Walsh made the trip by train with Lilly on the first day of December. She would spend just a few days away from the office to be with Walsh before taking the train back to Los Angeles. Walsh enjoyed the prior location filming of filming *Price of Freedom*. Close to the sea, rural San Luis Obispo did remind him of southwest

Ireland. Returning to Los Angeles, he looked forward to his second holiday season in Southern California. Lilly Romano brought him great expectations for the new year of 1927.

—

For Chadwick Hollister, there existed no expectations for anything good on the horizon. On the contrary, the outlook worsened over the past weeks. Not one for introspection that his compulsive conduct was the source of his problems, he instead focused on what course of action to now pursue. At best the Kelly scandal would continue indefinitely, but not without repercussions. The studio heads already seemed to be avoiding him. Lacking the ability to control the situation caused increasing paranoia. Seeing himself a possible target of the attorney general's investigation became a constant fear. Even without direct evidence, his circumstances might worsen.

There was no longer any way to deflect attention from his party. Regardless, the nonsense being printed by that idiot Hearst in all his papers printing innuendos about Chaplin's womanizing, would never cast suspicion on Chaplin as a suspect in the Kelly Affair.

Hollister rationalized that Chief Fletcher represented clear jeopardy should something come to light about his participation in the cover up conspiracy. His part in this was only bribery and obstruction of justice. Yet if Fletcher came under legal threat for conspiracy involving murder, he could easily make Hollister a prime suspect by a plea agreement to save his own skin.

The circumstances of that night made Gerhardt a prime suspect. That in turn made Hollister a suspected accomplice by association with the hush money to falsify the autopsy. The regrettable bribe paid to the pathologist now understood as a serious mistake. He should have relied on Fletcher to sufficiently scare Richardson into falsifying the autopsy. Once that happened, then let Gerhardt dispose of Richardson in the contrived accident.

For Chadwick Hollister, there was no way of removing either Fletcher or Gerhardt as potential threats. Fletcher thinks he is covering up for a famous actor and has no direct evidence linking him to Kelly's death. Unlikely that Fletcher would do anything since it would incriminate him criminally. Gerhardt was another natter. Should Gerhardt die, there existed no one that knew he murdered Tara Kelly. Yet there was no way that he could conceive of causing Gerhardt's demise. At any rate, Gerhardt's complicity in the murder should prevent his turning against him without also risking going to the gallows. The mental image Hollister conjured in his mind of himself ascending the gallows steps turned his blood cold.

Hollister never brooded. His instincts always were inclined to take action. Too often reactionary, he nonetheless felt more in control when doing something. Rely on his money, connections, and intelligence to realign circumstances in his favor. Blame others. Fabricate whenever it suited his position. When confronted, never retreat, just continue maintaining his position twisting facts as necessary. Although devoid of character, Chadwick Hollister was clever and knew how to work the system and coopt people to do his bidding. Although born into wealth, his ambitions and intellect propelled him to achieve remarkable success in business for his own narcissistic sense of importance.

Ordinarily he could keep his deviant appetites in better check than that night. Cocaine and a compromising opportunity with a vulnerable young woman combined that fateful evening to compel Chadwick Hollister to give way to his darkest instincts.

Faced with any problem, attack any problem forcefully and persist until achieving success. Refusing to admit the problem was a creation of his own making freed him from indulging in self-recrimination. As the first rain of the winter season sounded from outside the windows of his study, he lit a cigar, settling into deep thought. By the time the cigar was down to a stub, he concluded he might have found a solution.

The solution centered on again using Kurt Gerhardt. A reliable weapon without scruples, Gerhardt was so deeply committed that he might see this as their shared solution. The plan was simple. Gerhardt would kill Walsh in a situation that incriminated Walsh in circumstances pointing to him being responsible for

Tara Kelly's death. Accomplished by Gerhardt planting irrefutable evidence on Walsh that left no doubt of his involvement.

The evidence in Hollister's possession became available only
as another irrational act of the moment that might now prove
uniquely useful. That night as Tara Kelly lay passed out on the
bed, he unzipped and removed her figure-hugging blue dress.
With her breasts exposed but still unconscious, he removed her
underwear. In his state of feeling the effects of smoking cocaine
he violently sexually assaulted Kelly unable to resist as she suffered near unconsciousness because of her excessive cocaine in-
take.

Later, Gerhardt left him to clean up the soiled bedding which
he bundled and placed on the floor for the cleaning service scheduled to come in and clean up from the prior night's party. Smelling her sent on the garments, Hollister could not bring himself to
dispose of Kelly's clothing. Now those articles would serve to con-
demn Walsh. The state investigators would make the case that
Walsh either had a romantic relationship with Kelly, or was obsessed with her, raping her when she rebuffed his advances. It did
not matter with Walsh dead.

Hollister smiled with a sense of satisfaction. His scheme was
bold. An audacious stroke of genius. Granted it did not explain
the payment to Dr. Richardson. That unresolved question would
remain an unresolved mystery but not enough to sustain the scandal with the rapist-murderer identified.

His next step was to have his reliable right-hand Nathan
Schachter reemploy the private investigation firm surveillance of
Walsh. Schachter knew nothing about Hollister's or Gerhardt's
actions the night of the party. Once the newspapers exposed questions concerning the death of Tara Kelly implicating Hollister's
party, Hollister explicitly told Schachter that possibly one of his
guests did something that night. The police were not investigating
her death as anything more than an accidental overdose. However, this Walsh person was raising a public outcry. For the sake
of their clients, they needed to follow Walsh's private investigation and stay one step ahead.

As the matter progressed, Schachter suspected Hollister's actions as more than just looking out for the interests of an important moviemaking client. It mattered little to Schachter. His value to Hollister was doing the dirty business of spreading money to public officials for leverage. As a lawyer and expert in banking and financial transactions, his real value was in his creative abilities to conceal Hollister's illegal activities. He devised creative mechanisms to deliver bribery that obscured the origin of the money by disguising the money as explainable with fabricated documentation. The method of making regular monthly payment to Chief Fletcher and the hush payment to Dr. Richardson was his creation.

Schachter had no more scruples than Hollister. Learning of the vicious assault on Walsh after Hollister told him to discontinue surveillance on Walsh, made clear Hollister's deeper interest in the matter. By then Schachter already found the reported accidental death by hit-and-run of Dr. Richardson suspect. Sounded like the work of his counterpart Kurt Gerhardt. Both he and Gerhardt were fixers for Chadwick Hollister. The difference lay in their respective areas of expertise. Schachter thought of his endeavors as brilliantly creative compared to the cruder services he suspected Gerhardt provided, such as the attack on Walsh.

The following morning, Schachter sat in Hollister's office. "This matter of that actress's death has begun to threaten our position with our studio clients," Hollister said. "They are terrified of another scandal, and this has become increasingly worse. I harbored the suspicion that it could have been one of my guests that molested that actress that night. She was drunk. I showed her to a bedroom upstairs and told Gerhardt to check on her periodically. He reported only a short time later that she was sick in the bathroom and vomited all over the place.

"So, there was a gap of time until much later when Gerhardt and I looked in on her. She passed out on the bed. We had a difficult time waking her. She was fully dressed, a pool of vomit next to her on the bed. I could not conceive it possible that someone raped her that night. The woman was incapacitated that night.

304

"I originally suspected Charlie Chaplin might have done something. Don't think that even makes sense now. Chaplin likes women. Young women. That's no secret. But according to his reputation he doesn't need to force himself on women. Chaplin is also a short little guy. Can't image him manhandling someone like Tara Kelly, drunk or not."

Schachter sat listening to Hollister waiting for him to get to the point. Hollister was simply reiterating his reasoning for making the complex laundering of hush money with bearer bonds to Dr. Richardson.

"I spoke with Fletcher. Of course, he's pissed off with his name appearing in the newspapers. Worse now that he's become the whipping boy for the LAPD's incompetence. Probably blames me for that."

Schachter commented. "Don't worry about Fletcher. He is paid enough for doing what you asked. Just bad luck that Richardson decided to have a conscience."

"Anyway, during our conversation, Fletcher started speculating out loud. He suggested that my efforts to shield a famous actor might have been misplaced. What if Walsh was the perpetrator? The assault on the actress might have happened at her house the following morning. I replied then why did Walsh make such a public outcry? Fletcher replied that maybe he was getting out in front of the issue anticipating the autopsy would reveal the rape.

"I said to Fletcher, are you saying our efforts at cover up were successful? That Walsh had no way of knowing that Richardson would publish a sanitized autopsy, so he went off half-cocked to point the finger toward others? Fletcher said that was a possibility. Once the real autopsy report came out, Walsh and the Pasadena newspaper reporter kept suggesting that the police must vigorously investigate everyone at your house that night. Now you also find your name in the newspapers."

Hollister never had this conversation with Chief Fletcher.

Hollister then said to Schachter, "I never considered Walsh might be the culprit. Entirely possible after thinking about it. Perhaps Kelly rejected Walsh's advances. Perhaps they had a falling out. Jealousy because of another man? What if Walsh's newspaper

305

attacks were a way of deflecting attention away from him? What better way than to suggest any of several famous movie actors?"

Schachter followed the chronology as the scandal unfolded. As the attributed source to the *Pasadena Star-News* breaking the story, Schachter seemed to recalled Walsh raising the question about Kelly's death before the pathologist's original autopsy report came to light. If Walsh feared becoming a criminal suspect, why hound the LAPD in the press for complicity in a cover up? What Hollister was saying made no sense. Therefore, this was just a poorly constructed story for Schachter's benefit. He was paid too much to argue with Hollister over something where he had no vested interest.

Having presented the foundation for his argument, Hollister got to the point. "I intend to find out if Walsh is hiding something. We must find a way to stop the damage of this continuing public speculation about the death of a minor movie actress. Whether Walsh is somehow involved or not, if we can damage his credibility in some way, it may help to deflect attention away from Hollywood people. I want you therefore to reengage the services of the private investigation firm. Same as before. Put Walsh under twenty-four surveillance and provide me a report each morning."

"I'll get right on it," Schachter said wondering what Hollister really had up his sleeve.

CHAPTER 24

Los Angeles, California | 1926

Chadwick Hollister cared nothing about Schachter accepting his reason for reestablishing surveillance on Walsh. Schachter would do as he was told. Knowing nothing about the events that night, Schachter did not represent a risk. Guilty of all sorts of white-collar criminal offenses, including bribery and bank fraud, it is unlikely that Schacter would assist law enforcement. The complex trail of falsified transactions had Schachter's fingerprints not Hollister's. Schachter enjoyed controlling the devious world of his own making and being paid handsomely.

Hollister's plan was simple. Consistent with how he operated. Kill Walsh. Change the narrative. Confuse the official investigation. Do not overthink the details. Act decisively. Introduce chaos into the media coverage of the Kelly affair with the objective of deflecting attention entirely away from himself and Hollywood celebrities. Manufacture a big lie with enough credible circumstantial evidence while unwaveringly repeating the lie. The premise of the fabrication does not have to align perfectly with all the known circumstances.

The next hurdle was to convince Kurt Gerhardt to commit two more murders. A lesser man of Hollister's prestigious stature would recoil from the sheer magnitude of engineering multiple murders. However, introspection was not within Chadwick Hollister's egomaniacal makeup.

For Hollister's plan to work, he needed a scenario whereby Walsh is killed in such a manner that does not appear as assassination. Someway consistent with portraying his culpability in Kelly's death. That is where the inspiration to resurrect surveillance on Walsh came into play. The simplified scenario explained as Walsh discovering he is under surveillance and overreacts by shooting the private investigator. Gerhardt then kills Walsh, staging the scene to appear as an exchange of gunfire by planting the two different weapons used to kill both victims.

The second element was to plant incontrovertible evidence in Walsh's possession linking him directly to Kelly's death. His guilt becoming the reason for overreacting to the surveillance. That is accomplished by providing the blue dress, the blue heels, and the torn under garments of Tara Kelly from that night at his house.

Ignoring Gerhardt's instructions that night, Hollister could not bear disposing of them. Instead, he placed them in a safe concealed behind a framed oil painting of the Hollister family English coat of arms, hinged with a concealed release catch. As the scandal progressed in the media, he became apprehensive about the danger of trying to dispose of the evidence linking him to rape and murder. Those articles would now serve to directly implicate Walsh. With Walsh implicated and dead, the matter ends.

He might even be able to indirectly float anonymous stories to the tabloids suggesting lurid details of Walsh's relationship with Tara Kelly that eventually led to rape and murder. Truth was of no concern for sensationalist publications like the Hollywood tabloid *Look-See Magazine*. The Tara Kelly story had all the sensationalistic ingredients of celebrity, sex, and crime. Create enough chaos with misinformation that facts become obscured in a frenzy of conjecture.

With the death of Tara Kelly resolved and the perpetrator dead, the newsworthy value of the story would quickly subside. Lingering unresolved questions became irrelevant.

—

Hollister sat in his favorite chair in his study. Situated next to floor-to-ceiling windows and a walkout glass door to a covered balcony, the last of the day's sunlight streamed into the room. Across from him sat Kurt Gerhardt. Both sipped expensive single malt Scotch.

"I believe I have found a way to conclude this continuing threat over the actress's death, Kurt. Both of our names appearing more prominently in the press is troubling. This investigation from Sacramento reaches beyond my influence to exercise control. I also admit this is a problem of my own making. You have been extraordinarily effective so far in removing problems. Only one more task remains. If you pull this off, we are both become completely clear of suspicion. The whole fucking scandal goes away."

Hollister paused a moment letting his words sink in.

"What is it you need me to do, Sir?"

"Egan Walsh has been the problem from the beginning. I need you to kill him."

The statement shocked Gerhardt. Without revealing surprise other than carefully setting down his glass on the coffee table in front of him, he responded, "Not sure I understand how that helps us, Sir."

"More complicated than just killing Walsh. Let me explain. I had Schachter reactivate the surveillance on Walsh by the private investigative firm. Told Schachter that Fletcher speculated to me that maybe it was not one of my movie star friends that raped Kelly but maybe Walsh. That gave me the idea. The investigators from Sacramento will drag this thing out indefinitely. We need to stop the economic damage this scandal is causing to the movie studios and indirectly to Hollister Financial."

"How does getting rid of Walsh help?"

Hollister smiled. "Because you will shoot the private investigator using a British-made revolver like Walsh used in the Irish War and described in his book. Then you will shoot Walsh with a second gun. Both victims die in the shootout with you planting untraceable guns at the scene."

"What will the police believe the motive to be?"

"That Walsh panicked when discovered he was being watched."

Gerhardt thought that made no sense and raised his eyebrows.

"Listen to the rest, Kurt. After we learn particulars about Walsh's habits, you will construct a scenario to get the private investigator and Walsh together under some pretext. After shooting them and staging the scene, you plant the evidence. Evidence that will undeniably implicate Walsh in the actress's death and therefore serve as the motive to reacting violently when learning his was being followed."

"What evidence?"

"The blue dress and other things the woman wore that night."

"You kept them?"

"I know it was careless, but now it becomes perfect for setting up Walsh. Unable to refute anything since he is dead."

Although a hardened man with no regard for others, Gerhardt never experienced someone with Hollister's depth of ruthlessness in his years as a soldier in combat or as a LAPD officer. Hollister's diabolical cleverness was also not lost on him. His fate was inexorably intertwined with Hollister. Twice having killed on orders from Hollister left him little choice but to continue this macabre affair. He thought Hollister's plan more deranged than clever. Even if he executed the plan successfully, the outcome might not achieve the results Hollister expected.

Typical for Hollister to expect him to figure out how to construct a workable plan to accomplish the objective from Hollister's broad concept.

"Will you do this, Kurt?"

After a moment, Gerhardt responded, "Yes. If I'm able to figure out the critical details necessary to make this work. This state police lieutenant is no dummy. How to get the two targets close together someplace without witnesses? How to conceal myself until making my move? Timing becomes everything. The shooting must be done from very close to both targets. Where to plant the blue dress? Must be someplace that appears logical for a guilty man to hide something so incriminating. How often does Schachter deliver reports from the private investigator?"

"Every morning starting the day after tomorrow."

"Let me see them. How thorough is the surveillance?"

"Around the clock."

"Okay. After I get a feel for Walsh's movements and habits, I will take up my own surveillance. Going to take a bit of doing to put this together, Sir."

"Do what you have to but the sooner this gets done, the better for both of us."

"I understand."

"You pull this off, Kurt, and we can both rest easier. Getting rid of Walsh by setting him up as the perpetrator will end the investigation. The whole issue quickly fades from public interest."

———

A week later, Gerhardt knew enough to form a workable plan. Not perfect by any means with so many moving pieces beyond his control. Risky, yet possible. The risk came not from shooting both victims, but ensuring the scene appeared to fit the intended scenario. Otherwise, it just introduced an entirely new thread for the state investigators to pursue. A narrative that not even Hollister could control. Hollister likely never understood the possible unintended consequences if any detail went wrong. That was the way Hollister operated. Issues commands and expects people around him to find the means of making things happen.

Gerhardt spent most afternoons and evenings for the next several days following Walsh looking for possible places to stage the shooting. The best opportunity seemed to be the house in the Los Feliz neighborhood. The home of his lover Lillian Romano was also Walsh's new residence ever since Walsh left the hospital after the beating by the off-duty LAPD officers arranged by Gerhardt. The homes on the street were set on large lots. Enough distance between houses to inhibit observation by anybody looking out their windows. The street did not have streetlights making the plan possible. It meant choosing a time after dark when the Romano woman was not home.

Once he settled on the place, the next challenge was devising how to get Walsh and his watcher close enough together to simulate a confrontation. By now he identified two different people from the private investigative firm alternating surveillance on Walsh. As single watchers rather than a team, it forced them largely to remain in their automobiles to appear partially unnoticed, particularly at night. That also served the need for Gerhardt to approach the watcher unnoticed.

The solution came to him suddenly. Surprised that he did not think of it earlier. He will impersonate a plainclothes police officer. Armed with an authentic black-market LAPD detective badge.

The rough plan called for picking a time after dark which in December could be early evening. Wait close by in his car until Walsh drives up. Expecting the watcher to drive up immediately following Walsh's arrival, Gerhardt immediately exits his car. As the watcher parks his car, flash his badge at the guy behind the wheel. Order him out of the car while yelling out to Walsh, "I'm LAPD, Mr. Walsh. Wait up a moment." He will then pull the private investigator along by the arm and walk toward Walsh. Once close enough to Walsh, release the watcher's arm and show his badge to Walsh. Move next to Walsh and face the watcher. "Do you know this fellow?" he will ask Walsh. "He's been watching this house every night." Wearing leather gloves to avoid fingerprints, extract a Webley .455 revolver from a shoulder holster and shoot the watcher. Simultaneously then pull a .38 revolver from his jacket pocket with his left hand and shoot Walsh.

Check that both victims are mortally wounded or finish them by suffocating them. Then quickly place the weapons in their hands. Time now becomes critical. Retrieve a suitcase stuffed with Tara Kelly's clothing from his car across the street and return to place it in the trunk of Walsh's car. Leave the scene slowly with headlights extinguished until clear of the area.

Simple enough if the timing works to plan. And if no car drives by or a neighbor looks out a window and sees him leaving the scene. Even though too far away for anyone to recognize him, the involvement of a third person destroys the scenario of the two victims shooting each other.

Do the police accept the evidence planted in Walsh's car implicating him as Kelly's possible assailant? If so, do they accept that Walsh panicked and shot a private investigator? Do the police accept Schachter's and Hollister's explanation for hiring a private investigator to watch Walsh? That becomes Hollister's problem. No physical evidence exists to link him to the murders. The guns are stolen and purchased from a black-market source.

Before revealing his plan to Hollister, Gerhardt drove to Romano's neighborhood and walked the anticipated sequence of movements depending on exactly where the watcher parks his car. Using a stopwatch, he memorizes the steps and timing of the choreography to build a timeline. Back at Hollister's house, he rehearses in the backyard in real time. Executing the timing of every detail becomes critical for success.

When satisfied, he goes over the plan with Hollister. Asking only a few questions, Hollister is astounded by the level of detail in Gerhardt's plan, adding to confidence for its success. Gerhardt is an invaluable asset possessing remarkable capabilities. "I like it. When can you do this?"

"I'll make the first attempt tomorrow night. It will depend on Walsh arriving at the house and the Romano woman not being home. If that doesn't happen, then I keep trying each successive night until the circumstances are right. Either way, I'll return here immediately."

—

It took until the third night before the required circumstances aligned. Gerhardt first drove past the house to observe the location. Knowing the cars driven by Walsh and Romano, neither was in the driveway. He then drove a short distance away in front of the closest adjacent neighbor's house to wait. It was still early, shortly after sunset. An hour before darkness. A cloudy night with very little moonlight.

He knew where the surveillance car usually parked. A short distance from Romano's residence on North Catalina Street in front of a vacant lot on the opposite side of the street. Gerhardt observed the surveillance routine on several different nights. Walsh arrives and parks in Romano's driveway. The private investigator following pulls to the curb a short distance on the opposite side of the street and extinguishes his headlights.

It was a chilly Wednesday night two weeks before Christmas. The Romano residence was located on a corner lot on North Catalina Street and Bonvue Avenue. After observing that neither Walsh's nor Romano's car were parked in the driveway, Gerhardt parked on Bonvue. He could observe Romano's driveway from across the intersection of Catalina and Bonvue while waiting for the private investigator to appear and park on the opposite side of Catalina. Seeing approaching headlights, Gerhardt leaned down in the seat to avoid being seen as a car approached from the south. Gerhardt watched Walsh's car turn into Romano's driveway.

Within seconds another car pulled to a stop across the street and turned off the headlights. The watcher. Gerhardt immediately exited his car and strode briskly across the street coming up behind the watcher's car.

Wasting no time, Gerhardt pulled open the driver's door and stuck his badge in the face of the driver while yelling loudly, "Get out of the car! What are you doing here?"

The startled man complied responding, "I'm a private investigator. Watching someone."

Gerhardt grabbed the man's arm roughly. Looking across the street, he saw Walsh standing next to his car in the driveway looking toward them after hearing Gerhardt yell at the driver.

"I'm LAPD, Mr. Walsh. No cause for alarm. Wait up a moment," Gerhardt yelled out as he marched the private investigator by the arm across the street toward Walsh.

Arriving in front of Walsh, Gerhardt pulled his badge. "Know this guy?"

Walsh replied, "No. Who is he?"

"Claims to be a private investigator. We've also been watching your house on orders from state investigators working on the Tara Kelly case."

As Gerhardt said this, he turned to face the private investigator while stepping back next to Walsh. Reaching inside his jacket he extracted the Webley .455 revolver from a shoulder holster then fired two rounds into the private investigator striking him in the midsection. The large caliber rounds dropped the man instantly.

Walsh instinctively reverted to training. Dropping down on his left knee, he spun to his left to confront the shooter while drawing his own weapon expecting he might be shot next.

As Walsh turned facing Gerhardt, Gerhardt held revolvers in both hands. He fired a round at Walsh from his left hand holding a short-barreled .38. The shot missed Walsh from a combination of Gerhardt using his left hand and Walsh's unexpected defensive reaction now pointing a weapon back at him from his crouch position.

Walsh responded almost simultaneously as Gerhardt fired. IRA training called for firing twice in rapid succession to ensure downing your adversary. Walsh's first round struck Gerhardt in the lower midsection and the second into his upper chest.

Gerhardt staggered for a moment before falling to the sidewalk on both knees before collapsing onto his side, dropping both revolvers.

Walsh kicked away the two weapons. He then checked the private investigator. No pulse. After searching the man's body, he found a driver's license and private investigator's license.

Turning to Gerhardt, "Who are you?"

Propping himself up by one hand with difficulty, Gerhardt did not immediately respond as he struggled to breathe. Coughing blood indicated a round punctured the lung. Blood-soaked Gerhardt's shirt in an expanding stain from extensive bleeding of the wound to his lower abdomen.

Walsh removed the LAPD badge and Gerhardt's wallet. He found no identification as a police officer. The driver's license was in the name of Kurt Gerhardt. 1440 Benedict Canyon Drive

315

indicated as his address. Walsh recognized the address as the residence of Chadwick Hollister. "You work for Chadwick Hollister?"

Gerhardt made no response.

"Listen to me. If you don't get medical attention quickly you will bleed to death. What was your plan tonight?" With Gerhardt remaining silent, "If you don't give me answers then I'm going to stand here and watch you bleed out. You aren't a cop so I can claim self-defense. I even have a concealed weapons permit. You don't have much time left."

With difficulty, Gerhardt said, "I came here to kill you."

"The man you shot is a private investigator. Explain that."

"Chadwick Hollister hired the firm some time ago to follow your movements even before discovery of the actual autopsy report. I shot him with the Webley. The same weapon you cited in your book. Intended to appear as if you shot him. The revolvers are   untraceable."

"Then you kill me with the .38? Plant it on the private investigator to make it look like we shot each other?"

"Yes."

"The reason behind this?"

Gerhardt said nothing for several moments.

"You want me to call for medical help or not?"

"In my car I have evidence implicating you in the rape and murder of your actress friend."

"What evidence?"

"The blue dress she wore to the party that Saturday night. I was going to put it in your car. Make the shooting look like you realized you were under surveillance and panicked."

"Did you rape and murder Tara Kelly?"

"No. It was Hollister."

Shocked by the revelation, Walsh began piecing everything together. Whether it was Gerhardt or Hollister, Hollister was at least complicit. Obviously, Hollister was the source of the hush money paid to Dr. Richardson. Probably bribed LAPD Chief Fletcher.

"So why don't I just let you die?"

"Because I can testify against Hollister?"

"What good will that do you?"

"Enough to cut a deal to avoid the death penalty."

"Tell me how it happened."

"Hollister drugged the actress with cocaine-laced cigarettes then raped her. It went too far, or he just went crazy. He then gave her enough cocaine to kill her. Better dead than alive to testify against him for rape. I'll testify to that if you get me medical help."

"And Hollister kept Kelly's blue dress? Why?"

"Don't know. I told him to get rid of it."

"Did you take Tara Kelly home?"

"Yes."

"Was she already dead?"

"I think so."

"Did you kill Dr. Richardson?"

"Yes."

Gerhardt's replies came with increasing physical difficulty. Coughing up more blood and progressively appearing weaker from the loss of blood, he had little time left.

"I'll testify. Now call for help."

Walsh remained silent contemplating the alternatives. If Gerhardt survived, he would recant everything. Hollister would provide the best defense attorney. If Gerhardt claimed Hollister to be the rapist, there existed no evidence in support of that. The evidence points to Gerhardt being the rapist. The blue dress is in his possession. Nothing linked Hollister to providing cocaine to Kelly. Hollister's only exposure possibly the Richardson hush money. Even if Hollister proved to be the source, his lawyers could construct any of several different scenarios to obscure his culpability. With no direct evidence to corroborate Gerhardt's testimony, Hollister might never be charged. Gerhart instead likely to be convicted and sentenced to hang for Kelly's rape and murder.

Hollister's greatest exposure was the hiring of a private investigation firm to follow Walsh. Yet even that could be explained by Hollister's vested interest in following the damaging scandal closely. Might even use the motive that he suspected Walsh.

Although Hollister was undoubtedly the person that paid the hush money to Dr. Richardson, that might be difficult to prove, or otherwise defensible casting reasonable doubt.

After a long interval, Gerhardt rasped, "Well? Do we have a deal?"

Walsh looked down at the growing pool of blood forming around Gerhardt. Not likely that medical help could arrive in time to save him. No decision for Walsh to make. He assumed Gerhardt must have arranged for his beating by the dirty cops.

"Don't see any reason to help you. I'm going to instead just stand here and watch you bleed to death."

Reconciled to his fate, Gerhardt did not respond. Fading quickly, then toppling over unconscious, Walsh let a few minutes pass before confirming there was no pulse. No neighbor apparently heard the gunshots and called the police. No sirens in the distance.

Walsh made the telephone call. Not to the LAPD but to State Police Lieutenant Townsend at his temporary LAPD office number, finally reaching him at his hotel number written on the back of his business card. Lieutenant Townsend and Assistant Attorney General arrived within thirty minutes.

Fortunately, Lilly worked late that night. Could not imagine what might have happened had she been home when this happened.

Waiting for Townsend to arrive allowed Walsh time to recover his composure. Prepare himself for hours of interrogation. Figuring out what to do next. Should he tell Townsend and Assistant Attorney General Curry that Gerhardt claimed Hollister raped and murdered Kelly before he died of his wounds? What good would that do except embroil him indefinitely in this endless tragedy?

No evidence existed to implicate Hollister. The evidence directly pointed to Gerhardt. Gerhardt had the opportunity of raping Kelly at her home then murdering her. More likely than an assault happening upstairs while the Hollywood elite partied downstairs. Yet Walsh believed Gerhardt. Hollister might never be held accountable. The person responsible for three murders.

Walsh had no plan about what he might do except for immediate priorities. Say nothing about Gerhardt's dying declaration. Let Townsend and Curry figure out what happened by the evidence that made clear this was a failed attempt on his life and to exonerate other potential suspects. Let them find the blue dress in Gerhardt's car. If they believed Chadwick Hollister was behind this, it fell to them to attempt to make a criminal case.

Gerhardt no longer presented a danger. Only what would happen to Chadwick Hollister remained unfinished. Knowing what happened to Tara Kelly and what he endured to find her justice made the fate of Hollister intensely personal.

Walsh heard the distant wail of police sirens. Something provoked him to go back to Gerhardt's body. In his pockets he found a set of keys on a separate key ring from the car keys. Possibly keys to Hollister's house. Mindful not to keep them on his person, Walsh walked to a row of bushes close to the house and tossed the key ring behind the plants.

Having nothing specific in mind, Walsh only knew that keys to Hollister's residence might become useful. Hollister was a murderer many times over. Gerhardt merely his murder weapon. With Gerhardt dead and possessing Tara Kelly's dress from that night, no evidence directly implicated Hollister in her murder. Nor was there evidence that Richardson's death was even murder much less ordered by Hollister. Tonight's murder of the private investigator could easily be attributed to Gerhardt's doing. Hollister must be made to suffer retribution.

CHAPTER 25

Los Angeles, California | 1926

California State Police Lieutenant Duncan Townsend arrived with Assistant Attorney General Albert Curry at Lilly Romano's house minutes before two LAPD vehicles and four officers arrived.

They notified the LAPD after receiving Walsh's call since it was within their jurisdiction.

Townsend approached Walsh. "On the telephone you said you shot Kurt Gerhardt after he first shot a private investigator then tried to shoot you?"

"That's right."

"Give me your gun, Mr. Walsh."

Townsend pocketed Walsh's gun, taking it with a handkerchief to preserve fingerprints then began examining the two shooting victims.

Curry approached the uniformed LAPD sergeant and officers flashing his credentials. "This is my crime scene, Sergeant. It's associated with a much larger case that falls under my authority as special state prosecutor. You are to secure the scene but do not touch anything until State Police Lieutenant Townsend and I are through. Call this into your watch commander. Send an investigative team, photographer, and someone from the medical examiner's office immediately. Understood?"

The LAPD sergeant nodded as Townsend approached and tossed Gerhardt's car keys to the officer. "Find the car these keys belong to. Search it but do not move it."

Townsend and Curry stood next to Walsh. Curry said, "Okay. Tell us what happened."

Walsh describing the events, omitting only Gerhardt's dying declaration. If Curry was to charge Hollister with murder, he must find tangible evidence not hearsay from another murderer. The only links of Hollister to any crimes were circumstantial. Hollister was undoubtedly the source of the hush money paid to Dr. Richardson but likely not traceable to back to Hollister. Hollister probably hired this private investigator but that remains unclear. With the right lawyer, Hollister could explain away these circumstances sufficient to cast reasonable doubt in the mind of a jury.

Lilly Romano drove up and parked quickly in the street clogged with police vehicles. Seeing Walsh, she approached and looked aghast at the bodies of Gerhardt and the private investigator before embracing Walsh. "Are you alright?"

"Fine."

"What happened?"

Townsend said, "Who are you, mam?"

"Lillian Romano. This is my house. Egan Walsh lives here."

Curry said, "I am Assistant Attorney General Albert Curry, Miss Romano. I'm in charge of investigating the circumstances surrounding the death of the actress Tara Kelly. It seems that this matter tonight is another piece of the puzzle connected to that mystery. Let's go inside and talk further."

They all took seats in the living room, when the uniformed LAPD sergeant entered through the front door holding a small suitcase. "This is the only thing we found in the car, Mr. Curry."

Curry placed the suitcase on his lap and opened the latch using a handkerchief. Inside was a blue dress and matching blue heels. Underneath those items was a torn undergarment. Curry did not touch the items to avoid disturbing any forensic evidence. That will be all, Sergeant. When the officer left, Curry turned the suitcase around for everyone to see.

"Tara Kelly's dress from the night of the party I imagine. Completes the picture of what happened tonight. Gerhardt stages the shooting to make it appear that Mr. Walsh panicked when confronted by someone watching him. He's been viciously attacked previously. Now armed, he panics and draws his weapon. Shoots the private investigator who is armed. The investigator was not armed but Gerhardt brought a weapon to fulfill the charade. Gerhardt also brought the large caliber Webley he determined from reading your book as a weapon you might possess, Mr. Walsh. Do you have such a weapon?"

"Yes. My service revolver from the war in Ireland. Too large and heavy for proper concealment under a suit jacket. When I took the advice of a good friend to go armed after the beating, I purchased the smaller and Colt."

Curry said, "My guess is that Gerhardt had no idea you were armed. This was to be easy. Plant the Webley in your hand and the snub nosed .38 on the private investigator. Retrieve this suitcase with the incriminating evidence of the assault and murder of Tara Kelly and place it in your car, Mr. Walsh. Even with other inconsistencies, it could prove compelling evidence that you are responsible for the actress's death with your death denying the ability to interrogate you. Now walk us again through every detail of what transpired since you arrived here."

Walsh began methodically explaining. Townsend took notes as he and Curry asked clarification questions. Lilly sat transfixed hearing of Walsh's narrow escape. After two LAPD detectives arrived with a photographer and a forensics team, Walsh repeated the story for their benefit.

After concluding the questioning, the lead LAPD detective said, you will have to come with us to the Hollywood Division station, Mr. Walsh to make an official statement."

"Mr. Walsh is my witness, Detective. He just survived a murder attempt. His statement can wait until tomorrow. Any questions, have your commander call me at any of these telephone numbers." Handing the LAPD detective his business card, "Now we're going to leave Mr. Walsh and Miss Romano alone while we clean up the mess out front."

As they filed out of the house, Walsh said, "Thank you, Mr. Curry."

Alone and emotionally exhausted, Lilly hugged him. "Does this mean the ordeal is at an end, Egan?"

"For us it is. I still think Chadwick Hollister is complicit in this entire affair. Too many unexplained things have his fingerprints all over them. Kurt Gerhardt did not have the means to pay hush money or influence someone as high ranking as LAPD Assistant Chief Fletcher to help cover up Kelly's death as accidental. With Hollister's money and influence he might escape accountability. That is out of our hands now. Nothing more we can do. We can return to a normal life, Lilly."

She hugged him again and kissed him. "Not sure what normal will feel like. So far, life with you is never boring. I'll welcome peace and quiet."

Walsh replied, "Well, we have another movie to make. I'm more energized about that than ever. Right now, one last obligation remains. I need to tell Benny what happened. After all this, he deserves to break the story in his newspaper. I'll have him pick me up and take me to the LAPD station to give my statement tomorrow morning.

"Another media circus, but that will die away quickly. Essentially the story is finished."

However, in Egan Walsh's mind, the matter was not finished. That depended on Chadwick Hollister surviving Curry's investigation. Unless Curry uncovered something sufficiently incriminating, the circumstantial case against Hollister would not warrant charging him criminally. A very likely outcome. Even if brought to trial, convicting Chadwick Hollister was by no means a certainty.

—

The media circus began after Benny Zimmerman led with his story in the *Pasadena Star-News* that made the front pages of newspapers the following day across the country.

Tara Kelly Murder Reaches Milestone Conclusion

Hollywood, CA: Benjamin Zimmerman:

Two nights ago, the mystery surrounding the rape and murder of Tara Kelly came to conclusion. Reporter and friend of the deceased actress, Egan Walsh had led a campaign to discover the truth in what became an obvious cover up of Kelly's death. Walsh's efforts resulted in a brutal physical assault weeks ago that landed him in the hospital. On Tuesday night of this week an assassination attempt occurred on Walsh in the Hollywood Hills.

From the previous assault, Walsh was legally armed at the time. Walsh surprised and shot dead the would-be assassin. That person was Kurt Gerhardt, driver and bodyguard for Chadwick Hollister. Hollister is a prominent Southland commercial banker connected with the movie industry. It was at a party hosted by Hollister in Beverly Hills months ago that the actress Tara Kelly attended which was the last time she was seen alive.

According to the State of California Special Prosecutor Assistant Attorney General Albert Curry in charge of the Kelly investigation, Gerhardt attempted to stage a scene to incriminate Walsh as Tara Kelly's assailant. In the process, Gerhardt murdered another person at the scene and was found in possession of the dress that Kelly wore the night of the party. Possession of this evidence establishes Kurt Gerhardt's direct involvement in the rape and murder of Tara Kelly. Kurt Gerhardt either raped and murdered Tara Kelly or acted as a co-conspirator to someone else that directly committed the crime.

Zimmerman's column went on to describe the unresolved inconsistencies surrounding Kelly's death. Those details and Gerhardt's connection made Chadwick Hollister a suspect involved in the violent crimes against Kelly along with subsequent associated criminal offenses.

Gerhardt's murder of the private investigator and his attempted murder of Walsh made for a dramatic story that overshadowed Zimmerman's attempt at implicating Hollister's probable complicity. As with Walsh, Benny Zimmerman was certain that Hollister was behind the cover up and possibly even Kelly's assailant. Zimmerman's column called specifically for Chadwick Hollister to better explain what transpired that night at his house. He was the person that ordered his employee Gerhardt to drive Kelly home presenting the opportunity for Gerhardt to commit the assault then fatally poison Kelly.

Zimmerman's column attributed the resolving of Tara Kelly's death to the singular efforts of Egan Walsh. His portrayal of Walsh's tenacity, suffering a serious physical attack putting him in the hospital, then ending the mystery by escaping death at the hands of the person directly involved in the murder of Tara Kelly, made Walsh a national celebrity.

As Walsh suspected, after a week, the story no longer made the front pages. The mystery of Tara Kelly's death solved. The culprit identified by possessing evidence only the killer could possess. That Kurt Gerhardt might have engaged in trying to cover up the crime held decreasing news value. Even connecting Hollister to the murderer of the private investigator made little difference. Seizing the opportunity, Hollister immediately went on a media counterattack against continuing suspicions appearing in print as to his involvement in a cover up. He had the money to hire a team of the best criminal defense attorneys that threatened civil action for libel. Hollister also possessed influence with the publishers of the *Los Angeles Times* and the *New York Times* to downplay attacks directed toward him and print sympathetic editorials.

Walsh observed this as his concerns of Hollister escaping justice began materializing. He had keys to Hollister's residence. When he kept them, he knew he harbored taking some form of retribution against Hollister after Gerhardt confessed. Gerhardt might have murdered Kelly, but he did not rape her. If he murdered Kelly, then it was on Hollister's orders.

Walsh owed it to Tara Kelly to ensure Chadwick Hollister received suitable retributive justice.

—

His plan was simple. Yet it must remain his secret alone. He would not burden anyone else for his unorthodox decision to personally administer justice. The same decision that Wyatt Earp related making by avenging the murder of his brother and the assault on his family by outlaws protected by corrupt law enforcement in Tombstone, Arizona in 1882.

For Egan Walsh, times were now much different with the passage of decades. He could not do something as blatantly illegal in 1926 Los Angeles. What he had in mind held risk, but the circumstances existed for making it appear credible.

—

After spending a day working on the set of *Dying for Ireland*, Walsh telephoned Lilly at her Western Avenue Fox Films office.

Said Zimmerman left a message earlier that he wanted to discuss something for his next piece about the aftermath of the Kelly affair. Lilly Romano said she would then take the opportunity to work a while longer and see him at home later that night.

It was dark on this moonless December night. He came prepared for a clandestine entry into Hollister's home. A burglar's outfit. A set of black workingman's clothing, rubber soled shoes, knit cap, tight-fitting black leather gloves, and shoulder holster with the .38 revolver.

He parked a half mile down the hill on Benedict Canyon Drive from Hollister's estate. Climbing the eight-foot-high wrought iron fence not visible from the road, he dropped to the other side a couple of hundred yards from the house. Lights were on in the main house, but only on the second floor. No cars in the front driveway suggested Hollister should be alone upstairs.

He tried the back door leading from the kitchen. Locked. A good sign that things were buttoned up for the night. Hollister no longer had his bodyguard Gerhardt for protection. The housekeeping staff are probably in their quarters as evidenced by the lights on in the separate building.

Finding the correct key, Walsh entered quietly. Although he did not know the layout of the house, light from upstairs afforded some illumination of the staircase. Ascending silently and reaching the top, light came from an open door into the darkened hallway. Maybe a study or bedroom. For this to work, Hollister must be alone. If Walsh found someone else with him, he would mimic the entry as a burglary. He raised a black scarf from around his neck to cover the lower half of his face.

He approached an open set of double doors. Withdrawing his revolver, he took a careful look inside the lit room. Artwork adorned wood-paneled walls. Bookshelves lined one wall. A spacious room with large windows looking toward the back of the house with landscape lights visible in the garden walkways at the rear of the house.

In a comfortable high-back leather stuffed chair, Walsh could see the back of Chadwick Hollister's head. Smoke from a cigar circled upward as Hollister looked out the windows. Next to the chair a crystal tumbler with an amber drink sat on an end table. No one else was in the room.

No longer concerned about making a sound. Walsh quickly came around Hollister's chair.

Hollister jerked his head around taking in the shock of a masked figure wearing a mask pointing a gun. "What the hell! How'd you get in here?"

"Stay seated."

"If it's money you're after, I have a few hundred dollars in cash. No jewelry. I live alone with just a couple of household staff."

"Yes, I know. The staff live over the garage. Correct?"

Hollister was surprised by the question. "Yes."

"Then you are alone?"

"Yes."

"Is this a burglary?"

"Not exactly. Something far worse I imagine. I'm here to see justice done for Tara Kelly."

Now frightened more than if this was a burglary, "Who are you?"

"The person that killed your man Gerhardt."

"Walsh?"

"Before Gerhardt died, he told me what happened the night of your party. How you drugged Tara Kelly with cigarettes containing cocaine. How you raped her here in one of the bedrooms. How you then murdered her."

"Why would Gerhardt tell you all this?"

"Because he thought he might save himself. Rapidly bleeding out from two gunshot wounds I inflicted. After you ordered those corrupt cops to attack me, I thought it best to protect myself. Gerhardt never expected me to be armed."

"What do you intend to do? Shoot me too?"

"Nothing that easy. You need to pay a higher price for all the people you murdered. Tara Kelly. The pathologist. The private investigator. Better that you hang for your crimes. Waiting for the day when you climb the steps to the gallows is far better

328

punishment. So, you are going to write out a confession. Get over to the desk."

"If I don't do this, you'll shoot me?"

"That would not provide me with enough satisfaction. Now get over to the desk."

Hollister got up from the chair.

"Do you have a gun?" Walsh said.

"In the top right-hand drawer of the desk."

Walsh extracted a .38 revolver from the desk and put it in his pocket. "Take a seat at the desk."

Hollister complied. Writing a confession under duress held no credibility nor any legal weight as evidence. Walsh had no way to convey it to police investigators without incriminating himself. The best Walsh could do was publish the document which Hollister could deny. In the context of other issues surrounding the Kelly matter, this added nothing to his legal jeopardy.

Walsh said, "Take out pen and paper. Write down in your own words what you did from the time you gave Tara Kelly cocaine, to the sexual assault, then how you killed her. Tell me out loud what you are writing."

"And if I refuse?"

"Then you will go through a good deal of suffering. In Ireland a terrible fate for a traitor was to shoot him in both knees. Terrifically painful. Makes you a cripple. The result becomes the same so it's better to avoid that unpleasantness. The choice is yours."

"Mind if I have a cigarette? Hollister asked.

"One with cocaine?"

Hollister just nodded.

"Go ahead if it helps."

Hollister hesitated before beginning. Walsh stuck his revolver against Hollister's right temple and said, "Get to it."

Hollister inhaled strongly from the cocaine-laced cigarette. The cocaine relaxed him enough that after a few minutes he was briskly writing to conclude this ordeal.

Walsh took the opportunity to switch weapons without Hollister noticing. He now held Hollister's own revolver against his temple.

Finishing the confession, Hollister laid down the fountain pen.

Walsh said, "Sign it," while pressing Hollister's revolver more firmly against his temple.

As Chadwick Hollister finished signing his name in a flourish, Egan Walsh pulled the trigger.

Having moved slightly to the side, Walsh avoided the blood and tissue splatter from the bullet's exit wound. Pressing the barrel of the revolver to Hollister's head also had the effect of dampening the muzzle sound.

Leaving everything as it was, Walsh let the revolver fall to the floor. Leaving Hollister's study immediately, he crept downstairs. Looking outside the kitchen window he could see the lights still on in the staff apartments above the garage. He quickly exited the backdoor and locked it from the outside. The only illumination was a single exterior light next to the back door. It was a moonless night and once clear of the light, no one from the staff quarters could probably see him dressed in black with the darkened first-floor interior of the house.

He was across the lawn, over the fence and back in his car within fifteen minutes. Once back in the car, he put it in neutral and coasted for a distance downhill before engaging the engine. Before arriving back at Lilly's house, he pulled over to discard his burglar outfit in a trash bin and change back into his suit. In his trunk he found a rag in the toolbox kit and suitably soiled his hands and white shirt. His excuse for arriving late was because his car broke down. *Never made his meeting with Benny Zimmerman. Had to walk a long way to find a service station then pay someone to drive back to the car and tow him into the garage. The repair turned out relatively minor for a mechanic living next door willing to disrupt his evening to make repairs when I offered him forty dollars.*

Walsh hated deceiving Lilly, but this must forever remain his burden alone. While feeling no remorse, he felt himself a responsible member of society. The social order cannot function with individuals delivering their own justice. That part of him detested the compulsion compelling him to deliver justice for Tara Kelly. Both Hollister and Gerhardt were unquestionably guilty of murder. Both were guilty of attempting to kill him. Yet while

Gerhardt's death was self-defense, he could not claim the same for Hollister.

For the rest of his days, he would revisit the moral implications of his actions this night. Although a non-practicing Catholic since a young boy, remnants of early catechism instruction still left an imprint. Not enough to visit a confessional, yet enough to cause him to question the ethical implications of killing Chadwick Hollister.

———

The housekeeper discovered Chadwick Hollister's head slumped over the desk in a great pool of blood in the morning. The news made the newspapers the following day.

Tara Kelly Murder Mystery Solved

Hollywood, CA: Benjamin Zimmerman:

Yesterday, the housekeeper of Chadwick Hollister of the New York commercial and investment bank Hollister Financial discovered Hollister's body in his study at his Beverly Hills estate. The medical examiner-coroner's office ruled Hollister's death as suicide from a self-inflicted gunshot wound to the head. A suicide note found next to the body written by Hollister confessed his responsibly for the rape and murder of actress Tara Kelly months ago when she attended a celebrity movie star party at Hollister's Beverly Hills home. Two nights ago, the mystery surrounding the rape and murder of Tara Kelly appeared to come conclusion.

Hollister was under mounting suspicion following the death of his driver and bodyguard Kurt Gerhardt in the attempted murder of journalist Egan Walsh just weeks ago. Assistant State Attorney General Albert Curry commented that circumstances indicated that Gerhardt was attempting to murder Walsh and place evidence that would incriminate Walsh for Tara Kelly's death. Because of a prior assault on his person, Walsh was legally armed and killed Gerhardt in self-defense. At the time of Kurt Gerhardt's death, the media concluded that Gerhardt murdered Tara Kelly. With the confession and suicide of Chadwick Hollister, Gerhardt's role as an accomplice to Hollister comes into perspective.

Assistant Attorney General Curry believes that Hollister feared possible exposure and the possibility of being charged with a capital crime. Appearing under the influence of both alcohol and cocaine according to the autopsy, Hollister wrote out a confession that conformed to all the known facts surrounding Tara Kelly's death then took his own life with a bullet to the head.

With the deaths of Gerhardt and now Hollister, Assistant Attorney General Albert Curry announced that various evidentiary details established conclusively that Chadwick Hollister and Kurt Gerhardt were responsible for the death of Tara Kelly. Other aspects of possible cover up among Los Angeles elected officials remain under investigation, but the Tara Kelly case is otherwise closed.

Hollywood and movie audiences around the country can now breathe a sigh of relief. The tragic murder of the actress Tara Kelly was not truly another Hollywood scandal. It was nothing more than a vicious criminal act perpetrated by someone with enough wealth and influence to obstruct justice. Yet he could not escape the justice imposed by incurring the unrelenting pressure caused by fear of discovery and thereby dying on the gallows for his crimes.

Chapter 26

Forty-four-year-old Daniel Miller sat in a movie theater in Belfast, Northern Ireland. An afternoon matinee performance since he worked nights at the Harlan & Wolff Shipyards as a security guard. The theater is small. Music accompaniment to the silent movies is provided by a phonograph rather than a piano player. Located on Shankill Road, this was a working-class Protestant neighborhood. Politically, staunchly British loyalist. The northern six counties of Ireland holding a majority of Protestants chose by referendum to remain part of Great Britain rather than join the largely Catholic population of the southern twenty-six counties of the Irish Free State established following the Irish War of Independence.

Miller was only one of a handful of patrons in the theater. He came to watch the American-made movie *Price of Freedom*, set in what Miller called the Anglo-Irish War. Ireland's largely successful rebellion to disassociate from Great Britain. Having served with British security forces in the violent conflict to put down the Irish rebellion, the conflict was intensely personal for Miller.

Midway into the movie, a title card appeared on screen announcing the forthcoming encounter between the Irish IRA and the British Auxiliaries of the RIC known as the Kilmichael Ambush. Miller braced for what was to come on screen.

The film's physical surroundings brought forth a rush of vivid memories. The scene portrayed an IRA ambush of two British lorries carrying eighteen heavily armed RIC Auxiliary officers on a road in County Cork. Miller was there that day.

The scene opened with IRA fighters concealed behind a rock outcropping north of the road. Moving slowly along the road, the first British lorry stopped when an IRA officer in uniform appears standing in the road. The IRA officer then throws a grenade into the lorry. IRA fighters break from cover and open fire on the British Auxiliaries as they scrabble to get out of the damaged lorry. A bloody massacre leaves all nine RIC officers dead or dying after only five minutes, portrayed in two minutes of the movie.

The following film scene switches to the second lorry. In the actual event, Daniel Miller commanded eight other RIC officers portrayed in the movie's reenactment.

Miller sat forward in his seat in the darkened theater as the scene unfolded. With the IRA losing the element of surprise, the British in the second lorry dismount the vehicle. As they take up defensive positions, an intense firefight erupts. As the filmed action focuses on the starring actor portraying an IRA attacker, the scene then switches to the face of another attacking IRA fighter. This actor is extending his arm holding a Webley .455 revolver, the same sidearm Miller carried that day. A brief several-second closeup shows the actor's face as he fires his weapon repeatedly. The film then advances to the IRA's target, a RIC Auxiliary in uniform being struck down by the IRA bullets.

The shock of what Daniel Miller just saw on the theater screen was overpowering. He sunk back into the theater seat breathing rapidly. Impossible what he thought he just saw. Was his mind playing tricks? He watched the remainder of the movie, but the face of the IRA shooter never reappeared. The only way to be certain of what he saw was to watch the movie again.

He immediately purchased another ticket for the next late afternoon showing. Enough time to allow getting to his night shift job later that evening. He decided to settle his nerves with a couple of whiskeys before returning to his room and getting into his work uniform.

Seated again in the theater, he selected a seat closer to the screen. He watched the opening credits to understand what movie studio filmed this movie. Produced by Fox Films and filmed in Hollywood, California. The names of the actors displayed meant nothing to Miller. The man he saw on screen only appeared for a few seconds and might not be listed. However, he never learned the name of the man that shot him that terrible day in November 1920.

He braced for those few vital seconds to again reappear. Once those frames passed, he became certain the actor was the very same IRA gunman that shot him repeatedly that day in Cork and left him for dead. How was that possible? For the rest of the movie, he replayed events of that day over and over. A day that transformed his life. Could this really be the same man, or just someone with a close resemblance? Or was this a figment of his imagination?

The next afternoon he watched the movie for a third time. This time there left no doubt that the actor was the man that shot him three times that day. Cost him his left eye and limited use of his left arm. Left for dead after the victorious IRA left the battlefield, he somehow survived. As serious and painful as his wounds were, his ordeal remained far from over. He recalled enduring rain with a temperature cold enough for frost throughout the night adding greatly to his suffering until rescue arrived late the next morning. Daniel Miller became the only RIC survivor of the Kilmichael engagement.

The following day Miller went to the public library in hopes of learning more about American movie making, Fox Films, and this place called Hollywood. How could he learn the names of those appearing in *Price of Freedom*?

———

Daniel Miller's life changed forever in County Cork that cold November day in 1920 in County Cork. While the bodies of his comrades were removed from the battle site to Macroom Castle, the headquarters of his Auxiliary RIC Division company, Miller was taken to a hospital in Cork City. Ultimately, the bodies of the dead Auxiliaries would travel by a Royal Navy destroyer to Wales with an honor guard for individual military funerals.

While British newspapers eulogized the heroic service of the fallen dead, survivor Daniel Miller was soon forgotten. Following immediate surgery in Cork, he was transferred two weeks later to a British military hospital in Liverpool where he spent several more weeks recovering. The wound to his lower abdomen missed damaging major organs but should have proved fatal from loss of blood, hypothermia, or infection. In that sense, he was fortunate to be alive.

However, the other two wounds would change his life. In addition to the patch covering his empty left eye socket, a lengthy ugly scar extended from his cheekbone under the eye patch down the left side of his cheek. The round that struck his left arm rendered his elbow nearly useless with severely impaired range of movement. Damage to the ulnar nerve at the elbow also prevented full use of his fingers and left hand.

———

Unemployment in the British United Kingdom remained high when Miller demobilized from the Army in 1919 following the Armistice that ended the Great War. Economic recession followed the four years of WWI as the warring parties struggled to assimilate the staggering numbers of demobilized military. War debt destroyed many European economies including that of the United Kingdom. Northern Ireland suffered along with the rest of the UK.

Daniel Miller begin service with the Royal Inniskilling Fusiliers Regiment of the British Army in 1899 at the age of seventeen. Hoping to escape a workingman's life in the shipyard like his father a riveter, he joined the British Army just before the outbreak of the Second Boer War in South Africa. Distinguishing himself in that brutal conflict, he quickly rose to the rank of corporal. He subsequently served in postings to Ireland, England, China, and India. When WWI broke out the Regiment became part of the British

Army 36th Division, better known as the Ulster Division. Now Sergeant Major of the 1st Battalion, Miller saw combat at Gallipoli and later the Western Front at the Battle of Cambrai where he received an officer commission.

Although surviving WWI uninjured as an officer with the rank of captain by the end of WWI, Miller was decommissioned. His military career ended after almost twenty years. With the added deficit of being what was known as a *temporary gentleman*, his wartime status as a former British Army officer held little value in the difficult post-war economy of the United Kingdom. The pejorative label applied to a British officer that rose from the ranks rather than born to a position of wealth or class, a perquisite for acquiring an officer commission prior to WWI.

Once Daniel Miller lost his British Army commission with the massive post-war demobilization, his life changed abruptly. Cast adrift like hundreds of thousands of army veterans, he had no civilian skills to fall back on. Even for those that served only temporarily in the Great War, employment opportunities were scarce. The pension offered for almost two decades of service in the British Army was entirely inadequate to support a decent life. For an Irishman in England, opportunities were further limited. He returned to Belfast where employment opportunities were no better but where he had family, his older sister Kathleen and her husband Graham Abernathy.

His brother-in-law enticed him to join the Ulster Volunteer Force. Abernathy was a member of the militant organization formed years earlier well before the Great War to block domestic home rule for Ireland. With the Armistice of the Great War in 1918, the UVF officially demobilized. Yet it remained a haven for militant unionists as republicanism became pronounced in the Catholic dominated South following the 1918 election.

To Miller, the UVF was little more than a bunch of civilians talking tough. He began drinking too much. His frustrations led him to become increasingly arrogant about his military career after too much alcohol. Eventually, he concluded that he could not just remain idle and take his brother-in-law's and his sister's charity. Swallowing his pride, he accepted his brother-in-law's offer to help him find work at the shipyard. Unfortunately, lacking any applicable skills, the best his welding foreman brother-in-law could do was get him a job as a common laborer.

Daniel Miller suffered through the indignity of becoming reduced to such humble employment circumstances for almost a year. Salvation seemingly came in July of 1920 when the British government established the Auxiliary Division of the Royal Irish Constabulary. The brainchild of Secretary of War Winston Churchill, the ADRIC originated as a special paramilitary unit to conduct counter-insurgency operations against the Irish Republican Army's insurgency.

Membership in the ADRIC consisted of former British Army officers with combat service in the Great War. Many were decorated veterans serving on the front lines and many having risen from the enlisted ranks like Daniel Miller. Intended as a temporary service unit for one year, the pay of 7£ per week was double that of an ordinary RIC constable. Placed in perspective, an employment advertisement for ex-army officers to work charity coffee stalls at 2£10 shillings per week received five thousand applicants.

The ADRIC were to act as a mobile strike force. An elite unit with combat experience and deemed intelligent and motivated given their experience as officers. They were heavily armed and moved about in armored lorries and Crossley tender personnel carriers often armed with mounted machine guns.

The initial complement of 1,900 ADRIC quickly earned an infamous reputation in Ireland. Their official portfolio as a counter-insurgency unit meant they were to conduct what amounted to a reign of terror throughout Ireland. Their principal area of operation became the southern rural counties representing the most serious military operations of the rebel IRA outside Dublin.

Daniel Miller found himself right in his element. The IRA insurgency closely paralleled his experiences early in his military career serving in South Africa during the Second Boer War at the turn of the century. A guerrilla war unsuited to conventional British military tactics. The frustrations experienced by the British resulted in torture and murder of captured Dutch and French

Protestant Huguenot that constituted the enemy Boers. The situation in Ireland quickly proved the same type of warfare. The same brutal tactics resulted in similar atrocities.

Miller reverted easily to those engrained practices in the Irish conflict, quickly rising to a position of leadership in his ADRIC company. At the Kilmichael Ambush after serving for just five months in Ireland, Miller was second in command of the deployment that day.

———

Following his long convalescence in a Liverpool military hospital, Miller returned to Belfast a year later. Miller's disabilities forced him to again seek help from his older sister Kathleen and her husband Graham Abernathy. They offered him a room again. His brother-in-law also found him work at Harlan & Wolff. With his disabilities, this time as a security guard on the graveyard shift. The low paid position preferable to living off the charity of his sister. His meager WWI pension offered little more than bare subsistence.

Abernathy was a former member of the Ulster Special Constabulary established in 1920 after British partition of Ireland in the northern counties during the Irish War of Independence. Known as *B-Specials*, the paramilitary organization served as an unpaid part-time paramilitary force to fight the IRA in what became one of the bloodiest locations of the Irish War. The force was made up of militant unionist Protestants. Miller's wounds in battle against the IRA earned him respect among B-Special veterans. The comradery provided many a free pint of stout but little tangible benefits for reinventing his life.

———

Discovery that he might be able to locate the person responsible for his disfigurement and exact revenge proved invigorating. Regardless of the consequences, the possibility of satisfying his long-festering obsession now became a real possibility.

His first visit to the Belfast Central Library, however, proved frustrating. He realized just how much he was out of his element. In the years since his wounding, he subconsciously sought to avoid people. Not so much because of wearing an eyepatch, he felt more embarrassed by his appearance from the prominent scar on the left side of his face. The inability for full use of his left arm marked him as a cripple. The thought of being pitied instead crippled his social interactions. Overcoming his aversion, he forced himself to ask assistance of a young pretty librarian sitting behind a desk.

"Miss, might you help me?"

"Yes, of course."

"I am trying to get information about a movie made in America. The name of the movie is *Price of Freedom*."

"Oh yes. The movie about the War. Did you see it?"

Miller nodded. "Glad we live in Belfast not in the South. Missed fighting the Catholic rebellion but at least Ulster remained in the UK. Got these wounds in France in the Great War. That's where I lost my eye and disabled my arm.

The woman nodded with an expression of understanding. "War is so terrible. Maybe now we can have some peace. How can I help you?"

"Thought I recognized someone in the movie. The face of a comrade that served with me in the British Army Ulster Division in France. How might I go about researching more about this movie and maybe learn if that was him?"

"Well, that would be something if your mate turned up as an actor in America. Let's see what we can do. We have books about the motion picture industry in the arts section. How about we start there? My name is Alice. And you are?"

"Daniel Miller."

"Well follow me, Mr. Miller."

There were a surprising number of books about movies.

Alice said, "I love movies. Motion pictures shown on large screens in theaters found a beginning a couple of years before the outbreak of the Great War in Europe. In the fifteen years since, many countries began motion picture production. The United

States, Britain, France, Italy, Germany, Denmark, and Russia all produce movies viewed by audiences internationally. American-made movies now dominate the world market. Hollywood is the recognized center for modern motion picture production."

"Where is Hollywood?" Miller asked.

"Hollywood is a place in Los Angeles, California. Most movie production studios are located there."

"The movie was filmed at Fox Films Studios," he offered.

"Well, let's see what we can find about Fox Films."

Pulling a book from the shelf, titled simply *Hollywood*, Alice said, "Let's see what this might tell us. Probably nothing about *Price of Freedom* since that was just recently released, but enough information about Fox Films to maybe contact them."

She found several pages devoted to Fox. Photographs of the studio and stills from some of its most successful movies. A map showed the location of their ninety-acre studio and back lot in Los Angeles. Miller now had a tangible sense of where he might find his nemesis that has for years tormented his thoughts. All that remained was putting a name to the face.

Standing next to Miller, Alice said, "I remember reading a recent story about this movie in the *Belfast Telegraph*. Some sort of scandal surrounding the death of the female star of the movie as I recall."

"When was that?"

"Just months ago."

"Where might I be able to look at past newspapers?"

"Right here. We have a newspaper archive section. This year's copies of the *Belfast Telegraph* are recent enough to have not yet been moved to storage. They are in the basement. If you follow me, I will show you how to search."

The librarian settled Miller at a table and chair then brought out a stack of back issues of the *Belfast Telegraph*. She started in May when she recalled seeing *Price of Freedom*. The first articles Miller found about the death of actress in the movie appeared in June. The newspaper pieces provided no obviously useful information. There were many references to someone named Egan Walsh. This Walsh person apparently did not believe that the actress died of an accidental drug overdose. Nothing in these articles about the actress's death brought him any closer to identifying the face in the movie.

He exhausted his search going through every newspaper back issue from May. Returning upstairs to the librarian, she asked, "Any luck finding what you were looking for?"

"Afraid not. His name was not listed in the movie credits. Apparently only the featured actors receive name credit. He only appeared briefly for several seconds of the movie."

"Yes. You can imagine how many people appeared in that movie. Some with just a few seconds on film. Many never appear close to the camera. What they call *extras*. People hired to populate the background."

"That makes sense. I might never find him then."

"Perhaps this person performs as an extra in other films. They get paid. Probably not much, but it's work. You might try to connect with someone identified with the production who might be able to help. Perhaps write to someone at Fox describing this person."

That was an idea but did not seem to hold much chance for success.

Alice asked, "Did you ever read the book *Price of Freedom*?"

"Book?"

"Seems the movie was made from a novel. Written by someone that fought on the side of the Irish rebels in the South."

"Really? Does the library have a copy of this book?"

"Let me check in our card catalogue file."

She thumbed through the small wooden drawers filled with index cards organized by titles. After a minute she said, "No, we don't have a copy. That's not unusual. Probably not published that long ago. We don't usually get copies of new publications unless the publisher sends us a promotional copy. That wouldn't happen if published in the United States. You might try a bookstore though."

The first bookstore Miller tried did not know of the book. It was not far from the library to the west on Shankill Road in a Protestant loyalist area. Since *Price of Freedom* favored the cause of

Irish republicanism to free Ireland from British domination, he was more apt to find the book in a Catholic neighborhood in the Falls Road district to the south.

As he entered a politically situated bookstore, several copies of the book stood in a stack on a small table.

A background of the glossy dustjacket reproduced the green, white, and orange colors of the new flag of the Irish Free State. PRICE OF FREEDOM appeared in large font, underneath, A Novel by EGAN WALSH. Little wonder it did not appear in a loyalist area bookstore. The only reason for Miller's interest was to find something more about the author who apparently was very involved in making the movie. Miller was also Irish. Maybe he could use that to get closer to this Walsh if Walsh worked on the movie of his book. Miller knew enough about IRA activities in Belfast during the war from his brother-in-law to pass himself off as a former Catholic IRA fighter. Leaving Belfast for America became a logical reason for emigration because of widespread discrimination against Catholics in Northern Ireland.

Miller picked up a copy of the book and opened it looking at the inside fold of the dustjacket. He read the promotional text on the fold then turned to continue reading on the back fold. There on the bottom he looked at the photograph of the face of the man that shot him that day on a remote road in County Cork. No mistaking, this was the man he saw briefly in the movie. The man that took his life. Egan Walsh.

—

Miller read *Price of Freedom*, repeatedly rereading the description of the Kilmichael Ambush.

Armed with a name, Miller returned to the helpful librarian the following day. Showing her Walsh's novel *Price of Freedom*, "Is there a way to learn more about this fellow that wrote this book?" Reading the book, the author Egan Walsh undoubtedly took part in the ambush. "All I know is that he probably fought with the IRA in County Cork during the Irish War."

"Might be possible. With the settling of the war and establishing the Irish Free State in the South, followed by the terrible civil war, a lot of material on the IRA became public. Let me see what I can find. Give me a couple of days?"

"Of course. I appreciate you helping me."

"Well, that's what librarians do. My name is Regan Donovan, Mr. Miller. "May I ask why this Egan Walsh is important to you?"

Using his alternative explanation for his visible wounds allowed him to disguise his politics. Many Irish both republicans and unionists served in the British Army during the Great War. "I believe he might be a fellow officer I served with during the Great War. A good friend. Lost track of him after I was wounded at the Battle of Cambrai in France in 1917."

"Very well. I'll do my best. See you in a couple of days."

Regan Donovan took the opportunity to throw herself into this research project to enliven her otherwise boring library duties. When Daniel Miller showed up days later, she was gratified with what she had for this unfortunate man.

"Mr. Miller. Good to see you. I found a fair amount of information on your wartime friend. How 'bout we sit down over there, and I'll show."

Seated next to Miller, she laid down a typewritten sheet. "Did you know that your friend fought with the Irish Republican Army in the Irish War?"

"Only after I read his book. He never talked about politics when we were in France. Still, it came as a surprise. Then again, I knew he was Catholic from somewhere in the South."

"County Cork to be exact. Worked as a reporter for the *Cork Examiner* before joining the IRA. He saw some of the worse fighting during the Anglo-Irish War. Published IRA records say he fought with the IRA West Cork Brigade. Served with what was called a flying column. A mobile IRA strike unit. Walsh was part of a unit led by the notorious IRA commander Tom Barry. Seems Walsh rose to a position of leadership."

No question now that it was Walsh that shot him. "What happened to him after the signing of the Treaty?"

"He never fought in the civil war. Claimed no allegiance to either faction. However, he was interned by the Irish National Army on suspicion of providing intelligence to his former IRA colleague Tom Barry. No details I could find other than a brief reference that he was released after a couple of months confinement. Seems he left Ireland shortly after that for America."

"How is that he wrote this book?"

"That I don't know. What I found stated he resumed his former career as a newspaper reporter. Found a position with the *Boston Globe* newspaper in America. Boston was a logical place for an Irishman to resettle. As a reporter, your friend is undoubtedly good with words. Apparently turned to fiction writing. Used his personal experiences apparently to write an exciting novel."

"Why would he appear as an actor in the movie?"

"Well, the movie was based on his book. He is even credited with the script. I also discovered he was credited as a technical consultant for the movie. Probably just filled a position as an uncredited extra in the filming.

"But I found something more interesting if you are trying to get in touch with him. He is currently involved with what is called a sequel to *Price of Freedom*. A movie based on the Irish Civil War to be titled *Dying for Ireland*. The movie is currently in production in Hollywood, California at Fox Films Studios.

"I also found a lot of newspaper articles making reference to Walsh. The lead actress on *Price of Freedom* died under mysterious circumstance. Walsh led a newspaper crusade attacking the Los Angeles Police for covering up her death. His efforts caused him to suffer a terrible beating, putting him in the hospital as a warning to back off. Undeterred, his efforts paid off when evidence later emerged indicating the actress was raped and murdered. Your friend became a real hero in America."

CHAPTER 27

Belfast, Northern Ireland | 1926

Each day Daniel Miller relived that horrific experience in late November of 1920. Most nights he faced the same recurring nightmare of suffering through hours of cold before being found. The face of the man that repeatedly shot him blurred in memory until he saw the face on the movie screen. The face of Egan Walsh now served to focus his hatred on a tangible reality.

Walsh firing his Webley revolver on screen seemed an accurate reenactment. He only remembered the face of his assailant and the vision of the initial revolver discharge. Nothing further recalled until awaking from unconsciousness in the dark by the cold reviving him. Realizing he could see only from his right eye he touched blood-clotted tissue on his left cheek. With his right hand, he explored a deep open wound down into the muscle under his left eye socket. His left arm was immobile. His uniform tunic and shirt stiff with dried blood around his lower abdomen. He remembered the feeling of relief after determining he was no longer losing blood. He then crawled toward a dead Auxiliary lying close by, managing with his one good arm to pull off the man's field jacket and replace his own now soaked with blood. Taking the man's knitted, soft wool Balmoral cap to replace his own lost in battle, he stretched it down over his ears for added warmth.

The trauma and pain from the wounds that day became more difficult to recall over time. Not so with the unrelenting suffering stretching through the night until rescue came the following day. The damp. The bitter cold. The hallucinations. The lucid moments of coming out of unconsciousness. The despair of lying among the dead with every expectation that was to become his fate. The repeated nightmares since that night of waking up feeling cold.

The endless weeks spent in hospitals. The new despair of realizing that his debilitating injuries of losing an eye and most of the use of his left arm that restricted use of his left hand could never be reversed. A bleak future. The only thing that prevented him from putting a bullet to his head was a burning hatred at his core. Rage can be a powerful motivator. It sustained him. Discovering the identity of the man responsible for his damaged circumstances, rage transformed into revenge. With a name to put to the face, revenge took on tangible meaning. A real possibly to resolve his insatiable turmoil. A renewal of life by giving him a purpose for living after years of hopelessness.

—

How to get to America presented the first challenge in his pursuit of Egan Walsh. Money not only for passage but to sustain him while locating Walsh. If Walsh was working on another movie, that meant he was in Hollywood, California. Miller must first travel to the east coast of the United States by steamship, then make a long train journey to the west coast. How much time would it require to locate Walsh and make a plan to kill him? Hard to estimate what that might cost, but Miller knew he did not have anywhere near enough money.

His brother-in-law was the only person he could approach to ask for money. Abernathy was like family and his occasional drinking companion. Abernathy took pride in his service with the Ulster Special Constabulary. Feeling a kinship because of Miller's service fighting the IRA in the South, Abernathy might understand why he must go to America. Yet asking Abernathy for money would still be emotionally difficult. Asking for help was not in Daniel Miller's nature. As for Kathleen, he would plead the need to seek out better employment opportunities in Irish Boston.

Over pints of stout at their favorite pub on a Sunday afternoon with some of Abernathy's mates, Miller whispered, "Need to ask you something very important, Graham. Privately."

"Sure enough, Daniel." Abernathy spotted an unoccupied table toward the back of the pub. "Boys, I've got to talk over some family business with, Daniel."

Sitting down, Abernathy said, "What's on your mind, Daniel?"

"I told you the details about how I got this," Miller said lifting his damaged left hand to touch the scar under the eyepatch.

Abernathy nodded and sighed. "A right awful affair. A wonder you survived."

"Most would think I'm just another casualty of war. This was more than that. A soldier's duty is to wage war on the enemy. You do not kill prisoners, especially those wounded. That day, the IRA did more than wage war. They intended to kill everyone in our unit. All died except for me. Only a matter of chance with the IRA thinking I was dead and my will to live saved me."

Abernathy just nodded since Miller described that day many times to him before.

"I have thought of little else since that day that destroyed my life. A week ago, something happened. I saw the face of the man that did this to me. The man that shot me then left me to die slowly. The cause of my suffering that terrible night. My suffering every night and day since then."

Abernathy set down his glass hard on the table. "Where did you see him?"

Miller grinned. "On a motion picture screen."

"What?"

"Went to see that American movie about the Irish War. *Price of Freedom*. Saw the man's face portraying an IRA fighter reenacting the very attack where I was wounded. Even shooting another actor dressed like an Auxiliary. That was me! The sonofabitch on the screen was there that day!"

"How can you be sure it was the same man?"

"Thought the same thing, Graham. Maybe my mind was playing tricks with the memory. Watched the movie two more times to make certain. No mistake. That was the shooter's face. So, I set about learning as much as possible about this movie to discover his name.

"Seems the movie was based on a book written by an Irishman named Egan Walsh. Meant to be fiction, turns out that the novel was probably autobiographical."

"Autobiographical?" Abernathy asked, being unfamiliar with the word.

"Meaning the leading character in the book was probably patterned after the author's own experiences. Had a librarian do some research. Seems Walsh served in the IRA West Cork Brigade. Attached to the notorious flying column commanded by that murderous bastard Tom Barry. It was Barry's IRA unit that attacked us that day outside Kilmichael.

Walsh was arrested after the signing of the Treaty. According to the newspapers, he was suspected of providing intelligence to the anti-treaty faction when the civil war erupted in the South. Released for some reason after a couple of months. Seems he then left Ireland for Boston.

"Being a former newspaper reporter for the Cork Examiner before the Irish War, Walsh found a job with a Boston newspaper in America."

"Sonofabitch! And you're sure this is the bloke that shot you up?"

Miller nodded. "It was Walsh that shot me then left me for dead to suffer. Merciful thing to do was put me down like a horse with a broken leg. I suspect they shot others that were wounded since no one else survived."

"Damn! That's something to have tracked down this fucker after all these years. Now what, Daniel?"

"That's what I wanted to talk about, Graham. You are the only one I can trust knowing this. Cannot very well tell Kathleen what I'm set on doing."

Abernathy looked at him with a questioning expression.

"I mean to go to America and kill Walsh."

Abernathy sat up abruptly. "Are you fuckin' serious?"

"Yes. What else? Can't go on living knowing Walsh lives enjoying a good life while I can't even get meaningful work."

"But Walsh is in America you say."

"That's the problem, Graham. I don't have the money to get there and find him. After all you've done for me, I hate to ask but I have no other choice. Is it possible to lend me the money?"

"How much you are looking for?"

"I figure £300 more than I have. Cost of passage to and from America plus living expenses for maybe a couple of months."

"Fuck's sake, that's a lot of money, Daniel! Kathleen will have a shit fit. How you going to explain to her why you must go to America?"

"Better employment opportunities. I expect to pay you back once I settle this matter and return to Belfast."

"Then again, maybe it could go all wrong. Get yourself killed or sent off to prison. How do I explain that to her?"

"Should it come to that, Graham, I don't have a good answer. You and Kathleen are the only family I have. Nowhere else to turn. If you can't see your way to lend me the money, I'll understand. I'll find another way somehow. Not about to give this up though. Soldiering is all I know. I'll never find meaningful work. I either kill this ghost Walsh or kill myself."

Abernathy shook his head and exhaled deeply. "Jesus, Daniel. I can see how this is gnawing at you. We have some money saved up. Let me speak to Kathleen. You're family, Daniel. I'll go along with giving you the money if she agrees." Laying his hand on Miller's shoulder, "Let's have another pint."

———

His sister tearfully agreed to lend him the money to emigrate to America. Miller suffered a tinge of guilt over deceiving her yet rationalized it by the need to indulge in what now was an all-consuming obsession. The thought of going to America already uplifted his outlook as a means of taking decisive action. If successful in killing Egan Walsh, he harbored no allusions that it would change anything except satisfying his need for revenge.

Kathleen and Graham Abernathy stood waving to Daniel Miller as the ferry to Liverpool pulled away from the dock in Belfast Harbor. From Liverpool, Miller would travel by train to Southampton. From there, a berth in third class steerage on a steamer bound for New York. From New York, he would make the journey from coast to coast over the vast expanse of the United States by train.

CHAPTER 28

Hollywood, California | 1926

Daniel Miller arrived in New York aboard the steamship *RMS Cameronia*, at the Chelsea Piers on Manhattan's west side on the Hudson River. He was one of nearly 900 third class passengers. However, unlike the majority of those traveling third class, Miller traveled not as an immigrant but armed instead with a U.S. visitor's visa obtained from the United States consulate in Belfast. With no intention of staying in the United States, it was better to travel as a temporary visitor than becoming scrutinized for his disabilities which might preclude entry under immigration restrictions. The visa also avoided being directed to a ferry taking immigrant seekers to Ellis Island for processing.

He carried a single suitcase in which he concealed his British Army Webley .455 service revolver wrapped in a shirt although he did not expect that his luggage would be subject to a customs search.

New York was a bewildering metropolis. Rather than attempt to navigate the New York City subway system, he chose the long walk from the steamship dock to Grand Central Terminal in midtown Manhattan on East 42nd Street. He came armed with maps of New York City, the United States, and Los Angeles. Understanding maps from his military training gave him a sense of confidence in the otherwise overpowering experience of New York

City. He expected to confront a similar challenge once he reached Southern California. The metropolitan Los Angeles area surrounded by many suburban cities covered an extraordinarily large geographic area. The Hollywood district where Fox Film Studios was located was a considerable distance from central Los Angeles where he would arrive.

The massive New York City Grand Central railway station was itself an awe-inspiring edifice. Making his way to the ticket counter, he inquired about a ticket for Los Angeles, California.

"One way or round trip?" the ticket clerk asked.

"Just one way."

"Sleeper accommodations?"

"How long is the trip?"

"About 90 hours with stops and connection changes in Chicago. You take the 20th Century Limited from here to Chicago then transfer to the Golden State Passenger Line to Los Angeles. About a two-hour layover in Chicago."

"How much for the sleeper?"

"First or second class?"

"Second class."

The clerk checked the rate tables. "$123.50 for the entire trip."

Before departing Belfast, Miller exchanged some of his British pounds for U.S. dollars at a Belfast bank. The train fare amounted to about £31.

"Does Los Angeles have a subway system?" Miller asked.

The clerk said, "No. But they do have light rail serving the greater metropolitan area. Enquire at the Los Angeles Central Station when you arrive for a map of the routes."

It was only ten days ago that he left Belfast. Good progress. His train left New York at nine o'clock the following morning. Tonight, he would find a cheap hotel nearby. So far, his preparations have served him well. Yet once he reached Los Angeles, he faced a host of new challenges. How long would it take to become familiar with public transportation? He read that Greater Los Angeles was so large in area that most people required an automobile. He did not have sufficient money to even hire an automobile. How easy would it be to locate Egan Walsh? How long would it take to learn Walsh's habits? How long will it take to formulate his plan of attack? Did he have enough money? Could he find a way to kill Walsh and successfully escape? Could he make it back to New York then to Belfast?

Endless questions that could only be answered after arriving in Los Angeles. The only thing to do was to rest during the train ride. Yet the long cross-country trip across America only served to make him question the sheer desperation of this venture taking him halfway around the world. He must remain focused and not become overwhelmed by the unknowns. Remain confident that the fortuitous discovery of the man that maimed him was an omen that he could fulfill his destiny of seeking revenge. Achieving that perhaps might lead to a different life by finding accommodation with his physical disabilities and achieving some measure of emotional peace.

———

He awoke from the uncomfortable bunk of the Pullman car on the final morning of the trip. Making his way to the dining car, the view out the window was that of sunrise over the Arizona desert. Not only thousands of miles from Belfast but an alien landscape.

A few hours later the train pulled into Los Angeles Central Station on 5th Street downtown. Before exiting the train station, he purchased a map of Greater Los Angeles mass transit. For its vast geographic size, the Los Angeles Railway streetcar service provided transportation within the city and the interurban rail service of the Pacific Electric Railway allowed for reaching surrounding communities. The latter should allow him to reach the Hollywood district to the west of Downtown Los Angeles.

Miller found a police officer to ask for directions.

"Excuse me officer. Might you help with some directions?"

The officer looked at him subconsciously forming an expression in reaction to Miller's scar below his eye patch."

"Of course. Where you headed?" I have business with Fox Films. Their studios are on West Pico Boulevard."

"Best way to get there is to take the Pacific Electric Red Cars. Should get you to Pico Boulevard. Check the route map over on that wall," the officer said pointing. "Where you from?"

"London."

"A long way. You work in the movie business?"

"In a manner of speaking. I'm a script writer. British motion pictures. Have an offer to do some work here in Hollywood. Might I find hotels near the studio?"

"That I can't say but I would think so. Pico Boulevard is a major street in that area and lots of goings on with all the movie studios out that way. Good luck to you."

Stepping outside the rail station, Miller looked about at the buildings comprising Downtown Los Angeles. Nothing like the skyscrapers of New York. More like the modest heights of those found in Belfast. Yet unlike Belfast in November, it was a warm sunny day.

The Pacific Electric route map was bewildering. Difficult to pinpoint the exact location of Fox studios on West Pico Boulevard with the closest trolley stop. The best he could do was select the appropriate line and try to follow progress on his Los Angeles area street map. Once close enough, it was only important to locate an area that likely had hotels. Spend the night before reconnoitering the next day. His research served him well to get him this far. From here on he needed more immediate information from which to devise his assassination plot of Egan Walsh.

The gratification of avenging what Walsh did to him after all these years felt close at hand. Miller should have died that day, yet Walsh did not finish him off. For that he was made to suffer unending torment. Surgeons saved his life only to face forever the emotional isolation of his disfigurement.

There was a hotel just a few walkable blocks from the Fox studios. More costly than he hoped for, but he could afford it for the anticipated duration. To the desk clerk, Miller asked, "How does one go about applying as an extra in the filming of a movie at the Fox studios down the street?"

The clerk looked at Miller's face with some surprise at the question. The eyepatch was one thing, but the pronounced scar would likely preclude selection as an extra. "Well, you check in with the guard at the entrance gate. He'll direct you where to go. You ever done this before?"

"No. First time. I'm Irish as you can tell by my accent. Hope to get a part in the movie *Dying for Ireland* I believe Fox is filming."

The clerk smiled and handed Miller his room key. "Good luck."

Miller did not know if the movie was currently undergoing filming. If not, he had a backup plan. The objective was to somehow meet Egan Walsh face to face. The best opportunity appeared to be the filming studio where the librarian learned that Walsh was working on the sequel movie to his successful *Price of Freedom* adapted from his novel. Using the excuse of applying as an extra might gain him access inside the studio. If not successful, he would find other means of establishing how best to get close to Walsh.

Miller prepared and rehearsed a plausible reason for seeking Walsh since leaving Belfast. The basis of which was his service in the IRA in the Belfast brigade during the Irish War of Independence. As an Ulster Special Constable with the RIC during the war, his brother-in-law provided sufficient information about the Belfast IRA enemy to afford Miller material from which to construct fictional exploits as an IRA member.

The following morning, he walked to Fox Film Studios. Asking about where to apply as an extra, the gate guard gave a quizzical expression undoubtedly due to his appearance and then directed him to a personnel door labelled *Extras Casting*.

Inside there was a line of a dozen men queued up in front of a table. Two women sat behind the table. One appeared in charge holding a clipboard in front of her, the other working a typewriter.

As Miller's turn came, the woman in charge looked up and winced slightly. "Are you looking for work as a movie extra?"

"Yes, mam. Specifically for the movie *Dying for Ireland* if it will soon begin filming."

"It starts filming next week. But I'm not sure you would be right for a part."

"You mean because of my war injuries?"

"I'm so sorry, but your injuries are … such that they would not be suitable for any role available as an extra. I'm so sorry."

"Would it be possible to ask Mr. Walsh if I might be suitable?"

"Mr. Walsh? Do you know him?"

"Not personally. But we both served with the Irish Republican Army during Ireland's war of independence. That's why I wished to be in *Dying for Ireland* after seeing *Price of Freedom*. Might I at least speak with Mr. Walsh and explain why this is important to me?"

The woman thought for a moment before saying, "Let me check. Please take a seat over there. What is your name?"

"Daniel Miller. Thank you."

The woman dialed an extension on the telephone next to her. After a brief conversation that Miller could not hear, she motioned for Miller to come over.

"Mr. Walsh will come out to speak to you shortly, Mr. Miller."

Ten minutes later, Egan Walsh came up to the woman who pointed toward Miller.

"Mr. Miller? I am Egan Walsh." Miller stood and grasped Walsh's extended hand. "Do I know you from Ireland?"

Miller contained his visceral response of looking at Walsh's face by displaying a forced smile. Staring at Walsh's face left no doubt that Walsh was the one that shot him three times that day in November 1920.

"No, Sir. Only indirectly by your reputation. We both served in the IRA during the war of independence. On opposite ends of Ireland. I served with Roger McCorley and Seamus Woods in the Belfast Brigade."

"Did you receive your wounds in Belfast?"

"No, Sir. The Great War in France. Serving in the British Army Ulster Division at the Battle of Cambrai in 1917. Been a soldier all my life. Spent most of my time in the British Army at various postings around the world. Losing an eye and most of the use of my left arm caused my decommissioning as a captain and leaving the Army. The British Army didn't need a disabled Irishman. Returning to Belfast after recovering from my wounds, I experienced first-hand the level of discrimination for Northern Irish Catholics."

"Yet you were able to serve in the IRA?" Walsh asked.

"I secretly provided intelligence for the IRA. McCorley and Woods organized an Active Service Unit within the first battalion. I served as an undercover intelligence officer. I developed a reliable network of sources that provided good information they used to plan attacks on the RIC and the B-Specials. At the time I was working as a dispatcher for a trucking firm moving cargo in and out of the Port of Belfast so I could also assist with IRA logistics."

Walsh nodded. He knew of McCorley's and Woods' IRA exploits in Belfast. Every bit as fierce a fight against British security forces as in County Cork. "What brings you to Hollywood?"

"Without boring you with my life story, I left Belfast after the signing of the Treaty and hostilities ceased. Belfast was not a healthy place for a former IRA. Came to Boston where my sister immigrated years earlier. Resumed working in the freight business around Boston Harbor.

"Read your novel *Price of Freedom*. Your story so engaged my interest I began writing myself. Not a novel, but an autobiographical work about the War in Ulster. When the movie *Price of Freedom* came out, it had a profound effect. Encouraged me to pursue my own writing."

"Interesting, Mr. Miller. But why come all the way to Hollywood and become interested in appearing as an extra in a movie?"

Miller smiled. "Not just any movie but *Dying for Ireland*. I never experienced the civil war in the South, but *Price of Freedom* allowed me to relive my experiences of the Irish War. Hoped if I worked in the movie as a cast extra that I might have an opportunity to meet you, Mr. Walsh. Learn out how I might develop a new career as a writer like you did, Sir. Something more worthwhile than organizing freight trucks, which is about all I can do given my disabilities. That's why I came to Hollywood."

Walsh was sympathetic to this damaged man. Apparently emotionally struggling to have come to California for the reasons he stated. Someone that risked everything to fight for Irish freedom even after sustaining life-changing injuries in the Great War.

Yet, as an extra his facial disfigurements would be a visual distraction on screen.

"I must be honest, Mr. Miller. Your facial injuries might not be suitable for a part as an extra. Tell you what though, it is not my decision to make but let me speak to the assistant director in charge of casting extras. Come back at one o'clock and ask for me again at the same desk."

Walsh removed a notebook from his jacket pocket and scribbled a note. "Give this to the gate guard and see the same woman at the extras casting desk this afternoon. Even if you can't appear in this movie, I'll spend some time giving you some helpful ideas about writing. Least I can do for a former IRA comrade."

Miller returned promptly at one o'clock. The woman at the casting desk made a telephone call. After a short wait. Walsh and a younger man approached.

"This is assistant director Walter Downing, Mr. Miller." Walsh said as Miller and Downing shook hands. "What do you think, Walt?"

Downing let out a deep sigh. "I don't know, Egan. The eyepatch is okay but that scar. Sorry to be so blunt, Mr. Miller, but we have a movie to make."

"What about if the makeup people *fix* the scar, Walt?"

"Jesus, Egan. He's just an extra."

"As a favor, Walt. Use him as an officer standing next to McLaglen in the scene at the Four Courts when McLaglen's character leads an assault to dislodge the anti-treaty occupiers. The eyepatch will give a dramatic touch of a veteran that has seen his share of combat."

"Okay. If John doesn't go along with it though, you tell him it was your idea not mine." Downing was referring to Director John Ford who controlled every aspect of film production.

"Well, Mr. Miller, looks as if you are going to be in the movie. We'll give you your former rank as captain. This time though as an officer in the Irish National Army."

"Thank you, Mr. Walsh, and you too, Mr. Downing. What do I do next?"

Downing said, "Come with me and I'll see you get a pass. Show up here on Monday at six o'clock in the morning. Don't be late. Need the makeup people to see what they can do to make you look … better."

Miller had several days before going onto the set. No telling how much longer before actual filming began. During that time, he must determine where an opportunity might occur to shoot Egan Walsh.

It immediately became clear to Miller that he would kill Walsh on the movie set. Even without the precise details worked out, at some point he would have the perfect opportunity to smuggle in his loaded Webley and find a way to get close to Walsh. Get as close as when Walsh shot him. A fitting end by killing his sworn enemy in a recreation of the actual event in Ireland. Ironically possibly ending his own life in a movie titled *Dying for Ireland*. This was Miller's destiny. Satisfying his obsession for revenge could never change the difficulties he must endure for the rest of his days. Forever a repulsive cripple struggling to eke out nothing more than a solitary existence.

Miller immediately realized that he deluded himself in believing there was a way to kill Walsh and escape. Walsh's assassination on a movie set would become sensational news. Successfully making his way back across America with his disfigurement thereby became unrealistic. The only solution was to end it here. Shoot Walsh then go down fighting when inevitably confronted by police. A soldier's death in a worthy sacrifice.

Removing the need to plan for getting away freed up his thoughts. His mood elevated. There was little to prevent a committed assassin from success if willing to sacrifice his own life.

With little else to do until Monday, Miller's thoughts turned to envisioning the many possible scenarios of seeing Walsh's face just before he died. Miller would enjoy his remaining days until the right opportunity occurred.

———

Monday morning, Daniel Miller felt a sense of inner calm not experienced since before his injuring. Walsh was there to greet him when he arrived at the studio. "Director Ford has no objection to an eyepatch if the scaring can be overcome with makeup. Follow me and I'll take you to the makeup people. The Director wants to see what you look like with your face fixed for the camera. After that I'll take you for your uniform costume fitting. Want you looking right smart when you meet the director and the star of the movie Victor McLaglen."

An hour later, Walsh was astounded by Miller's appearance after the makeup artist worked on his face. "Amazing. Let's see how you look in uniform."

After Miller changed into the uniform of a captain in the Irish National Army, Walsh declared, "You will do just fine. Let's hunt down Director Ford."

Today's rehearsal was a run through of a sequence of action scenes. The back lot setting duplicated the Four Courts Buildings in Dublin. The Irish National Army led by Michael Collins was preparing to shell the complex to dislodge anti-treaty dissident IRA that took over the government buildings. Victor McLaglen, starring as Brandon Flynn played a senior officer in the opening scene leading an armed attempt to enter the buildings to dislodge the dissidents before resorting to a destructive artillery barrage. A dramatic action sequence in which Miller appeared as an aide standing close to Flynn. Assuming John Ford approved the extra with an eyepatch.

As the cast assembled, Ford along with Victor McLaglen walked toward Walsh. Walsh asked, "What do you think of the fellow with the eyepatch, John?"

Ford walked closer to Miller and said to Walsh, "Okay. Looks like an officer. Just make sure makeup makes him look this good on film."

Walsh nodded to Miller with a smile.

The rest of the day they ran through the choreography of the scenes while lighting technicians and the cameramen found their positions. In the afternoon John Ford announced, "Tomorrow we begin filming. Appropriate firearms will be issued to those designated by the armorer. The ammunition will be blanks with special powder loads to produce appropriate gun smoke for appearance. Seven o'clock everyone."

So, there it was. Tomorrow presented the perfect opportunity. His role called for holding a revolver as he directed firing of those with Enfield rifles as part of an attempt to assault the Four Courts Buildings from the rear. He must find a way to smuggle his own Webley onto the set and substitute it for the prop revolver at an opportune time. The problem resolved itself quickly when the assistant director announced that all extras were to return the following morning dressed in costume ready to begin filming. The firearms were returned to the armorer as everyone departed the studio at the end of the day in costume.

The plan became exceedingly simple. He would kill Egan Walsh the following day. All he needed to do was stick his loaded Webley in the rear of his waist band concealed by his uniform tunic and walk into the studio. When issued the prop revolver loaded with blanks, he would perform the scene as rehearsed discharging blank rounds to produce the desired smoke effect for the filming. After the final take as the cast dispersed, he would return the prop revolver to the weapons cache table. Without being seen, would then extract his loaded Webley from his waist unseen, placing it in the holster. He could then approach Walsh and when close enough, withdraw the Webley. Shoot Walsh from a distance at which he could not miss.

———

Egan Walsh was on the set early. Lilly Romano also attended with him as did co-screenwriter Ray Schrock. This was one of the most elaborate filming sequences as the Irish National Army prepared to dislodge anti-treaty rebels by shelling the buildings requiring extensive special effects. This morning's scene was a fictional contrivance written into the script as a means of providing closeup action of the lead character. Brandon Flynn would lead an assault by a unit of soldiers before the historical accurate scene portraying the bombardment scheduled for filming that afternoon.

As a special favor to his friend Wyatt Earp, Walsh and Lilly picked up the aging gunfighter that morning. Telephoning him the previous day, "You'll enjoy Wednesday's shooting, Wyatt. Action sequence with a large cast of extras. Lot of shooting. Tom said he was going to try to also show up. We'll all then have a fine dinner tomorrow evening."

Miller arrived earlier to allow makeup artists to conceal his facial disfigurement. He sat next to Victor McLaglen also being prepped. Having a shared background of being in the British Army, they chatted amicably.

As they finished and stood up, McLaglen said. "You look like a true British officer, Mr. Miller. Even wearing an Irish uniform. "You know there are surgeons today that could fix up your facial scar to look the same as all that makeup. Something to think about."

"I will. I imagine, however, that must cost a lot of money. Appreciate your advice though, Mr. McLaglen. Anyway, do I look good enough to stand at your side in today's filming?"

McLaglen smiled his huge engaging grin and slapped Miller on the back. "You look right smart." McLaglen then gave him a salute which Miller returned.

Once everyone was assembled after being issued firearms, and the assistant director completed positioning everyone for the beginning of the scene, John Ford said, "Everyone ready? Remember the scene choreography and timing. This is a complicated scene. Any mistake by anyone makes for a retake. Got lots of work planned for today so I don't want to be bogged down with unnecessary retakes."

Walsh sat close to Ford. Both held megaphones to communicate instructions to the cast. They ran through three rehearsals of the long scene without filming before Ford was satisfied to begin the cameras rolling.

The shooting went well that morning. Approaching noon, they were facing a third take. Ford announced. "That last take was much improved. Still needs to be more fluid. A couple of you extras appear hesitant. Think of yourself as actually engaged in a battle, people. Move like you mean it. Get it right then we break for lunch and move to the special effects bombardment scene this afternoon. Take your beginning positions."

This take went flawlessly. Ford kept nodding his head affirmatively as the scene unfolded. When concluded, he yelled, "Cut! That's a wrap people. Good work. Let's have lunch and relax a bit. I expect an equally good performance this afternoon."

For Daniel Miller, this was now the perfect opportunity. He stayed back as everyone moved toward a large tent assembled with tables of food and chairs. Without being seen, he exchanged his prop revolver with his loaded Webley, placing the studio weapon in the back of his trousers waistband.

A deep breath readied him. He began walking briskly from the set toward Walsh. His eyes were fixed on Walsh who remained seated talking to Director Ford. At a distance of twenty feet, Daniel Miller pulled his Webley revolver from the holster and kept walking. Extending his arm while holding the weapon on target, he stopped ten feet from Walsh.

Walsh looked up just as Miller fired. The round struck Walsh in the upper left side of his chest. The large caliber round knocked Walsh backwards to the ground. Miller fired a second time aiming at Walsh's head, but the round missed.

The reaction of those in the vicinity took several seconds to materialize. Only a short time before, the set was filled with the sounds of gunfire in a pitched gun battle. Lilly Romanc was the first to react with a sustained scream seeing Walsh knocked violently backwards from his chair. She had started to walk toward Walsh just before she saw him go down.

Miller turned and began running from the set to make his escape. As he ran, he turned his head over his right shoulder to see if anyone was pursuing him.

Seventy-eight-year-old Wyatt Earp was seated well behind where Walsh and John Ford were located closer to the filming set.

Earp never ventured out unarmed. Still concerned that someone from his past, or a relative of someone he killed might come looking for him, he intended never to be caught by surprise. The same advice he imparted to his friend Egan Walsh. Earp now carried a Colt .45 revolver similar to the weapon he carried throughout his law enforcement career. The difference being this firearm had a more manageable 5.5-inch barrel, shorter than his former cavalry model with a 7.5-inch barrel. Easier to conceal in a shoulder holster under his suit jacket.

Watching the real scene of Walsh collapsing to the ground, Earp instinctively drew his Colt. As Miller approached on the run with his head turned backward, he did not see Earp with his drawn revolver. Even with a shorter barrel, the Colt was still a heavy weapon, fully adequate for Earp to use his preferred method of confronting lawbreakers by *buffaloing* rather than shooting.

Earp delivered a full-force blow to the left side of Miller's head. Miller went down sprawling headlong onto the ground unconscious. Earp kicked away Miller's Webley and pointed his Colt at down at Miller's head as several other men converged around him.

—

Lilly Romano cradled Egan Walsh's head in her lap. He was conscious but his breathing was coming in labored spurts. Within minutes, the studio attending physician arrived. Looking at Walsh's wound, he directed John Ford to help him role Walsh onto his side. As suspected, the doctor found a large exit wound. He immediately applied a large gauge bandage to stem the bleeding from the gaping wound. To John Ford he said, "Hold this bandage and keep up the compression. "Keep him on his side."

Someone found a blanket to cushion Walsh's head as Lilly Romano positioned it under his head. The doctor began cutting away Walsh's shirt to examine the entry wound then began compressing the wound with a bandage. The siren of an ambulance could be heard approaching closer.

"Will he make it, Doctor?" Lilly Romano asked.

"We'll do our best," the doctor said.

Walsh was taken to Queen of Angels-Hollywood Presbyterian Medical Center on North Vermont Avenue in East Hollywood. The same hospital following his beating months earlier. The studio physician accompanied Walsh in the ambulance along with John Ford and Lilly Romano.

"How bad is it doctor?" Ford asked.

"Hard to say. He's lost a lot of blood. Got to operate quickly. A surgical team will be waiting. Depends what kind of damage they find."

As staff wheeled Egan Walsh into surgery, John Ford comforted a distraught Lilly Romano in the waiting room. Victor McLaglen, still in costume uniform with Tom Mix and Wyatt Earp arrived together a short time later.

The surgery lasted four hours. Eventually the surgeon appeared. "The surgery was successful. The surgical team is guardedly optimistic about recovery. Mr. Walsh remains very weak from loss of blood but is receiving plasma to recover his blood volume. The large caliber round delivered at such short range smashed his second rib then exited through the scapula. The course of the bullet damaged his left lung causing it to collapse. That happens as air enters the abdominal cavity and compresses against the outside of the lung inhibiting normal function. We expect him to recover use of the lung. Had the bullet's path been a couple of inches lower, it would have struck his heart and been fatal. The most pressing post-operative danger remains infection. It will be days before we can be sure he is out of the woods."

"When can we see him, Doctor?" Lilly asked.

"He will be in recovery for several hours. Once he recovers consciousness from the surgical anesthesia, he will be groggy from morphine to control the pain. The nurse will let you see him then. Only one person at a time and then only very briefly. Mr. Walsh has suffered an extreme trauma. He requires rest. At best, he must remain in the hospital under monitoring for some time."

When he regained consciousness, Lilly Romano was again sitting at his bedside.

Touching his face, she said, "The doctor expects a full recovery barring infection. As they put you in the ambulance, I thought I had lost you." She broke down and began to sob.

He struggled to say something but the oxygen mask assisting his impaired breathing prevented any audible words. "Don't try to talk. Just rest and recover," Lilly said. "I love, Egan Walsh."

Reaching his hand to the mask, he pulled it away enough to speak. "I love you, Lilly. We're good for each other."

She nodded wiping away her tears. "Why did this man try to kill you?"

Walsh replied, "I don't know. Told me he served with the IRA in Belfast during the Irish War. I suspect that was a lie. I helped him get a job as an extra in the movie. Seems now that was to get close enough to shoot me. Something must have happened in Ireland he believed involved me. Too many ghosts from that war."

For Egan Walsh, why Daniel Miller tried to kill him would remain a mystery. Days later, his friend Benny Zimmerman published his column in the *Pasadena Star-News*.

Attempted Murder at Movie Studio

Pasadena, CA:

Benjamin Zimmerman reporting:

Three days ago, a spectacular event rocked Hollywood. Like something from a movie script, a cast extra participating in the filming of the movie *Dying for Ireland* shot the movie's technical consultant and screenwriter Egan Walsh. Somehow, Daniel Miller smuggled a loaded revolver onto the back lot set of Fox Films Studios on West Pico Boulevard. Although seriously wounded, Mr. Walsh underwent immediate surgery and is currently recovering although he remains in critical condition. A spokesperson for Fox Films said the chief of medicine at Queen of Angels-Hollywood Presbyterian Medical Center stated the surgical team remained guardedly optimistic about Walsh making a full recovery.

Egan Walsh is well-known to this reporter while working together to expose the tragedy of the death of actress Tara Kelly earlier this year by rape and murder. Mr. Walsh was instrumental in exposing a coverup of the crime. His efforts almost cost him his life and eventually led to the suicide of prominent banker Chadwick Hollister as the person responsible for Kelly's murder.

Interviewing Mr. Walsh after this recent unrelated attempt on his life did not shed light as to the motive of the assailant Daniel Miller. Walsh was able to reveal that he had a brief conversation with Miller who was to appear as an extra in the movie. Miller claimed to have been a veteran of the Great War fighting with the British Army in France. He further claimed he was from Belfast, Northern Ireland and served in the rebel Irish Republican Army during the Irish War of Independence several years ago.

The hero of this bizarre event surprisingly is legendary Old West lawman Wyatt Earp. Earp was famous for his law enforcement exploits in Dodge City and Wichita, Kansas, then later in Tombstone, Arizona. He is best remembered for the historic gunfight known as the Gunfight at the O.K. Corral in Tombstone in 1881. The now seventy-eight-year-Earp seems not to have lost his touch. Known to prefer using less than deadly force to subdue unruly outlaws and drunken cowhands, Earp was famous for his quick hands and using his revolver as a club to the head in what became known as *buffaloing.* As a friend of Egan Walsh, Earp was on the set of *Dying for Ireland* during filming. Carrying a Colt .45 revolver in a shoulder holster, Earp disabled Daniel Miller with a blow to the head as Miller attempted to escape following his shooting of Walsh.

Wyatt Earp apparently always went armed with a permitted concealed weapon fearing someone from his past looking for revenge. Earp's vigilance may have saved the lives of others that would have surely pursued the armed assailant, Daniel Miller.

Daniel Miller recovered from Earp's blow with only a concussion. He has so far remained silent undergoing police interrogation. All that is known is Miller carried a British passport and entered the United States on a visitor visa two weeks ago. The Los Angeles Police are investigating Miller's background with British authorities. Miller is currently in custody awaiting arraignment for attempted murder. Miller has declined to speak to investigators to provide a motive for attempting to kill Egan Walsh.